A Fire in the Earth

Marcos McPeek Villatoro

Arte Público Press
Houston, Texas
1996

This volume is made possible through grants from the National Endowment for the Arts (a federal agency) and the Andrew W. Mellon Foundation.

Recovering the past, creating the future

Arte Público Press
University of Houston
Houston, Texas 77204-2090

Cover design by Scott Fray

Villatoro, Marcos McPeek.
   A fire in the earth / by Marcos McPeek Villatoro.
      p.   cm.
   ISBN 1-55885-094-5 (cloth: alk. paper)
   1. Women—El Salvador—Fiction. I. Title.
PS3572.I386F57   1996
813'.54—dc20   95-37662
                                                               CIP

The paper used in this publication meets the requirements of the American National Standard for Permanence of Paper for Printed Library Materials Z39.48-1984. ⊚

To my mother, Amanda del Carmen,

Gracias por la sangre
y la historia

A
Fire
in the
Earth

Prologue

Old Don Pablo lifted the wood pipe to his lips and sucked deeply. Neighbors called it *vuelveteloco*, the "return to insanity" herb.

A few were perturbed by his use of the weed, as it made him talk strange, though unlike a drunken man. Others couldn't care less that old Don Pablo burned the dried-out leaves which only he found on the outskirts of the city, and then only at certain times of the year. They had remembered their own grandfathers, most of them Indians, using something very similar in old rites from a bygone, pagan time. Don Pablo was the only one left from those days. He sucked the tiny pipe and smiled, as if some ghost from that favored past told him a well-spoken riddle. The weed, he always argued to his granddaughter, kept him young, so that at the age of one hundred and forty-five he still enjoyed passions young men fantasized, enhanced by the wisdom of old age. He was still known to bed a few women in the barrio. It was his smoking that allowed this. It erased the border between past and present, taking his spirit back to inhabit the body of the young man he had been a century before, in a time when he would undress a lady with his lips and fingertips and hold her hips high in the air.

Don Pablo sat in the shade of some pines. The trees trembled suddenly, not from wind but from a force that pulled at their roots. The old man reacted slowly to the roar that bellowed underneath his feet, muffled by several feet of rock and earth. "Ay," he muttered, once it registered that he was sitting on top of an earthquake. "It's been a while. Are you planning to eat the city?" he asked the earth, pointing with his lips toward where the capital stood. Today his wanderings had taken him far from home. "If you do, perhaps we will be smart enough to go away, and build far from your nest."

Don Pablo had lived through many tremors. Still, he was not very good at gauging which were threatening and which were merely assertive signs from the earth in its desire to be known, to be remembered. He had seen the destruction of whole towns by the mere spitting of the planet's crust, endeavors made to knock the sun out of the sky.

The tremors ceased. Pablo glanced about, smoking. Looking upward toward the blue heavens, he saw three large sets of wings approaching. "Well, this could be a sign," he mumbled, knowing what type of fowl they were.

The vultures, like black angels, formed a circle in the distance. They gyrated slowly downward in no hurry, as their target was not going anywhere.

"You've found something. Was it a gift from the tremors?" He chuckled, then looked down at the now passive ground. He took a stick to the dried-out sand and dirt between his legs.

The shadow in which Don Pablo sat moved three feet before he looked up from his scribbling. The shadow's edge approached his toes, and the sun silently threatened to heat up his dry oasis. The three vultures flew away from the meal they had picked with such care, and sat upon gnarled limbs that stood a field away from the old man. Momentarily satiated, they held their heads up like surveyors. The living creature on the other side, spewing smoke out of his mouth, neither threatened them nor offered them food. Sometimes he would make a noise, speaking to them from a distance. "You think you'd like to eat me?" crackled the laughing question. "Well, perhaps not today. But someday you will, and that's fine. Then I, in turn, will one day swallow you, true?" He chuckled at his own riddle, digging his toes into the ground until the dark veins of his feet were like roots pushing out from the earth.

The birds paid him no mind. Their perceptions were preoccupied with the movement under the ground, the rumbles that they could feel more quickly than any maladroit mammal in the area. It approached again, like a moan muffled by a huge blanket. The vultures stared, and began to squawk. The world turned quiet. They waited. Suddenly another wail bellowed, thick and deep, as rock rubbed against rock under the blanket of black dirt and dried grass. They stared at the land before them, at the field, and at the old man who sat, oblivious, still muttering philosophy. Their branches shook. The largest of the vultures screeched while all three flapped their wings for balance. Then the rumble broke through and screamed at the sun.

To the east, hundreds of yards away from both them and the old man, the earth opened. Something underneath spat out black clods and hurled them straight upward. The globs lost momentum and fell to the grass. Other blocks followed, with rocks, stones, sod. This was too much for the birds. They fluttered and squawked at the scene, then took off from the branches where they were perched and spread out their bodies, flying northward to one of the higher hills overlooking the valley.

The field had been abruptly altered. Once the underground howling weakened into a cry and became silent, it left not a hole, but a large, round hill of dirt and stone.

Don Pablo sucked the last of his third bowl. He looked up, as if touched on the shoulder by a friend. The field before him stood silent, the dried grass moved only slightly from a careless wind. He looked to the right. "Oh. Look at that," he muttered, the light pipe bobbing between his cracked lips. There sat the dark, fat mound. Don Pablo believed it was looking at him.

"Now where did you come from?"

The old man stood, pulling his feet from the cool sand and earth. He walked toward the new mound, adjusting his hat slightly to better take on the sun's beating. It took him a while to arrive at the edge of the hill. He grasped a handful of the moist, cool soil which, minutes before, had been deep beneath the place where he trod. Yet the sun was beginning its baking, already sucking out the first layer of moisture.

"Well, this is lovely indeed."

The slight, sinewy frame touched the mound along the base, petting the beauty of its darkness. He muttered phrases about planting, placing seeds carefully, only with permission, mind you, following the ancient rites. The sun spoke to Don Pablo, reminding him of its power. The old man stood upright again, rubbing the small of his back. "I've got to go home; it's a long walk before supper." He turned and headed toward the distant town. It would take him a few hours to arrive, where he would hear his pregnant granddaughter scolding him—that here he was wandering out again in the forest, that how silly it is for an old man to take such chances, and where in the world had he gone anyway?

Before heading over the first hill on the edge of the field, Don Pablo turned and looked one final time at the new little mountain like a master calling a dog to follow. He smiled, chuckled with pleasure at the newborn, and then took off, muttering questions to himself as to who would be so fortunate to touch this bit of earth daily.

Part One

Chapter One

Holy Week, circa 1870

Amanda Velásquez leaned up against the adobe threshold of the door to her home and watched the old man amble over the hill. Her arms were crossed, and they rested upon her large, pregnant belly. Amanda shook her head slightly from side to side. "God knows where he's been," she said to herself.

She had given up worrying about Don Pablo long ago, learning that there was nothing she could do or say to keep him in one place. Today, however, lent to some concern. The rumbles had been felt all through the city a few hours ago. Two of her ceramic pots had fallen from the table and shattered across the hard, mud floor. Now, resting upon the cool adobe of the threshold, she breathed easier, knowing that the earth had not swallowed her grandfather.

"Hello, girl," said the old man as he walked by her.

"Hello, Papi. How was your walk?"

"Nice. Always very nice. I watched the birth of a mountain."

"That's good," she responded. Along with worry, Amanda long ago gave up trying to completely understand the old man's stories, especially when he had the pipe wedged between his lips.

〰️

The earth trembled throughout Good Friday. By Holy Saturday, all was calm again. This being the holiest season of the year, theologies developed around the earthly phenomenon. Many thought God would protect them. The Lord could not allow Hell to attack during this holiest of times. The spiritual curmudgeons proclaimed the oppo-

13

site. They said that this was the opportune time for God to cleanse the earth of its sinful filth by allowing Hell to do the destruction. In the course of the three days that followed His death, Jesus had descended into Hell. When He came back up again to sit at the right hand of the Father, the Devil could escape too, perhaps out of the same crack through which the Lord had emerged. It was a convincing argument.

Although she tried to work, Amanda could do very few chores without tiring quickly. Her neighbor, Silvia Córdoba Montenegro, helped her. Silvia spent a part of every day with Amanda. They had grown up together in the barrio. "Sit down, girl," Silvia demanded gently. "I will take care of the tortillas."

"You know we need very many for tomorrow."

"I know, I know. I will make yours and mine together. Here, sit down, rest. My God, ready to give birth and you want to clean up the whole barrio. I'll fix you something to eat first."

"No. I'm not hungry."

"Come now, I'm sure you have not eaten since breakfast. What are you doing, fasting?"

Amanda did not answer Silvia's teasings.

Silvia turned to face Amanda, then placed her hands upon her large, round hips and proceeded to scold. "Fasting? True? Now? God doesn't want that from you! Why? You are about to have a baby. You have a child in you that is hungry!" She turned to the warped table on the side of the room and dusted the fine, dry dust off its top. She pushed more wood into the small adobe-brick pit upon which they did their cooking. She paid no attention to the sweat that beaded across her forehead. "Besides, yesterday was a day of fasting, not today."

"You fast when you want, friend. I want to fast today. This is a holy day, too. I must feed this child's soul as well as his body."

"Wonderful. You and your child will share a cloud in heaven on the same day if you don't eat. Those are stupid laws for rich people who can afford to fast. Here." Silvia handed Amanda a clay bowl of rice and beans and a cup of hot, sweet coffee. She then called into a dark corner, "Don Pablo, are you hungry?"

"Yes, girl. Always."

14

A Fire in the Earth

"Let me fix you something. Here. How are you feeling in this heat today?" Silvia spoke loudly, thinking he did not hear well, a common but mistaken assumption. He heard everything.

"It has been hotter, child." Pablo answered, turning his head away from Silvia's pitched inquiry.

"Yes, I'm sure you've seen worse." This was not a snide statement. Silvia spoke the truth. Don Pablo was the oldest man in the barrio, maybe in all of the city. The people respected him, and waited for him to return from long walks, such as the one he had undertaken yesterday. He always had a story to tell. The night before, people had gathered around his porch to hear him tell of a strange mound of soil that had been born right before him. Now he was eating his rice and beans slowly. When he finished, he lit an old pipe filled with the dried leaf. Laying his head back into the dark corner, he sank himself into the act of reliving dead days suddenly resurrected.

Silvia took from a dwindling pile of corn that sat on the floor. She scraped off the kernels and tossed them into a large bowl. Filling the bowl with water, she tossed lime and ash in to prepare it for tomorrow's tortillas. She worked, oblivious to Amanda who quietly placed the clay bowl of rice and beans beside her chair. A pitiful dog came in from the street, trying to escape the heat and the drunken festivities of Holy Week. The animal wandered about the room, his tongue dangling.

"How are you feeling?" asked Silvia.

"My belly is rumbling. But I don't think it's time yet."

Silvia turned and looked at the girl's abdomen, then turned back again. "Your belly hasn't dropped much. I believe you will have a girl."

"I hope it's a boy. Somebody who will go out and work for me, bring in some money."

Silvia said nothing, afraid that whatever words she uttered would sound judgmental. Amanda had suffered enough from the community's reproof since that day when a man came through the barrio enticing her with all sorts of promises. Amanda's beauty, others always said, would be her downfall. Silvia wondered if Amanda's religious zeal, which had grown in the past nine months, was but a wall of

15

defense, a way of shielding herself from the sin that now lived within her belly.

Silvia looked for other subjects of discussion. "The sun is about to set. The field workers will be home soon. That should be interesting. My man took his Holy Week bottle with him, so I doubt they got much done. Especially after that scare yesterday, with the tremors." She turned to Amanda, who had remained silent. She was asleep. Silvia picked up the bowl beside the chair, empty of the rice and beans. She smiled at the pregnant woman and took the bowl away.

Silvia's husband Juan came by. Knowing that his wife was no doubt visiting their neighbor, he stopped to greet the women. The dog, licking bean gravy off his chops, walked out to greet him.

In the cathedral towers the bells rang loud and long Easter morning, clanging together haphazardly, echoing the celebration throughout the alleys and streets. No one went out to the fields. The women had prepared food for the celebration early in the morning. The priests set off on a long procession along the main streets of the city. With their incense and their holy books and their gold and white liturgical clothes, they led the people to the city's cathedral, where the bishop would greet them. The procession went by the countless adobe houses, past the newly built walls of the country's university. Young men on the way home from school strengthened the crowd's numbers. This was a good sign, people thought. The university, with its import of foreign professors, had been suspected of teaching atheism to the students.

Other people leaned out of windows. Adjacent to the majestically carved and painted university walls sat another set of adobes, their walls thick and rough. The multicolored murals of the university, with religious motifs strewn upon them, loomed over the adobes, daring and proud to stand tall upon the earth.

Silvia and Amanda made their way to the cathedral. Don Pablo was not with them. He had never taken part in any Church celebration. He had, in fact, scorned religion, claiming it a farce. Amanda had

16

insisted on going, although the rumbles within in her abdomen grew stronger.

People filled the cathedral to capacity, then filed around the walls. The mass was much longer than usual, and the weather the hottest and driest of the year, as was the case just before the rains. The bishop droned on, preaching ethereal words to deaf, sweating bodies gathered in the pews.

Amanda had obediently not eaten anything this morning. Sitting in the pew, she stared at the huge bloody crucifix that loomed over the old bishop. She sat in the very back row, tradition not allowing a pregnant woman to sit closer, especially one who had fornicated. White blobs danced before her eyes, shielding her from seeing the prelate. The crowd of women around her grew, as did the heat from their bodies. The air died and turned stale within the four walls. The high ceiling offered no help. The hot, humid air hovered around them, enhancing the smell of the multitude. Sweat soaked her dress until she could sweat no more.

The crucifix bled from behind the white spots before her eyes. It bent and flexed until Jesus melted into a mass of pink and red. The bishop held up the bread above the altar, with his back facing the people and his mumbled Latin barely audible. Little bells held by an altar boy who knelt beside the holy table clanged against one another. The blotches of white exploded and swallowed Amanda.

$$\approx$$

They took her home. Amanda's contractions began their own rhythm. She called for Silvia, who stayed by her side all day. Through the pain she breathed out to her friend, "It would be a blessing, true? To give birth on Easter Sunday." Silvia smiled at her, brushing the sweat off her face with a damp rag.

Don Pablo walked by. He glanced at the woman in labor, then shuffled back to his bed and lay down.

Silvia, incredulous, said to her friend, "What is he doing here? He shouldn't be in the room!"

Amanda glanced back. She winced in pain as a contraction ended and allowed her to look toward the old man. He was enveloped in smoke.

"I don't think you will get him to leave. He's already entered his other world."

The two women worked together. Night fell, and Silvia lit candles all around her friend. Amanda shed clothes as the contractions deepened, as if to free her body from a growing, intense heat. Silvia gave her water. Amanda's dark skin sweat, and her belly shined like a world in a flickering universe. Sitting completely nude upon the bed, Amanda's head swirled between contractions. Silvia looked at her friend's body. It was an image of beauty. Silvia, just a few years older, had caught a number of babies born in the neighborhood. Her reputation was growing. Her confidence had also matured, and she knew by silent knowledge that, though Amanda now suffered, this birth was quite normal. Silvia smiled for a moment, admiring her friend's thighs and the globe that sat in her lap. Young to midwifery, she could still be amazed by the moment. Silvia took a cloth, dipped it in water, and wiped it slowly across Amanda's breasts, her shoulders, her nape, while Amanda closed her eyes and whispered moans toward another impending contraction.

Suddenly, thunder rolled underneath the two women. Before Silvia could think of rain or formulate any other excuse, the thunder bellowed under her feet and made the dry mud floor vibrate. Screams came from down the street, which were soon lost in the rumble that bulked upward like a bubble from the ocean floor. A house on the other side of the street shook. Silvia watched the scene through an opening in the wall. The tile roof of the building caved inward, beginning from the bottom and cracking upward, showering shadows of broken block into the light of fallen torches.

Suddenly it ceased. The buildings and brick roads stopped dancing. A few weaker buildings still crumbled, while the thick walls of adobe houses muffled the wailing of the wounded and the dying.

Panic trickled onto the road. Men yelled to their sons to prepare wagons and horses. Women packed food and clothes into cloth sacks. Domestic animals neighed and yelped, confronted with the newborn

A Fire in the Earth

evil. Children cried and clung to parents' legs. One little girl held a dog in a tight, panicked grip. It pawed away, digging and scratching into her stomach.

Silvia's husband, Juan, had already grouped his children together, and was packing belongings in sacks and throwing them over his two horses. The decision to leave was made, without any need for discussion. Everyone knew that it would not be safe to remain inside the city, where adobe walls reached up two meters below a man's head. Juan led his horses toward their neighbor's house. He watched his wife and Amanda walk out, the pregnant woman waddling as she wrapped loose clothes over her. Amanda clutched something in her hand, a fragile black pouch; she held it as if it were a life.

Juan moved the wagon just in front of the door. Amanda half-plopped into the bone-dry hay. Don Pablo followed, hobbling to the cart with Silvia's help. The old man yawned, then muttered something about what the fuck was all the commotion for. His eyes were still red; not even the earth's birth pangs could shake Amanda's grandfather from that strange fairy-tale world he preferred to inhabit. In his gnarled hand Don Pablo clutched a cloth sack that held his precious, simple possessions—his flute, the pipe, and dried tobacco.

The convoy stopped only when they reached a distance from which they could contemplate the whole city in one glance. From a kilometer away, the capital sat in darkness, barely visible by the weak moonlight and the thousand torches flickering inside dwellings.

In cases of childbirth, Silvia became the commander. She shooed her family away, told her husband to lay out several serapes, and ordered her four children to tear out dried grass and tall weeds to use as bedding. Amanda's water had already broken. "Come on," Silvia ordered, "we must move over there."

Half picking her up, Silvia brought Amanda to a stout tree that stood away from any torches. She placed Amanda's hands on a low, thick branch and ordered her to grab hold of it. The young girl sat back until her spine rested against the trunk. First Silvia held her upright by the waist, then she put her own hand between the girl's legs. "Spread them apart," ordered Silvia, and Amanda willingly, in spite of her grunting and moaning, moved them.

19

Juan looked at the two women up on the hill. He could hear the inhuman sounds, noises he thought should never come from a woman. Turning away and squinting, he helped his children set up their camp for the night.

Others did the same. Bustling in every crevice of the night, the caravan organized itself and set up shelters with nothing more than serapes and sticks. Chickens ran about, confused by the new environment. Women followed, throwing down small palmfuls of rice to keep the animals from wandering away. Two brothers struggled with a fattened pig. Others gathered wood and built small campfires. Over the flames, women stirred rice and beans that had been snatched from their clay stoves. Everyone worked. Everything became organized. The night had suddenly turned into a day of busy labor, interrupted only by an explosion that came from behind.

〰〰

The earth's womb expanded sideways, then fell inward toward the rumble that escaped and shattered the main street of the city. One thousand adobes bent toward one another before surrendering to the anger that raged beneath them. The cathedral church bells clanged and tumbled down. The earth chewed, crunched, sucked inward, then finally burst upward, spitting the shattered remains of people, animals, and structures. Then the planet stood still. Buildings fell, stones and tables and carts and horses and human bodies plummeted from high above, dropping from heaven. Fires struck the wood of older, dried-out buildings. Hell's passing storm had finished its deed. Within thirty seconds it had come and gone, leaving nothing behind.

〰〰

Silence whispered into her ear. Silvia awoke, blood dripping through her long, young hair and over her cheeks. Night still lay upon her. From below she could hear the bustle of people, the droning arguments over whether or not to go on, to stay, to return and look for neighbors, relatives, friends. She turned her aching head down the hill

A Fire in the Earth

toward the city. In the weak light of the moon overhead, she looked for the small, low skyline of the capital, but could not find it. The cathedral tower, which had always slit through the sky, had vanished.

"Juan, Amanda...Juan, where are you?..."

She picked herself up and wandered about, wiping blood from her eye with the corner of her dress, looking for family and friends. Her hand ached. She felt blood dripping from it, and wrapped her dirty apron over the wound. She fell into a wide, shallow indentation that previously had not existed, stood up again and kept moving. Her mouth felt parched, and dust caked her blood-stained face. She called out her husband's name until she heard her own in response. A torch quickly approached her and an arm encircled her waist. She asked for the children, and Juan showed her they were safe, huddled together and weeping. Old Don Pablo sat among them, his arms sheltering them with a large blanket. Juan's voice fell in impotent shakes, groping for control.

They looked for Amanda. They began with the tree she had used for birthing, now felled by the tremor, its roots reaching upward like a dead spider grasping the moon. They found her on the other side of the hill, about thirty feet below them. Juan held the torch over her. Amanda lay on her back, blood, mucus and feces all over and inside her dress, her abdomen sagging like a deflated bag. Silvia looked for the chord. It was nowhere to be found.

They carried Amanda back to the children. Juan made a bed for her while Silvia lit a torch and wandered about the small hill. Away from her children and husband, her chin trembled. Tears mixed with blood; her tremulous voice stammered and fell into the dead night air. She called out to a god that beat against her chest. She stumbled to an area of bunched weeds, and from the edge of the sun-scorched grass Silvia heard the stammering cries of a newborn.

The baby lay halfway on dry grass and halfway on dirt and small rock. Dust covered her. She choked in tiny coughs as the dirt continued to settle. Silvia dropped to the newborn's side, heaving with gratitude. The flame of her torch revealed the long chord, still attached to the newborn. The other end, wrenched prematurely from the womb, bled profusely. The midwife knew that remnants of the placenta had

21

remained attached to Amanda's insides. That would be a problem to deal with. Silvia clutched the new child, then pulled away, afraid of moving broken bones. There was little blood on the infant, though dust penetrated many scratches.

Gathering the chord and torn afterbirth like a pile of soaked clothes, Silvia held the newborn to her chest and walked carefully and quickly back to her caravan on the other side of the hill.

$$\approx$$

It took a full day for the dust to settle. It covered walls, bricks, and corpses. Men worked together to move rubble off the suffocating screams of those trapped below. This also meant digging through dead arms, abdomens, a half-crushed head stamped with fear, the corpse of a baby choked by silt. At times they reached the screams. Other times they scratched at the tremendous mountain of rubble in vain. The hand-sized rocks they managed to remove amounted to nothing next to the remains of a crumbled wall. Hours passed; they made no progress. The screams continued. A long and cruel howling set the men to scratching and clawing away, for the cry demanded something from their souls that forced their bodies to beat against unmoving stone until the final blessing came, when the scream finally stopped. Then they began again, only to fail one more time.

At times the earth trembled, a sleeping, angry dog shaking away pesky insects. As the rumbles continued, the people abandoned the city and ran back up the hills to their caravans. Priests came out from among the survivors. Finding it impossible to bury them all, the ministers held general eulogy services for those still under the stones, with one curate taking an area where Barrio González once stood, and another preaching over the dead neighborhood of El Dominio. They preached in various corners of the crushed capital, trying to put the silence to rest.

A pack of dogs ran by, growling at the death they were leaving behind. The pack was composed of skin-drawn mongrels that suddenly made no sign of recognition towards their masters. Those were the ways of the fire in the earth. The dogs would never return, as if they

A Fire in the Earth

had been called back to some demanding, primeval source. The old dog that had eaten Silvia's beans scampered by Amanda and her newborn child. It growled at the screaming baby, then kicked bits of dust and joined the pack.

People began to move away. The passing of days forced them to leave. The stench of their loved ones leaked from beneath the dried mud blocks and forced the survivors toward a slow pragmatism.

Outside help came to the area of devastation, from Sonsonate and Santa Ana, bringing food and potable water, wood for temporary shelters, and other materials for survival. Leaders from other towns came to help with the building of the future capital. The central government moved to Sonsonate and ran the country from there. It was then that the people of Amanda's barrio had actually seen the president and his small retinue. It had been a fleeting moment, an accident really, to glimpse those who controlled the country. Yet again they were gone, whisked away to the safety of another city, returning to their world of the Unseen.

Many people, especially children, died from lack of food and an abundance of disease. A woman sitting close to Amanda's shelter clutched her dead baby; diarrhea streamed down its legs. The people grew irritable and lashed out at their sudden, enforced exodus. They demanded things from the area leaders who stayed behind. But they could deliver nothing except plans and goals. Meanwhile they waited for equipment to arrive.

An official organization was formed by those in charge. The mayor and his crew, who kept in contact with the departed president, informed the people as to where they would soon move. They spoke of going east, toward a lake named Ilopango. There, commerce and reconstruction could be more efficaciously carried out, and all would benefit from the new geographic location. Excitement was forged out of necessity, and word spread throughout the various groups that huddled in encampments upon the hill. In no time, people had found their places once again—the middle class to one side, the elite to another, and the poor on the periphery of planning.

It was in the periphery that people spoke in whispers. There were no assurances that Ilopango would promise them the good life. Yet they had never known what it was to be secure. The only security offered them was the voice of old Don Pablo, and he spoke quietly, as if not wanting to share his thoughts with the leaders who spoke over the throng.

"I know a wonderful place to live."

That night his neighbors followed him. It was a small group, only the families who had lived up and down the street of his barrio, all friends to a degree. They found it easy to follow the old man. No one else was interested in joining them. To gather near the banks of Ilopango, according to the official campaign, promised a safer future.

The exception was a young, white-skinned, brown-bearded curate. He stumbled behind, asking some of the fifty-odd people in Don Pablo's group where they were going so late at night. No one could tell him. "We're following the old man," said a little boy.

The priest, named Mateo, asked if he could go along. They agreed. Father Mateo was not sure why he made this choice. He knew he could have been utilized in the rebuilding of the capital, that he and the other priests would now doubt have homes built for them before anyone else. Such were the ways of society. Perhaps he had left for this reason. He left without telling his superiors, hoping they would think he'd died in the destruction or from the ensuing disease. He enjoyed that thought. He was filthy. A family gave him clothes. He donned the short, loose shirt and pants made out of heavy cloth, strapped on work sandals, and tried to blend his bearded, white-skinned face with the ruddy, dark faces of the crowd.

They walked through the night, following the glow of the old man's pipe. Don Pablo extinguished the smoke, too busy to enjoy it, preoccupied with finding the new friend he had met days earlier. No one spoke through the night hours, trusting their future to the elder up ahead. Just before the sun rose, as they began to distinguish the trees and hills from the night sky, Don Pablo smiled.

"There it is." He walked at a faster clip.

They stood on a hilltop and looked into a deep, long valley. Volcanoes smoked in the distance, far away from this place. In the middle of the valley protruded the huge, fresh heap of ground. In the first hours of morning it was difficult to see what it was.

A Fire in the Earth

"Has that ever been there before?" asked one of the men. No one answered him.

The caravan marched down into the valley and gathered around the earthen monument, amazed at its size, and especially at its texture. There was little rock covering the mound. Its outer surface was composed of a rich, black soil, so thick and loose that the people sank into it down to their ankles. One man precariously crawled up the black, loamy sides to stand atop the knoll as his friends laughed at his maladroitness. The other farmers who observed him figured its height to be perhaps fifteen meters. It smelled rich and freshly dug. Yet there were no tracks to indicate that it had been carried from another location. Many theorized that it had dropped from the sky. Perhaps Mount Joya had spat it out, and it had landed here. Others disagreed, as they pointed to small holes and cracks around the mound where other tiny piles of the same rich earth lay scattered. "Hey, This is what Don Pablo had told us about!" The old man said nothing, but smiled as he gazed upon the new hillock.

Women began building fires and fixing the evening meal with whatever they had carried. Men continued to walk around the mound of earth and discuss possibilities. The priest, Mateo, joined in with them. He picked up a clod of moist dirt and compressed it between his soft fingers.

"Is this good earth?" he asked.

Someone mumbled a response, "Yes, Father, very good earth."

"It is a gift then," he said.

"Yes, Father. It seems that God has already tilled and plowed it for us!" said Juan, Silvia's husband. "We need to work it some, but it would not take long to plant upon it. We could have food in a few weeks. It's very wet now, as if it came from ground water. But it will dry soon. If we plant quickly, we may be in time for the rains."

They began planning. They would need to fortify the loose earth with a stone base so that the rains would not wash away the good soil. They spoke quickly, men to men, and did not stop until they heard old Don Pablo's voice.

"We must apologize for tilling it. We must be thankful for its gifts."

No one said anything, save Father Mateo, "Yes, it certainly is a gift from God." He spoke excitedly, joining in the moment with Don Pablo.

"God. But God...not your god." Don Pablo looked up, a small, young flame flickering in his eyes. The response was hushed and clear like a stone dropping into smooth water. It silenced the men.

"I saw this thing born. The earth gave it up. We need to give it back to her."

Silent embarrassment encircled the group, tied and knotted by the old man's words. Someone endeavored to change the course of the conversation to keep him away, for now, from his stories. "Well, yes, Don Pablo. How do you think we should plant?"

Don Pablo looked up at the rich, black knoll. "The stone wall is a good idea," his voiced settled into the soil. "But when you plant corn, do so with the rod, and not with furrows. I hate furrows. Two seeds in each hole made by the rod. The same with other such foods. We must disturb this earth as little as possible. And when you plant, plant with sorrow."

Again they turned silent. They thanked the elder, then walked toward a campfire, too excited to listen to his ancient commands. He smoked, bent toward the mound, grabbed a handful of the soil, kneaded it in his palm. "Do it correctly," he mumbled, his words crackling with age. Rarely had he been so serious. Clumps of the black sod fell between his fingers and returned to the mound. A tear crawled in and out of furrows of his skin, the first rain of the season. It fell and splashed like a blessing upon the clods of soil.

Farmers gathered around the campfires. They threw ideas back and forth. They gently argued over how to preserve the mound. The women called them to dinner. Dozens of people sat down to eat. The men shoved down rice and beans while still planning on how to preserve the rich soil that was their new bounty.

They worked a full day constructing the stone foundation. The curate joined in, though no one cared to work with him. This was man's labor, they mumbled, not a priest's. Yet he insisted, and the campesinos gave him room, quietly rearranging and rectifying the mistakes he had made, replacing his stones with others. They were

A Fire in the Earth

glad when he rested every half-hour, and hoped that by the next day he would realize his limits as he dragged his stiff, dolorous body out of sleep.

That night they baptized Amanda's baby and gave her the name Romilia. In the midst of friends who gathered around with torches taken from various campfires, Father Mateo dug from his heart the new feelings he was experiencing. He spoke of the miracle of what is born anew in the midst of death and destruction, and how this meant that all of them, though experiencing pain and loss, could come out of that pain with a sense of resurrection. His words were young, much younger than the life-wrought faces gathered around the peace of the night. Yet he drew tears from them. The people went to sleep with those moist gifts, given by a real priest who, though a lousy day worker, had actually chosen to live among them.

♒

They constructed huts for each family from wood out of the nearby forest. Others built the retaining stone walls, cultivated the mound and planted seeds they had brought from their destroyed homes. They worked the earth daily. Some men hunted and collected edible roots, nuts, berries and leaves. This supplied the community during the interim between planting and harvesting. Don Pablo preferred to stay with those who tilled the earth. He and the crew were in contact with the mound daily, digging all around it, smoothing the soft ground with the tips of their hard fingers. They planted seeds carefully, as the old man had advised them, finding wisdom in his words. It was a tender earth, untilled and in need of much care. It seemed to heap higher from their daily touch. The rains hit and moistened the world, penetrating deep into the soil of the new hill. At harvest time, the earth broke forth abundantly.

The new village celebrated. A few men built a small hut atop the knoll, with a wooden cross on its little roof. They presented it as a gift to young Father Mateo, along with a new home at the bottom of the mound. Another, more substantial church would be erected later, big enough to fit all. For now, the little chapel would do. All smiled at it,

27

except for Don Pablo, who mumbled words from an old, forgotten language. He would walk around the hill late at night, then stare up at the temple like a lover who has lost his woman to the convent.

They named their pueblo El Comienzo, for there they began their life again; it was their beginning. The mound, that black rainbow of earth which promised no more rumbles of destruction, made them strong and self-sufficient. They grew the bulk of their crops upon it, beans, tomatoes, onions. Around their homes they formed other gardens of corn, yucca, rice. After a few years of subsistence farming, they would grow an area of coffee trees, a crop large enough for their own consumption. Yet it took many years for this to come about. The trees had to be started from seed, and once they became trees, it was necessary to wait three years for the first beans to appear. Other fruit was never lacking: the nearby forest offered a natural garden of mangos, bananas, papayas, oranges. Cows from the fields of the destroyed capital had been brought in during the exodus, along with goats, pigs, and horses. They would raise the young of these animals, fatten and milk them.

In the beginning, some families came together and built a root cellar at the bottom of the mound. They dug a cave deep into the rich earth and lined it tightly with rocks. Here they kept cool their cheeses and milk. The root cellar was open to all, both to add to its contents or eat from them. This was the town in which Amanda Velásquez would raise her child Romilia, in an ejidal owned by no one in particular, but held by the community as a whole. Here Amanda could forget her past life. The ignominies of having a bastard child seemed to lay dead and dry-boned in a heap of rubble several hills away.

〜〜
〜〜

In those hills, three angels slipped through the still sky like black shreds of silk. They whispered over that heap of rubble, flying lower and lower each time they encircled an unseen path in the air. They landed. Thick dust jumped and rolled around their tough, wrinkled knuckles and claws. Everywhere they walked or landed dust greeted them, the same dust that covered the bones of the dead city. Food lay

28

everywhere. Others of their kind came, until they blackened the site with folded wings and gnarled, strutting heads.

One of the creatures dropped down upon a branch that protruded from a low pile of rock and clay. The branch bent deeply, more than the stick of a tree. The dark angel jumped to an adjacent rock and stared at the limb, which was thick with dust except for where the angel's claws had dug in. Again it hopped onto the branch, jumped up and down violently upon the soft limb, shaking off the dirt. Food lay underneath. The angel picked at the limb, tore at the cloth that wrapped it. A gold ring encircled one of the twigs that had curled upward in a dead endeavor to clutch the sky. At times the ring got in the way of its beak.

Earlier, the angels had seen a small group of the upright beings moving north, and a larger group moving east. Someday, perhaps, they would follow them. Someday. For now there was so much to do here. They were a patient breed, and even though they peppered the rubble by the hundreds, they perched silently, picking, breeding in their new land of plenty. It was quite a kingdom.

The woman seemed to have been born from under their wings. Old, ragged, she shared the same gnarled sympathies that clung to their faces. She held a walking stick. The black ones had the complacency of carrion. They paid her no mind as she walked among them and squinted her wrinkled eyes to the hills that surrounded the rubble in which she stood. She looked up a hill and perceived that people had once been there. The abandoned campfires and poles that had been used to hold up cloth for temporary shelters were still there. Yet no one remained. And no one had found her among the rubble, although they had looked for survivors after the devastation.

The rags that she wore dripped from her like rotting moss tearing off an old, knotted tree. She walked out and away from the rubble, leaving the undisturbed black creatures to continue their feasting. There were several trails in front of her. She easily found the clues and marks that indicated the direction people had taken when they abandoned the city. She could also tell what kind of group made which trail. These two, for instance; they led in opposite directions. One was littered with tortilla halves, parts of mangos, some spilled rice. Obviously a trail of the affluent, those who could afford to drop such things, who were not accustomed to emergencies, who still had to learn to save everything. Their trail went eastward, toward Ilopango.

The second trail was clean. The people who followed it had dropped nothing. They could not afford to; they had little in the first place. And they were barefoot. She saw this etched on the thick dust of that dry season—clean toeprints of men, women and children still untouched by the wind. They had gone north, into the mountains.

She reached down on the trail of the affluent and snatched a dry, crusted, forgotten tortilla. She chewed it slowly, silently, hunched over slightly, a reflection of the black ones behind her. She would follow the northward trail, the path of the poor. It was not a true decision; she knew she must follow them. She had, after all, lived among them for hundreds of years. Certainly those who had travelled to Ilopango had talked about people like her—witches and warlocks, a story or two about vampires. Yet to the rich, these were just stories. To the poor ones who had travelled north, the old woman was a part of their heart. They had practically created her. She finished the tortilla. It was enough for the journey ahead.

Chapter Two

"Yes? And what does faith have to do with her getting better?"

Old Don Pablo rested against the rickety chair that he had made during the first years. He drank his coffee after putting the question to Father Mateo, who was visiting the Velásquez family, and who had just said to Amanda that the woman's faith had brought her sick daughter Romilia back to health.

"Papi, do not start with that nonsense. Quiet," Amanda gently hushed her grandfather, knowing that the old man's questions were inroads toward a conversation to attack whatever he wanted to attack, especially religion.

"I am not starting anything, girl. I am just asking a question of this young man." He wrinkled a smile and invited the curate to sit down.

"Father has no time for your nonsense, he must visit others, too."

"No, no, I do not, Doña Amanda, really. I have some time before mass this afternoon. Now, Don Pablo, you don't believe that Amanda's faith had anything to do with little Romi getting better?" The priest pulled a chair to the other side of the doorway. He had waited for an opportunity such as this to speak with the old man, who was known to blaspheme. It was a rare privilege to save a pagan, since almost everyone else was somewhat of a Catholic. Before him was the first man Mateo had met who openly professed heresies that harkened back to primitive, indigenous ways.

"What is this faith of yours? In some god, up in the clouds, beyond the clouds. That I do not understand. Where does all this come from?"

"Well, it comes from our Lord Jesus, from our belief that He died and rose from the dead for our sins. As Christians we believe that Christ helps us in our everyday—"

"No, no. I have heard all that. I cannot help but hear it," Pablo rolled his eyes toward his granddaughter, who worked in the kitchen. "But *where* does this come from? Come on, you know what I mean. The Spaniards."

"Excuse me?"

"The Spaniards brought all this belief in Christ, all this religion."

Amanda brought another cup of coffee and a piece of sweet bread for the priest. She turned to sweep up the floor. She had just cut the old man's hair. Tufts of silver grey gathered in piles. While the two men chatted, Amanda bent down, grabbed a lock, and wrapped it with a dry corn husk. She pulled a small black pouch from the pocket of her dress. Opening it, a few chained beads fell out, one decade of her rosary. Amanda shoved the wrapped lock of hair beside the rosary, then placed the pouch safely in her dress pocket.

"Well, yes, the Spanish did bring us religion," said Mateo, "because all the people were pagans. There was no religion here."

"Wrong. There *was* religion here. But your people choked it to death." Don Pablo pulled out his pipe. Mateo had never studied the pipe this closely. It was made of old bone, and its stem, some type of hardwood. The old man took dry leaves from a cloth sack that dangled from his rope belt. He stuffed a thimbleful into the bone. "Girl, bring me some fire." Amanda did so, carrying a thin slice of torchwood from her stove. He puffed and spoke between breaths. "Now we have this, what you call it, this religion from the sky."

Mateo stumbled for words. Perhaps, he thought, the old man was a great revolutionary, since he spoke against the Spaniards with such a grumbling attitude. He tried to placate him. "Well, it certainly is a good thing that we are now free from Spain, true?"

White eyes peered through brown, wrinkled slits of skin and cut through the bitter smoke. "Free? What is freedom? Boy, we are all infected. The water has been crossed; they have come and gone. We are still infected." He spoke almost lethargically, as if he had thought through all this many, many times. "Look at this." Pablo moved next to Mateo and rested his arm upon the priest's long dress-like cassock. The curate's hand next to the old man's appeared white, sickly. "They're in you completely. I can barely see a trace of our blood in you." Pablo puffed, allowing himself time for thought. The priest looked at his own hand, at what he had always cherished. Now, before this old Indian, his white skin seemed shameful. Pablo continued. "Even I have been infected, though not as deeply as you. But my name, Pablo, what kind of name is that? One of your saints."

"You are Indian?"

"Pure."

"Then, then how did you get such a name?"

Age looked at youth directly in the face, with the loaded ammunition to prove his beliefs. "One of those Spanish missionaries who wanted to save our poor pagan souls told my father that if he did not want to see me burn in Hell, he should have me baptized. The priest was the one who named me."

"So you are baptized?"

"Yes."

"And, and what type of Indian are you?"

"I am originally of a Pipil tribe."

"Can you speak any of those languages?"

"Of course. I have forgotten much. When I was a boy, we were told to talk Spanish, those of us who lived near villages. So I have lost it a lot. There is no one to share it with."

Silence fell between them. Mateo watched the smoke blow through the old man's nostrils. The ancient one did not seem to mind the silence. He looked out at the darkening street. A neighbor passed by. Both men greeted the woman as she walked on.

"What is that you are smoking?" the priest asked.

The Indian smiled and took off his hat, since the sun was no longer beating down. "I cannot remember its original name. It comes from the hills over there. It is a very dark, green leaf before you dry it." He puffed twice, then a third time. "Would you like to smoke?"

"Oh? Me? Oh, well, very well. I do like cigars, if it's anything like that."

"This is a little different. You have to suck deeply. Like making love to a woman."

They shared. The younger man, unaccustomed to harsh smoke, choked at first until Pablo taught him the proper way to breathe the smoke in. Amanda walked by, saw the scene, and protested. Her grandfather silenced her with reprimands. She did what she was told; she marched back into the kitchen.

They smoked more. The street turned dark, with only the tiny ember from the pipe barely illuminating their faces. Mateo had forgotten about his afternoon mass. Those who planned to attend soon learned where he was. It was not uncommon for him to miss mass at times. He was the only priest in town, and made a point of visiting people in their homes. When word circled the village as to where the priest was, the women nodded and smiled in approval. It was time, they said to one another, that someone tried to save that old Indian's soul.

"You are very infected with it, boy. You are so white, almost as light as a Spaniard. Not like me. I am *moreno*, dark as the earth. And you grow hair on your face. Your blood is very confused."

Mateo touched his forehead with his fingertips, as if discovering it for the first time. "But...but was everything the Spanish did so bad? They gave us religion... I do not mean to say that they were good to us completely. We had to, to break away from them. But can't we take from the good things that they—" he muttered.

"We haven't broken away from them. Emancipation cannot stop the infection. They took everything away from us, and made us believe in some god that we can't even see, and call him king, ruler. We believed in a god that we *could* see, the earth, the trees, the river. That is the god who feeds us, who takes care of us. It was not faith that cured the little one. Do you know what cured Romilia? Maguey!" He shoved the pipe into his mouth.

"Maguey?"

"Yes. That plant next to the river. Pick the flower, boil it down, take out the oil. The child drinks it, you rub a little on her chest, and she is fine. I picked it yesterday; we gave it to her this morning. Tomorrow she'll be helping her mother with the tortillas."

Thoughts blocked and formed together in the young priest's head, movements of color and light, of heat and youth. He turned and looked into the darkness of the adobe home, saw a woman standing over the glow of dying embers. There she drifted back into a deep shadow and pulled a slim wooden beret from her head. Her long thick hair fell over the floor, snaked across the room and wrapped thick over the curate's lower abdomen, and tightened between his inner thighs.

"You know, old man, I cannot marry."

"Why not?"

"I am a priest. It is the law of the Church. I cannot marry, for I must serve with all my being the people around me, and be chaste for the Lord."

"That is stupid."

"Fuck! What is happening to me?... The walls, they are breathing..."

The old man grabbed the priest's arm, smiled at him as the youth turned his head back and forth, his eyes closed tight, his mouth hanging. "Get quiet, get quiet. Just listen to me, boy. Follow me this way. Let's take a walk. Over there, to the mound. It's good to walk at night. Easy to find one's way, with the moon as bright as it is. Look how it drops light upon the mound, see? How beautiful, the crops now. The men have done a good job..."

They walked around the mound three times before the priest spoke again. His mind cleared some with the reassurance of the old, decrepit Indian who was holding his arm. "How old are you?"

"Much older than you."

"Yes, but how old?"

"I don't know. One hundred, one hundred and fifty. Difficult to say."

"One hundred? How can you—" He stopped, seeing the hunched figure of an old woman walk by, a small torch in her hand. Father Mateo whispered excitedly, "It is she! I have seen her so few times. I've tried to find her house. There she goes..."

"Oh, yes. The witch, as you people call her."

"That is what they say. No one knows where she is from. She talks with no one. Do you know her?" Mateo asked.

"No. She is one of the witches from your religion. To me, she is an old woman, old like myself. Now, the Ciguanaba, I have seen."

"You know the Ciguanaba?" spoke the priest, incredulous. His childhood came crashing into his skull. The Ciguanaba always came up at the kitchen table where he listened to the stories of the old serving women. The Ciguanaba always appeared as a beautiful young woman, half-dressed, who walked through the forest as if she were lost. She was always "found" by a young man who could not control the muscle between his legs. Instead of helping the girl, he would decide to take her. Then the young beauty always changed into a hairy beast who would begin eating the young rake's stomach first, not stopping until she cleaned out his bowels, chest, and abdomen. Father Mateo waited to hear the old man's version of the very old story.

"Of course I knew her. It was not very long ago, perhaps forty years or so. I was old enough to keep my wits about me, yet young enough to enjoy a good solid roll with a woman." Pablo smiled. "I am perhaps the only man on this land who has gotten his wishes satisfied by the Ciguanaba without getting his guts torn out. You know how it goes. You're out in the woods, she appears, and says she's lost. Men either show her the way to a town, for which she leaves behind a small pot of gold, or men try to fuck her, and of course they end up with their stomach ripped open. Well, I suppose I was more careful. I was out in the woods one evening, looking for a plant under moonlight. She appeared. Of course, she said to me that she was lost, and wanted to know the way to the nearest village. Oh, yes, she was beautiful, young, and somehow her eyes beckoned me to reach under the clothing that covered her. She showed just a little bit of thigh. That, of course, is the trap. It is not so much her eyes but your loins that set the trap. I was old enough to control myself, for the moment. I told her where she was, and how to get to the capital. She thanked me, smiled, and turned away. I could see over to the left, in the forest's shadows, the golden glow of the treasure she had left behind. But to me, such treasures are worthless. I mean, if all you get is gold, what fun is that? I called out to her, just before she became a spirit and disappeared into the moonlight. She turned and looked at me. I said to her, 'Excuse me, ma'am, but I believe you left something behind.' 'What?' she said, confused. 'That,' I said, and motioned toward the golden glow. She laughed slightly and said that it was mine to take. I told her, 'Ma'am, I have no need for such gifts. Others need it much more than I. I am happy with this,' and I motioned to the woods that surrounded us. She turned her head slightly, as if amazed at a man who would turn down her riches. 'You are happy with your lot?' she asked me. 'You have no wishes, no desires?' I answered her, 'My child, I am a man. I have the desires of all men. Yet I also desire that no person be harmed.'

"That made her smile. We spoke awhile longer, about many things. She asked me a lot of questions about men, and why we act the way we do. I doubt that any man had ever spoken with the Ciguanaba like that. And she, though a force of magic, is also a woman. She gets lonely, I'm sure. She told me how difficult it was to watch men think with their balls, and how it angered her when she came across men who tried to take advantage of her. Of course, their fate was then sealed. When she spoke of those men, who were stupid enough or horny enough to reach under her dress and grab her buttocks, I saw in the moonlight the tips of her fingers and the talons that were beginning to grow out, long as blades. How many stupid men had she gutted? I thought. Then the talons disappeared. 'You are different,' she said. 'You act like a man, not a beast.'

"It was not long before we were together. She was like some young rabbit on top of me, kicking away. Then, the moment after we both cried out, she put her lips on mine, pressed hard, and vanished.

"I saw her a few times after that, and we went at it more and more. But after a while she kept on following me around. That can be embarrassing, you know, having a witch follow you everywhere."

Both men stood in front of the root cellar at the bottom of the mound. Father Mateo, sitting on one of the stones next to the cellar door, stared at the old man throughout the telling of the story. As the tale ended, the young man's jaw dropped completely open.

Don Pablo sighed, then smiled down at Mateo who sat before him like a disciple. "Let's keep walking. I want to show you something."

Pablo reached down and helped Mateo pick up his own body, for it was separating from and reconnecting to his brain every few seconds.

"Where are we going?"

Pablo said nothing. The youth followed the man as they walked quietly up one of the hills that guarded El Comienzo. Once atop it, both stopped to inhale deeply the cool night air. The moon splashed a blue haze over the grass and trees among which they stood. Don Pablo pointed towards a distant mountain. "Do you see that?"

"What?"

"You can see it better in the daytime, but look closely. See how dark it is, dark green?"

"I...I think so."

"It is a large coffee plantation."

"Oh."

Save for their heavy breathing and the scream of a thousand crickets, silence once again fell between them. Mateo's mind grasped onto his body more tightly after the long trek.

"It is much larger than before. It used to cover only half the mountain. Now that whole side is covered with coffee."

"Someone in the capital must own it."

"I don't understand. Why so much coffee?" asked the old man, as if asking the moon. "There is no one who can drink that much coffee."

"Well, I have been to the capital recently, and it is growing much bigger. Perhaps, well, perhaps they are drinking it." Mateo tossed out suggestions of answers, half-committed to the conversation, not understanding why the old man had dragged him up to see coffee trees on a distant hillside.

"There was once a banana grove on that mountain. And a forest."

"Yes, well, perhaps they did not need all that anymore. Perhaps they have enough."

The old man shook his head, bewildered. Soon he began walking downhill. Mateo stumbled behind. Don Pablo spoke no more, except to utter a "good night" to the confused priest as they separated at the base of the mound. Pablo drifted off to his home where his granddaughter awaited him with a scolding. She insisted that he never do that to the priest again, and that she would be very embarrassed the next time she went to mass. Meanwhile, the priest fell into bed in the small rectory, closed his eyes to the darkness, and watched as the eyes of Pablo's granddaughter came closer. Her hair fell once again, drifted over his stomach and buttocks, and wrapped itself tight as her face bent downward and grabbed his manhood in a multicolored whirlwind, pulling his body down a slippery hole, deeper into the thick, heavy brilliance he had been swimming in all night, until he ceased to exist, like a match swallowed by an ocean.

$$\rightsquigarrow$$

The Comenzaños heard little about what occurred outside their community. News travelled slowly, usually by means of some passerby who wandered into the village. Through the years they learned that the newly formed capital was growing very quickly, that it had a mayor, a town council, a national police force. Outside help had come to the capital, not only from other cities, but also from other countries. From El Norte, the United States, a lot had been sent to reconstruct the city in terms of building materials. Europe, in turn, had sent considerable financial aid. That was the extent of what the Comenzaños knew, since rarely did any of them venture out to the new city. What other news they received remained vague. At times they heard about a group called "The Families." They did not know who they were, other than the fact that they were Europeans.

After her seventh birthday, Romilia worked steadily beside her mother in the kitchen, washing clothes, or pressing them with the hot irons she had learned to dexterously place in and pull out of a fire. There was not, actually, much work to be done in their home. Don Pablo was the only man to be cared for, and he demanded little. Yet Amanda still worked, as if the few simple chores of her day meant her existence. When they were not working, they prayed, or at least they assumed a prayerful position. Amanda took the girl to church every afternoon, just before sundown. Even though Father Mateo would not always celebrate a daily mass, mother and daughter would sit in the pews, clicking rosary beads.

The strange stories that Don Pablo told his great granddaughter fascinated Romilia—stories about a city that once had stood huge and majestic, and that in a matter of seconds had been swallowed by the earth. And he and her mother had lived through it! In many of the old man's stories, certain themes arose again and again—death bowing to life, life losing all to death. Sometimes it was difficult for her to understand which side the old man stood on. "You were born in that turmoil, girl," he would mutter to her. "Do not forget that you were born then."

His stories took on new meaning the few times Romilia felt the earth shake. She did not panic until she looked around her and saw all her neighbors crying and running. Yet she could hardly believe that these tremors that did no harm to El Comienzo could destroy an exalted city such as the one Don Pablo spoke about. Romilia wanted to see the ruins of the old capital. Amanda never allowed it. "It is unholy ground," she said. "God grew angry with us that day, so angry that He destroyed us on the holiest of days, Easter Sunday. That is unholy, dangerous ground."

Her religion had spoken. It was useless to try to reason. Any reference to the old city tossed her mother into apocalyptic conversation. Usually Romilia saved her questions for Don Pablo, who was more than happy to elaborate on them. "Yes, girl, the earth grew angry with us. The fire in the earth consumed most of us. We had raped the land with the ugliness of that city. But the earth is not merciless, child. See what she did for us? She gave us this," he said, raising a hand and his pipe toward the mound.

It was all still very strange. When she heard the old man speak, Amanda would either rush from the doorstep where they sat or ask him to please stop bringing up the past. Afterwards and without fail, whenever Romilia walked by, her mother Amanda would bend down, grab her, and clutch her tightly, as if she feared her daughter would be swallowed into a pit. Romilia failed to respond in any way. Her mother's embrace was something abnormal to the child, something originating from an old chaos the girl had never experienced. Romilia would freeze in her mother's arms, waiting, wanting to wriggle away, but remaining there out of a child's sense of duty.

She watched, in the afternoons, as boys her own age walked toward the small church with a downcast look on their faces. They were going to school. Padre Mateo taught them math, spelling, and catechism. He taught Latin to some of the older boys, hoping to recruit someone who, as he had said many times, "May take my place here." None of the boys showed such interest. Three hours later the boys ran

A Fire in the Earth

home, their faces high. They wrestled together in the streets, laughing, free.

"What do you do with Father Mateo?" Romilia asked Juan Pedro, a boy her same age.

"We learn this." He showed her a scratched, beaten slate, still not wiped of the numbers and figures he had tried to work that day.

"What is it?"

"Math. It is difficult."

"Show me."

Juan Pedro began explaining to her how all the numbers worked together, adding, subtracting, adding again. They worked together for several afternoons. It had taken him very little time to explain it. She memorized the numbers and understood the theories quickly. Romilia helped Juan Pedro with his mistakes in addition and subtraction. Her life had prepared her for calculations such as these. In the kitchen she had to figure out how many eggs to add to a dish when a neighbor stayed over for supper. Sitting on the river rock, she counted away the dirty clothes to determine how far she was from finishing. The two children made a game of the schoolwork, and both looked forward to working together after his classes, until her mother caught them scratching math problems and numerals in the dirt behind the house.

"You have no need for that. It is knowledge for men. You need to learn what I teach you."

Romilia was scolded all the way into the house. Juan Pedro lowered his head, glancing at the slate of numbers.

Romilia returned to her work of cooking and sewing. Darkness fell over her chores. She entered her mother's kitchen as a shadow. At the end of the day she left the room with bitterness toward the cooked food and the hot, stoked oven. She still worked mathematical problems at times, writing on an old strip of cloth with a sharp piece of cooled charcoal from the fire while the moon shined through a hole in the roof. She played with the numbers dexterously, or so she thought, not knowing whether or not they were correct.

As Romilia grew, her workday became longer. Her mother decided that making goat cheese was the girl's specialty. Romilia hated the goats. They were filthy animals that ate everything, that awakened

41

her during the night as they poked their heads through a hole and let out their sudden, nasal bleating. She hated the cheese trough. Yet Amanda had taught the girl well, so that she could milk the animals and set the milk to curdle in the trough. She would stir it constantly, cover it with a thin cloth so it could rest, and finally pour it into wood trays. Later the cheese was packed and cut into small, chalky blocks that flaked apart easily. The girl never ate it.

Romilia listened less to the old man Don Pablo. His stories had gradually run together and become a babbled past. He no longer told those ancient accounts with the same fervor, and the men of the village no longer stood around him to listen. The time for that old wisdom, they said to one another, had slipped away. People walked by his doorstep, greeted him respectfully, but did not stop and talk. He did not notice. He smoked his pipe less, as if he no longer needed the tobacco to reach into that other world. As she worked in the kitchen, Romilia heard him speak of the fire in the earth, its power, of an old god that flew around and above the volcanoes, spitting them out, relighting them by lowering the sun down. Romilia grew accustomed to his broken sentences, until one day, as she carried a wooden bucket of water on her head, she saw him stare at her from his seat on the doorstep. He was not smoking the pipe at the time. She could see his boned chest move like a wind bag. She lowered her own eyes to avoid the old man's stare. It was as if he had found something in her, a thing, an object that she did not know she possessed. His head moved with affirmative understanding, yet the pipe remained still. Words fell like spring water over the pipe's stem. "Girl, it's coming. It will follow you all your life."

She said nothing. It frightened her, and the bucket on her head almost tumbled as he continued with the message, now fragmented, "It's coming...very quickly."

His voice mumbled dead. She stood there in the dread of respect, the water bucket still balanced on her head. He smoked again, and she quickly walked away from him.

Don Pablo said no more. He took a chill and turned sick. They put him on a sack of soft hay and covered him with three old blankets. Amanda stayed awake with him as the fever dug deeply into his chest.

A Fire in the Earth

Neighbors had given her extra candles. She sewed and mended clothes by the flickering flames while sitting beside him. In an opposite corner slept Romilia.

During the day friends came by. Although his mind had regressed in those weeks, the whole town still respected him. He was their living past. Tears fell from older people's eyes, old friends, still much younger than himself, people who remembered sitting on his lap in the old city, listening to the stories.

At night he whispered in groans. His voice periodically clicked with an unknown, indigenous language that sporadically tumbled along with his Spanish. One late night he moaned out, enough to awaken Amanda, "The girl, where is the little one?"

"She is fine, Papi, she is here, sleeping."

"Where is that child? Where is she? Girl!"

Romilia awoke. She raised up and stared at the old man, who was now on his elbows. The blankets fell from his upper chest. In the candlelight she saw him, staring out like a blind man. "Girl! Be careful, it is coming, it will arrive with the coffee trees. It will take you up and toss you down..."

Amanda tried to quiet him, but he said it over and over again until the message mumbled away into weariness. Romilia hunched up underneath her blanket, afraid to look out. Her dreams, working in community and against her, welcomed the old man's voice, not letting her escape the hollow echo of his words.

The next day people continued to visit. "He is worse," whispered Amanda. "It is near." Father Mateo had come by each day, and on this day said another prayer for the old man's soul, preparing it. As the sun fell over Volcano San Vicente, a crowd of people entered the small adobe home. It remained silent inside, except for a few women muttering prayers. The men held their hats in front of themselves.

The old woman entered the room and stood silently behind the others. No one knew anything about her, except for the myths that had been created in recent years. They didn't even know her name. Suddenly the old man laughed. It burst from his chest as if it were too large to escape through his mouth, and the people stood confused as Amanda rushed closer to him, smoothing his forehead, whispering to

43

him. The guffaw trickled to a chuckle, and he soon fell silent again. The crowd of friends turned to one another and whispered. Those who had stood around her noticed that the old woman had left.

That night Amanda began the bedside ritual. She lit candles, sat next to him, sewed, waited. Romilia fell asleep. Soon Amanda nodded away in her chair, her sewing resting on her lap.

The old man threw off the blankets. With some difficulty he stood up, rested on the side of the haystack, then picked himself up and walked out. Neither heard him. The past several days of waiting for death had wearied them, and they had collapsed into dreams that demanded their full attention.

He walked out into the moonless night. Though blind with fever, he still walked directly to the mound, bent toward it, and snatched a handful of its dirt. He staggered onward, a scarecrow of a body, clothes barely hanging from his limbs. He moved away from the center of the village as if escaping an infection, and with the strength of all the dead, moved toward the nearby woodland. His feet bled from stepping on sharp rocks, and the crimson of his blood washed into the shallow of the river that he crossed, running toward unknown forests and valleys that had no borders. Above him rested the stars, bright with happiness and splendor. They welcomed him to the forest. The trees greeted him as a fellow and the moss offered comfort to his feet. He held to a vine for security, and with the other hand, still filled with earth from the mound, he smeared the wrinkles of his face, rubbing again and again, caking the cracks with black soil.

> Shihuí shiquica nuna-huey
> palti fagaque tey mina
> taga azu-inte nemetzhmaca
> Naja-niáu nacrímulina

The wind whispered through the tree branches in gratitude and approval of the prayer, one not heard in these woods for well over a century. Animals ran about, squeaked and cried out in joy, and a small creek that lay behind him trickled away. Many long-dead leaves lay before him, waiting for him to rest. His bones and muscles, hundreds of years old, heavy with the generations that called out for him to join

A Fire in the Earth

them, fell forward with the confidence of a stone that had been dropped and slammed silence through the forest.

〰〰

Three days later they found the body. This disrupted the people's growing belief that he had been spirited into heaven or swallowed by the earth. Amanda wept when he disappeared. She turned confused and angry at the stench rising from the corpse. They placed the remains in a wooden box, and that morning men took time from their work to dig a grave in the small cemetery. Father Mateo buried him with liturgy. He spoke to the whole village gathered around him about how the old man had shared so much with them. He sprinkled water upon the coffin and uttered dead, Latin words that fell unheard against the pine box. Earlier, they had held a mass for him, but kept the rotting body outside since Don Pablo had never admitted to being a Christian. Still, they had the mass said. It seemed the best thing to do, the only gift the Comenzaños knew to give. But it was of no more importance than the liturgy at the graveyard. Don Pablo was inside the earth. They covered him with dirt. Later, in the continual moments of rains and dry seasons, Don Pablo smiled at the coffin that enclosed him, laughing at its rotting collapse to the greatness of the earth. He reached out to the clods of dirt and stone about him, and embraced them with great longing.

Chapter Three

Romilia had as much information on the old woman as anybody. She, along with the other young people of El Comienzo, always sought more. The myths had grown like the vines that hold together a decrepit adobe building and then grow into it, breaking the dry clay apart. Such were the children. The stories had been rooted into them more deeply with the witch's life span. Their parents said that she had been with them since the beginning. "She looked that old when I was young," said others' parents, awakening the boys' and girls' curiosity. What does she do? The children learned the answers and could recite them like correct statements to catechism questions. She steals the Eucharist from the church when Father Mateo is not watching, and dips it in her beans like a tortilla. She eats the hearts of children. At night she flies over the town, pissing on it. They knew.

During the day, though they feared the witch, the boys challenged her with taunts and laughter. She was *la bruja*. They could taunt a witch if they wanted to. It was their right to throw rocks at her, to gouge sticks into her adobe house and knock out hard clumps of clay until she ran out the door and waved a tall walking stick at them, screaming creative profanities that added dimension to their myths.

"Mamá, what is the witch?" Romilia once asked Amanda.

"Witch? She is an old woman," the mother spoke while ironing a dress, next to the burning stove. "Why?"

"I heard the boys talk about burning her."

Amanda chuckled. "Yes, that is the thing to do. Burn her, burn her. As if she had killed someone. Someday, when enough people are saying that, they will do it."

"But she *has* killed people!"

"Oh yes? Who?"

46

A Fire in the Earth

"Well...children."

"Ah, yes. What were their names? Do you know of any murdered kids?"

Romilia said nothing for a moment, then asked, "You don't think they should?"

"What?"

"Burn her."

"No, of course not. She has hurt no one. She does not do anything, true, but that is no reason to burn her, just because she never works. If that is witchcraft, then some men in this town are guilty of the same practice. Get me that *chamarra*, girl."

Romilia brought her the blanket. "It is said that she is guilty of the, of the destruction of the old city. Maybe that is a reason—"

"She did not destroy that old city, Romi. An old woman cannot destroy a city. God did that, because of our sins. And do not speak of it that way."

"What way?"

"That...that way, just throwing it around, talking about it that way."

"Papi said that the earth did it, swallowed the city up because it was angry."

"Papi said a lot of things, child. He had a different way of looking at life."

"But where did she come from, what does she do..." Her questions kept coming, as was normal for the pre-adolescent that she was. All she could get from her mother was that the town witch was nothing but a harmless old lady who never worked.

Others parents spoke at more length about her powers and her impossible age. Romilia relied on neighbors, as well as on the experiences of people her own age, for that information.

While Romilia questioned her mother in the kitchen, the old woman passed slowly by. She had just left the church. Father Mateo had seen her there. She had stood in the back of the simple building, leaning upon her staff, staring at the tabernacle with unblinking eyes. A strange position for prayer, thought the curate; nonetheless, she *was* in the church. Later he told others about it, hoping to quell some of the rampant stories. She had turned to him and stared at his back as he walked away. As soon as the pastor had exited, she did the same.

It was afternoon. Most people rested from the morning's work. She clutched her staff with a gnarled hand and shoved it in front of her while plodding onward. Two men passed by. No words were exchanged. Humped over, as if looking for something on the ground, she walked toward her old adobe house to escape the noonday sun.

A rock hummed by her left ear and cracked against a nearby building. She turned slowly, quietly, towards the corner of the alleyway where she heard the children's voices scampering away. "Concha vieja!" *Filthy old cunt.* They disappeared around the corner, into the harsh sunlight that protected them.

In the slight shadow of the alleyway stood a lone boy. A building sat squarely behind him. His one hand clutched some ammunition; the other stood empty, guilty. He did not speak, but she could hear his breathing, could feel his heart beat against his ribs like a caged animal. It was all she needed.

Her cowl fell back slightly as she raised her head. She tossed him a grin. He could not move, for she had ordered invisible claws to burst from the street and clutch his quivering ankles. Above her smile the wrinkles broke and cracked. One of her vulture eyes tore open the stiff skin surrounding it and excreted a teardrop that fell over her cavernous cheek. Another followed, and the two teardrops joined to form a red liquid flame that trickled out and grew in its descent. It slid over her soiled neck, fell to the dusty road, and crawled toward the boy. He stared at other red drops which fell from her head and joined the original flaming tear. They bulked together and grew in size and weight. The giant liquid flame raised over him, and a head pushed outward. It had bloodshot eyes and several mouths with the fangs of a crazed dog. Crimson dripped from the teeth, and the monster smiled like she smiled. They encircled him, rose high above, then crashed down.

He dropped the stone and fled from the deserted street, which echoed with the laughter of an old woman.

48

A Fire in the Earth

The two friends said nothing to each other while they walked toward the young cemetery. Both Silvia Montenegro and Amanda Velásquez carried flowers which they had created from scraps of old cloth. They placed them at the base of the blue, wooden cross that marked the peace of Amanda's grandfather. The women knelt down and held their position while the beads of solemnity clicked against one another with whispered winds of prayer.

Few crosses protruded from the earth, as there had been little death. To Don Pablo's left lay a woman that had twenty-four grandchildren and ten great grandchildren. Just above him rested the aged bones of someone's grandfather. No one lay to his right or below him. Above him, farther up the hill, stood the three small graves of those who had died in childhood. That was all. Their town was blessed, to have only three deaths of children in the thirteen years of its existence. Those had passed away in the very beginning, when the silent violence of disease and hunger still threatened them.

After the prayer, the two women spoke of inconsequential subjects: the lack of water in this seemingly never-ending dry season; little Romilia and her adolescent inconstancy; the wonder of where the old man's soul was now, not in heaven, and yet not in hell either; perhaps not even in purgatory. God must have some comfortable place for stubborn old Indians. Perhaps on some quiet old mountain where fruit trees grew, along with the old man's favorite plant.

For a long moment both turned quiet, comfortable in their friendship. Something suddenly galloped from behind and kicked up dust like laughter. Silvia released a string of small, interlocking curses as both women shielded their eyes from the dust. They looked up and saw that a horse and carriage stood next to them. A head stuck through a small window. They had never seen such a strange, sickly looking face. The man's hair was blonde, like that of children who suffered malnutrition. Yet this man seemed healthy, except for his red nose that looked like someone had held a burning ember to it.

"Good morning, women. Sorry I am for the dust storm. It is impossible to not upset it, true?"

They looked up at him. He smiled, perfect teeth reflecting a hot sun. He spoke their language brokenly, tossing the salutation to them like shell fragments. A stranger, most certainly.

The being stepped out of the carriage. He was dressed in new brown leather, all over, from his neck to his boots. Pieces of metal pretending to be diamonds dangled from various parts of his body, and a smart hat, too new to have seen much use, topped him. He was a young man, perhaps in his twenties, the women could not be sure.

From the carriage top a second man came down. He was older, though he too dressed well. Though dark-skinned, he was obviously a man of high learning. He had no callouses.

The pale man spoke. "I am named Schonenburg. Hans Schonenburg." Amanda and Silvia turned slightly to each other, and endeavored in whispers to pronounce the confusing, obviously foreign last name. With much timidity they mumbled their own names, which fell like dead leaves onto the dry earth of the man's unhearing ears. He continued. "Could you please direct me to your mayor's office?" They stood silent, as if afraid to talk, not because they did not know the answer. They wondered how to speak to someone who so butchered words and phrases.

"Excuse me? Excuse me? Ma'am, could you please...ma'am, please, what is name your?"

She repeated, though more slowly, "Silvia Córdoba Montenegro, at your service."

"Ah, Silvia, pleased I am meet you. Could you say me where office mayor is?"

Silvia glanced quickly at Amanda, and they argued silently with their eyes as to who would say it. They both did, their words meshing together, "We do not have a mayor."

"No mayor. How not have mayor? No one for town runs it? Who is man who, who directs?"

They were silent again, then their own silence frightened them. "You could talk with any one of the men. They are not the leaders. But you can still talk with them."

A Fire in the Earth

"Yes. Well," he waited a moment, looked about at the simplicity of the town, then stared back down at them. "You are...ejidal, true?" he asked, like a child learning the sins of another child.

"Well, yes, it started that way, I believe so, isn't that true Amanda?..."

"I see." Schonenburg turned to his companion and mumbled in the clarity of a proud language, hard yet moving gibberish to the women, "Yes, I have heard of these places. But I have never seen one. My ideas were correct on what they are like. Thank God for the new laws." He turned back, smiled, and once again spoke like a baby. "You, thank you, women." He wiped the smile away while opening the carriage door.

More dust kicked off the mockery of wooden wheels. The women shielded their eyes, while Silvia compared the rich young man with the pubic hairs of an old dog. They picked up their buckets and walked home, where they spoke profusely with other neighbors.

News travelled from the moment it was created. The young rich fellow had gone to the heart of town, had back-slapped some of the men as if he knew them well. "He is from the capital. He just moved there recently, from Europe," neighbors told Amanda. "Can you believe he told Don Aldo to give his horses some water from the inside drinking trough! As little as there is now, and he is racing his animals all over the countryside, and telling us to give the animal our drinking water!"

"What's that name of his? Jyona...Jyoh...something like that."

"Is he from Spain? He kind of looks it."

"Certainly does. But he speaks some other tongue."

"I heard them talking about coffee. That is when the men started getting hot. I am not sure what they all said, but they said something about buying land."

"Land? What land?"

"I have no idea."

"Hhmph. He probably wants to sell us some of his land." Silvia looked around at the women in her kitchen. "Well, I'll get the straight story tonight. Juan was with them. He'll tell us what happened."

Marcos Mcpeek Villatoro

The women continued weaving speculations of why such a nobly dressed yet sickly youth was interested in them, in their village, of why, in the constancy of a dry April day, he appeared like a clean, leather bat flying through their village. Though they performed their chores, they wasted no opportunity of seeking out one another at the well, at the root cellar, in the shade between the adobes, where they tossed the subject from one to the other until the focus of the story, the young man himself, galloped through the main street of the village and spat out two words he seemed to have memorized. He uttered them clearly. "Campesinos tontos!" *Stupid peasants!* It halted all gossip. The carriage disappeared in a cloud of dust.

The encounter was a reminder to them all. The young man's insult resurrected a feeling of forgotten submission. Those who suddenly remembered were stunned by a reality which said to them with a sardonic voice that life is very long, and freedom very short. When Juan Montenegro arrived home, he stared dead at the floor as he spoke, relaying to them in a monotone words that the young rich man had said through his translator. Promises were made. Confusion had erupted. Words had been tossed about like chips on a gambling table, money, land, buying produce, coffee. They had spoken mostly about the latter. Schonenburg owned the large coffee fields on the other side of the hill where the sun set, far in the distance from El Comienzo. They were growing. The crop was expanding, and a cold green lava of trees spread out and away from La Joya Mountain. "He said that he wanted us to grow coffee here, that we could make money from it. Everyone would make money, according to the stranger. Then everyone could buy the food they needed, instead of growing it."

"How did the other men speak?" asked Silvia.

"José was for it. You know. When the man started talking about money, José jumped right in. But Carlos, he did not care for the idea. Me? I do not know. It would mean a lot of changes." Juan looked down again and chuckled. "It began to get a little hot for a moment. At the end he talked about how backward we are out here, cut off from the rest of the world. He said, or his interpreter told us, 'You do not know who the president of the United States is?' Then he told us, it was Gran, Grand, something like that. Then he said something about some other president up there getting kicked out of office sometime back, that it was the big news all over the world. I do not see why, we used to go through that all the time. Then he talked about the railroad that is being built. You remember that? They were building it when we were still in the capital. Then he started up about being free from Mexico. It was then that Carlos started burning. The stranger asked, 'You *do* know that we are free from both Mexico and Spain, don't you?' Carlos got pissed off with that. 'Yes,' he said, 'we know about our independence. We know how free we are.' I know that Carlos is not interested in raising coffee. He doesn't trust the stranger."

"Why so much coffee? Did you ask why him they're raising so much over on Joya?"

Juan breathed out heavily. "He said something about how it is helping the economy of the whole country to raise only one crop. Then they ship it to other countries and sell it there. Then our country gets more money. He said that there are a lot of people in other countries drinking our coffee."

"There must be hundreds, with as much coffee growing on Joya." Silvia spoke with a naive cynicism. "So what's going to happen?"

"Carlos said we had to think about it. That's when the young goat got angry. He started telling us that we would always be backward if we did not join in with the rest of the country in order to help the economy. That we're the only *ejidal* left in this area, and that it was towns like ours that kept the nation from getting any better. Then he took off. His servant said nothing, but climbed up on the carriage. No handshakes or nothing."

"It's better that way," came a voice from the door, interrupting the general conversation. "I'd rather not shake the hand of the man whose balls I'm going to blow away." Everyone turned. There stood Carlos, the man of Juan's story. An old rifle dangled from his fingers, its barrel suffocating in rust.

"They're going to try to take our land! My son has been to the capital. He told me what people told him. They want to take it all!"

Except for Juan, who turned his head as if in embarrassment, they all stared at Carlos. He ranted on, not stopping even for Silvia's interruption when she told him to put the weapon away. "We can't let them do it! This is our land, they will not take it!"

"They can't take it, Carlos. The stranger wants to *buy* it from us."

Juan's words offered little consolation. All the neighbors soon left, except for Carlos. He hung the rifle on a peg in the wall. Silvia invited the angry man to eat. She prepared the evening meal in an attempt to calm things down. She piled plates of food for her husband, for Carlos, and for the three children who sat silently at the table. Juan Pedro, the only boy and the eldest, the child who had taught the few lessons of mathematics to his neighbor Romilia, watched intently as the fervent conversation between the two men continued.

"We will fight for our rights! We do have rights, we are protected, we must—"

"How will we fight? You own the only gun in town, and it's got only one bullet. Besides, perhaps we will not need to fight at all. We will simply say 'no' to whatever offer they make."

But, Juan, you know that there are others here who will accept the offer. It is temptation, money. And my son kept talking that the offer would be for *lots* of money, shit! And if they do not listen, then we must fight. If they do not hear our 'no,' then they will listen to that." He pointed to the rusty weapon.

Either weariness or Juan's appeasement calmed Carlos down slightly, but not completely. After another hour of incessant talking, the conversation began to run in circles, and they were repeating the same phrases, ones that resounded in Carlos' ears like chants urging people to revolt. Finally the phrases dwindled and vanished into the night. Carlos excused himself, thanked Silvia for the meal, and walked home, clutching the rifle.

A bugle blast was the only warning. Then came the high wave of dust, kicked up by the hooves of thirty horses. The men who rode into town wore little leather badges branded with an official government seal on their uniforms. The Comenzaños had never seen them before. They had only heard about them. Perhaps this is what they call the

A Fire in the Earth

Guardsmen, many said in whispers. Behind the horsemen, Schonenberg's carriage followed. The German was still well-dressed. He wore a different pair of leather chaps and a different cowboy hat. Two men in derbies sat next to him, talking with animation to each other.

The caravan of Guardsmen rode up to the mound, directly in front of the root cellar's door. The farmers working on the mound had watched the band ride into El Comienzo, and now stood and waited. The new arrivals broke into groups and rode through every street of the small village. They circled the mound. "Gentlemen," spoke one of the officials, "by official decree of our government, we have come to El Comienzo." He reached into the vest of his uniform, pulled out a slip of paper, unfolded it, and began reading in a loud, monotonous voice. "This is from your capital. A new law has been passed and will now be enforced throughout the country. Please listen." Around him the scuffling and loud mumbling of the Comenzaños tried to drown out his voice, but he waited until everyone turned quiet.

He read:

The House of Representatives of the Republic,
CONSIDERING:
1. That agriculture is the nation's chief source of life and prosperity and that it is the duty of the Legislature to remove any obstacle to its development;
2. That a principal obstacle is the communal land system in that it annuls the benefits of ownership of the larger and most important lands in the Republic now used for less intensive forms of cultivation, or causes the abandonment of land due to its precarious and uncertain tenure by its holders, thus preventing them from the right of developing the said land;
3. That resolutions passed to abolish the common land system by indirect means have not achieved the purpose of the Legislature;

HEREBY DECLARES THAT:
Article ONE: The system of the *ejidal* throughout the country hereby is abolished...

The official's voice droned on, spattering the details of the newly passed law. The people heard him no more, but turned to one another in panic, searching for an answer. Angry retorts wove in and out of the crowd.

"What do you mean that it is abolished?"

The man stopped reading. He looked down as if bothered by a persistent child. "You are wasting the land. You are not exploiting it as well as you should. This is a very slow way of farming." He motioned to the mound that had recently been seeded with various vegetables. "The whole country feels this waste, you see. We must use every acre, every inch of land for the good of the whole country, for its economy, you see. For the sake of everyone, this law has been passed."

It was obvious that he had been through this before, that he had rehearsed it over and over again before other multitudes of farmers who had asked the same questions. He continued reading the proclamation, ignoring the growing mutterings and shouts from the crowd.

"What about us? This is our land. You cannot take our land!"

"This is the law," answered another, younger official, standing near the farmer who questioned. "It is a law that protects everyone in the nation. You are part of the nation, so you will be looked after." This only pacified them for a moment. The ranking official continued reading words which, to him, were clear and precise, but to the Comenzaños were nothing but drifts of charred wind. Many heard the word "auction" from the official's droning lips. Some shouted the word back in disbelief. As the farmers argued amongst themselves, the official on horseback rode the animal like a plough through the crowd and cleared out an area on the street. The men in the carriage crawled out, brushing the slight dust that covered their suits. Schonenberg gestured his companions forward. They walked between the horses of the armed officials. The three talked amiably, looking over the papers.

The official pulled out a second sheet of paper. "Your attention please," he called out. "This public auction has now begun. All are invited to attend. The auction is for the purpose of selling this land on which we stand, which extends from the foot of Mount Joya to the west to the foot of Cerro Negro to the east, from San José Guayabal to the north to the site of the old capital to the south. You can have the rubble, too."

Only the three businessmen chuckled.

A Fire in the Earth

"This is a total of 56,000 acres. The bidding begins at fifteen colones an acre. Do I have a bidder?" the Official hurriedly called out.

The three well-dressed men thrust their bids over the crowd that stood at a safe distance, behind the strong, threatening horses with the tall men upon their backs. The amounts of currency in colones flashed between the three men in close competition. There was barely any hesitation between one loud bid and the next. Then the official-turned-auctioneer's voice echoed the offers, "Twenty colones from Señor Hills, twenty-five colones from Señor d'Aubuisson, thirty from Señor Schonenberg, forty from Señor d'Aubuisson..."

The crowd had turned silent, not knowing these men, nor their names. The three spat out the weight of their wealth in a pitched battle of figures, vying to win the game. The auctioneer rattled the names with a familiarity that spoke of friendship, never hesitating over the difficulties of foreign pronunciation. The people stood and stared, their mouths still mumbling about land, home, crops. Old men squinted in the sun, some women cried, yet no one moved until hope rang out. First the force of gunshot, followed by the angry courage of the phrase, "Damn all of you, you cannot do this!" But then came a second shot, different from the first, more clean and accurate. Juan's farming partner Carlos fell to the ground, clutching his stomach.

One soldier on horseback held his arm where the farmer's only bullet had wounded him. He looked down at the bleeding villager, cursing him with vehemence. The official who shot Carlos jumped from his own horse, kicked the rusted rifle to one side, and held his boot into Carlos' stomach where blood stained the heel.

"You are under arrest."

Other officials crowded around, tied the wounded man's arms from behind, and flung him over the back of a horse. The animal, smelling the blood and feeling the weight of the man drop onto its back, bucked to throw it off. Carlos fell to the ground face first, his hands held together from behind.

"Leave the prick there," barked the commander.

They did. The auction had ended. All had been settled. Hills had bought a third of the land to the west; d'Aubuisson the third to the east; and Schonenberg owned the middle. Because of the gunshots, the armed officials stood ready, guarding the streets all over the little village. Other officers handed picks, shovels, and hatchets to the farmers, and at gunpoint told them to begin uprooting.

"And set fire to the shit on that mound."

Upon hearing the order, Schonenberg, who was speaking with one of the other buyers about how much coffee they could plant, turned. He spoke in his broken Spanish. "No, wait. They keep if want."

The senior official standing nearby turned to Schonenberg. "No, Señor Schonenberg, it is best not to. If we gave them that hill to do whatever they wanted to with it, then we would have to give other villages some pieces of land, too. We have not done so. We must keep the farmers on equal footing, or they will hear of the inequalities and rebel."

Schonenberg pulled a thin cigar from his vest while listening to the explanation. He understood fragments, then turned his head to the interpreter. Behind the officer's truth stood the reluctant farmers, climbing the mound with picks and small torches from various cooking fires. A man yelled from the foot of the mound, protesting, almost crying. An official told him to shut up, pointing a rifle at his face. Schonenberg barely glanced at the official who spoke with logic. The official's face, hard with authority, spoke again. "See how difficult they can be? But not impossible." He tipped his hat to the young landowner and walked away to perform more duties.

Schonenberg bowed his head slightly to the government official while sucking the cigar. He flicked dead ashes upon the dusty road. A slight wind gathered them up and deposited them into the burning, dried-out cornfields.

Silvia's husband Juan climbed the mound with a torch in hand. An official down below instructed him to light the few old dead vines and plants that enwrapped the mound.

"But we just planted seed here."

The official looked up at him, saying nothing.

"You cannot expect us to burn all our seed. At least let us dig it out."

Again the soldier answered with a stare. The senior official rode over, shouted at Juan to get his balls moving, that it was not his land.

A Fire in the Earth

Juan stood, empty as an eggshell. He bent down and set the torch to an old, dry vine. The flame ran through the vine, consuming it, continued through another, which snaked under the ground. It popped and cracked the seeds that sat in the womb of the dry earth, waiting for rain. The fire crackled slowly, and Juan followed it with dry, sunken eyes. He looked down at the land that burned before him, watched his townspeople as they scattered about with their cries and wails, watched as the officials, with all their handsome rifles, endeavored to silence them all, shooing them away from the jerking body of the wounded, bound Carlos. Silvia, Amanda, and Romilia stood in a bit of shade, weeping. The priest ran about, trying to talk some form of reason, of morals, to the new owners of the land who turned deaf ears. Above Juan the dirty church smoked, the old, parched wood spitting flames like torches. The tongues of fire danced upward from the little church to snatch at other clouds, true clouds, pure and gray, swollen with rain. Within the hour it unleashed the new, wet season that all had been expecting with anticipation. The blind water showered down upon all—rich, poor, armed and unarmed. Mud mixed with soot and ash, washing soil away. The new owners jumped in their carriage and were carried to distant homes where the Unseen dwelled. The official Guardsmen guided their horses to refuge under lean-tos. They remained in the town and became the newest residents. The people took their tears to their homes. And the rains came on, promising the sublime hope of new crops.

〰〰

In January, coffee was harvested throughout the country. The area around El Comienzo, however, though thick with healthy green branches, stood bare of coffee beans. A two-year wait stretched before they would put out beans, and a third year beyond that before a decent crop would be ready to be picked. The people sold nothing and bought nothing their first year. Neither did they store. There had been no chance to harvest months before when the government officials first entered their village and the men with the strange names bought the land. The root cellar was barren, for the cheese made from the goats'

59

milk was consumed almost immediately. The goats could not keep up with the demand. Many cows had been slaughtered during the November-to-January interval to supplement the scarcity of rice and beans. Soon there were no cows left. The soldiers told them to ration the remaining rice and beans, while the capital tried to send them limited portions. They also sent one of their own men, a professional, to implement an official form of rationing.

Romilia lost much weight during that first year, and turned sickly. She had always been a plump, healthy child. Eating less had taken its toll quickly on her. Her fifteen-year-old face became hollow, turning inward. She kept a fever for several days and had to remain in bed. Throughout the days of the girl's illness, her mother remained next to her, placing rags on the young woman's face, giving her sips of water. While Silvia watched Romilia, Amanda visited the church, praying for an hour at a time, ignoring the pains in her brittle knees as she leaned on the hardwood floor before the tabernacle.

The girl had to eat. That was the only cure Silvia could offer. "How are you doing with rice, beans?"

"Fine, we are fine. Yes, I will get her to eat more, but it is so difficult for her to sit up, and with her throwing up so..."

Amanda soaked and boiled the beans. A half a pound of beans was left. It sat in a shadowed corner, protected. They had no rice. There were no other condiments, no onions, peppers, or salt. Yet the beans were full of strength, Amanda knew that.

When Romilia could finally sit up in bed, Amanda gave her some of the liquid from the soup to drink, then fed her the beans once she saw she could keep them down. Romilia ate a small bowlful. She drank more water, then some sips of sweet coffee. A day passed. That night she ate another bowl. When Romilia fell back to sleep, her mother massaged her forehead with the tips of her fingers, then rubbed old, warm skunk fat on her bare chest, hoping to loosen some of the sickness. She rubbed continuously, hoping for a cure with each stroke. The skin up to Romilia's neck glistened with the melted animal fat. Amanda smoothed the fat over the sunken, wood-dark breasts, making the child's nipples stand up. Amanda sang an old children's song that calmly pleaded for the little one to sleep. The mother tried to keep her

A Fire in the Earth

voice from trembling as she almost whispered the words of the song, "¿Por qué lloras niña? Por una manzana que se había caido debajo de la cama..." Amanda covered her, draping two blankets all the way to Romilia's chin, and then she got in bed next to her daughter, praying them both into dreams.

The following morning Amanda awoke early, before the sun. She relit the fire to boil the beans and added more water. Again Romilia ate, drank half a cup of coffee, and returned to her sleep. Amanda cleaned the house, waiting for lunch, when she could once again give food to her girl. The afternoon passed listlessly for the mother, and when supper came, she gave Romilia refried beans, smashed into oil, with borrowed tortillas from a neighbor down the street. Romilia ate, then slept deeply that night. The fever seemed to have broken, and Amanda once again smoothed her fingers over her daughter's face and rubbed the hot fat deep into her chest before getting in bed next to her once again.

For the next two days she followed the same pattern, feeding the child beans, walking her to the latrine, bringing her back to bed, feeding her again. When Romilia finally spoke, for the first time in days, she asked for a piece of sweet bread. Her mother smiled. The girl was finally hungry. Yet, Amanda had no bread. She ran out to the neighbors' homes, asking for one piece, just one, for her sick daughter. All the town knew of Romilia's fever, as they knew of late of several children getting sick. They turned shameful glances toward Amanda, saying that they would give her their last piece if they had any. She walked away gracefully and sought out someone else. Her blind asking led her to the witch's house, an adobe shack she had never visited before, not in all her years of living in El Comienzo. Her child's hunger drove away all the taboos and legends surrounding this house. "Please, would you happen to have some sweet bread, just one piece, to give me? My daughter has been sick, and she needs to eat..."

Her breath stopped, suddenly realizing where she was standing. She brushed back a long lock of hair that had fallen to the side of her face. The old woman looked up at her, said nothing, and waited for Amanda to finish talking. She chewed on a tortilla, and Amanda could hear the wet smacking of teeth and lips.

"I have sweet bread. It is worth five pesos apiece."

"I, I have no money. I cannot buy anything."

"Very well."

Amanda stood, confused. The old woman continued chewing, not moving from her rickety chair next to the doorstep.

"Could you please...my daughter Romilia has been sick, could you please give me one piece?"

The old woman chewed. She glanced down at her dirty lap, at the stains upon her old, rotting dress. This was the first time Amanda had seen the full of her face—wrinkled, cracked, lacking in emotion, a rocky cliff beaten by the weather and ill treated by the world since the beginning of life. Suddenly the legends echoed in her head, the myths that the children cherished.

The woman creaked off her chair, walked into her hole of a kitchen, and returned with a small piece of sweet bread, still warm from a burning adobe oven. "Here. You owe me twenty pesos."

Amanda hesitated at first, then snatched the bread and thanked the old woman profusely. She walked away. As she was about to turn a corner, she heard the old woman's voice. It seemed to be pulling Amanda's long hair, tearing at the scruff of her neck.

"Remember, you *owe* me!"

Amanda spun around, nodded her head in confused obedience, and walked on. Her mouth filled with warm mucus and she almost shoved the bread to her lips. But she remembered what it was for and tried to ignore the huge white blobs that blinded her sight. She walked the streets, turned the corners, and reached her pathway. Someone said hello; she could not distinguish who. Her body searched and demanded, a wild dog hunting, thinking of nothing else. She walked through her door, almost tripping on the step, turned to the bed and smiled at her daughter.

"I have some bread for you."

"Thank you."

Amanda handed it to her, walked to the stove, and stirred the beans. "Can you eat some more?"

"Yes. Perhaps a bowl."

A Fire in the Earth

Amanda poured the beans into the clay vessel, brought the bowl to her child, turned towards her own straw bed, and then walked away and out the door. "I'm going to rest for a little bit," she said as she stepped outside. She could see the pot of hot beans on the stove, the coffee that licked around the white blobs of light before her eyes. She felt her abdomen twist inward, which forced her legs to buckle down.

The neighbors came running when they heard Romilia's screaming. They tried to control the contortions of Amanda's body. They placed her in the straw pallet. Silvia looked around Amanda's kitchen. She found the sack of beans with barely one handful left, as if Amanda were saving it for the final moments.

The women managed to find handfuls of beans and rice in their own homes, along with half an onion, a tomato pulled from a hidden plant behind one of the adobes, and a subversively grown pepper. They filled one pot with rice and one with beans, and cooked supper in Amanda's kitchen, undoubtedly the richest meal in town that evening. They started out by feeding her first the liquid from the beans, and then slowly introduced the other foods.

Silvia shook her head at Amanda, who was beginning to awaken.

"What good are you if you starve to death? Oh wait, don't tell me. You were fasting for the Lord." Silvia turned and looked at Romilia, who had propped herself upon the bed, staring at her mother with worried eyes. Romilia's long hair flowed over her shoulders, and her renewing health brought some beauty to her hollowed cheeks.

"No, perhaps not for the Lord," remarked Silvia, and she turned to her friend, who had fallen asleep. Silvia touched Amanda's face, feeling for fever. She kissed her forehead and made sure the serape was tucked under her chin. Later she told the other women of her plans to spend the night.

♒

In February, the coffee harvest ended. Thousands of pounds of beans were sent in sacks from the capital. Small trains carried them to southern seafronts. From there they were shipped to buyers in Europe, the United States, to all who would buy. It had been a bumper crop. The families with the strange names came together to celebrate the growth of their new economy. They each had sent a free sack of coffee beans to their relatives in the old countries as a symbol of their recent successes.

In the capital, Schonenberg, d'Aubuisson, and Hill planned and worked, making sure that their lands near the city of Sonsonate would yield as good a harvest the coming year. They speculated on the newly acquired plantations near the old capital. Within the next two years they hoped it would begin to produce. Until then, they knew it was necessary to continue sending some resources to that village. They had heard that they were losing people, that families were moving away. They knew that they had to keep them on the land, at least for another two years. Resources would help, more beans and rice, an occasional barrel of cream. And new laws, of course, were necessary. They worked on the latter after ordering their warehouse managers to send a few more bags of beans and rice and two barrels of cream to the village of El Comienzo. "That should make them happy," said Schonenberg, smiling.

They also sent notes to the government, with advice and ideas on the regulation of movement in the country. It would be better, they said, to keep people in the areas where they already lived. These and other requests were enacted into law with prompt action on the part of the legislature. Beans and rice continued to be sent to the village; periodic checks as to the maturing of the coffee trees also continued. The Schonenbergs and d'Aubuissons congratulated themselves for their adroit business activities while they continued to plan together.

The two years whittled away, and officers from the families with the strange names came out to the little village more regularly. They brought with them more pressure to be exerted, along with a promise: Keep working towards a good harvest, or there won't be as much beans and rice; and, when the coffee comes in, you will get money.

With the third season the trees sprouted buds that bowed heavy and crimson. The people of the village rejoiced with the arrival of the juicy red hope that hung from the branches. Money would soon come, as soon as they mustered the strength to pick the beans. Cash would replenish their old way of living and bring along new buildings, small markets, new people.

~~~
~~~

At the beginning of the rainy season that year, a young man on a strong horse rode through the streets. He tipped his hat to a passing guard, apparently out of forced respect. The man tied his horse to a trough near Amanda's house, and wandered about, searching. He turned to Romilia, who was standing outside, washing clothes in a huge, wooden tub and rubbing them brutally against a rough, flat stone the size of a small table. She threw water on the clothes from a rain barrel.

"Excuse me, miss, is there a hotel nearby?"

She looked toward him, then pulled her eyes downward, away from his direct stare, his expensive riding suit. She turned carefully from side to side, wishing he were addressing someone else. Her hands were still scrubbing the clothes on the large slate, only more slowly now.

"Hey, miss. Yes, you. Could you help me, please?"

She stopped her work, stared with a bowed face at the man. He had addressed her as *tú*, the familiar form, used between intimate people, friends, loved ones, children. He appeared somewhat older than herself, though she no longer looked like a child. Life had brought her to womanhood over quicker roads. Yet he had thrown the word *tú* at her flippantly, as if they had known each other for years.

"We have no hotel."

"What? You have nothing? What do you do with passersby?"

"We...the town, someone takes them in if they need a place to stay."

"Oh. And who might I talk to in regard to this?"

"If you know someone in town, you could talk with them—"

"Wonderful. I don't know anyone." He turned, and mumbled something that she did not understand, some alien tumble of words.

"What?" she asked.

"What? Oh, that. Just an English phrase. 'What a heck of a place.'" He spat it off his tongue like a true *gringo*, or as she believed a gringo would speak. The young man grinned proudly for a brief moment, knowing he had impressed her. Then he quickly became stern again. "Look, where is your father? Can I talk to him?"

"I have no father. You speak English?"

"Yes, I speak English. Listen, it looks like I know only you. Do you have a husband? No? Well, could it be possible to stay at your place? Is your mother home, or someone I can speak to about this?"

To talk with her mother, to sleep with them, the use of the word *tú*... She shivered from his frivolity, his disregard of certain taboos. Or was life outside of El Comienzo so different now?

"Look, my name is Patricio, Patricio Colónez. I'm from the capital, and I need a place to stay for a couple of days. I...I will just sleep on your porch or something. Look, do you have any family? Could I talk with someone else?" He was young and strong in speech, and acted as no other man she had ever met. Perhaps it was the English.

"Do you have a mother?"

The rise of his demanding voice pulled her out from her thoughts. She went to retrieve her mother. Amanda came out and stood on the porch, tall, much older than both of them, her arms crossed over her chest and her eyes directly upon the stranger's face.

"May I help you?"

"Uh, yes, like I told your girl there, I am in from the city, and I need a place to stay for a couple of days. I am building a brickyard on that hill up there, and I need to check out an area to build my house."

"You are building a what?"

"A brickyard. You know, for making bricks."

Amanda looked toward the hill. "That is farmland."

"Not any more, ma'am. I just bought some of the land from the Schonenbergs. Some of their leftovers. Just east of this little village of yours there is plenty of good, red clay for brickmaking. They burned that area down, you know. Thought they would grow coffee on it. It didn't have good planting soil. But I heard about it and saw the possibility for another business in it. Being close to this village, I can hire several workers. Looks like work is needed here. Anyway, I need a place to stay for a couple of nights. If I could just stay on your porch. You can give me a serape or something. I'll be fine."

"I'm sorry, but perhaps you should go elsewhere, perhaps to the church."

"No, I do not want to stay there, God, no." He turned away. "Look, no one else knows me here. I am only asking you for the porch. I will be gone in a couple of days. I can pay you, and if you feed me, I will pay you for that. And I can wash down at the river."

Amanda stared at him, but her eyes wavered at his proposal. She looked down to the ground, her arms still together, then looked back at him and slowly accepted the offer. Patricio smiled and graciously thanked her. After Amanda returned to her house, the young man winked at Romilia, which sent her cowering behind her wash water and wet, dirty pile of clothes.

∿∿
∿∿

Patricio Colónez slept on their porch, and left two nights later. Two weeks afterwards he returned, and again requested the use of their porch until he had built his house. He slept on Amanda's porch for a month while hired men from El Comienzo built a quick, one-room adobe house, along with shelters and work buildings for the brickyard on top of the hill. Once he had moved into the adobe house, he behaved like any other neighbor, as if he were accustomed to such limited conditions of life. Yet Patricio's dress and overall appearance were not those of a man who would live in an adobe. People were correct in their estimations of him. While they constructed the brickhouse, ovens and warehouse, the men also built his home on the same hill as the brick factory. It was much larger than any other adobe, made of small bricks and lumber. No one had a house of lumber.

Patricio spent his days at the construction site, many times stripping off his string tie and coat and lending his hands to the labor. Later, he worked every day with them. As the weeks passed and Patricio became a familiar figure, all the men tried to be hired on at his brickhouse. Colónez paid more at the factory than did the Schonenberg family for picking coffee. Working on the hill was far better than

67

walking out into the wide ocean of coffee bushes, where deadly marching ants and serpents awaited.

While still dwelling in the small, temporary adobe, Patricio periodically visited Amanda and Romilia, asking how things were going and whether or not they needed anything. Blatant and crude, he stumbled over his questions without any indication of the formal mannerisms to be expected from a man of his financial status. He brought gifts with every visit. He littered their house with odds and ends brought from the capital, useless knick-knacks that they would never buy themselves, but that the two women adored, especially Romilia. On nails dangled small crucifixes dipped in fake gold paint, and a cheap copy of an Aztec insignia. Little bowls of tiny clay fruit were scattered over a table. A new serape of brilliant colors was draped over an old chair, covering its age and dilapidation. Sometimes they found a ten-colón note tucked under one of the serapes. Once, badly hidden under a new, minuscule bowl of clay fruit, there was a fifty-colón note folded many times over.

Sometimes, after a visit to the capital, Patricio brought them freshly cut steaks or ocean fish packed in cool water and rags. "Look, just this morning this thing was swimming in the Pacific Ocean, right outside the beach at La Libertad!" he would say. Neither woman had been to the ocean, though they had heard much about it from friends who had worked there in younger days. Amanda could not reject these gifts, or they would spoil. And she and her daughter were hungry. She fixed the fish the same way she fixed any fish from a nearby stream, frying it in deep animal fat. She always asked Patricio to stay with them for dinner, an invitation that stemmed from pride. He always accepted. He sat at the loosely nailed table with them, seemingly comfortable on the splintered bench, content with placing his elbows over the creaking wood. He lived as if he had known this before. He welcomed such invitations to eat with them until it was no longer necessary for her to ask him. While Amanda cooked, Patricio glanced periodically and smiled at young Romilia who worked in another corner of the kitchen, and who knew not what to do.

"He wants to marry her," Silvia said to Amanda as they made tortillas together one morning, sharing the rationed corn flour, and hop-

A Fire in the Earth

ing to make it last longer. Silvia was tasting a morsel of cold fish her friend had saved for her.

"Be quiet. That is not true. Besides, that can't be. He is not one of us."

"You are either blind or lying. Friend, you know how he looks at her. The other evening when I walked in, he was staring at her like a snake at a baby dove."

"Yes. That is love, most certainly."

"It is only a matter of time."

"Time. Time and money. Silvia, he is a rich man! There is no way—"

"Rich, yes, and he shovels shit, too! I have seen him working in that brickyard of his with all the rest of our men. He's not afraid of sweat. He may have money, but he's a *labriego* in his heart and in his arms." A compliment for them, to call someone a peasant, made Amanda smile. She knew the same word for others was pejorative: *labriego*, to those people, meant poor, dirty, stupid.

"Why fight it, Amanda? Just think, you could have grandchildren who could speak English." Silvia laughed at her own joke.

"Stop that. You are going too far, friend. I do not know where Señor Colónez learned his English, but that does not mean my grandchildren will speak it, too—"

"Ah! '*My* grandchildren!' So you *have* been thinking about it!"

"Shut up! You said it first!" Amanda smiled with embarrassment while still shaping a tortilla. Before thinking, she threw the raw, flaccid dough at Silvia, who ducked, but not in time. The two lifelong friends welled with tears of laughter until Romilia walked in, a bucket of water on her head.

"What's the joke?" she asked, looking at the dough on Silvia's cheek.

"Oh, nothing, girl. We're laughing about rich and poor, you know," said Silvia. Amanda fell into more suppressed laughter. They both started up again.

The confused young woman set the water down and walked to the only adjoining room, separated from the kitchen by an old curtain. She breathed out a slight huff of adolescent anger at not knowing what the women were joking about.

The girl snatched one of the trinkets Patricio had given them and held it to the sunlight stealing in through the small window. The clay bananas were painted red and yellow, the mango green, the papaya a darker green. To the side of the bananas sat two apples, both of them a deep red. It was a deep lie. She had never eaten an apple, or seen one for that matter. Apples were not indigenous to the country. They had to be imported. Romilia had heard that they were crisp, tender and very expensive. The rich could afford to eat them, and had them brought from a place called California. Perhaps Patricio had eaten one before. Ironically, the clay bowl had been made here, in a land lacking in apples. Patricio explained the tiny clay sculpture. "A new trinket for foreigners. They are sent to Europe, to the United States, everywhere we send coffee. Now all the world knows about our little country."

All the world. The phrase had no real meaning for her. She looked out the window, and all she saw were more adobes, rows of them, clay- and dirt-packed. What else was there in the world? And then, above them all, the newly built, almost completed house Patricio was build- ing on the hill. It answered her, There is the world. It had to be. The new house stood straight and even, made of tight, small brick and hard lumber.

The world. Patricio had brought the world to El Comienzo. She would seize it. She knew she had the chance. And she knew what her mother and the neighbor were laughing about. They were correct, and she was correct: She was the chosen one. She looked down at her palm, at the miniature bowl of food, at those two fake apples. Slowly her fin- gers wrapped about the fruit of clay.

Chapter Four

"It is with much happiness that I stand before this young couple. It only seems like yesterday that I was pouring the water of salvation over this young lady's forehead. Romilia and Patricio, we gather here today to bring you two together in holy matrimony..."

Amanda looked on, dropping tears. A large crowd had gathered in the church, none of them relatives except for perhaps a few distant cousins. Some were friends; many, however, were not friends, but onlookers, jealous gazers, judgmental watchers. This girl was marrying the wealthiest man who had ever visited El Comienzo. Perhaps, some speculated, one of the richest men in the country. Others rejected that theory, for obviously he was not one of the Unseen. Still, it was an incredible occasion. To have one of their own suddenly be hauled up to higher ranks was no small event.

The news had spread like fire. Many things were said about the rich man, about the woman and her daughter—that they had lured the man into their home; that they had promised him things; that they had worked on his youth, his temptations; that Romilia was probably pregnant. "Well, if only he had stopped at *my* door his first day in town!" some would say. It all amounted to hope, lost opportunities, never to happen again. The rich do not marry the poor, that was the law of generations. It was now being broken. No one knew the punishment.

Almost immediately after the ceremony, the couple left. Patricio had a newly-painted carriage waiting outside, black with gold trim, complete with horses and driver. Romilia had time to kiss Amanda, Silvia, and Juan, and wave goodbye to everyone before the smiling Patricio pulled her into the carriage. The driver cracked his whip. They pulled away from the waving people.

They were taking the intercontinental train to Guatemala for their honeymoon, then on to Mexico City. From there they would travel to the Mexican beaches. They would be gone for two months. During that time, Patricio's house was to be completed. Patricio would be disappointed. Although the laborers worked long hours, the house was too big. It required more time, more lumber that had to be sent either from the capital or from the Sonsonate region. But lumber was in great demand, and the supply small, so that prices had risen dramatically. When the *patrón* arrived, the workers were still waiting for materials.

"What do you mean you couldn't finish it? My God, you had two months! What did you do, sit on your dicks all day? Damn, I can't believe it!..." The wealthy youth paced about the incomplete structure.

"Señor Colónez, if you would please permit me, we have worked hard, but the lumber, you see, it has not come in. When the last load came, they told us not to expect any more for the next three to four weeks. It should be arriving soon."

Patricio turned, his fists to his waist, and looked at the older man standing before him. His name was Pepe, and he was the foreman. His face was as calloused as his hands. The slight hunch of his back showed the vast burden of the work he had carried. He was very healthy, though. The past three months had been good for him. He had worked for Colónez and had made sufficient money to feed his family and himself.

Patricio looked down to the ground, ashamed, as if he had just scolded his father. "Yes, well...look, I know you have worked. It is just that I was ready to bring my wife here. But look, it seems good so far. You have done fine work..."

"Well, Señor Colónez, if you will permit me, the house *is* ready for habitation. At least, most of it is. The bedroom, and the kitchen, they are ready. And the bathroom is almost complete. That man you had sent from the capital, he did the job quickly, and so all the latrine work is done, if you do not mind the walls not being completely finished. So Romilia ca—I mean, Señora Colónez can have her own private bathing room..." The old man, hiding his embarrassment, motioned to the youth to come inside and look.

72

A Fire in the Earth

Romilia watched all this from outside the carriage. She stared as her husband ranted and shouted before calming down to a disappointed whine. When the old man took Patricio into the unfinished building, Romilia paced from one end of the carriage to the other. The town lay before her, below her. The picturesque view made her smile. She had never seen it from here. It was a beautiful little village. Smoke rose gray and white from holes in the roofs, signs of cooking. The tile and thatched roofs were dark red and yellow from the years. A group of children played in the street close to her mother's home.

The vacation had been exciting, full of good food that had put pretty weight on her. Seafood, beef and desserts surrounded her at every meal. She laughed to herself while remembering a short conversation that she and Patricio had in a beachside restaurant in Iztapa, a small ocean town a country away. "You must be pregnant, Romilia, look how beautiful you are!" *Que hermosa*, how beautiful, how healthy. But she was not pregnant. It was all fat, lovely fat, a blessing to the eyes of the Comenzaños.

Beautiful. It was true, she was beautiful. He had told her that, many times through the honeymoon, especially when he had to coax her out of her clothes. Never had she been naked in front of a man. She had only dreamt of it, creating in her imagination lurid moments out of a dearth of knowledge. This had proven frustrating. Patricio at times had grown angry, much like the anger that he had displayed to Pepe the foreman. Yet soon after, he always calmed down to an apologizing whine, then would coax her in other ways. When finally naked, in the pitch dark of the hotel rooms, he had pulled her head down toward his abdomen. She had resisted, confused, and had clamped her mouth closed, especially when she had felt his hardness brush against her cheek. She heard him whimper. Feeling her hesitation, he had pulled her body up, flipped her on the bed and had fallen on her, the fury of his love fighting against her passivity, making up for something lost. He just wanted to see her, he had said, to see her full beauty in the light. Beautiful. She was so beautiful. He had taught her that English word, as he had taught other words and small phrases to her during their trip. Now she said it to the little village of El Comienzo below her, "Booteful. Booteful." She crossed her arms over her large

73

breasts and laughed, squinting her eyes to the setting sun that cast an easy red glare over the hills and shed peace on her lovely town.

※

The old woman witnessed many strange things. Perhaps that was what set her apart. When she told others about them, they looked at her first in disbelief, then with acceptance and finally in fear. She could not help that. It was not her fault that such incidents occurred. And she had to tell someone.

Once a cow had died in the field, and the witch had told a passing neighbor that a throng of bats had descended upon it the night before, that there were so many you could barely see the animal's white hide. They had fed on the creature until all the blood had been sucked out, "and I saw it collapse in the field last night." Never mind why she had been out there in the night, watching bats kill a cow. She dared the farmers to slit its throat open and watch it not bleed. They had not. She warned them of the possibility that the cow would rise from the dead and walk about at night, seeking out other victims. They were thankful when the carcass began to rot on a hot sunny day. Once a dog had torn a chicken apart on a street corner near her adobe, and she had announced to some folks standing nearby that someone would die soon, near that same spot. No one wanted to hear that. Juan de Dios Herrera, a seventy-eight-year-old man, walked by that corner a week later. He keeled over, falling on his walking cane. He had died from old age, but the snapped cane sticking through the weathered, crackly skin of his abdomen made others thing differently. No one went by that corner anymore, but rather on the other side of the road. And no one doubted her word.

She had the habit of walking about at night, through moonlit streets and small alleys, as if she were looking for something. She moved quietly, stealthily, able to sneak behind anything. When the young people came out to play in the evening, they avoided her as if she were poison. Yet there was not much diversion going on at night anymore. It had disappeared with the coming of the coffee crops and the armed Guardsmen who walked the town. Those who were caught

74

A Fire in the Earth

spent the night in the newly built jail cell, and woke to embarrassment and peer mockery the following morning. Young people, along with a few drunks, were the only ones who utilized the small adobe cell with metal bars over the windows. Many babies were conceived in that cell. It was the only one in El Comienzo. A couple that was caught in the root cellar or at the river or in alleyways could not be locked separately. "Jail babies" became common, and new grandmothers laughed out the nickname as they held the life in their arms. Father Mateo frowned at this and tried to teach against it. But with the grandmother lovingly holding the jail baby, cooing at it while the teenage mother stood by, there was not much a priest could do except offer idle theological threats about the afterlife.

Few times did the old woman end up in the cell for a night. She moved so silently, the soldiers rarely saw her. When they did, they ignored her, seeing no harm in her night amblings. Yet sometimes a zealous young lawkeeper who was new in town found her, brought her to the cell, and left her there for the night. She never complained. She said nothing to the officer, but obediently followed his orders. Usually she spent the night alone, but on one occasion she was blessed with the company of two very young teenagers who had been caught in the root cellar.

The witch sat in a corner chair. Though the moonlight beamed through the barred window, it missed her, leaving her in the shadows.

The young couple looked at each other, embarrassed, talking in half phrases about what to do. They did not see her. It did not take long for young fear to engage fervent touch. The boy, José, kissed Marta on her cheek from behind. He unbuttoned his pants, and his hands found her small nest of soft pubic hair. They rustled into position upon the hay. José's hands pushed her acquiescing wrists up and away from her head as she arched her back and feigned a soft struggle. The unbuttoned blouse fell to both sides, and the boy placed his lips on her nipples. He arranged her arms into a crucifix-like position, pushing her left hand into the shadowed corner. It was then that her fingers brushed up against the old woman's naked toes.

"Hello," spoke the shadow.

Marta screeched. Both jumped. The girl ripped her hands easily from his grip and clung like a humpback cat to her lover. He backed them both into the safety of the opposite corner.

"Hello," José spoke. "Who are you?" he asked, although he knew.

"Only an old woman."

Their eyes soon adjusted. She did not look toward them, but rather darted her own eyes about in the darkness as she chewed on something, perhaps a mango. The boy was not sure.

Marta fell against the locked door, all the time fighting with the buttons of her blouse. "Please, please let us out. We can't stay in here."

"Quiet," spoke the officer. "You'll be out tomorrow. We can't have you walking around the streets this late at night."

"No, please, you do not understand. *She is in here!*" She whispered her squeal.

"Oh? Oh, yes, your witch. Don't worry, she won't hurt you. Just don't get her angry." The man chuckled toward another officer. Both ignored the girl's squeaking pleas. She gave up, huddled next to her lover, and they both set to whispering to each other to stay calm, to sleep, to escape her until morning.

José woke to a scuffling noise. He looked up. The moon had moved, its light now shining on an empty corner between them and the old one. A sniffing, fat rat scurried in the light, running around in a tight circle. The boy's sleeping eyes drifted toward the animal, then looked up at the old woman. She was staring wide-eyed at the rat. Confused, he rubbed his face, then looked again and saw a bony cat hunching in the moonlight, hiding in the shadows. The rat could smell its enemy. The witch stared like a silent owl as the cat arched its back and then suddenly leapt onto the small animal, tearing at it with its claws. The cat pierced the rodent's underside again and again, and the little animal kicked and squeaked loud enough to wake Marta. The girl opened her eyes in time to see the cat rip open the protruding stomach of the rodent and pitch out several wet balls of half-formed lives. They spilled out of the womb like rotting preserves from broken clay. The cat clamped its jaws around the rat's head, then dug and dug at its meaty supper.

A Fire in the Earth

The girl buried her head into her lover's neck, whimpering. José stared at the old woman. She was staring at the corner where the killing had taken place. The girl prayed to Mary, the mother of God, for the night to end, wept and prayed, while the old woman began repeating several times over, "It is a sign, it is a sign," moaning like an old donkey. This pitched Marta into wails and louder prayers. She woke the guard, who shouted through the door to shut up, "Or I'll keep you in there all day tomorrow, little bitch."

A lifetime later the sun rose, and the girl clawed at the door, cursing and pleading. The boy failed to calm her down, as he too cried out for mercy. The guard shoved the wooden latch back, and they scampered from the cell.

The young guard had to nudge the sleeping old woman out of her corner. She mumbled under her breath and scratched her undersides as she sleepily walked out the door and toward her adobe.

〽〽

Romilia stepped lightly into the almost completed house. She shied before the impeccable rooms. Smooth tile mapped out the floor in various patterns of red, green and white. On the plaster walls, paintings hung, ones that Patricio had brought from his old home in the capital. Workers brought in furniture, large pieces made of heavy wood. American or European? she wondered. Friends had told Amanda and Romilia how to determine someone's wealth by the origin of his furnishings. If the furniture and clothes came from the United States or Europe, he was a very rich man. If from Mexico or Brazil, moderately wealthy.

Romilia asked one of the workers who helped move the furniture where had it come from.

"Mexico, the D.F."

"Well, it is very nice furniture."

The worker agreed, and joined his companions as they hustled about the house, zigzagging through the corridors and rooms, placing pieces in various corners. They kept asking her where she wanted things. "Put it there, over there, yes, that is fine," and they placed the sofa in the kitchen, as she ordered. The beds went in the bedrooms, that was simple enough. But she had the master bed go into a child's room, and a small guest bed into their master bedroom. A fireplace carpet—a gift from a North American business associate, which Patricio never used, as he had no fireplace—went into a hallway.

The house had steps. She followed them and saw that they did not lead to the roof, but to a whole other house that sat on top. It was composed of various bedrooms and a bath. She inspected it, figuring it to be a latrine; but to have it on the second floor of a building! Staring at the toilet, she remembered the stories that had passed through her mother's kitchen, how the machine used pure water to wash away the waste. She taught herself the technique, pulled down the dangling chain, and jumped back as the water rushed down the tube from the receptacle on the wall and into the bowl.

Patricio had already hired the first household servant: the cook. She was a large round woman named Santo, who had come from a neighboring country half a life before. She was as dark as Romilia, but held herself as if she was accustomed to working in a lighter-skinned world. She spoke quickly as she went about the large kitchen, putting away utensils and metal pots, shining and apparently new. "Good morning, Mrs. Colónez, I hope you slept well. There are people outside waiting for you, townspeople who want to sell you some things. I think it is best you deal with them, considering there is not a scrap of food in this kitchen, and the *patrón* would enjoy eating something this morning, as well as this afternoon and tonight." She clanked and shoved metal into various compartments inside counters and cabinets. All the kitchen cabinets seemed to be made out of new wood, clean, sanded, covered in some shiny clear paint.

"Who, who are you?"

"My name is Santo Antonia García, at your service." The older woman held out her arm to her young mistress. Romilia grabbed it from behind. They shook elbows customarily.

"Mr. Colónez has already hired you?"

"Oh, yes, ma'am." Santo laughed. "I have been with the Colónez brothers for many years, probably since you were but a baby."

"Oh."

A Fire in the Earth

"The people are waiting outside," she said, and pointed with her lips toward the back door of the kitchen.

"Oh. Yes, thank you."

Romilia walked to the back and looked out the window of the second door at all the people standing below her, at the foot of the wooden stairs. She turned back to the cook. Behind her she heard them all, calling out in monotones, advertising their wares, *"Bananos, tortillas, queso, guajada, bananos, quesadillas, pan dulce, cosas de horno, cosas de horno."* They were all her neighbors' faces, all from El Comienzo. Over two months had passed since she had looked upon those faces, had talked with them. The new young mistress of the house turned to the cook.

"Doña Santo..."

"Yes, we will need some *guineo*, if they have any. I know that it is difficult to find in this blessed area, but the master likes his fried *guineos*, and cheese of course, perhaps three blocks of it, since it can keep awhile. No tortillas; I make all the tortillas myself. He likes his fresh, not half a day old. Of course, he would never complain, but I always have made them fresh for him. And we have milk, too, of course. The men will bring it in from the barn directly. But some sweet bread, that is good for this afternoon with coffee..."

Santo suddenly turned around toward her teenage *'amá*, her mistress, but the *'amá* looked as if she were experiencing chaos, or sudden sadness—something, the cook could not distinguish. "What is the matter with you, ma'am?" She spoke in the tone used towards a young girl, a child who knows nothing about this life.

"I, I need to make these decisions?"

"Well, yes, I thought that since you are the mistress, you will know what we need to buy in order to cook. Of course, I am here to help. But you must choose which—"

"I know all these people."

"Oh. Well then, it will be easy to buy. You know which food is better than which other. That's an advantage." The woman smiled a large, fat smile, then turned and worked on filling one of the cabinets with her utensils.

79

Marcos McPeek Villatoro

Romilia turned back to the small crowd of women outside. Most of the faces were older, though little girls also stood among them. She forced herself out the door, and picked up the hem of the new dress Patricio had bought in Mexico during their trip. She walked into their midst. They smelled of tortillas, of strong coffee, of deep, moist adobe homes. "Well, let us see, us, yes, good morning, everyone." They all greeted her, "Good morning, Señora Colónez." She breathed out something heavy from her chest, much more than just breath. "Let's see, I will take some sweet bread, perhaps twelve pieces, and some banana, uh, does anyone have *guineos*? None?" No one said anything. "Well, we need some guajada, and some cheese, yes, cheese, ah, you have some?" Her eyes opened bright to the young girl, barely over ten years. "What type? Goat cheese! Goat cheese..." She began to giggle like a child. She tried to suppress it, but failed. "Good. I love goat cheese. It is our favorite here." She giggled again, a kid who has won a trick. The women smiled politely. Others fabricated laughter, which quickly died.

Romilia bought something from everybody. She had them place the foods on the table in the back porch that connected to the kitchen. Santo gathered the food and placed it in appropriate areas of her domain. She covered the cheese in order to keep flies away. She complained furtively, "Ma'am, I said we did not need tortillas, that the master likes his straight from the fire. And you do not need to buy a dozen pieces of bread. The women will come every day; I thought you would know that, but I suppose you're not used to having a wad of bills in your hand..."

Romilia mumbled affirmations to the master cook, not really hearing her, for she was busy putting away the bulk of colones back into her little purse pocket, both the money and the purse a gift from her husband. She walked out of the kitchen, excusing herself from the older woman, and continued exploring this home that she had suddenly inherited. They had called her Señora, the old neighbors from down the hill. And Doña Santo, the cook, had called her the mistress.

She wandered from room to room, wondering why so many. A few bedrooms for children; it had been said that this was necessary. And of course, guest rooms for friends who would come in from the capital to visit. Such things were to be important now. Men brought in cabinets and placed them in the master bedroom, then returned to the large carriage that still held more belongings from the *patrón's* old home in the capital. The workers grunted beneath the weight, then placed them around the mistress, tipping their hats to her while returning to the carriage. The room she stood in was full. The workers began filling other quarters. She was left alone. She drifted from cabinet to cabinet, touching the fine, finished wood, then opened the drawers, seeing what was held inside, what her man owned. Several watches, with their chains dangling together. Handkerchiefs, perhaps three for each day. String ties. Papers. Letters. Under some socks and shirts, in different drawers, lay books, small, with no titles upon them. She opened them. Everything was handwritten, a strong handwriting, though she could not yet determine that. She could not distinguish the emphasis placed in one area, or the shakiness of another. She could not read. Yet she knew these were his. All she could read were the few numbers placed above each set of paragraphs. They followed each other consistently: 29/3, 30/3, 31/3, 1/4, 2/4. So then, he writes. What did they say? She stared until her eyes almost ached, then suddenly breathed angrily, knowing that she held in her hand the knowledge of her husband, perhaps his whole life. Yet a cage of glass kept her from learning. She could see, and yet not see. She shoved them back in the drawers with impatience, as if demanding the sudden ability to decipher.

Patricio entered the house, sprang up the stairs to meet his wife. "My love! Where are you?" She answered him, and he came to the room. "You've found our bedroom, I see. Where is our bed?"

"This is it." She pointed to the small, single mattress.

He chuckled, raising one eyebrow. "Romi, this is not our bed. If we sleep here, one of us will wake up on the floor." He walked about the room, then into the hallway, checking all his belongings, seeing if they were nicked or scratched in the moving, which they were, and which made him curse under his breath. "Romi," he spoke from another room, and she followed. "What is our bed doing in here?" She tried to explain, and he laughed with love and endearment. He walked about the house, doing the same thing, seeing where the various furniture pieces where, laughing at them, then kissing her on the cheek. She followed behind him, silent as each peck of his lips scorched her with shame. He burst with laughter when he saw the couch in the kitchen. Santo vainly tried to heave it away from her wood-burning stove. The *patrón* laughed even harder when Santo leaned on it, puffing, explaining to him that she had not wanted to say anything to the mistress, so she was going to move it herself, and that the lady had a great deal to learn about this life. Romilia walked in from behind, looked at the *patrón* and the servant, two old friends from a lifetime together, now laughing. Romilia turned and ran out.

$$\approx$$

During the following weeks other servants were hired: a woman who cleaned the house every day; a helper in the kitchen to work with Santo; two men to keep the grounds clean, the bushes clipped, the grass cut low. Four other men worked on the small farm behind the house, caring for the hills of beans, feeding the cattle, keeping up with the 22 privately owned coffee trees that had been planted under a part of the remaining, unburnt section of forest.

To the east of the small ranch stood the brickhouse. Huge, square kilns where a hundred bricks could bake together at one time had been molded into the walls of the buildings. There would be no regular adobes. Colónez's factory meant to ship the wares to other parts of the country. These bricks were of the highest quality, much smaller than an adobe, and exact. The perfect rectangles were composed of a mixture of both clay and crushed shale, which made them more durable. The corners slid over another brick with a tightness and perfection never before witnessed by the town. It promised to be a grand operation. Men would soon be hired on, as the rumor had it, up to 200. More money, it was said, would trickle down the hill, as it was known that this young man Colónez was a generous fellow. Money, the whole town desired it, not only the ones ready to work and manufacture, but also the new ones, those town merchants who had come in with the growth of the ubiquitous coffee trees. New shops, small businesses, and stores had dotted the streets in recent seasons. They had foreseen the coming of coffee as a good omen. The rising of the brickhouse completed the vision.

A Fire in the Earth

For the ranch Patricio hired the men and women from the village, but he also brought his own, a number of people from the capital who had served him there. They acted as trainers for the Comenzaños, teaching them how the ranch should be run, how the *patrón* preferred that it be handled. Neither group was Romilia's. To the workers from El Comienzo she could say nothing, as they were people whom she once addressed as *usted*, as *señor*, and *señora*. Now she was to use their first names, and told them what to do. And they were to answer her quickly, with a final "Yes, Señora Colónez" that tumbled from their mouths like tiny pebbles over a steep grade. How could they change so quickly? She could not understand it. The servants from the capital had a different attitude. Whenever she met them in the hallways of the house or near the kitchen, she stumbled against them like a running child falling clumsily before a tall, uncaring stranger. All the servants from the capital were saying the same thing with their silence. At times their secrets, hidden in the air, crystallized into murmured phrases, "Lucky little rich girl, jerked out from the dirty alleys. She is lost, she does not know what to do."

Santo had that way about her. The words burned against Romilia's chest as she stood just outside the kitchen doorway. When she entered, she first saw Santo, who went about silently as if she had not spoken since she got out of bed early that morning. Her assistant, Cristina, a little, sharp Indian, more so than either Romilia or Santo, worked stone-faced beside the old cook.

Romilia smoothed down her stiff dress. "Well, how is everything here?"

"Fine. Everything is fine, Señora. We will eat in the next hour, as always."

"Good, good. Patricio will be hungry, you know." She smiled.

They said nothing, gave her not even a glance, but stood cooking in a silent righteousness. She left the kitchen. They began speaking again in low, safe tones.

Romilia ran up the stairs to the master bedroom. She looked about her quarters. There was nothing for her to do. One of the maids had already cleaned up the whole upstairs. She looked out the glass window, touching it like an alien object. Outside, the men were working on the farm. Far behind them, on the eastern edge of the ridge, workers beat away at the day, shaping some of the first bricks, carefully placing them in the large ovens to bake. She stood at the window unmoved. Soon the men slowed down their work and moved down the hill to eat their dinners. "I let my men go home and eat," Patricio had once said proudly, perhaps for his humanity. "What good is a hungry man? Nothing. He is worth nothing. Let him eat, and he will work for you. He will work like a beast." A just, rich young man, that was his reputation in the beginning. How lucky, she had heard the Comenzaño servants say, to have him as the *patrón* of our town.

Patrón. He did not own El Comienzo, yet the people already spoke of him as if he did. It had taken no time at all. They took on this—to her—new language as if returning to an old life. The servant women from the village had little problem with the change. In creating for him the position of master, the people had automatically placed Romilia in the post of first lady. It was, however, nothing more than a title. She stumbled through this exulted life like a fish jerked out of water, slapping against the beach, dying. The servants began to understand that there was no need to refer to the mistress since they could ask Santo. She knew everything about how things should be taken care of. Thus everyone played their roles except Romilia. The farmers and brickmakers sweated for them, the servants waited on them, the cooks fed them. She did nothing for no one. The *'amá* was obsolete. She found herself at the bedroom window several times during those first weeks, where she stared out at the working world. Tears filled her eyes, and she drowned the vision of the brickmaking men as they walked away from the factory to their adobe homes. She blinked her eyes and they were set free, and she saw, once again, their weariness take them down the hill.

"What do you mean you do not know what to do?" asked her husband, chuckling slightly as he shoved food into his mouth. "Romi, you are the head of this house! You do not have to do any work." He gulped coffee then, setting down the cup, looked at her with a smile. "You will have enough to do in the time ahead, taking care of our little ones. Do not forget that you have to fill the bedrooms upstairs."

She smiled politely. "Yes, but Patricio, should I, well, should I not do other things, too?"

"What do you want to do?"

"I don't know. I suppose I am just used to doing something."

"How industrious." He smiled, then barely glanced about the room. "Look, Romi, you are accustomed to working all day long. That is all behind you. You do not need to work anymore." He smiled, as if evoking some perfect existence.

"I do not want to just lie around all day long." But this was not the point, and she knew it. Yet the point could not be touched, for it was like touching smoke. It would also mean to touch friendships, his with the old cook. The new marriage was just that, new, and it could not overpower the history of years between Patricio and Santo. To speak in those terms, about boredom, about work, seemed much safer.

"Well, you know that you could work with Santo. Now, of course, you cannot make any more goat cheese," he said, barely chuckling, "but as the mistress, well, you have the right and responsibility of watching over the whole house."

"I think Santo, well, she works in her kitchen; it is her area. I do not believe she needs me, no," she began to mumble, reflecting the vagueness of the issue and her inabilities which, in his shadow, seemed to be numerous. She could not speak as clearly as he spoke. That skill had come with education, obviously. And she was learning, listening. But in moments of bottomless uncertainty, she fell back to an old accent, that of the village girl. It did not seem to bother him. "And, well, there is not that much left to do in the house…"

"I believe it will just take some time. You will become accustomed to this life. Just do not begin by washing windows or cleaning the house. Leave that to the maids; it is their job. You, my lady, are the delegator. Do you know what that is?" She did not. "That means you are in charge. Tell them what needs to be done. Remember, this house is your domain." He stood, wiped his mouth with the cloth napkin, tossed it on the empty plate. "Well, love, I best get back to the brickhouse. The men are surely waiting for me." Today he wore his work clothes, his jeans, the dark-green work shirt. He was laboring with them these days. He kissed her on the forehead and placed his hat onto walk out.

"Patricio, I have a question." He turned back to her. "Why is it that you go out and work with your men twice a week, and I cannot do any work around here? Her smile pretended innocence, which he believed.

He grinned, almost laughed. "Because, Romi, it is different. The work out there is hard work for a man, only for a strong man. It is good, it is necessary for a man to work, for a man to be a good man," he stumbled along, trying to dig some sense of philosophy from fabricated thoughts. He seemed appreciative of the opportunity. "But the work here, in the house, that is work for a maid," he spoke in a whisper. "No, I am not saying that they are worth nothing. We need the maids. And they want to do the work. And they do it well. But it is not work for a young wife of your, well, of your status. Especially not for any wife of mine." He leaned over, and kissed her forehead again, then smiled to her. "But that is a good question. You are, what is said, inquisitive."

"What does that mean?"

"Well, it means that you want to know a lot about a lot of things." He spoke proudly, as if a goal had been established for her.

"Oh." While he still leaned over, she asked, "Patricio, I was wondering, you know, I have not met any of your family yet. Your brother, what is his name? Antonio? Yes, well, I would like to meet him, and his wife. Perhaps we could invite them out here sometime."

His smile melted into vagueness. "Yes, I think we should wait awhile though. We've only been here a month or so. I think we should wait awhile longer, you see, to, well, let you get more accustomed to this place."

"Oh. Fine, that is fine." She smiled cordially. He kissed her again and walked out the door. She stood up from the table and watched him through glass as he walked from the grand house, her tall, thin, young husband, strutting toward his brickhouse. She watched him interact with the workers. He was much taller than they. Smiles broke between him and the men. *To get accustomed to this place.* The words

A Fire in the Earth

rang through the hollowness of truth trapped in her brain and translated into the true meaning: to not be a peasant girl anymore.

She stared into a mirror. Mascara from the States lay on her face, brush strokes of age rubbed upon a child. The long red dress almost touched the floor, and it bunched around her waist. A necklace dangled like a stranger on her neck, earrings flopped on each side of her face. It was all too blatant. She knew who she was. A girl, that girl, the goat-cheese maker, painted up in riches, her body covered in the glittering sackcloth and ashes of her newly married wealth.

$$\wedge\wedge\wedge\atop\wedge\wedge$$

Doña Amanda expected no visitors that day. She was sitting on a small stool, in the corner, far from the lit stove, sipping cooled coffee and eating a small piece of bread brought to her by Silvia earlier in the day. She stared through the half-dreams rising from the afternoon heat.

The black one-horse carriage ambled down the street. Amanda jumped up, almost spilling the coffee. She placed the cup on the stove and began cleaning frantically, hopelessly, throwing old, half-burnt cooking towels into a hidden area under the wood table, taking the straw broom to the dirt floor, sweeping the few chicken droppings quickly into the street. The carriage pulled directly up to the door. The driver jumped down and opened the carriage, then held out his hand for Romilia to use as a polite handle. She did not see it, climbed out by herself, and walked into the familiar adobe home. Her mother pushed her hair together, combing it with her palm, trying to pat it down into a presentable pile. "Hello. Well, girl, I never expected to, today, to see you..."

The girl voiced "Mamá," and grabbed Amanda. A tear dropped on the older woman's dress. Romilia smelled it. She smelled the kitchen, the old corn flour, the work and age in her mother's dress. It had been over three months, enough time for things such as odors to create a memory: the odor of need, of uncleaned days of sweat. Her tears fell, confused, yet she still held her mother. The smell encircled her like an old dog wanting to become reacquainted. She pulled away slightly.

87

"How are you?"

"Fine, girl, very hot of course. I have just finished eating, waiting for the day's heat to go away, you know..." She laughed with embarrassment and tried to push down her tousled hair. "And you? How was your time after the wedding? Your trip? Are you pregnant yet?"

"No, not yet, I don't think so."

"Well, with some women, it takes time. Silvia, now she gave birth to her first one, Marta, a short time after they got together. But I know some women who wait months for something to start growing. But for you, I know it will come soon." She smiled, offering that blessing.

"Yes. How are you, Mamá? You look as if you have been sick. Have you been eating—"

"Oh, I'm fine. Well, I was a little sick, a week ago or so. Just a fever, nothing to worry about. I am better now." They stood facing each other, not touching. Amanda's hand smoothed down her loosely crossed arm, as if petting herself. "So how are *you*? How do you, you know, how do you like it?"

"Me? Oh, it is good, yes, just fine."

"Yes. How beautiful, your dress, oh yes, that is good, strong cloth."

"Thank you. Patricio gave it to me during our trip. It's from Mexico."

"Mexico! How nice."

"Yes, yes."

They said nothing. Outside, Romilia's driver stood, checking the spokes of the wheels, as the wood was chipped slightly from small stones on the road.

"I have missed you, Mamá."

"Oh, and I you. I have missed you, too." Something fell, a hardness, cracking like the brittle bark off a tree. "But I have prayed for you every day, especially while you were in Mexico. It is so far away."

"Well, we were fine." She smiled at her mother for a long moment. "Mamá, it is difficult."

"What, girl?"

"It is, the life. It is all so different."

"On the hill, you mean?"

88

"Yes. They are all so, so mean, so far away. I do not know. It is as if they laugh at me constantly." Her chin trembled.

"Come on, child. Who laughs at you?"

"The maids. And the cook. I think they hate me." She told a few stories, like a soldier in from battle.

"And the other Comenzaños, the folks from town?"

"I don't know what to do around them. They were once my friends, now they act like, like servants. I don't know..."

Amanda touched her daughter's hair, gently pushing it down. "Well, it is your world now. Much different than here, we all know that."

"I don't know if I can live in it."

"Girl, you have to live in it. You married it. And think, it is a good chance. Romilia, your children will never go hungry. You will do well; he will treat you well. He is a good man, very generous. He has been generous to the people of this town. For those few years after the coffee first came, we went through bad times, but Mr. Colónez, your husband has brought back some life. And he knows what it means to work."

"Fine. That is all fine. But what do I do?"

"You..." But she stopped. She knew nothing about the life on the hill. Yet she was a mother. There was something in that. "You are his wife. You have something to say. Just...just stand your ground." It was fabricated, but like a rope down a well that reached for water in the darkness, it pulled out a deeper truth. "You must leave all this behind."

"What?"

"All this. You cannot play in both worlds. You must, well, you must leave this."

"Mamá, I do not want to leave you."

"Oh, you will see me! I do not mean that. I mean, you must not be who you were before, understand? Look, Romi, you are no longer poor. You are rich. You cannot live in both places. You would not want to."

Romilia looked confused. Abstractions blinded the young woman's mind. She was sixteen-years old and still lacked experience to grasp the mother's words.

They remained together several more moments. Outside, the driver grew impatient and began circling about the carriage. This surprise trip to the village was not on his agenda, not that he had a full agenda. Yet the *patrón* did not know about it. He paced nervously. Inside, the conversation slowed. The women spoke softly, preparing to part.

"Does your new husband know you are here?"

"No, no he does not."

"You had best get back, girl."

"He should not mind. I should be able to visit my mother! Besides, Mamá, you know how he is. You have seen him; he works with the workers at the brickyard. Just like you said, he is good to everyone here. I can come down here if I want."

"Yes, well, there is no doubt that he is good. But I do wonder, well." She looked for words, studying the dirt floor to find them. "Like I said, they are different, up there and down here. He tries to work with the workers. But he does not have to. I do not know how long he can live that way. It is like the reading last week in mass, about not belonging to two different worlds, something about not belonging to God and something else at the same time." Romilia again was confused. Amanda saw this and tried to make a clear sweep at once. "What I say is that I think he may still be upset that you came down here. I may be wrong, but, well, it is better to not take chances." She smiled.

They said goodbye. The girl cried slightly as she left, as if there were a danger in departure. Yet the encounter had given her strength. The source of that strength held firm, leaned on the adobe doorway, smiled and waved as the carriage pulled away. She battled the echoes of the newly married little child. Mamá, I do not want to leave you. And Amanda had denied that such a thing could happen. I am your mother, that can never be broken. Amanda had lied very well, and she knew it, for she knew that none of it was true. While the horse hauled the carriage away, Amanda's chin trembled as mumbled prayers for all her family, the dead, and the distant living, poured out from her lips.

A Fire in the Earth

♒

Mother wisdom dug slowly into Romilia's abdomen. During the interval between the conversation with Amanda and the world that awaited her on the top of the hill, she forged a new determination. As she sat in the carriage, she forced herself to think about it, about the person she would have to become in order to survive. Her hands closed into tight fists of anger. Approaching the hill she saw it all—the house, the brickyard, the small farm behind it. Her home. Their brickyard. The echo of the mother's words brought her down to reality. The carriage pulled up to the front door. The driver jumped off, opened the carriage door, held out his hand. Romilia took hold of it with a delicate movement as she stepped out. "Thank you, Diego," she said, forcing her voice into a feigned mastery. She walked into the home.

The heat of the day dried out what was left of Romilia's tears, the last tears she would ever shed as a child. Inside, she stopped, looked around at the paintings, the rugs, the plaster-white walls. She looked at the door to the kitchen. There was no need to wait.

She walked through. Santo, working in one corner, glanced to see who had entered, then turned back. Little Cristina worked on the other side. She said nothing.

"Doña Santo, what have you thought of making for dinner tonight?"

"We will have refried beans, some rice, and tortillas. There is also some picadillo left from lunch, if Mr. Colónez would like. I have also made some orange *refresco*, since that is his favorite—"

"I would like chicken soup."

Cristina looked up, turned to her fellow servant, who in turn looked at the young wife. "How's that, ma'am?"

Her voice trembled slightly, but a quick, angry force pushed it forward, "I said I want you two to make chicken soup for tonight. Patricio likes chicken soup. He had it several times during our honeymoon. I want to have it tonight."

Santo attacked slowly, then gained speed like a distant train, approaching. "Mrs. Colónez, we cannot have chicken soup tonight. I do

91

not have enough time to make it, and besides, I was planning to have it Thursday night, and it is not good to have it *twice*—"

"Time is not a problem, Santo, for when Patricio comes home he will retire for his bath. Tonight it will take him an extra hour to clean up and prepare for dinner. Therefore you have an extra hour to prepare the soup. Patricio and I will come down together at 8:30. We will eat then."

Romilia turned to leave. The cooks stood open-mouthed from surprise. Before opening the door, Romilia turned to Cristina and gently said, "Cristina, tonight please boil four buckets of water for the bath instead of the usual two. Thank you." Then she left.

Cristina turned to Santo. The large cook stared at the door as it swung slightly back and forth. Neither Santo nor Cristina uttered any words for several moments; then Santo made up for the silence and burst forth with a river of filth and anger. The things she said made the younger cook cower behind her work.

〰〰

Patricio walked up the stairs wearily. It had been a long, good day. Brick dust covered the tops of his boots, and a wide stain of sweat ran down his shirt. He was so tired that he did not even stop by the kitchen to greet his old friend Santo and find out what was for dinner. Rather, he plodded up the stairs to the waiting bath.

In the bathing room next to their bedroom, he barely noticed a hand placing a bucket of steaming water onto the floor. "Good afternoon, Cristina," he greeted, unbuttoning his shirt. He sat in a small chair to wait for the servant girl to leave the room.

"It is not Cristina."

"Oh. My love, what are you doing, drawing my bath?"

She said but a few barely audible words. He picked up his weariness and took it to the door of the bathroom, smiled down to his wife as she poured hot water then cold water into the large tub.

"That is not your job, woman."

"I do not think of it as a job." Candles lit the room. Though it was still light outside, Romilia had pulled closed the drapes, darkening the

A Fire in the Earth

bathing area. The candles flickered around her, reflecting upon her eyes as she smiled, tiny stars in the night of the room. She stood before Patricio, took the unbuttoned shirt off him, unbuckled his belt, and ran her hands slowly into his pants, grabbing him. She then led him thusly toward the large wooden tub. Like a child, he giggled, questioning all the way. He was quickly naked. She slid him into the vessel of steam and water and then began washing his body with a soft, wet sponge thick with soap.

"How was your day?" she asked calmly, looking, almost studying, each part of his body as she washed it—his thinness, the muscles of a hardworking, well-nourished young man.

"Fine, just, just fine.... Yours?"

"Oh, good. I am learning more about our home here, my love. That is good, so I can run it like a good *'amá*." She laughed like a woman. Suddenly she sounded older than Patricio. She spoke nothing of the trip to the village. Now was not the time; perhaps there would never be a time for that. She told him of supper, of the chicken soup, and asked him about other foods that he enjoyed. He mumbled off a short, unthinking list. Food had no relevance at this moment, "Oh, beans... rice...crab...uh, beans, they're good...."

She pulled out the cork plug from the bottom of the tub. As the dirt and soapy water receded around him, she poured more warm water over him, not allowing his skin to shiver in the barren air. That water also left the tub, ran through the hole of the long metal drain which emptied it outside. Such was their wealth, to have a bathing tub on the second floor. She plugged it, then with the two extra buckets of hot water, now just slightly cooled, she covered her husband, slowly pouring it all over his body until he sat in it to his thighs. Then she stood directly before him, and in the candlelight, began to undress. He watched. His mouth drooped open, and the fullness of his youth grasped toward her. She pulled the pins from her hair and it fell like a black blanket over the pure earth of her shoulders. Naked, she touched herself with her fingertips, filling her nipples and opening her thighs toward him. This was all new, and yet it was allowed, and she moved with a newly acquired strength to take her position as mistress. She leaned over and kissed his lips, holding the sides of the tub with

93

her arms, then brought her head downward to his chest. He barely held her with weakened fingers. She spoke as she loved, whispering various words as she lowered her head toward his desire, "Perhaps, Patricio, we could soon entertain some of your friends—yes, my love— and we could invite your brother here for dinner, I'd like to get to know him better—yes, my love—and I would like to meet more of your associates from the capital, and perhaps I could do some things different with the house, the furniture, and the workers, it would be good if they wore some sort of uniform—yes, my love, oh yes, my love, yes."

Once he had agreed to all, she stopped speaking, then parted wide her lips to his anguished, youthful need.

Chapter Five

Romilia planned for their guests as if a Holy Day approached. She followed her husband around, asking him questions: Who were they, how was he associated with them, how long had he known them? Then she listened to him intently, watching his movements and method of speaking. Comparing his speech with her own, she recognized the vast chasm that existed between education and ignorance, purchased knowledge and a starving mind. She and the rest of the people of her village had the habit of "swallowing" syllables and consonants from each word. After realizing the difference, she tossed aside shame and worked fervently to change that habit. Soon she spoke each word of her sentences with clarity and distinction, like Patricio, to the point of clipping her syllables more than he did. The act of imitation became all-encompassing, the language, the subjects spoken about, the way of laughing properly. It was a dramatic change, one which he noticed.

Patricio's older brother and sister-in-law, Antonio and Gloria Colónez, visited the ranch at least once every two weeks. The corpulent Antonio always showered profuse blessings upon Doña Santo for her extraordinary meals. She had cooked for the older sibling in earlier days. Antonio had agreed to let Patricio hire her when the younger brother decided to move out into the country. "It was for the best," Antonio once explained to Romilia as the four sat and ate. "This boy here would starve to death without a good cook. It was necessary to keep her in the family." He laughed, for he knew Santo listened to him from the kitchen. "See what she did for me?" He rubbed his fat stomach wrapped in a vest suit.

"Yes. She is a very fine worker," smiled Romilia.

Gloria said very little, but not because she was shy. If she spoke, her words usually honed against her lips before striking at her husband. Patricio also spoke little in front of his only brother. Antonio filled the room, leaving little space for others to comment.

"Hhmph. It still amazes me how this little runt survived and got where he is today. Do you know the story about your husband, Romilia?" His question flowed over a raised glass of wine. She smiled, shaking her head to indicate she hadn't. "While I was out beating the alleys for business—I was working as a realtor to buy land for the railroad coming through—this runt was running around the capital learning English! Can you believe that? You remember that, don't you, little brother?" Silenced by Antonio's overpowering laughter, the younger brother nodded his head in a small affirmation. "He would have rather studied English than eat. And I think you did go without some meals. God knows we both did. Our parents gave us nothing, because they had nothing, and that father of ours acted as if he wanted nothing. We were lucky to get some form of education, since our father could read and write. Well, here I was, the first person in our family to make money, and this guy is running around trying to learn English. I felt I had some responsibilities towards him, you know, me being the older one. So I sent him as a kid—you were just a kid, weren't you? Yes, I sent him to English school. The new one that had just opened up in the capital. I handed the money over for a year's tuition."

Patricio sat, staring at a stripped chicken bone sitting on his empty plate. His hand rested on the arm of the chair. His fingers pulled at his lip, an old, teenage habit, suddenly revitalized as a tiny defense. He listened to the story, unsure of how true it was, at whether or not what he was hearing was Antonio's voice itself, or an echo. *So I handed the money over for a year's tuition.* The money had not been meant for his schooling, though Patricio had put it to that purpose. It had been a payoff, a bribe to forget the ignominies which clung to the young brother like sap to a dying tree. The real story, hidden beneath the tale Antonio was spinning, rotted away in silence, creating a void. Patricio tried to ignore it, and feigned interest in his brother's version.

"A year or so later he comes back to me. You were about fourteen, true? About that age. This husband of yours, Romilia, comes up to me and says, 'May I buy a dictionary?'" Antonio laughed between phrases.

A Fire in the Earth

"And I say, 'What kind of dictionary?' 'An English dictionary.' So I asked him how much it cost, and gave him the money. You already had a book, a grammar or something like that, right?" Patricio nodded silently in agreement. "But I remember. You kept going on about how the grammar did not have enough words. Yeah, I remember. So he buys this book and takes off studying.

"Then some time passes, a year or so. I brought in these fellows from the States, big guys, ready to strike a deal to buy some land out west, near Sonsonate. I thought it would be fun to have them talk with my little brother, you know, since he knew a few words. Now, there was a translator there, someone I borrowed from the government. I paid him well. Jesus Christ, I had to. The government, no wonder it has money! Anyway, I wanted my kid brother to talk with these guys because I had watched him out on the streets of the capital, talking with the passing gringos who shopped for tourist stuff out in the market. He just insisted on speaking English with them. This boy was a wildcat! It was like you were trying to suck the language from them, brother! And they would laugh. I figured they must have found it cute, a little Latin boy trying to speak their language. So here I bring these two businessmen from the States and had them meet Patricio. And here they go, talking, and talking, and talking! I could hardly get a word in Spanish edgewise. You would not stop talking with them, would you Patricio? And the government translator's eyes were wide. He could not believe that a kid like you could be speaking English."

Antonio laughed as he talked, forgetting the other parts of the story, the gaps that festered in his younger brother's head. Memories rushed into Patricio's mind, adhering to the vapors of the dinner wine. The huge Antonio coming back home after that meeting with the gringos, screaming at the teenager, then kicking him hard—once, twice, then a third time—kicking away his own embarrassment that his younger brother was smarter than himself. When the gringos returned a year or so later, they found Patricio working in a brickyard on the lower end of the capital. The gringos were passing by, watching how the primitive people made bricks and commenting on how slow, how backward, the natives were. Then they saw Patricio. One of them called out to him in English, testing to see if it were the same boy they had met a year earlier. "What are you doing here?" They asked him, knowing that Antonio, his brother, was doing well financially. Patricio answered slowly, methodically, yet flawlessly. "I must work in order to give money to my family, to my mother and father."

The two gringos looked at each other. Their cream-white skin was protected by derby hats from the heat of the midday sun. They held a quick, private conference. Suddenly they turned to Patricio with excitement. "How would you like a job? A real job?" Patricio stared at them, unable to speak. While two gringos stood looking at him, waiting for an answer, he was barely aware of the work going on behind him, the laborers bursting their lungs with the weight of bricks, lifting them, heaving them to another side of the brickyard.

"Finally, here was my little brother working for the Intercontinental Railroad, a translator for all the gringos coming in through the capital, making good money.

"Then he started climbing. I could not believe it. Now what would have happened, Patricio, if I had never given you the money to buy that dictionary, or to send you to school?" Once again Antonio finished retelling the familiar story. Again he passed over the important details—the flickering candles and cigarettes burning between the young boy's fingers as he stayed awake late, drilling in his mind the rules and regulations that governed an alien tongue, turning slowly the pages of a grammar book, a dictionary, turning them only when the previous page was completely absorbed.

"Yes," spoke up Gloria, "and here he became general manager of the whole region between Sonsonate and the capital for the Intercontinental Railroad. A very impressive position, Romilia, for your husband. Not just going out and gambling all night long in order to make fast money, like other people do." Gloria did not turn to look at her own husband, ignoring his grunts of defiance. "You did so well in that job, Patricio," Gloria added.

"Yes, brother. I still do not understand why you gave it all up," Antonio said. "Only seven years at it, and you decide to take all your belongings and move out in the woods—"

A Fire in the Earth

"Patricio can do what he wants, Antonio," said Gloria, a cymbal clashing upon the table. "And that is enough. No more gossip about Patricio in front of his new wife."

Antonio turned again to Romilia. "You did not know any of this, Romilia?"

"No, not very much, we—"

"Jesus, brother! You marry her, and she does not know you? What did you two talk about during that long honeymoon of yours? Living a secret life, so secret you do not even invite your family to the wedding." He laughed out with a heavy cynicism.

"Antonio stop talking like that—"

"We married because we know what we like." Romilia dropped her words slowly to cool down the fomenting argument. "We do well together," she directed the phrases toward Antonio, "because we both work hard for what we earn."

The evening conversation, out of necessity, turned to other subjects. Soon the wives went touring about the house. They talked about furniture, about buying quality to decorate objects with. Romilia listened intently, something Gloria did not notice. She talked on, not knowing that she was teaching the young mistress of the house many things about this new world she had entered.

The men retired outside to smoke. Both lit cigarettes imported from the States. They were a new, prepackaged type that had just recently been offered on the local market. Affectedly, Antonio plugged his cigarette into a streamlined brass holder and then clamped it between his teeth and lips.

"So you like it out here?"

"Yes. That is why I came."

"Well, that is good, that is good. It is nice here. Quiet. Of course, you are missing many things in the capital. Big things. So much is coming in and out of the city, exporting, importing. A trainload of goods comes in twice a week from La Libertad. They just keep shipping shit in from San Francisco. That is where these came from." He pointed to his cigarette. "Rich, true? That is where it is, little brother, that is where the action is. Keep close ties with the gringos, and we'll keep smoking these. That is why I still think you should come work

99

with me. With my ideas and your English, we could end up living in San Francisco, California. Or perhaps New York! But here you want to stay, in this little town." He flicked ashes that drifted into the sinking day. In the village below candles flickered around cooled wood-burning stoves. "You know, I have never noticed that hill sticking out in the middle of town. That is a strange thing. It looks like, what...beans growing on it?"

"Yes," spoke Patricio. "For a while Schonenberg tried to grow coffee on it. It's his property. But coffee would not grow there. The trees died. For some reason, the ground never took them."

"Hey, listen," the large man smiled and burst out laughing as he changed the conversation. "Are there any places to visit down there? I know it is small, but still, there must be some places a man could put his pepper into."

Patricio forced a smile as the dry rot of memory crumbled open in his skull. "I do not know. I have not visited any."

"What? Well come on, let's go find out. We can go after the women fall asleep. My bitch always falls asleep before I do. We will not be leaving until later tomorrow morning, so we can sleep late."

"No, I don't think so. Not for me."

"Oh, what is it, Patricio, afraid the new wife will cut yours off if she finds out you stuck it somewhere else?" He reeled slightly backwards. Patricio tried to answer the guffaw, to escape the suffocating aura his brother had cast.

"No. I just do not need to go get some anywhere else." He turned for the first time that night, looking sharply toward his brother. "Some people do not need to look elsewhere, when they have a good, solid woman."

"Is that true? Well some of us *do* look elsewhere, even if we do not need to, because we have enough in us to give to other bitches." Antonio breathed out his defense. The hidden anger on both sides receded, knowing it was best not to allow it to crawl closer, two animals of the same breed avoiding one another to forestall the dangers of their violence. Antonio turned the conversation elsewhere.

"How is it going at the brickyard?"

"Very well. We are sending out a load a day."

A Fire in the Earth

"I see more homes being built out of brick. Then they cover it with cement.

"It's become popular. Stronger than adobe."

They continued talking about the demand for brick and how well the factory was functioning. This kept them away from dangerous topics.

"I suppose you really do not need my name on the papers anymore, true?" asked Antonio, referring to the title to the land where Patricio had built the brickyard. They had bought it together.

"What? Well, no, if you want to pull out you can. Of course, you will lose your share of the profit."

"Yes, well, that would be fine. I can do without it. It would not cost you much either, to buy my small piece. Perhaps we can take care of that business soon." The older brother spoke congenially, as if offering an apology. Patricio had used Antonio's name in the contract in order to strengthen it. Those who did not know of Antonio's gambling habits thought he carried more weight with the money holders of the country than did Patricio. They uttered light, half-spoken phrases concerning the transaction, one that would never come about, as it amounted to very little. They finished their cigarettes. Antonio, always prepared, pulled out a glass flask of whiskey and gave it over to his brother. Pride emanated from his words whenever he could boast of new acquisitions from the land of the gringos. "This came from a state called Kentucky. It is very rich, true?" Patricio swallowed, coughed on the burn, then felt the smooth heat run through him.

They both sat down on the wooden porch of the home, lit two more cigarettes, spoke more, drank more. The full moon burst the air with a subtle, furtive light. The mountains and volcanoes failed to hide themselves in the darkness. "Well, it *is* beautiful out here. I can see why you moved, little brother. Look. Thousands and thousands of coffee trees. That is a field of money in front of us. Do you talk with d'Aubuisson much? How is he doing with the crops?"

"Hhmph. d'Aubuisson never comes out here. None of the d'Aubuisson's do. Just their messengers, the guards. The crops are not doing well now. The *pendejos* burnt down almost all the forests, wanting to plant more coffee, just plant more coffee, put trees all over. Then the

101

coffee trees burn up with the sun because there is no shade, because they have burned down all the forests. Stupid fuckers, all of them." Antonio chuckled at his little brother's whiskey-warmed curses. "Now, one time Schonenberg came out here. You know, the boy, what's his name? Rodrigo I think, yes, the one who dresses like a queer cowboy, all the leather strings hanging off his ass. His father is that German fellow, Hans. I talked Rodrigo into getting his father to let the people grow beans on that hill. Otherwise, it was going to waste."

"Don't worry. The crops will come back. They are working hard to get a rich harvest this year, I understand." Antonio spoke out of complete agricultural ignorance, and half-heartedly defended the family names. "When it comes to crops, there are good times and there are bad times. In seasons, I mean. You know. That is to be expected." He swallowed more whiskey. "But you know, Patricio, you look all over this country now, and what do you see? Green. Green trees. Coffee trees, from one end to the other of this little country, you would think we were in Brazil. And that means money, little brother! There is a restaurant down at La Libertad, El Rincón is the name of it. One day last February a friend of mine and I ate there, talking business, and we sat and watched the longshoremen working like wildcats to get hundreds of bags of coffee, already dried and ready to grind, loaded onto the ships. And there they went, to the United States, to Europe, all over the world. I said to my friend while we ate, 'You know, the world economy, Fidel, the world economy. Our little country is in it now!' And we are, Patricio. We are in deep. And that means money. It was time, too, it was time. Now we are progressing, we are moving ahead." He gulped more whiskey. Patricio said nothing. He barely listened. He had heard it all before. In his old life, progress had been the only topic of conversation.

After a long while, Antonio finished developing his thesis. He lowered himself back to the wall, rested his chin on his chest, and fell asleep. Patricio sipped more, stared out at the town below him that blew out its many candles and crawled in bed. Antonio jerked awake, mumbled something, then pulled himself into the house. Patricio heard him greet the women, then stumble toward the upstairs guest room. The younger brother still held the flask, and sipped deeply. It

A Fire in the Earth

was good, hot, it soothed many inner tensions which he did not know he felt. It also opened sealed hatches of his youth, of brotherhood, of an enraged, older sibling who beat his frustration incessantly against the boy Patricio, taking the point of his boot to the child's pelvis. Patricio now coughed to one side to spit it away.

While staring at the flask, another Antonio, the recent one, echoed through the slosh of whiskey. *Keep close ties with the gringos.* Close ties. Patricio had not talked with a gringo in several months, and had no other opportunity to speak English. He was afraid of losing it. He spoke out suddenly, reaching toward the town below. "The night is beautiful because the moon is so very full. It shines its light upon the earth."

It was all correct, every single one of the English words. He smiled, a large child's smile, because of the whiskey, because of his grammatical perfection in the foreign tongue. "I should teach her how to speak it," he said aloud, again in English. "I believe she would like that. It would please her a great deal." Perfect English. It was a gift of several years of work. He spoke it with a sublime power. After working with the gringos for seven years, speaking with North Americans every single day, he spoke it with as much ease as donning work clothes. That was the only thing he missed about the capital. Suddenly he believed his brother was right. He should stick with the gringos. Not for money; he cared little for that. More, perhaps, for the energy, the crossing over, the linguistic power. A sudden anger blossomed toward the town below, an anger toward ignorance, its inability to speak in the splendid foreign tongue. But his wife—"I can teach her." If anything, a few words, phrases. That could be a beginning.

Beginnings. This was all a beginning for him. He believed in the legend of his people: He, with his own actions, helped to recreate that legend in himself, that theirs was an industrious race. Not like those others who had come from afar, bringing foreign money, "Buying land that they knew not how to till." The English leaked from his lips and spoke back to him. In the capital, in an earlier life, it had become mandatory to know the ruling families, to slap their shoulders and kiss their wives and drink with them. He had not expected this during his rise, during his journey through mandated labor, the underground work of baking bricks, the clash and clang of railroad ties, the bloody sweat from accidents. He had seen it, had stood alongside it, the heaving and the hunger necessary to keep the foundation of the city, of the country, pumping strong. Which was better, poor sweat or rich whiskey? he asked himself. Both existed, was the answer, and he had reconciled the two by moving away to this little town.

The following morning Antonio handed Patricio a newspaper from the previous day. He had read it in the carriage on the way to El Comienzo. "Here. So you can keep up with civilization."

Patricio folded it and placed it on a reading table. That morning he had put on a suit and string tie so as to see his family off. But as soon as the horses pulled away, Patricio changed into his work clothes—jeans and a sweat-dried shirt. Then he stole away to the brickyard and spent the entire day with the hired hands. That evening he returned, bathed, and sat down to read the newspaper from cover to cover. His eyes took the words in hungrily. He supposed then that it would be good to buy a subscription. There were no newspapers in El Comienzo. There was much more traffic between the town and the capital than ever before, and he could receive the paper every week when it was only three days old. It would keep him marginally informed of that world he had left behind. Receiving news four to seven days late reminded him of his distance, here, on the periphery, where a dweller is the last to hear, where the news skidded and stopped in a cloud of dust.

〰〰

In the following months the newspaper's arrival became a part of his rituals. Twice a week he sat down to read. As months turned into years, the couple grew accustomed to each other's idiosyncracies. Romilia knew not to disturb her husband once the periodical arrived.

In the heat of this past Sunday evening, March 31, violence broke out in an eastern barrio of Sonsonate. Several drunken youths attacked various local establishments. The marauders were quickly subdued by the local guard, and peace was restored to the little barrio. There were no injuries. Four of the uprisers were killed.

A Fire in the Earth

Patricio read the newsbrief on the eighth page of the paper. He mentally counted. This was the third outbreak of violence caused by drunken youths in two months, according to the paper. The others had occurred in the capital. The capital, of course. Such things always seemed to happen there, that hub of the world that was the point of departure and arrival of everything and everyone important. This, however, was the first report of such an incident happening in Sonsonate.

Below the two-inch long article was another. It concerned the birth of another child to the Schonenberg family. It was the end of the story from page one. Patricio slapped the paper closed and then reopened it to page ten.

He had worked all day with the men. Now he was clean, his face newly shaved, his pitch-black hair neatly combed. At times he glanced at the wedding photo on the bookshelf in front of him. He was standing behind Romilia, and she was sitting in front. Neither was smiling, just as the photographer had ordered. There she sat in her white dress, quiet and calm and innocent. Patricio's eyes kept shifting from the newspaper to the photo. He was no longer impressed by the press as in his younger years when he lived in the capital. In those days he received the paper a mere two days after the news reported had taken place. It would arrive crisp and new at his office in the Intercontinental Railway Administration Building. Now he yawned as he flipped through the final stories. His eyes crossed from fatigue, so that to focus upon his life became doubly difficult, specifically on the first four years after his marriage. There were still no children. This troubled him. He was reaching thirty and his seed had yet to bear fruit. The deadline of his disgrace approached. She had just turned twenty. There was no more room for excuses, no more answers such as, *Well it is understandable, she is still only a child in many ways, some women take longer, the body must develop, science will tell you that*. And who could question science?

Science had spread quickly by then throughout their developing little country. It gobbled up tradition in their cities and towns, and showed them the modern life. Science and technology came on the trains, whose tracks wrapped about the tiny nation like a tight metal cocoon, yanking it out of hiding from beneath the rest of the American republics and hurling it into the mainstream. Progress had come to his doorstep, had shown him how to develop his business. Science had brought him a new machine to his brick factory. Obstreperous and rude, it cut the soft clay tidily into perfect bricks, ready to bake in ovens. There was no more need for the block setters, the men who took all that time to pour the clay and slate into the wood mesh that shaped only two dozen blocks at a time. Science came and doubled his production rate, while the old block setters were flicked off the mountains like crumbs, rolling deep into El Comienzo, slamming into a field of neverending coffee trees. *It was all for the best*, according to his brother's often repeated phrases.

"It's for the best. This technology is your salvation!" Antonio had said. And what of the block setters? Work awaited them in the coffee fields. "Don't worry, you are not the god of jobs around here, you know." Romilia had laughed heartily, as she had always laughed at her brother-in-law's jokes. She had found the jolly businessman to be a joy, and had insisted on inviting Antonio and his wife to their house as often as possible, sometimes once every week. In those four years they had become a scheduled element of their married life. The pattern was set: The weekly visits, the drinking, the older brother wanting to go down the hill, wanting always to fuck, always pulling at his little brother, "Let's go fuck a bitch, let's go fuck." In the twilight of sleep, with the newspaper dead at his feet, Patricio's defenses dropped. The doors once sealed against memory opened wide. He looked up and in his mind's eye...he saw his brother no longer bald, but with thick hair, the enraged youth kicking him until his manhood sucked into his pelvis, disappearing. Such had been childhood, his brother emasculating him on a routine basis. Even when Patricio had been taken to the local clinic for internal bleeding, his brother wove a well-acted story before the doctor of how his poor little brother had fallen spread-eagled onto sharp stones while playing outside. It had happened repeatedly, not stopping until Patricio had grown old enough to defend himself. Now they never mentioned those days, not the beatings, even through the years of barrenness in the Colónez ranch home.

A Fire in the Earth

Patricio grunted in his chair to forget, to escape into some corner of sleep. The newspaper rustled off his foot. He felt a hardness in his pants that drew attention to his brother's proposal—go to the little village, fuck, love up some young women. Now it did not matter, not in sleep. It had been four years, and sex with his wife was less explosive and more of a chore. There was no vital purpose; there were no children. It was merely the need to calm manhood, believing he was planting in barren ground. Perhaps it was time to go down the hill; perhaps it was necessary to have illegitimate children at least. But not with his brother. He would never go with his brother.

Patricio's face slumped down, drained from the day's struggle, from thought, from failures. It was best to sleep. Had he been sad these days? It was difficult to say. He worked in the brickyard, especially after letting go of the old block setters. It was as if he was trying to save something, to grant salvation to those who remained, to promise them something better, to plead with them not to get drunk, from knowing, from living on both sides, seeing rich and poor. But he knew how the mind worked when it ran with necessity, what happened to thoughts of simple day-to-day needs, when the brain has little to eat, when it sleeps few hours. Then, Patricio knew, the mind boils to an ache. *Do not attack, like in Sonsonate, like in the capital. We are at peace here, we work, we eat.* His mind screamed silently at his workers.

The empty children's rooms above weighed heavily upon his head, pushing him deep into the sofa. The weight of the emptiness joined the heavy load of those stupid fights with his wife, the barren one, when he demanded why Romilia would not produce, why had it been four years, why she made him the laughing stock of the workers. Patricio had yelled at her, blaming her for coming from a small family. He went on about his mother-in-law loudly, she herself who had produced only one child, he would brutally scream amidst curses, as if Romilia being an only child carried weight in their present situation. Romilia, in turn, shouted words that were knives. She had an ability to cut, a talent that grew more and more each day, each year. He had threatened her. He would find others that would give him children. It was necessary to do so. She had sliced back, "Go ahead! Go ahead! Perhaps you will find out that what is failing is your *prick!*"

It had silenced him. Patricio stared at his wife, as if to ask her had she seen the scars when they made love? Yet the shock of her cursing statement allowed no questioning. He walked away, mumbling, as if reminding himself that he had not been stripped of potency in his childhood; he could still bed his wife and satisfy her; the problem was not his.

He did not go to find others. He waited. The third year passed, and there was nothing still. The bitterness infested every part of their lives like a plague, until the screams of blame fell to the floor, impotent and sad, crawling away into corners. They said little to each other. They had sex, coming to each other out of duty. Mornings followed evenings, and then it was the fourth year, and still there was nothing. He bought more land, finding something in it, more money, a little more power, more control over the dried-out whispers that defined his life. He began inviting gringos to come out, handing them over to Romilia like a gift, believing that they would help, that it would coax her into fruitfulness. The gringos came, bringing gifts. One gave them a gilded statue of a great eagle, holding branches in one claw, arrows in the other. The gift dispelled her fear of the foreigners, her fear of her own inability to interact with them. She placed the eagle upon the wall, admiring it with the few minute English phrases she had learned from her husband, "Haw, booteful, hawpretie."

The gringos laughed with delight. Sometimes they looked at her with peculiar smiles. Patricio saw that, and quit inviting them. Yet she had tasted them, it was too late, and she demanded that they visit again. The small pilgrimage of gringos came, arriving in carriages every month or so, friends from his old days, business associates who offered many things to the once-young man who was beginning to show age. They offered more money, more power in the city, where they had once worked so closely together, *Because, Patricio, my boy, you speak such damned good English.* But he had refused. They then turned and planted the idea in his wife's ear, struggling through their poor Spanish, telling her, *You could live in the capital. You could visit the United States*. That was all she needed. She began insisting. Patricio held fast: They would never go, not to that city, not to that life.

The rift grew larger, cleft with barrenness and refusals. The fourth year came. They were wealthy, and had become wealthier. All this he well remembered in one moment of mean sleep, hunched into the soft chair, with relaxed muscles and a dropped newspaper at his feet. His eyelids slammed together in silence and he drifted away, no thoughts, no memories, only a transient peace that distanced him from everything.

Romilia brought him back, waking him up. His eyes snapped alive to the dying daylight that sneaked away from the west window, and he stared up at her. Romilia, lovely, alive, looked down at him after kissing him awake. She smiled and made an announcement that offered a spark of hope, "I believe that I am pregnant."

⩕
⩕

The news trickled down the hill into town: A new job would soon be opening for a midwife.

People gathered about, talking, adding to the news, keeping it alive with the delicacy of rumors. The *patrón* and his wife were ready for the birth of a child. What woman would be chosen as the baby catcher? "Someone who needs to make a little money, that is for sure."

"It will probably be her mother. Doña Amanda will do it."

"Doña Amanda? She has little experience. Besides, Romi has forgotten her mother like a bad dream. Doesn't even visit her, the ungrateful little bitch."

"Well, it will not just be anyone. I bet I could do it."

"You? Marialena, you don't even know which end a baby comes out of. You'd be looking up her ass...."

The chatter ran from house to store to church, until a black horse named Relampago galloped down the hill one early morning. Then the running voices stopped and waited. Patricio's horse trotted past adobes and small stores. It stopped before a door that was always open. He stared into the dark threshold until he made out the presence of the older woman. "Good morning."

"Good morning, Mr. Colónez. How are you this morning?" greeted Doña Amanda.

"Very well, thank you." He climbed down from his horse and waited for her invitation.

"Come in, please."

She brought him a cup of coffee and a piece of bread. He sat down at the old table and ate. She leaned against the doorway with her arms crossed, looking down to the ground, flipping a rock with her toe.

"Are you eating well?" he asked.

"Yes, very well, thank you. I ate the chicken last night. There was so much meat on it, I shared it with my neighbors. But I saved the other two for eggs." She pointed with her lips toward the back lot.

"Very good. I am glad."

Silence fell between them, an attempt to reflect calmness, to gain for each of them time to think.

"You know, my wife is pregnant."

"Yes," she replied, and an uncontrollable smile snapped over her face.

"I need to hire someone to help her, someone who can be with her during this time. Then someone to make sure your grandchild comes into the world healthy." He smiled for the first time. It turned quiet again.

"Do you have anyone in mind?" she asked.

"Well, yes. I wanted to ask you."

"Me? Oh no, I do not believe that would be wise."

"Why?"

"Because, well, my daughter and I, you understand, we are in different worlds, and she being my daughter..."

"I understand, I think. I thought this may be. Still, I come to you for advice. Do you know of anyone, someone who is responsible, whom I can trust? I don't want to hire just anybody."

Amanda waited a moment to answer, as if pondering. But her answer came too smoothly. Obviously she had known of someone ever since the news arrived in town. "Yes, there is someone I know who is very good at that job. She has done it for many years. And, if you take her, Mr. Colónez, you will be doing her a great favor...."

A Fire in the Earth

♒

"I believe you two already know each other."

Romilia looked at Silvia, now an older woman with a few white streaks running through her black hair. The *patrona's* mouth dropped slightly open. She answered her husband without looking at him.

"Yes, we do. How are you?"

"Very well, thank you, Mrs. Colónez."

Patricio spoke. Neither of the women seemed to hear him. He talked about responsibilities, eating times, of where the baby was to be born, what room was best. He was speaking of the midwife's sleeping arrangements when Silvia spoke up. "I believe, Mr. Colónez, I should go home every night and sleep with my family. Of course, during the last month, I will remain here if you wish."

"Oh, well, yes, of course. I can understand that. And the last month, that will be the most important time. Well, I will leave you two to visit. Romilia, you should show Silvia the house, where the things are, introduce her to the other workers." He excused himself. Both women stood in the drawing room. Romilia waited until she no longer heard her husband's footsteps.

"What are you doing here?"

"Your husband hired me, because of your pregnancy, Mrs. Colo—"

"Don't call me that. Call me—don't call me anything. Just let me show you the place. Here is the kitchen. Come."

They walked through the house. Santo worked away, preparing for the largest meal of the day. She greeted the *patrona* and respectfully listened as Romilia presented the new midwife to both her and Cristina.

"Welcome to your new work, Doña Silvia," spoke Santo. "You have been a midwife before?"

"Oh, yes. I have done it many times, all over. I probably have caught some people even you may know." She chuckled.

"Come, Silvia, I will show you the upstairs." Romilia rushed her out. "Here. That is the first bedroom, for the first child. Over there is the second. That is Mr. Colónez's and my room. You may stay in this room when you wish, especially during the last month, so you will be

111

close by. If you want, you may help with some of the other chores. Santo can show you what needs to be done.... What are you doing here, Silvia?" The question, fomented by a plea, seemed to emanate from a little girl.

"I was hired by your husband—"

"Yes, but there are others. How did he know, why did he come to you?"

"It was your mother's idea."

"Patricio talked with Mamá?"

"I, I do not know. Perhaps someone told him to go to her, one of the store owners in town." She stumbled from frankness, "It came at a good time for us, Romi. We were...we almost had to move out into the coffee fields, you see, money was—"

"What is this going to *do* to me?" Romilia turned away, hearing nothing of the life below. "I mean, Silvia, you *know* me." Sardonic laughter fell. "I can't have you be my maid."

Silvia looked to the floor. "Romi, I do not mind. It's necessary; it's good for me to work. I want to do it." She smiled carefully, petitioning for permission. "And you know I can do a good job."

"Yes, yes I know you can. I know you can. Yes, it is good that you are my midwife. This is good, good." She muttered it to herself, as if memorizing. She voiced nothing else, floundered in silence, until Silvia nudged her.

"I should know where you are, how you are doing with your baby. How long has it been?"

"I'm not sure. I think I vomited every day for about three, four weeks. But I'm not doing that anymore, thank God."

"Yes. Some of the gifts of creating life. How do you feel?"

"Good. I feel fine. Oh, I get tired sometimes, but that is because there is so much to do. Like last night, some friends were here from Sonsonate, and that takes me two days to plan. And come Friday, some more acquaintances from the capital will come out. They want to go hunting Saturday morning, so we will be entertaining them for the weekend. You can help with those things, too. There is always some-thing to be done. And we are building on, as you can see. Since I have

A Fire in the Earth

so many guests, I insisted that we have more rooms added to the house. And with the children coming, we will especially need them."

"Well, you should not entertain as much now, since you are pregnant." Her voice moved back from that of a maid to that of someone from the *patrona's* childhood—strong, slightly daring. "You need to slow down and have fewer people visiting. You need to rest. When a woman is pregnant, it takes twice the energy to do the same—"

"We will entertain as we have always entertained." Romilia turned and looked at the new maid. "That is my job; that is my position here. We will not stop that just because of a newborn coming."

"But, Romi, you must think about your health. And if you are celebrating until all hours of the night—"

"How do you know what we do here? How do you know how long our parties last? What, are the people in town talking about us? That is none of your business anyway. You will not be here at night."

"I'm just telling you what is best for the child, Romilia."

"And I know what is best for us." Romilia's words clicked together, little sharp tacks that dared the midwife to enter between them. "And do not call me Romilia, especially in front of the others. You will call me what they call me.

"But you just said to call—"

"I am Señora Colónez to everyone here. It is best that way."

"But how are we—"

"It is best that way."

The words snapped through the hallways and down the stairs to a listening pool of ears. The snap turned to whispers, and the whispers stretched and formed into other words. Editorials were added, by the gardeners, the cooks, the cheese sellers. They took the words like a gospel to the little town below, where all learned about it, as they all learned every detail of the life in the rich house up the hill. It became known that there was a conflict in the upper rooms of the Colónez estate, one between mistress and midwife, between former friends from a distant life. The Comenzaños had something new to chew upon, to spit out and study. It would keep them busy for the following months.

113

〰〰

The Schonenbergs came to visit. It was Romilia's idea. "Since they are practically our neighbors. They own all the land around us. We should be cordial, should we not?" This meant inviting them from the capital, as the Schonenbergs rarely came out to see their land in El Comienzo.

Tomás Schonenberg was the son of Hans, the man who once rode into town proclaiming the Good News of the Free Market. Tomás had been born in Venezuela seventeen years before. His mother—herself a Venezuelan—demanded that they give their son a Spanish name and that he learn Spanish. Yet Tomás still admired his father and imitated his manner of dress. He wore bright black leather with furls and a strange cowboy hat that did nothing to protect anyone from the sun. A painted woman, whose last name Tomás had yet to learn, dangled from one of his arms. She cooed and giggled and pointed at the quaint little mansion "sitting out here in the woods. It is so pretty!" In his left hand Tomás Schonenberg held a small wood case. He handed it over to Patricio.

"I promise you, this stuff will put you under the table, my friend. You will not see anything like it anywhere in this country, except in my bedroom closet, where I have a case of them." He told the story of a gringo friend who worked with the great and growing telephone company of the United States. It was he who had brought Schonenberg the case of whiskey which he had shipped all the way from Scotland. "It is a new distillery, just a few years old. But it is becoming very popular in Europe."

Patricio stared at the bottle, at the majestic head of the many-pointed-antler deer staring outward to the drinker. He politely and quietly thanked Schonenberg. They filled four glasses.

"Hey, Patricio, how do you pronounce this word? 'Soch?'" asked Schonenberg.

"Scotch," he corrected, with perfect pronunciation.

"Ah, yes, soch. Scoch. It is difficult, the gringo language. Father spoke only German, of course, and could not speak it here, except with a few friends. And my little mother knows only Spanish. Teach me more, Patricio!" They all laughed except Patricio, the one man who prided himself on his bilingual abilities. He only smiled and poured.

The four drank for an hour before dinner. Patricio, Romilia, and Tomás learned the name of Tomás' companion, Carmen. "We just met a few days ago, isn't that right, my love?" She cooed an affirmative reply. "It was at a business meeting. Who were you with? Oh, yes, Hills, that old shit. But a good man, a good man!" He slipped more whiskey down his throat. "Ah, this is such good stuff, but it puts fat on a man's belly. But that means I am beautiful, true?" He laughed, and Carmen squeaked a giggle. "Hey, here's a toast. I forgot about this until now. Romilia, you are expecting a little one running around your feet soon! Huh! How wonderful! Let us toast...everyone get your glass up, come on. Here, Romilia, you need a bit more. There we are. Here is to the little one to come into the Colónez family. May he have good health, and a...a fine life, and very good health!"

They drank. Patricio sat back in his chair, smiling when necessary. "Hey, Patricio, let's go outside before the sun sets. I want to see the little town my father gave me."

The two men left, glasses in hand. Romilia sat back in her chair, listening to Carmen's running words about how she had been pregnant before. But that was years ago, and it had been taken care of.

The two gentlemen stood outside on the front porch. "You really like it out here, don't you, Patricio?"

"Yes. It is my home."

"Well, that is good. It is beautiful, very nice. How do you say it in English? 'Booti, bootifl?'"

"Beautiful."

"Ah, yes, that's it. You do that so well." He drank more, talked about the coffee, how it was doing much better now that some new laws concerning the workers had been passed. "Yes," Tomás said, "those working the land now live out in the coffee fields, right in the middle of the trees. There they are, in a free house. Just as long as they work that area of land around them. That was such a wise law, true? My dad says it's a great law. He proposed the idea, you know. Now every worker is responsible for a piece of land, for getting it all picked, taking care of the trees. We were almost losing the trees before now. Fuck. Some of them were dying right in the ground during the dry season. Being eaten up by...by whatever destroys coffee trees, you know? Bugs, insects, weeds, whatever it is. But now, well, just look at it."

They both looked out at the green fields and hills, at the various little adobe houses standing among the foliage, with whispers of smoke that the night swallowed. "That is how it should be, Patricio, my friend. Everyone working for the good of the whole country. That's what Dad says. We are such a wonderful country. You know that, don't you?" Patricio barely shook his head, half-listening to Tomás' impassioned speech. "*Un país rico.* How do you say that in English?"

"Country. A rich country."

"'A reech cauntre.' Yes. I like that. How wonderful. You speak it so well. Look, teach me some phrases. I want to use them on my woman. She will love it. How do you say, '*Tú eres hermosa*' in English?"

For the first time Patricio looked the young, little man in the eye who wanted to say "you are beautiful" to his lover. Patricio suddenly felt much older, and a great deal wiser, standing before such inanity. He sipped from the glass, swallowed, and answered.

"You are a whore."

"Jyu ar a horr. Jyu ar a hor."

Tomás practiced it, several times. He laughed, a rolled giggle, as Patricio smiled at him and nodded in affirmation.

"Wonderful! Now, how would I say, '*Yo soy un hombre guapo?*'"

"I eat shit."

"Ay eet sh...sheet."

"Good. Try again. 'I eat shit.'"

"Ay eet sheet. Ay eet sheet. Hey! I spoke English!" He burst out with a thick, robust laugh. "Ay eet sheet! Ay eet Sheet! It is true, true?"

"I am sure."

Schonenberg turned with guffaws and repeated the foreign syllables several times, practicing, not wanting to lose them in the scotch. Ay eet sheet, jyu ar a hor, over and over again. He brought the offerings into the house and used them upon his girlfriend, who giggled with glee to hear the foreign words come from her new man. Patricio smiled passively. Romilia said little, her head nodding back and forth with sleepiness, offering a cordial, periodic smile, waiting for supper to come. The young Schonenberg practiced all night and promised another box of that good scotch to Patricio whenever he came to visit. The following day he would carry his new words to his home in the capital, repeat them periodically, proudly, laughing with friends, with his father's business associates, using them on the wives of the gringos, always laughing through another box of imported happiness.

♒

"She should not drink so much. I have seen it before. It will hurt the baby."

It was all Patricio needed to hear from the midwife. The parties would come to an end, he announced, until the baby was born.

"What right does that woman have to control what we do?" Romilia boomed her anger at her husband in the bedroom. "We will continue entertaining. That, that is our duty. I cannot have some bitch—"

"Do you want to harm our baby? And how can you call an old friend a bitch—"

"This is my house! She will do what I say!"

"I am the man of this house, Romilia. And we will take care of our child. The drinking hurts the baby while it is still in you."

"What does it do?"

"It...I do not know. It just hurts the child. Silvia said she has seen babies of a mother who drinks too much come out badly formed. Some of them die. Do you want to kill—"

"Don't tell me that! Don't blame me. I am caring for my child!" She stormed to the window, scowling, mumbling inaudible words, the aches of past years. "Old bitch, old bitch, always telling us what to do, what was best..." She sighed a heaviness toward the window that looked over the distant brickyard. "Look, if it's the drinking that you are concerned about, then fine. But that does not mean we must stop the parties. The baby is in me, not in everyone else. I can stop drinking, if that is the case."

117

"Still, I do not want to have the parties anymore."

"Why not? Why must we suddenly ignore our friends?"

'Those are not our friends, dammit! They are a bunch of rich asses who want to get drunk all the time!"

"And what are we? Poor? No, we are one of the bunch. We just happen to live out here in the country because we do not have enough sense to move to the capital. I will go and invite them. *You* had best be suitable. They are your friends and you know that. You can't separate yourself from them that easily. And I will not let you. You hear me? Ey! I will not let you—!"

He had walked out of the bedroom, had walked down the stairs, her screams running behind him. "It is that way with pregnant ones," said his old friend and cook Santo. And the new midwife Silvia had concurred.

"She was such a silent child, but I always thought there was something else in her," Silvia confessed to the cooks and to other workers standing nearby, who listened intently. This had occurred before, this talking among the workers. Silvia knew so many of them, as they too were Comenzaños. The others from the capital were also of her stock. They spoke to one another in an affable manner. She told them of her life, of knowing Romilia as a little girl. How she had always wanted to learn mathematics and to read, but her mother, Doña Amanda, had never allowed for that. *She cannot read. Our* patrona *cannot read.* This was enough for them to chew on for a while. They had heard the rumors, how she had lived in poverty, how Mr. Colónez had arrived and had jerked her out of all that, brought her up the hill, gave her money to play with. With Silvia around, they learned even more how their *patrona* came from their own stock, or perhaps even lower. Living, active questions came out of this. How is it we take orders from one of our own? She dresses in money, but she is one of us.

Santo helped feed the fire. "Well, you know she knew nothing of what to do when she first got here, couldn't even choose which cheese was necessary to have with what meal. And here she is now, strutting about like a rich goose. We should chop her little brown neck!"

A Fire in the Earth

Such talk moved quickly. It chattered behind the closed kitchen door, during temporary moments of privacy for the workers. They never heard the swish of a matronly dress slip behind the door.

"No, no. She is where she is because of blessing," Silvia spoke, trying to calm the turn of conversation with the other maids and cooks. "She was blessed to be brought here. We don't know why. Perhaps she did not deserve it. Perhaps there is no reason why. But she is here, nonetheless. And so is he. And since he is here, look how much he has helped the town."

The conversation followed her lead, of how the town had practically been saved by the Colónez's money. "It is just like him," said Santo. "He has always been generous. To a fault." For the moment they counted their blessings to one another, offering pious thanks to show that they held no animosity toward anyone.

"I would not be working here if it were not for Mr. Colónez," continued Silvia. "Because of him we have enough money to remain in El Comienzo. We do not have to move out into the coffee fields. Why, if it were not for him, right now I would be deep in coffee with my family, sweating fat drops in order to pick beans, just barely surviving. I do not think we could make it."

She knew this, yet she said very little to Romilia, for the latter as of late had no words to share with her. Barbed with silence when together, Silvia checked the growing, expecting mother like a field of dynamite. Something warned her, perhaps the silence.

There were other warnings, feelings not based on fact, but things she sensed. There was her inability to sleep at night; looking into a black sky and feeling an impending future darker than the night itself. Along with the ability to perform her work and derive whatever precarious rewards, midwifery often carried mysterious talents such as these. Every morning Silvia awoke with the heaviness of little sleep, and trekked up the hill to watch over the future mother. The midwife ached with tension as she touched Romilia's abdomen, running her hands around the expectant mother's waist, checking, feeling for any deformities under the soft, smooth skin, feeling for the size, for the texture of the carried womb.

"It is very small."

"It has not been long," asserted the pregnant woman. Silvia said nothing else, though she knew it had been several months, that the womb should have been larger. She questioned Romilia about her health, how she felt.

"No, I feel fine. Fine. I am just tired, and my ankles, look at them, so swollen. God, how ugly a woman gets when pregnant!" She looked in the mirror, checked her neck, her profile. "But I will pass, won't I, Silvia?"

"Yes, ma'am." She will pass; the midwife whispered a quiet prayer. Let her pass, let her pass. Forget the over-swollen legs, the headaches, the past week of sudden vomiting. With time, Silvia spoke less to the other workers, walked the hall with a careful lightness, waiting for other signs that inevitably came. Romilia kept asking to close the shades, "For God's sake, close them. The sun is blinding me," though it did not fall on her. The rays fell to the other side of the room. She grew more weary, and relied on Silvia to help her across the room or down the stairs. "Ay, dammit, watch it," scolded Romilia after gently brushing the corner of a cabinet with her thigh. Sudden tenderness in the skin. Silvia touched her, caressing a half-sleeping snake, running her fingers over the abdomen again, checking, holding her arm to walk across the house. This was her job. She was the midwife, the one responsible. Everyone knew that; everyone knew what weight rested upon the shoulders, the mind and the soul of the midwife. Silvia was the famous one, having wrenched this rich young woman out of a womb that had been torn open by that old fire in the earth so many years before in a rotted city. She was famous, had seen very few babies die, a miracle in this land. This was not the time to see one more death. So she prayed, prayed for safety, for new life, for an end to the signs—the wretched symptoms of which she had had the curse of witnessing before with some teenage mother in some poor barrio of the old city. *If it is to die, let it die small*, whispered her prayers that turned drastically other ways, looking for escape, for the least painful way out, one that would not force her to make decisions.

She could no longer escape the signs. Time was exacerbating them: The vomiting, the heaving out of anything that came in, the complaints of slight blindness, and her words, "Close that fucking window, the sun is blinding me!" Silvia shut out the sunlight for the expectant woman and calmed her, rubbing her forehead, false calmness trying to plough through the fear that rooted in her intestines. *Please let it die soon, before it is so large*, before, she knew, it would sit in her, rotting in her middle, with no way to get out except to call a doctor from the capital. They could do that, for they were rich, not like that poor teenage girl who had jerked through a convulsive death. Yet Silvia had heard about the doctors and their new, scientific ways, about running a knife over the woman's genitals and reaching in to yank out the young carrion, then cleaning the womb with an ammonia-soaked rag. That's what the specialists did, clean it out, disinfect it. The older woman walked the halls between kitchen and bedroom, stopping the husband from entering and visiting, telling him she needed the rest, to let her rest. "She is a little sick, but she will get better." She walked the silent hallways which knew nothing of these things, bedrooms and kitchen that waited in expectation for a new little life to crawl through them and play, hallways suddenly shaken by the scream "SILVIA! COME HERE COME HERE COME HERE!" She bolted up the stairs, lifting her dress to take them two at a time, and burst the door open to see the pregnant one on the floor, fallen, her sweaty hair tousled over her face like black moss and her whole left cheek twitching toward her nose. Crimson and mucus spattered upon her white nightgown.

Silvia reached for her, responding with some vague and final gentleness. She brought the frantic woman to the bed and tried to soothe her. While Romilia slept, Silvia changed her nightgown, pulling at it like removing evidence. Again she felt the abdomen, naked and bulging. There was no movement, none at all, not like there had been, those little bumps and kicks of the living.

It was obvious. She prepared for it. She gathered several towels, a large bowl of water, soap, a short-blade kitchen knife. She placed all this in the bedroom.

Sitting in a chair in one corner of the room, she waited. She wept. All this meant too much. Judgement would soon come. She wept silently, thinking of her old neighbor Amanda, thinking of the woman in bed, that little girl who had dreamt. There was only the waiting.

Nothing else existed in the great house which stood above the little pueblo that slept, waiting for the rich prince to come to the world and look out over that coffee field and brickhouse kingdom.

♒

The convulsions began at four in the morning. Silvia jumped from the chair to the side of the bed and tried to hold Romilia's arms down. She screamed Santo's name down the hallway three times. The old cook entered the room and stared with cracked-wide eyes at the violent labor.

"She is not having the baby; the baby is dead. We must get it out of her."

Silvia had Santo hold down the jabbing limbs while she helped Romilia's womb expel the unwanted corpse. She pushed down with her palms from the top of the womb, massaging, then resorted to blows against it until the mass moved. One half-hour later a gray, solid head pushed out, something for the midwife to grasp. Another contraction pushed it, making it seem alive. For a moment she was not sure. Santo, who had managed to grab Romilia's arms, turned her head away as Silvia brought the kitchen knife between the *patrona's* legs. Santo still heard, through the convulsive screams, the slicing.

In the next several minutes it was out, laying like a bag of wet, gray meat on the bedsheets. Silvia cleaned out the bearer's insides with towels and water, while Santo turned and vomited from the stench of the bloody newborn and the rotting viscera inside the unconscious mother.

"We must make sure she is as clean as possible, else she will get infection."

Santo followed orders. She brought in a tub of boiled water. They cleaned and wiped the seemingly unmovable stench and stains from the bed, changed the bedsheets around the sleeping woman, dressed her in new apparel. From her womb crimson and mucus still flowed, enough to rouse the stench. Silvia cleaned and dried through the early morning into the light of new day. "She is very sick now. A fever. She is pale. She will be like that for days. We will need to watch her."

A Fire in the Earth

Words dropped from the midwife like debris from a destroyed city, words that revealed nothing of the miracle before them, that the woman had lived.

Romilia did not waken until that evening, only to look up at the pulled, drawn face of her husband. She smiled at him, then suddenly scowled, then closed her eyes again, not opening them for another two hours. Silvia comforted him with age and experience, telling him time and again that she would be fine, but that it would take time.

That day they buried the body in the back yard of the home. Patricio had gone down the hill into El Comienzo to fetch the priest. Father Mateo was unaccustomed to riding in the large carriage of the *patrón*, and said very little to the young man who sat next to him, staring out the window. The priest only muttered, "I am sorry, Mr. Colónez."

"Thank you, Father. So am I."

The carriage bounced up the hill and pulled to the back of the large house to an open area near the trees that stretched out to the remaining woodlands. Don Roberto, one of the old farmhands, had dug a hole, small and deep, near some of the trees. He stood sweating when the priest and the *patrón* approached. Soon all the workers had silently gathered together, offering a crowd of mourners. Patricio stood like a blinking corpse, then stared around at the growing crowd. He spoke out as he saw Silvia. "Wait, wait, where is Doña Amanda? She is not here, she should be here...." Someone spoke up, that they could go get her from town, if everyone would wait for a short time. Again the carriage was sent, and within half an hour it returned. The chauffeur Diego helped the aging woman out of the coach. A stench became apparent, rising from the small wooden box that sat next to the hole, reminding them of why they were there.

"Okay, Father. Bless it." Patricio took off his hat and held it in front of him.

The old priest opened his book, looked up the blessings for a Limbo-bound baby, and began reciting them. The words circled around the crowd with some sense of honor, the old priest knowing how to speak to them. The *patrón* looked on, ignoring the words, the priest, saying nothing but "Thank you, Father" after the liturgy, and handing him a ten-colones note. The crowd broke apart, with the women taking their drying tears back to the workload and the men donning their hats to again approach the melodic toil under the promising sun. Patricio turned to the brickhouse office. He remained there all day, talking with no one, doing necessary paperwork. The chauffeur carried Amanda and the priest back to El Comienzo.

The mother of the dead baby slept, knowing nothing of that day, dreaming about adobes, walls and bricks; and of goat cheese, its smell, a stench like that of rotting life that still leaked from her. Dreams of a mother, distant and young, working, praying, refusing to let those numbers, that education for men enter the brain of the little girl. Such were the nightmares that came with sweat and fever, covered with the reality of rich serapes that held in a rising heat, trying to break a threatening temperature.

A day passed, then its night, and the sweat cooled away the violence from the young body. The midwife wiped the dark, smooth skin clean of salt and water, wiped with care and sincerity the unconscious body, cleaning, crying, touching one last time. The eyes of the *patrona* opened, though her head did not move. She looked at the surroundings, almost forgetting all that she possessed. She looked to her side and saw, through haze and weariness, a figure disappear around a door. That woman's figure, she could tell from the simple dress that escaped like a ghost. Then the man came in, her husband, and stood by her bed, touched her forehead, saying something to her. She could not understand his mutterings. The cook stood behind him, looking concerned, *That fat bitch lies; she wishes that I had died.* With that, reality rushed back like an ocean. She remembered who she was and who had disappeared previously like a ghost through the open doorway. She remembered all that she possessed; and she would never forget all that they said about her behind closed kitchen doors. Everyone discussed her position in life, analyzed who she was, who she should be. Thus she feigned sleep, and in her slow convalescence, created an arsenal of clarity for them all—the cooks, the workers, the *patrón*, that midwife. Once she awoke, they would know exactly who she was.

Deep night flooded the upper bedroom. Her eyes stared open at the stars which smiled through the window. They seemed to give her permission, as if to say *The final separation, this will be the final sepa-*

A Fire in the Earth

ration, all will be clear, we will all know our places. Another star flickered in, carried by an old hand that had touched her over and over again, helping her through the process of giving birth that had failed so miserably. The tiny candle-star danced, then sat upon the small table that stood next to her bed, flapped above the pillar of wax to show the shadows of both women's faces, one ready to wipe more sweat off the sick one, and the sick one, feigning sleep, eyes closed, with the flame's light almost afraid to touch her. She shattered the silence with a razor-whisper, "You killed my baby." Then the twist of a silent blade, approved by the stars, by the night, "Get out of here. Get out of here."

♒

"We will not stay there long. We will leave; there are other places. The ocean, the sea. It has promises, more food, different fruits. We can live elsewhere. But we will not stay out *there* for long."

Juan Montenegro, Silvia's husband, pointed toward the coffee hills. Silvia did not answer. She sat, leaning against their dilapidated table next to the adobe stove, and slowly pushed some dirt with the tip of her index finger.

"When do you have to leave?" asked Amanda, sitting before her, her head cocked to one side, her hand twitching at a long strand of hair.

"They told us this week. Since we could not hand over any money, they told us then and there. Like they were waiting for the day." Juan tossed his words about like boiling water. "Just waiting for us to have no money, to lose a job." Slowly he walked back and forth between a corner and the stove, looking down, fiddling with a nervously rolled cigarette. "It is as if Schonenberg knew that the baby would die." The words left him and beat his wife to a crumble. Amanda tried to hold her, yet the man beat reason against her. "Woman! Listen to me. It is not your fault! How many times do we need to say it?" Seeing he did nothing but break her down more, he walked out. He stood next to his old cart—as old as El Comienzo—the one which they had used to carry Amanda out of the destroyed city. Through the years he had added

125

parts, pieces of wood for spokes, for the lining of the sides. He had kept it operable all this time. Now it was full of all their belongings, old serapes used forever, a few clothes, cooking utensils stacked one on top of the other.

Inside, without a man looming over them, the two friends spoke. "What will happen to this place?" asked Amanda.

"I do not know. Probably he will rent it to someone, whoever would live in it. I suppose it is better than many places. At least it has a few inside walls. But I do not know. He did not make it his business to tell us." When she said "he," she did not mean Schonenberg, for they had never seen him. One of his messengers had been sent, a local who did all this sort of work for the landowner.

Silence fell between them. They were both accustomed to it, especially during these hard, sad times. "What part of the fields will you live in?"

"The local guard told us over to the west, beyond the first hill. You cannot see it from here. Juan says that is good, because they cannot watch us as much, so he thinks we can slip away sometime."

"I have heard that some people do that. The Oseguedas, they slipped off last year. I heard they went to the ocean, too, or was it Guatemala? I cannot remember. There have been quite a few slip away." She hesitated, then asked, "What...what would happen if they caught you?"

Silvia breathed out heavily, as if smoking. "I do not know. I have heard many things. They take you to the capital, throw you in jail. Now that it is law, I do not know. It seems they can do it. But maybe, maybe they will just make us work the coffee more...."

Amanda sat in a silent guilt, being the mother of this dilemma. "It is a bad law," she contested, making up for her sin, for her daughter's actions. "That is just not right. I do not see how they can do that at all. This new president, he only listens to those who shove colones into his pocket. It is not just, not at all." Silvia barely answered her. Her listless voice dragged across the dusty table. She mumbled something, that they can do whatever, for they are the law. The almost inaudible conversation went on for several moments, nothing else to fill the moment of parting. Juan moved back and forth between the kitchen

A Fire in the Earth

and the street which ran in front of the house. His grandchildren played outside, rolling down the streets rusted metal hoops from old wheels. They used sticks against the hoops, hitting them in a run, forgetting that in minutes they would soon move away and never again play on this street. They were the laughing, playing remnants left them by children who had gone away to the city to find work, a job that would offer them and their family survival. Little had been heard from them. No money had come. The grandchildren kept playing through it all, up until the final moment when the local official knocked on the door and told them he was the man to show them their new home. The children packed up their rusting hoops and put them in the cart, hanging them through a broom that stuck upward through the back. Their grandfather helped their grandmother climb in. They watched the grandmother lean over and kiss her friend, old Doña Amanda from next door. She held Amanda's face by the cheeks, dropped several tears, and mumbled words that barely clung together. The grandchildren tried to climb in, too, but their grandfather shooed them away, telling them with slight irritation that the old cart could not hold all that weight. "You will just need to walk along with me." They stood to the side, waiting for the crying women to release each other. A tremulous voice could be heard, "Forgive her, please, I am so sorry." The cart cleft their sorrow as the old mule pulled away. They looked back for a moment and watched old Doña Amanda, who seemed to curl up. Then the children knew this was a time of sorrow, and with purity of sensibility, of the vicarious, they let their own tears flow, suddenly aware of what was happening to them.

~~
~~

The house stood empty for several weeks. Thinking she heard something, Amanda peeked through a window of her home to look over. A man entered. She heard the banging of hammers, the noise of construction. A storefront was built. One of the small openings that served as windows was enlarged to make a shelf that faced the street. A lean-to roof was built over it. Food, dry coffee, beans, rice and soaps made by people on the other side of town were placed on the shelf every day. People walked by, bought and traded. In October and November fewer people came. It always seemed to happen that way, that in those months, no one had money for buying. Come December, however, the stores were once again busy, with people bringing small palmfuls of money that they had made from picking coffee, taking control of the marketplace for a transient moment.

Amanda did not know the new store owner. This was unusual; she knew all her other neighbors, and felt a responsibility to meet this one. He was from out of town, obviously. She could tell by the way he dressed. No one had ever seen him before he built the store. Someday, she told herself, I should get over there. She finally did. He was a nice young man named González, who spoke amiably for several minutes between customers. But as she talked with him, she looked around the store and remembered it was once a home. Rarely did she return to chat.

January came, the busiest, richest time of the coffee harvest. Every day, as long as there was sunlight, people walked through the hills and between the rows of trees. They pulled at the red beans and threw them into baskets strapped adroitly around their backs with crude ropes made from banana leaves. The workers stripped the red fruit from the branches. They worked from top to bottom, picking, pulling, dropping the beans into the growing heaviness of the basket. They filled thirteen to fifteen baskets each day, dumping the fill into large bags placed at the end of each tree row. They stopped only to eat at midday or to rest subversively between the thickest trees one could find. The other workers said nothing. A guardsman always threatened to turn in anyone he caught resting. They had no idea what would happen were they turned in, and no one cared to find out. At sundown they returned to their small, sunbeaten adobes. The pitiful clay huts popped from the ground every few acres, clumsy gravestones in fields and hills of living green.

Four men dressed in official uniforms rode through the village streets and into the coffee fields. They galloped violently through El Comienzo. Amanda watched the dust they had kicked up in front of her house. They rode away and disappeared behind the great mound.

A Fire in the Earth

The hundreds picking coffee lifted their heads and looked up at the four horses that trampled through the fields and into the hills. The officials stopped before one small adobe that sat alone in several acres of trees. The coffee had not been picked yet. Some beans had fallen to the ground and were rotting, a sin that threatened the sinner's mortality.

"Look at this! Fuck!" grumbled one of the men. "They have done no work here!"

"How many in the family?" asked another guard.

"Two adults, three children. Just recently moved here. Plenty in the family to do the work, that is, for one of our own. They're not some lazy *chapines*. I checked the records before we left. I always check for that. Not that it is an excuse, but it usually falls true."

The second guard hesitated, confused by his colleague's charismatic prejudice, wondering what Guatemalans had to do with all this. He mumbled, "Well, it is a good amount of land for only five people to pick. And you know that kids don't work as fast."

"It is not that difficult. Not if they worked hard, not if they were industrious. We are workers, Aldo," said the high official with cocked pride. "We are workers, and we let nothing go to waste. Except, of course, these fucking lazy Indians are another matter."

Aldo made no reply, knowing which way the conversation would go.

They checked the adobe house. There was no sign of life nor any belongings. The four remounted their horses and rode to where another nearby family was busily picking ten-acres worth. The main official spoke to an elderly woman who bent over to the lower branches of a tree. "Woman. Hey, you there! Old woman! Where is the Montenegro family?"

She looked up and squinted her eyes at the sun obscured by the large man on horseback. She stared at the living mass of horse's flesh, wrapped and tall and strong. "Don't they live over there?" she asked, pointing toward the empty adobe.

"They are not there anymore."

"Oh. I do not know where they are, sir."

"Why aren't they picking their coffee with the rest of you?"

"Well, they've had sickness, I do know that. Their mother and children—"

"Where are they now?"

"I do not know. I believe I saw them yesterday. Perhaps they are in town, looking for a doctor." She talked while looking back at the tree, pulling coffee from it. She put them more carefully into the basket than usual, under the shadow of the great horse and the large man.

"Well, they are being arrested for abandoning the land and crops, you know that, don't you?" The woman answered with a low, careful, "oh, yes, sir." The official looked out at the vast fields of green. "And anyone harboring them will also be arrested." He barked the threat, but looked out at the multitude of working campesinos and said no more, knowing the difficulty of such an impotent search through so many adobes. It would be done, however, for they had done it before.

The elderly woman did not speak. The four officials rode away, leaving the campesinos to continue reaching and picking, reaching and picking. Two of the guards began searching houses; the other two rode into the nearby woodland. The old woman could hear the quick screams of children running out of the adobes as the men entered them, but she dared not look up. She heard them tossing about the pieces of crude furniture made of tree stumps and logs, tearing away cloth that served to divide the huts into rooms, but she still did not watch. She could not look, not even when she heard the high moan of an older girl somewhere behind her, while men beat her with hungry laughter and took turns upon her, pelting against her through ghostly wails. She could not look up, for it would mean too much, too many things. Nothing could be done. Hunger had etched into her soul the need to acquiesce.

Night rose from the east. Several women left the hills and stoked fires in front of their adobe homes. Small children hovered about them. One mother cradled a babe in one arm as it nursed from her full breast. With the other hand she stirred the contents of a pot half-filled with watery bean soup.

Some families ate together, sharing beans and rice, a few tortillas, and water carried from the little river nearby. The old woman and her

A Fire in the Earth

family joined some relatives. The women cut tomatoes which they grew covertly amidst clusters of coffee trees. The tomatoes were tiny because they received little sunlight. The men worked for another hour, though as the day came to an end they stretched upward more often, and stopped to rest from time to time. This day they looked about before resting, searching out the majestic horses that had remained with them all day. One man yelled to another across the field, "Hey, Roberto, you thirsty or hungry?"

"I am hungry and thirsty," he answered, chuckling lowly.

"Come over. We'll take care of both tonight."

The sun dropped as it neared the old volcano. The men washed their hands in wooden buckets of water, cleaned out the new cuts and abrasions over their fingers, lesions that would make for thicker, more protective skin. The old woman dished out beans on the tortillas that acted as plates. She looked about while she worked, glancing up like a deer that carefully drinks from a stream. The ghostly scream, she wondered. Had it been Sarah, that girl in the far adobe? Had it been Carmen? Thinking she heard the snorting of a distant horse, she dropped her glance toward the beans, feigning disinterest toward the horsemen. Throughout these years they had all learned adroitness, when and where to look or not to look; when and where to care, not to care, to remain still.

Arturo, who had promised his friend both food and drink, brought from his adobe an old ceramic flask. The two men began consuming the homemade *chicha*—corn liquor, made from the stolen remains of tortilla corn flour which Arturo had snatched when his wife was not looking. The women gathered around one another, cleaning and talking after the meal. The children played in the small dusty area in front of the adobe, fenced off by the thousand rows of coffee trees. As the light at the end of the day dimmed, so did their play, and the children fell to exhaustion inside the adobes.

The old woman laughed openly at what someone had said, and chuckled at the men now under the control of the *chicha*. "They feel nothing tonight; they will feel the world tomorrow." It was a blessing to have such close neighbors, a rarity out here. This was what she had always liked about living in El Comienzo: To have a few other women

131

with whom to walk, to wash, feed and clean her family. Such had been the case in the days before the forced removal of the people into the coffee trees. She smiled at the two drunkards like a mother, approving of whatever happiness they had achieved. The younger woman beside her frowned, knowing what awaited her tonight. He would be all over her and grunt desires, pelting them against the cloth wall that separated them from their children. The young mother would attend to bruises tomorrow, as he would inevitably fail to—as he had said before, in other inebriations—please her with his hardness. For the old woman, that part of life was far behind her. Now she laughed at the antics of the two drunken young men.

A shrill whistle pierced the evening air. Everyone looked up and watched as four men on horseback rode slowly out of the small, nearby woodland. Juan Montenegro jerked from behind their horses. He was tied to one of the saddles with a long rope. His arms were strapped behind him. His woman followed, Silvia, the failed midwife that had been hired by the *patrón*. She held a grandchild in her arms. Her screams blended with the guard's whistle that was calling out to all the workers. The official paraded his strength and pride in his work, a wild caveat to the other remaining peasants. The grandchildren walked beside their grandmother, stumbling, crying because their grandfather had been cursed at, had been hit and tied by these strangers. The man with the whistle, the same one who had talked with the old woman earlier that day, yelled to the group eating out in the coffee plantations, "Ey! I found my lost Indian!" The other officials laughed as their leader smiled toward the old woman. Behind the little crowd of horses, children, and the bound man, a broken-down wooden cart full of old belongings burned and crackled, licking out flames to the encompassing night.

"Now all of you have work to do. Do not let the coffee they were supposed to harvest go to rot. Start picking it tomorrow. I will be here the day after tomorrow to check your progress."

The soldier who held Juan jerked the rope a few times, knocking Juan to the ground on his face. "Come on, you stupid dickhead." The others laughed with him, even the soldier who had shown a sliver of sympathy earlier that day. Their laughter died away, then echoed through the old woman's head. Earlier she had promised Silvia and Juan, "I will not tell them. Go. Go, God bless." She now turned silent, as did the other women with her. Laughter rang again, and she turned her oblong eyes toward the oblivious, drunken men behind her.

~~~

The four horses rode through the small town, dragging behind them Silvia's family, with the husband bound like an animal with his wife and grandchildren tripping behind him. When they passed by Amanda's house, their old neighbor jumped from the safety of her adobe and ran to her friends. She grabbed at them, clutching them against her breast, trying to stop their forced parade through town. The head horseman barked at the family's old friend, calling her names. The horses broke the final embrace, leaving the two women's tears to clot the dusty road.

The horses walked by the great mound that stood in the very center of town. They soon came to the outskirts of the community which faced the road to the capital. A new shiny carriage with the last name of some family, followed by "Alimentos Especiales"—Specialty Foods— painted on its side, passed them by. It kicked a cloud of dust that swallowed the weeping family. The horses of the tidy carriage turned right and trekked up the hill. It stopped in front of the ranch house. The driver handed a cloth bag to Santo, the portly first cook. She dropped two bills and some change into his palm. The driver smiled and turned back to his carriage.

Santo took the sack through the kitchen and into the dining room. There she emptied the contents into a colorful ceramic bowl. She handled the apples with great care, knowing how easily they bruised.

She took the bowl upstairs and placed it on a small table in a far corner, next to the master bedroom. She knocked. "They are here, ma'am." She turned away, completing what she had been ordered to do.

Seconds later the bedroom door opened. A dark figure stepped halfway out. At first Romilia took only one apple, but then she changed her mind and grabbed the whole bowl. Though small, the bowl seemed very heavy to her drained body, still convalescing from the pain and damage of giving birth to death. The door closed. The sounds of rest and exhaustion could be heard, breathing through a private silence. Then came the triumph, the crisp crunch of a red orb, juice spraying out of that foreign, imported fruit.

$$\approx$$

"What are some of the problems you have?"

"My baby died, a boy. He was sick for a long time, with the runs."

"Why did your baby die?"

"...My wife, she tried to get it to eat..."

"Yes, but why *did* it die? Why do so many of you, of us, die?"

"...Sometimes it is because of the evil eye, somebody who is sweaty comes in, they've been working all day you know, and he looks at your baby, and without wanting to, gives it the evil eye."

"Yeah, but you know, if you take a raw egg and rub it all over the baby, the baby will get better. Of course, the egg will be cooked hard—"

"No, no, no! This is no time to talk about such things, such stupid beliefs. We have to let that stuff go. Let's look at the analysis: Why do you die? Come on, don't just look at me, answer the question: Why do you die?"

"We, we are hungry; we do not have enough to eat."

"That is correct. Correct! And why not?"

"Because, because we have no money. We have no crops."

"You have no land because someone else owns it, true?"

"Well, yes, where we live here, *Patrón* Soundy owns it, as does the Parker family. They own all this land."

"That is correct. And they are making you grow something on it that you cannot eat. Coffee. But what would happen if you, all of you, owned the land in common? What? Come on, someone answer."

"We would grow more food, I suppose."

"Yes, we would grow more food, like we used to. I remember, this place was once all beans and vegetables. Now it is all that fucking coffee."

"Good! That is correct! More food should be grown here. Look how many of your children are thick-bellied because of not eating enough. Is this just? No, of course not. The land should be yours, and not belong to those few rich men. In fact, it is yours. If you had it, there would be no rich men telling you what to do. All of you would be the bosses, and all your children would eat. It would be for everyone's benefit."

"But we cannot have the land; we cannot buy it. It belongs to the *patrones*."

"But like I said, it *is* yours. It is everybody's land. It is everybody's and nobody's, you see. It is equally distributed so that everyone owns it in common. The power in the proletarian that will create an unbalanced social thrust that inevitably will... Well, just listen. This is what you must do. You must take it back from them."

"Take it? We cannot take it, the law says that it is their land. We cannot break—"

"Forget the law! The law is made by rich men, so they can get richer! Don't you see? This is all set up to suck you dry! Take the land back, that is what we need to do, take the land! The law is bad. It is wrong. We need to take the land in order to do it right."

"Yes, sir; yes, sir. The law is...it is wrong, yes..."

"The land should be ours."

"The law is wrong. Yes. Well...the law, I suppose, it is wrong."

Chapter Six

The hawk took little notice of the hunched figure walking away from town. It flew on, searching for a morsel out in the field, something to feed its young back in a distant nest. The earth-bound figure below stumbled east of the little village that sat like a muddy obstruction in the middle of the hawk's lovely, hill-protected valley. The figure left the road and walked toward the small forest. She found the edge of a natural rock quarry and rested in a deep crevice. The hawk, disinterested, flew away.

The old woman moaned and cursed as she lowered herself into the rocky area, cutting one of her fingers on a sharp stone. The rock above tossed some shade, cooling her. Once in the shadow, she breathed deeply, methodically, pulling in and releasing out the air of the fields and sky. Deep and sonorous, the breaths expelled something from her, a great pain, a universal obstruction, or perhaps just a cold in her throat. Such was the weather in the last damp days of November. The sun only added the misery of humidity as it beat upon the earth. "Damn cold," she muttered. "Damn lousy weather."

She moaned from an ache, a misery, not knowing its origins, disgusted with it. Perhaps it was the misery of reputation. She certainly had one. Everything she did met the townspeople's expectations. The story of the rat gutted in the jailhouse had quickly run through the streets, saying that it was she who had caused the Colónez family to be barren. Everyone also knew about the curse she had cast upon Amanda years ago, when Romilia had been so hungry and sick. No doubt she had cursed the town in many ways. Most difficulties, both individual and communal, in time became the fault of the old woman.

So she accepted this pain, too, sitting in the shade of the rock quarry. She rested, exhausted from the acute, rhythmic pains. They

136

came more quickly, then she grunted loud and long, and the spasms finally ended.

She wrapped the wet bundle in old cloths, then rocked it slightly, holding it to her wrinkled breast, concealing it in her age. The thing inside coughed and cried. She hushed it, cooed at it, and tapped its head slightly, almost gently, with her scaly fingertips. "Now, you be a good boy. A good, quiet boy."

The hawk shot over the little forest, ignoring her presence in the crevice. Suddenly it descended like a bolted message from heaven, its claws extended downward as if to snatch the whole earth and carry it away. The bird barely tapped the rocks just a few feet above the woman's head. She watched the hawk jut upward, with a tiny, writhing creature in its talons. The baby snake snapped back and forth, searching for its nest. Being who she was, the old woman saw so clearly, so significantly, the little snake as it turned its writhing head toward the hawk's belly and shoved its tiny mouth open to the hidden skin under the glorious feathers. She knew, as did all older people with time and experience, how a baby snake was much more danger-ous, as it could not control its bite, and would sink all its venom into an attacker. She waited for the upcoming drama, staring toward the snake's head that had been swallowed up in feathers.

The hawk circled once, twice, then faltered. It sought out one of the tree branches behind the little rock quarry. Failing, it tripped in its glory and majesty through uncaring air and slapped against a sun-baked stone. It still clutched the tiny serpent. The old woman looked down at her new bundle of life. She pursed her lips together and bobbed her head slightly in quiet understanding.

In the far distance, perched upon a dead tree branch, one of those black beauties had watched all this. It waited, then flew near the rock where the dead bird lay and circled quietly, calmly, not needing to rush.

♒

On the day of their tenth wedding anniversary, Romilia would give birth to a son.

Marcos McPeek Villatoro

The decade before that birth spiraled downward. Everyone knew she was barren, so they logically figured that no one would inherit the throne at the top of the hill. No one in that lineage would take command of the brick house, nor look over the little town of El Comienzo as had Mr. Colónez. Only he knew how to juggle generosity and aloofness. It had to be that way, the Comenzaños knew that. There had to exist a barrier. They could not expect him to sit elbow to elbow with the workers over a beer in the lower regions of town. Yet the generosity, it had always been there, the number of jobs, the decent pay. How would that end? Parents in town hoped that the child born to the Colónez's, would be as good a *patrón* as the father. After a decade, such conversations withered to nothing.

Suddenly, in the ninth year something took root. Not exactly hope. They gave up using that word sometime during the sixth year. In this circumstance hope had nothing to offer them, no meaning nor desire. When she realized she had become pregnant, Romilia did not know how to approach Patricio with the news. There would be questions, some not inaccurate. She almost wanted someone else to tell him. She knew, from her own cryptic reasoning, that this child would not die and rot away like the first one, but would be born healthy, safe, alive.

After the death of the unborn, Patricio had dug himself deeper into office work at the brickyard, never coming home until the sun had completely set. He returned to a lifeless ranch. For three months after the miscarriage the *patrona* remained in the master bedroom alone, convalescing, sweating through fevers, with a nurse imported from the capital placing wet rags on her forehead and mixing dissolved pills into her water. "This is what real medicine is," she once mumbled during a lucid moment. She cursed all forms of home remedies in general, and one midwife in particular.

Patrona and *patrón* saw little of each other. Every day Patricio had entered the room to be with her for a few seconds that barely added up to a minute. No words were ever exchanged. She usually was sleeping.

In the fourth month Romilia opened the master bedroom door and walked out. She was wearing her best and favorite black dress which fell the length of her legs. A blouse was pumped forward by her bound

138

A Fire in the Earth

breasts. Her hair was gathered in a bun and stabbed with a spangly comb from Mexico. She smelled of rose petals, and her face was highlighted by the best cosmetics. The nurse, now dismissed, packed her belongings and waited for the carriage to take her back to the capital. Romilia walked down the stairs and to the kitchen, and gave the surprised Santo a list of duties concerning the get-together that she planned to have the following week.

The parties resumed, resurrected from the ashes that drifted between Romilia and Patricio. After work Patricio walked home to parties, already in progress. His brother Antonio came every week, dragging his wife Gloria along. On every trip to the country, she flung her caustic, garrulous complaints about the carriage, about everything out in the country. Then her face metamorphosed into a smile that held all night long, every week, week after week, falling into years and years of smiles.

The two couples drank and ate all night. Throughout the years they gave it a nickname, *martes de parranda*, Orgy Tuesday. When those new progressive machines called telephones were installed in the country, Antonio insisted that his brother have one out at the ranch. Antonio would call on the invention, and after announcing who he was and stating, as customary, "I am ready to speak now," he would ask, "Are we ready for Orgy Tuesday?" One of them, Patricio or Romilia, always confirmed it; he with resignation, she with fervent excitement. It was practically the only use they got from the phone, although his business associates would utilize it, calling to ask such things as when their supply of bricks would be arriving to the capital. He would inform them that he had sent a letter, as always. Yet they still called, getting their use from that incredible, expedient machine. He lived with it, since his brother had paid for it. Each time he came to visit, Antonio would ask Patricio how the phone was working, and Patricio would always report, "Fine, just fine." Antonio then would raise his glass and toast the telephone.

They celebrated every Tuesday evening as expected, and they all slurred to bed in the early hours of the morning, soaked in whiskey. During the night, as the household slept, Antonio would walk quickly back downstairs, leaving his sleeping Gloria to the sheets of their bedroom. He would sit on the sofa after lighting a candle and placing it upon the bookshelf where the marriage photo of Patricio and Romilia stood. He would pull his pajama pants down and touch his drunken hardness, and stare at the young innocence of the dark-skinned bride dressed in white flickering in the half-swallowed light of the flame. It did not matter that she was sitting before his brother. She was so dark, so obviously Indian. His jaw always dropped as he relished the breaking of the taboo.

At the factory the money rolled in as the bricks were carried out by horse-driven truckloads. Patricio's production line grew to twice its original size, which meant hiring more workers from El Comienzo, many sons of the men who had been working there for years. They would be hired. A year later they would be let go because of progress—new machines that cut the bricks, new feeders that tossed firewood into the large ovens to bake the clay into stone. Soon others had to be hired, those who had the ability to manipulate the new machines, but who could switch quickly when the machine inevitably broke down and wood had to be fed in by hand.

After the miscarriage of their first child, Patricio worked less in the yard and more in his office. The three days a week that he once had shared with the men became two, then only one day. Soon that also stopped. Some speculated it was because he did not want to take one of their jobs. But Patricio also talked less with the men. He spoke to them only when necessary, when an order arrived for Sonsonate, or when they had to ship double the number of bricks because new office buildings were being constructed in some city. Once an order came in for a certain style of brick, a little larger, with a slightly different shade of red. Patricio rejected it. "This is for stupid rich shits who lick the asses of gringos and follow their style." He denigrated them quietly, for they were the same men who brought the gringos to his door, to the parties, where he spoke English with them, and smiled with them, and even laughed with them over a joke told in English. There he walked, between the brickyard and the estate, between the uneducated and the gringos, between rich and poor, not knowing, never deciding where to stand, or whether to stand at all.

A Fire in the Earth

Those nights that his brother came, they always sat outside, smoking cigarettes from the States, talking business. Antonio always tried to persuade his little brother to go down into town to grab a woman. "Come on, Patricio, one of those country girls? You know, they work so hard all day. They're solid ones, something tight to put your whip in." Crudity, once a week, Patricio could count on it. Yet he never accepted the offer. He still had access to sex. He had his woman, the beautiful *patrona*, still quite lovely and smooth, even after the miscarriage. In some ways she had become more radiant, a cold recalcitrance that cut her ties with mourning and pain. Yet as time ate away at life, they came to each other out of need, the demands of their bodies, and the desire still, that fervent prayer to the flesh that Romilia conceive.

When the years told him that this would not happen, that she would never give him a child, Patricio finally resorted to look elsewhere. Not with his brother, never with Antonio, knowing the shallowness and silent scandal the older sibling would cause. He went alone, during the day, the few times that it was possible. It was a welcome sight. The people of town had wondered when Mr. Colónez would be like all men and take into his arms the round of other women. Slowly, with gradual whispers, a voice ran with the story through the various homes, the different stores, especially with the women, and casually with the men, The *patrón*, he made love to Carmen, he made love to my daughter Elisa, it is true, Marialena told me, she does not lie, he lay with her yesterday evening. The town lifted open its doors to him and opened itself to his need. He planted here, there, quietly, modestly, not with the conquering desire of his brother, but with a timid, passionate want to create. Most times he did not bother to take off all his clothes, but rather spent the scarce minutes to perform the act in the cool darkness of an adobe and be gone. The young faces he left looked up at him, smiling at the privilege, staring with hopeful, oblong eyes at his gentleness, his modesty. Afterwards he fled back up the hill. Then, after he had sown for several days, the people waited. He waited silently up in his brickhouse, at times looking out his office window with a pencil in hand, playing with it, staring at the town as if searching for some sign. And all this time his wife entertained, tossing invitations toward the capital, mixing with the right people, rarely glancing down the hill.

Nothing grew. Then the other voice ran through town. *It is not the* patrona *who cannot make children.* Up to this point it had been Romilia's fault. Another truth formed: Mr. Colónez's seed never took root, no matter where it fell. Not even here, in moist ground, in rich, virgin soil.

Patricio returned to his brickhouse to work, his shamed manhood burning like hot sand over a wound. For a handful of years he tried. Three or four times a year he visited town, found women, silently entered them. Illegitimate children were at least half as valuable as a son by his wife. Yet there was nothing.

In the mornings he ate in the kitchen, with Santo working around him and Cristina over to one side. They talked, as they had always talked through the many years encircling them. Every morning he ate a full plate. Santo had always prepared them especially for him, ever since his younger days when he began climbing up to financial success at the railroad company. They had eighteen years together, as cook and boss, eighteen years that nothing could destroy, not even Patricio's marriage to Romilia. The cook always reminded him of this. She would repeat the same things to him, and he would accept them with his eggs and coffee.

"Do you think she will ever learn to get up when you do, Mr. Colónez?"

"Don't know."

"I doubt she will. I understand she grew up working, but now, I believe you have spoiled her in many ways. Never wanting to get up until the sun is hot, having such parties, staying up late by herself, when the rest of the world sleeps in order to prepare for another day. And it all ties together, you know that, don't you? The parties, the late night, *the drinking*...you know that is why you have no children."

"Yes. I know. Thank you, Santo. Once again, a good meal."

He would toss his napkin on the clean plate and walk out the back to look at the gardens before heading toward the brickyard. He shrugged away her maternal warnings, especially when she began her discourses on drinking. Santo was not Catholic. In earlier years she had discarded her self-blessing, genuflecting habits for the scrutiny and discipline of one of the Protestant religions that had been imported into the country. That made drinking alcohol an evil as far as the cook was concerned. It was consuming the devil's elixir, which brewed away a sober mind. She took every opportunity to remind her boss of this teaching. He let it pass by, even more quickly than the standards of his long dead Catholicism.

∿
∿

Such had the hours, the days, and the years lapsed like the ticking of a clock. All this became ordinary. No one suggested a change. All of them—the cooks, the workers at the brickyard, the gringos and the families that came from the capital, El Comienzo's young virgins, the *patrón* and *patrona* of the little town—knew nothing else. This had become their life, their routine, a life that the child to be born would enter, abruptly, in the tenth year of Patricio's and Romilia's marriage.

As always, that September flooded with daily rain, and mud slopped all over the world. That month Romilia failed to bleed. Somehow she said nothing, and waited another month. Then she knew, for there were other signs: the vomiting, the sudden abhorrence to alcohol and tobacco smoke at the parties. She concealed her condition, knowing there would be questions.

She waited. Looking out the window from her bedroom, she held the curtain with the back of her fingers. Patricio walked briskly away from the office, slamming closed the door behind him. He took a few steps, stopped, then turned back around, remembering something in the office. He was gone a short while, then again he walked out, closing the door, walking with his hands in his pockets as he skipped quickly from stone to muddy stone, large rocks that he himself had placed down between the brickyard and the house as stepping stones during the rainy season. This was the night to tell him. Only the news, only the truth. No theories, none of the possible, perhaps probable reasons. Only the fact, *I am pregnant.* She would endeavor to hide fear, along with any accounting of recent times.

It had been two months since her brother-in-law Antonio had come from the capital that Tuesday, another Tuesday as usual. That day he had arrived without Gloria, who was sick. The wet season always brought her down with a cold—sneezing, coughing, taking advantage of her weakness. "I will go by myself then," he had said to her.

Gloria had turned angry at this, questioning, "What do you mean by yourself? We always go together; it is Tuesday." She conveniently forgot her hatred for the countryside.

He had cooed her back to bed, "My love, you are in no position to go. Stay home tonight, sleep, sleep. It will do you well. The children can take care of you."

She had protested, telling him that the children could not take care of a pig, let alone their own mother. But again he had said that it would be best to sleep. Finally he had won, talking her into a drowsiness that had already possessed her.

The coachman had driven him, whipping the horses through the light rain of that July afternoon, over a newly-dug road that stretched across the country. Before the sun set he had reached El Comienzo. The coachman had opened the door for him. Antonio had stepped outside, and from the pockets of his loose pants the key to his many locked possessions fell. "Damn pants," he had mumbled. "I must have them taken in," he said, bragging of an imagined weight loss. The coachman had stooped over, had given him the keys, wiping them off before putting them in their owner's hand.

Antonio had walked by one of the ranchhands who worked in the bean field. "Good afternoon, Germán. How are you today? Where is my brother? Still at the brickyard?"

"I don't believe so. I believe he is somewhere in town."

"Oh? What is he up to?"

"I would not know, Mr. Colónez." Yet Germán had smiled slightly, as if holding an amusing secret.

Antonio had paid no attention, and walked on to the house. Inside he had made himself a drink, helping himself to the bar full of whiskey, pouring two fingers into a glass and carrying it around with

A Fire in the Earth

him while ambling through the quiet house. He could hear the cooks banging pans in the kitchen. They had not heard him enter.

Walking about, he had lit a cigarette, had flipped through a book, not reading it. After several moments of strolling, he had taken his overnight bag upstairs, walking quietly over the carpeted wood floor, and had tossed it onto the bed where he and Gloria always slept every Tuesday night. He had walked on, hearing some movement in one of the other bedrooms. After some hesitation he had cracked open the door of the master bedroom. In the large mirror beside the bed he saw Romilia pass by into the adjacent bathroom. She had nothing on and was wet from bathing. She had disappeared at the edge of the mirror.

The whole earth propelled him forward. Sipping from his glass, he had stepped quickly into the bedroom. His weight pressed against the mattresses as he sat down.

"Patricio. You are early."

"Uh, no. It is I."

"Oh, Antonio." The sound of scuffling could be heard. The half-closed bathroom door had shut completely, muffling Romilia's voice. "I did not hear you come in. Where is Gloria?"

"She is not here. She is sick. But she wanted me to come on out, and she sends her apologies."

"Oh, sick? I am sorry. I hope she gets well soon. But this weather, it turns against everyone." He could hear her quickly dressing. "I...I will be out in just a moment."

"Fine."

He had looked about, smiling for no appropriate reason besides the whiskey. He could hear her mumbling. She spoke to herself, a habit she had developed through the years—preparing herself for the evening when she would complete her daily duties. "The dinner, at six thirty, so drinks before, about five-thirty, and the desert, it is sweet cake, it is already made, according to Santo...." The mumbling faltered, aware of the presence of the brother-in-law outside. It suddenly had stopped, and in the deep silence she had opened the bathroom door and had looked him square in the face. "Antonio. What brings you into my room?"

145

"I thought I would wait here. Your husband—Patricio is not home, and Gloria is not here. I have no one else to talk with." He had grinned.

"Oh. Well, Santo is in the kitchen. I am sure she would like to see you."

"Yes, well, she is very busy. I do not want to bother her."

Suddenly she had busied herself with her hair, putting both hands to the combs. "Well, yes. Glad you could make it this week... Why don't we go downstairs, so I can fix me one of those." She had pointed toward his glass.

"Yes, perhaps in a minute." He had turned to the side, smiling, trying to rid himself of the smile. "You know, my brother was right in marrying you. You are a beautiful woman," he muttered, rubbing his thick lips with fingertips. "I saw you in the mirror, just a moment ago." He had spoken somewhat sharply, giving himself permission, the whiskey already acting upon him.

She had said nothing. She sat in a chair, looking down, so unlike herself, strangely stripped of strength and aggression. She was overcome by the drowning, shameful thought that someone had seen her nakedness. Suddenly she had blurted some impotent phrase, about him coming in without permission and looking at her like a pervert, saying nothing. But the phrase had passed him, swallowed by the thick walls, with no remnants of an echo. Nothing more had been said. He had given himself permission. And he was the rich man, richer than Romilia who had been nothing but a poor goat-cheese maker before the Colónez brothers had come to El Comienzo. Everyone knew that. Thus he had the right, and he took it.

At first she relented. She knew the rules created by a whole culture and planted in her, as in all women. The act reminded her of who she was, a dark-skinned woman with a lot of Indian blood and very few rights. The moment after he placed his empty glass down, Antonio had pinned her against the large bed and began shedding her fresh, new clothes, all the time inhaling her smoothness, her adorned richness. He cooed old, withering words into her ear, words used before with younger girls, women who always reached into his back pocket as he cooed, stripping him of money as he held them. He had whispered

146

A Fire in the Earth

to her in the same manner, as if this were the only way left to make love in the world, calling her my heart, my beauty. The little body under Antonio had kicked slightly, a rabbit trapped under the weight of a bear. He had no problem unstrapping himself.

Something rolled through her like thunder. Some would have said that the Indian rose in her. Whatever it was, it had brought her sharp-tipped hands to his neck. She had grabbed his flesh as if to swing from a thick tree branch, and had shoved him away.

"Get off me, you sweaty, filthy pig."

He had choked on spittle. After swallowing, he had stood above the bed.

"You little bitch."

She heard the anger. She could see the shame of a man calling upon an older, original force that would rely on no cooing, no placating words. On that rainy July afternoon he used his weight to hold her down. She had cried out against him, and her cry was heard only by herself. While he clumsily pumped out his need, she groped for the kerosene lamp next to her on the bed table. As he ended and groaned and grinned, she had brought the glass lamp down upon his balding head.

Antonio bumped from the bed to the floor. Romilia sat over him, heaving breaths, looking down at the heap of his half-naked body. She stared down between his legs at the tiny, once-hard head that shrivelled up as it spurt like a tiny cut hose.

She jumped over him, cleaned herself in the bathroom, redressed, then left the bedroom.

The cooks had heard the sudden scream emanate from the upstairs. "What was that?" Cristina had asked, and then answered herself, "I believe it was she. Should we check?"

Santo had looked out the window in that same moment, had seen the carriage of Patricio's brother, the chauffeur standing next to it. She answered, barely grinning, "Don't worry. I am sure she is fine."

147

After dressing, Romilia stepped over Antonio's body that slowly gained consciousness. She walked to the kitchen and began a conversation with the cooks, chatting, asking about preparations, succinctly placing demands here and there in each corner and chair and place-mat. She waited, listening, running out of reasons to speak, until she heard a distant creaking of the floor. The brother-in-law came into the kitchen, holding his head. Santo jumped to his side with a "Glory to God!" and a mouthful of spewed questions. He explained, the loose rug, the falling down the stairs. "I will get some cold rags. Come." Santo and Cristina took him to a couch in the next room. Romilia wait-ed, staying with the small crowd that hovered around the *patrón's* beloved brother.

Patricio returned later from town. Unknown to Romilia, he set out on another season of sexual endeavors in El Comienzo. That evening he had walked through the kitchen door, quickly taking the stairs to the upper bedroom, relieved to be able to bathe in solitude. There, while undressing, he glanced down and found in a shiny heap, next to the bed, his brother's keys. He picked them up, studied them for a long moment with sorrowful eyes, with memory that chalked up childhood losses to an older brother.

During the quiet dinner he placed the keys on the table, saying nothing. The brother, halfway through a bout of laughter, had let his chuckles dissipate like some river in dry season. Romilia looked down upon the key chain as if waiting for them to move, or speak.

"I believe these are yours." Patricio glanced at his brother.

"Uh, yes, they are. I did not even miss them. Where did you find them?"

"On the floor in our bedroom." His voice cracked.

"Oh, yes. They must have fallen while I was sitting, talking with Romi. You know, these pants, I'm losing weight, and they fall out so easily. They fell out while I was stepping out of my carriage, you can ask my driver on that one...." Antonio had continued, speaking through a whiskey that failed to soak the pain in his head. Somehow he had sidestepped the cultural issue, of being alone with someone else's wife. Romilia had stared at him for a moment as he slid past the silent lie, and shivered only slightly at his use of the pet name "Romi."

A Fire in the Earth

She had let him slide, not knowing or perhaps ignoring how that cultural taboo, of having a man in his bedroom with his wife, had burned against Patricio's soul. She knew nothing had been said—could not be said—without destroying the community that she had strung together between brothers, friends and relations in the capital, and business associates from the States. Antonio, with his adroit ability of avoidance, had won his safety. Thus, for self-protection, she had claimed the incident as petty, and did not allow it to tear at the netting that she had woven between the many different lives that danced together. Petty incident, not worth the scandal. She would never tell. Fervent speculation told her there was no need to tell. She analyzed the moment of forced coitus, and decided that though Antonio did ejaculate, only the first shots had entered her. She had made love to her husband several times since then, with her taking the initiative, bringing him into her with a force, opening wide to him in order to shut down thought or rumor. She had said nothing, and hoped that the reality of time, of ten years without birth, would say nothing either, would not question, would not ponder.

Thus, while watching Patricio step from stone to stone on that muddy October evening, coming home to eat supper, Romilia forced upon herself some sense of control. She stared at him from the window of the bedroom, holding the curtain to the side with the back of her fingers. With the memory-worn knowledge of what had passed between her and Antonio, she watched the *patrón* of El Comienzo walk into the bedroom. She smiled at him, yet the smile dropped to the floor like dead seed, and he looked at her with a vague sadness as she, for the second time in their married life, proclaimed good news.

♒

Six months later the carriage pulled up to the old, sunken door of the adobe house. Next door, the store kept busy, but the storekeeper named González looked up at the rich carriage and waved as Patricio stepped out of it. Patricio returned the greeting, touching his hat back at him, and walked to the neighboring dilapidated door. He hesitated a moment, then knocked. A voice crackled for him to come in. He

149

stepped through, took his hat off, looked toward the woman who sat next to the stove. Her eyes brightened, seeing him appear, yet her weary body was unable to stand and greet him. She mumbled a salutation, asked him to sit down, apologized for the chair being so dirty, and told him how she hoped he would accept her simple hospitality. "Of course," he mumbled, and he sat, his legs apart, elbows on his knees, turning the rim of his hat with nervous fingertips. They engaged in light fragments of conversation, her health, his work. Very quickly he announced his reason for visiting.

"I have some good news for you. Your daughter just gave birth to a baby boy." His face broke into a smile as he watched her age shine with the inner joy of one who had hoped for peace for a very long time.

She asked automatically, "What is his name?"

"Francisco Patricio Colónez y Velásquez."

"Ah. A little Paco."

"Yes, a little Paco."

"Is he big? Healthy? How is he?" She smiled through her questions, and tears ran the length of her wrinkles. "I have hoped and prayed for his safety, for his health, and for hers..."

"They are both well, both very healthy." He smiled, then looked down at the dirt floor. For the moment he forgot everything else, witnessing the woman's joy. "I would like for you to see your grandson."

"Oh, oh how good of you.... But I cannot travel up that hill; I am not doing too well now...."

It took little to talk her into it. In minutes, after she donned her nicest, cleanest scarf, he was helping her up the large step into the carriage. He climbed in after her. All the neighbors stopped their lives and watched the horses pull their burden away and up the hill, carrying in its stomach the rich man, the indigent woman.

He told Diego to be careful on the bumps, and thus the trip took longer than usual. That did not matter, though they said little to each other while in the cab. He looked out the window at the town they left behind them, staring, leaning his arms on his legs. She stared straight ahead at the partition in front of her, listening to the hooves of the horses, the crunch and crackle of wood and metal on rock and soft, drying mud.

150

A Fire in the Earth

Diego opened the carriage door in front of the large house, and both men helped Amanda out. Patricio escorted her, holding her arm as if she were a noble woman, all the way through the door and into his home. They climbed slowly up the steps to the second level, through a corridor to an upper room. She glanced at the walls, paying little attention to the paintings, the rugs, the intricate, heavy candle holders protruding from corners. She stared ahead, toward the blessing that lay in one of those upper rooms. She only asked, "Is she asleep?" and when he answered that he believed so, she walked on more assertively. There the door opened, and in the soft, controlled daylight held in check by the lovely curtains lay the woman, sleeping. Between her large, naked breasts rested the boy, sucking ceaselessly upon a nipple that for now gave no milk, but the thick, clear liquid colostrum of the first hours of life. In the silence Patricio could hear Doña Amanda swallow, a heavy, consumptive sound, emanating from her thin, calloused skin. She touched the baby, clean but still wet after the doctor's quick wipe-down. The young physician stood outside while the family visited. As Doña Amanda touched her grandson, the boy's eyes moved nervously under weak lids, then ceased moving, as if content with the new touch.

"He is so beautiful," she whispered. She turned to Patricio, but did not look him in the eye. "I know you will raise him well, that you will teach him many things, many good things. He already has that blessing, that *you* are his father." She said it in a way as if to set history straight, as if to silence whispered rumors. He accepted it as a gift from an old friend.

"Thank you, Doña Amanda, I—"

"I want to give him a present." She reached into a fold of her soiled dress and pulled out a small, black pouch. Carefully she laid it upon the baby's side. With her thumb she traced a cross over the boy's back and mumbled with an old, contemplative honor, "In the name of the Father, and of the Son, and of the Holy Spirit.

"This is a rosary, an old rosary that belonged to the boy's great grandmother, my mother. She died when we were still living in the capital. I brought it from the old city. It was the last thing I grabbed as we ran out." She grew quiet for a moment, then added, "Inside there is

151

a piece of corn husk, with a lock of hair in it. It is hair from my grand-father." She chuckled. "I do not know why I ever did that, but...I took a lock from the old man one day after cutting his hair. I put it in with the rosary. His name was Pablo. He was not Catholic. Pure Indian. He thought the Church was a stupid thing, a silly thing...

"But he was a good man. And so I saved his hair, kept it with me. When the boy is older, I want him to have it."

Patricio reassured her that the boy would receive it in coming years. One of Romilia's weary eyes drifted open, stared out, and fell upon Amanda. The new mother's hand dropped from her stomach to the bed in some failed endeavor to touch. Sounds murmured through the new mother's lips.

"I should go," said Amanda. "The baby should sleep, and not have people staring at him." Quickly she turned and left the room first, passing by her son-in-law. She stopped in the hallway. Patricio walked out, closing the door behind him. He helped her down the stairs and back to the carriage.

"I am very thankful for all you have done for me these years," she said.

"Fine, fine."

"The food...soon you will not need to send it to me anymore. So please, if you so desire, send it to Father Mateo. He will make sure it gets to people who need it. And the money, too."

"Doña Amanda, why do you talk that—" But she had already turned from him and had begun to climb into the carriage, asking for his help to get in. She thanked him once again. "You are a very Christ-ian man. I know I will see you in the Lord's Kingdom." Again she had spoken authoritatively, a woman prepared to meet that kingdom. "I am ready now," she said, sitting snugly in the carriage seat.

Patricio gave Diego the word to go. The coachman snapped the horses into movement, and the son-in-law watched the carriage descend into the little town.

There at the adobe Diego left Amanda. He climbed up the hill again and left the carriage in a small building next to the big house.

Night swallowed the weary, relenting day. In the flickering candle light that tried to dispel the darkness of her adobe home, Doña Amanda lay her head down to die. She held a cross in her hands, instead of the rosary that now belonged in the big house on top of the hill. She said several prayers, methodically, wearily. Closing her eyes, she mumbled, "Forgive me, Father, please forgive me, I have sinned, I have sinned. And please forgive her, please forgive her, too... This was not what I wanted at all, this was not it, at all..."

Neighbors around Amanda's home had eaten well the past three days. Every evening Amanda had come to their houses, giving one family a chicken and several potatoes, a second family a large cut of meat and a bag of beans, a third the same as the second, and to the family on the other side of the store, another chicken, with a sack of beans and another of rice. These people, who were as poor as Amanda, had received such gifts from her before. She had distributed much of the food and money from the Colónez ranch all those years, receiving a bag of supplies every other day. The money had gone to pay rent, keeping her out of the coffee fields. The food was so abundant that she could never eat it all herself. In the past four nights, however, she had given away all the supplies, whole chickens, huge cuts of meat. "He is being more generous," she had told them, laughing. "He wants to make me fat and beautiful again." They laughed with her, thanking her with silent smiles. It had become a ritual for them to receive the food. Soon Father Mateo would be delivering it instead. They realized this the following morning when some of the mothers came to visit Doña Amanda and found her dead in her straw bed. Later they noticed that her kitchen was empty of any food.

They carried her with tears and prayers, and placed her in a small pine box. The box bobbed with each step of the men carrying her to the cemetery. A hole had already been dug next to the grave of old Don Pablo, her grandfather, and the *campesinos* lowered her remains in with the tenderness and respect they awarded the old when they died. In Amanda's case, for one who had been claimed a living saint. Father Mateo said his prayers, then spoke about the woman, about who she had been, how he had known her, how he had been welcomed into her home when the little village of El Comienzo had first begun. The people listened. They agreed, shaking their heads slowly, bringing their scarfs to cover their faces.

Marcos McPeek Villatoro

The dirt fell and crumbled against the flatness of the coffin, sank into the cracks around the box, bringing a life to completion. Behind the weeping crowd Patricio placed his hat upon his head and walked to his waiting horse. As he turned he tipped his hat to the old priest, who waved back to him. He rode away, up the hill. Soon he was followed by the tolling of the church bells in the village. They were tiny, made of cheap, bolted metal. They clanged together like oversized buckets. Patricio swished the reins again and again.

The children of the village asked why the bells tolled for so long that day with the death of Doña Amanda. They were sent to grandparents, who explained it all, enjoying the opportunity of being listened to. They told the kids that the bells rang the longest for the older people of the village, for it was a reminder of when the earth swallowed their old city, and when they had to travel here to begin a new life. They rang the bells longer for those who had survived because they had been the builders of El Comienzo, the ones who had worked hard and long to create the little village. The were told of a time when a multitude of colors danced with the wind over the mound in the middle of the town. That was when many different vegetables grew upon it, when fruits and vegetables and cows and chickens were everywhere. Then the dead-skinned men came in, started coffee crops, and separated many families when they sent people to work far away in the fields. The bells rang through the children's confusion. The sound itself, the cheap clamor of rusty bolts and old metal, promulgated throughout the land with a strange pride of who they were, and what they had lived through. It tolled through memory, through forgetfulness, commanding people to stop, look, seek out whatever enlightenment there is in death, life, hunger, and plenty, and how all these things lived here, in this valley, right at that moment.

The bells tolled through dream and desire, and clashed against the mind of the dead one's daughter who slept deeply, free from reality, past or present. Floating in darkness, Romilia opened slightly the door of her eyes and saw an old woman who became the young mother of a past life that the *patrona* had escaped. The daughter reached out for her, grasping, crying out, "*Mamá, Mamá,*" but the mother did not

154

answer. She turned away, and the daughter cried out again, "Mamá, please, I did not mean to."

She watched as her mother took a machete in a calloused hand and split little splinters of firewood off a large stick to ignite a flame in the mud and clay stove, to cook some beans, rice, a little coffee, tortillas, and she cried as her mother spoke to her while handing her a small bag, "Here, take these onions over to Silvia, she will need them for supper." And the daughter pleaded, "No, please Mamá, I do not want to go to Silvia, I cannot go, please." "Child do not argue with me. Come now, take these over to her." She took the bag of onions. Meanwhile Silvia came from behind the stove. She stood tall and sure of herself, always too sure, and the daughter carried the onions to her, put them in her hands. The tall neighbor thanked her, wanted to touch her, but the daughter pulled away. She turned to her mother who held a rosary in her hand, fondling it, running the black beads through dexterous fingertips. "We must ask forgiveness, we must ask forgiveness." She repeated the words over and over again, telling the child to ask God to forgive her. God, who tolled those tinny bells, crashing them together loud and long, so long.

"Mamá, please make Him stop it." But they continued, crashing through her window until they fell upon her, all the tolls, clamorous and rude, crashing against her chest like the throb of a savage heart, a weight against her breasts, biting her nipples, trying to stop her breath. She tried to pull it away, but it was so heavy, it did not move. It only cried aloud, screaming to crush her, wake her. She looked down to the baby sprawled over her chest, crying into one of her naked breasts, and the doctor came over to pick the boy up, hold and caress it, quiet it. The rosary fell to her side, and the tolling from below them in the valley suddenly stopped crashing against the window of Romilia's master bedroom.

His name was Francisco. They nicknamed him Paco.

"I just can't get him to do it correctly. He keeps biting me," Romilia had said in the first days of the boy's life. Others tried to help her, but as much as Santo and Cristina explained, they could not show her how to make nursing more comfortable. It became too much. Her nipples turned tender, almost to the point of bleeding whenever he tried to suck. She pulled him away, filling his mouth with an empty wail. Special bottles had to be ordered from Sonsonate in order to feed him prepared cow's milk. Soon Romilia's supply dried up.

She tried to raise him in all other ways, but depended upon the experience of the old cook to help her along. Santo seized the opportunity and held the baby as if he were a grandson. Romilia actually allowed her into the master bedroom during the day.

The parties slowed down during those first years of Paco's life. Antonio and Gloria also visited less. "We're so busy," said Antonio over the telephone, "that we won't be able to make it Tuesday evening." Orgy Tuesday had begun dwindling early in the pregnancy. Patricio did not see his brother for weeks at a time.

After the boy's birth the *patrón* turned silent, as if he were waiting. Patricio gave over to his wife the first two years of Paco's life, knowing that the women of the house had to care for him. He seemed extremely patient during this time, so much so that no one expected anything from him concerning the boy's upraising. No one realized that he was preparing for the day when he saw Paco walk through the house, speaking in long sentences. That day quickly came. That same evening he said over the supper table, "The boy is coming with me tomorrow. He will spend the day in my office."

"Oh. All right. Why?"

"Because I want to spend time with my son."

At first it had been difficult, as Paco was not accustomed to so much time with his father. In those first days father and son left the ranch house with the boy screaming all the way. As the days passed, and Patricio kept taking the boy to work, the cries diminished. Romilia watched her husband walk Paco about the brickyard grounds, holding his hand with a certain, strong gentleness. Thus the ritual began, one that would last through the child's third, fourth, and fifth years. At times Romilia protested. But it never lasted long, especially with her husband's adamant staring at her, as if to question, "Why do you deny me time with my son?"

A Fire in the Earth

Time and consistency raised the boy. Paco became so familiar with the brickhouse that the few times Patricio did not take him, the child screamed and cried, angry at his mother and at everyone in the home. Romilia swirled in dismay and anger, vainly trying to quiet him down. She could not understand this new system that seemed to go against the ordinary ritual of a mother raising a child. A threatening revelation came upon her the afternoon that Paco walked through the door, racing into the house ahead of his father, and announced, "Hello Mamá, I want milk," in pure English.

She had stared at the four-year-old who walked by her and into the kitchen, her mouth drooping open. When her husband entered, she glared at him in shock.

"Paco just said something in English."

"Oh, yes? To you? Good."

"So is that what you do? Teach him English?"

"Well, partly, yes."

"All day? What are you doing, sitting him down and forcing him to learn—"

"I do not force him to learn anything. I just talk with him."

"In English."

"Yes."

"Why?"

"Why? Why teach him another language? Why do you think?" He walked by her and headed upstairs. "It will help him in life. Whatever he does, knowing two languages will help him immensely."

"So you teach him English all day long. How do you expect me to be able to talk with him, to, to be with him, to be his mother?"

"Romi, he still speaks Spanish. You can still talk with him."

"But not in English! I cannot speak to him in English!" Yelling, she turned away, showing more fear than anger.

"Then do not. Speak to him in Spanish."

"Patricio!"

"Hey, what are you frightened of? Be happy that your son can speak both—"

"He will be speaking behind my back before I know it. How do you expect me to live with a son that can do that?"

"Do I speak behind your back in English? Come now."

"No. But now he will have someone to speak to in English. You!" This silenced the room for a moment. She added, with her arms folded, "Why don't you teach me English?"

"What do you mean? I tried, but you did not want to learn. It takes time to learn a foreign language. It takes up most of your days. You either have to study it as if nothing else in the world matters, or learn it young, like Paco."

"Are you saying that I am too old to learn anything?"

"No, not at all, I—"

"Yes, you are. You think I am stupid, that I cannot learn another language or anything. Well I tell you, I was learning mathematics very quickly as a child, faster than any of the boys. I was teaching them how to do it correctly until my mother took that away from me. I can learn anything. I can learn anything I need to."

"Very well, very well, I will teach you some English," he promised several times, as he had done before.

For Patricio, teaching his wife English was a forced discipline. It would not last very long, even though they both tried. During a handful of evenings, Paco walked into a small room of the house and found his parents repeating phrases, one very eloquently, the other speaking with a heavy Spanish accent.

"Bueno, mi amor. Dime 'adios,' goodbye."

"Gootbiee, gootbie."

"Muy bien. Ahora, 'cuidate,' be careful."

"Bee cadful."

"Otra vez."

"Bee cadful."

"Bueno, ahora, 'Te quiero.' I love you."

"Ay luf jyu. Ay lufjyu."

During evening gatherings she used these phrases upon guests who smiled at her, especially the North Americans who told her in her own language, "¡Qué lindo!" How charming, how wonderful, you are trying to learn English.

It went no further. On the occasions that Paco walked in on them, he saw the stress of ignorance weave and tighten in his mother's face as his father calmly repeated phrase after phrase to her. She continued to stumble over an indigenous accent. Then it would all explode when his father would laugh endearingly in response to her pronunciation. The laughter would jar Romilia and unleash a deluge of pride and anger. She would go on and on about ignorance, lack of education, lack of love. Paco would turn and leave. Soon his father would follow suit, leaving his wife frothing with rage, burning off the collected frustrations of a lifetime.

She spoke of the language barrier no more. Sometimes she turned a corner in the house and found father and son sitting on the porch behind the kitchen, speaking, tossing about inaudible words and phrases like stones into a pond. They would then fall back into Spanish, weaving back and forth a web, a cloth, strong and natural and lovely, as if the sounds had color and texture. One said something in English; the other answered at times in Spanish. Mostly they remained on the same plane in the foreign language. The child became fluent, and lived and walked through the house, speaking with his father as if it were nothing out of the ordinary, as if this were just the way a boy his age was supposed to speak. He did not speak to the others in English, for they never triggered him into that language. He also learned, from his mother's wrath, that to speak the other tongue with those who did not understand could be volatile. But when the gringos came ("Never call them 'gringos,'" explained his father. "They do not like that. That is our little joke-name for them"), and he heard their words, he fell into that language. Romilia watched with sharp eyes as the gringos raised their eyebrows in sincere surprise, delighted with the boy, showering compliments and praises upon him before his mother who forced a courteous smile forward.

The men at the brickhouse took to Paco as if he were their own son. The boy was always at his father's side when Patricio walked about the establishment, checking the work, talking with the workers. "Hey, Mr. Paco, come here, boy!"

Paco smiled at Enrique, the brick setter. He ran over to the man and the machine that crashed and clanged against the world. Dust billowed around the tiny leather boots that Paco wore. Enrique had huge arms. They were light-skinned and hairy, unlike those of any other man Paco had ever seen. His eyes were as blue as cold, deep water.

"His father," explained Patricio to his boy one day, "was a gringo soldier who came and left in the night."

White streaked the worker's hair, concealed under a farmer's hat. Enrique lifted Paco in his arms like a small bird. He held him against his chest and rubbed his unshaved face against the boy's skin. It felt like sandpaper. Suddenly the boy was raised up over all the men's heads and sat upon Enrique's stone-like shoulder. He waved at his father. Patricio smiled and shook his head in approval.

"Hey, Paco, come here, we got a present for you."

A handful of the men took him over to a corner of a shed and told him to go to a small room and pull out something standing on the floor. Seconds later the five-year-old boy raced amidst the laughing men with a tiny wheelbarrow clutched tightly in his small hands. He pushed over the dust toward Patricio, yelling in excited English, "Daddy, Daddy, look what I got!" Patricio laughed at the wheelbarrow, made especially for Paco to carry bricks. He asked who had constructed it.

"We all carved a piece of it," said Enrique. "Orlando made the wheel."

"Hey, Mr. Colónez, he will be a regular *labriego*, true?"

"Perhaps. But do not tell his mother."

They chuckled with their boss, sharing the moment of laughter. They knew that the boy had brought the *patrón* back into their midst. In these days Paco watched his father don old working clothes and join the men in their labors. With his new toy, Paco carried chips and pieces of broken bricks, discarded to one corner of the factory. He filled the wheelbarrow with as much as he could carry and sweated alongside the men and his father. He dumped the pieces in another shady site, then built his own miniature house and another small edifice. He constructed roads between the buildings, and in other places he built from sticks and mud the other houses that he could see everywhere in the town below them. Paco did not rush. He built slowly, methodically, to the laughter and gentle jokes of the workers. At the end of the morning, before lunch, he placed his wheelbarrow back in the shed and put broken bricks around his little town. He warned the men not to break it. They left the town just as he had built it and waited to see what kind of construction he would add the following day.

Each day Enrique took a few minutes to inspect the progress. With the wheelbarrow, Paco had carried dirt from the vegetable garden of the ranch. He piled it in the middle of his construction site and was smoothing it down when Enrique approached him. "Ah! Now what would that be?" asked the worker.

"It is the hill in the middle of town," answered Paco. He squinted at Enrique, confused at this adult's inability to see the obvious.

"Oh. I was going to guess that. Is that the church over there? And that, is that the market where Doña Santo shops?"

Paco answered affirmatively.

"So you have made a little El Comienzo. Very good! What are you going to do with your mound?"

Paco did not answer, but scrunched his face, trying to remember the mound itself. He looked down at the real town, then answered, "Plant something on it."

"Oh. Great. What will you plant?"

"Mmm," the boy muttered, then looked up and stared at all the hills that encircled them. "Coffee!"

"Oh. Okay. Well, what will the people do with all the coffee?"

"Drink it. Do you have any more string?"

"Yes, let me get you some." Enrique stood up to go to the shed. When he returned, Paco was still patting down the mound. "So you want to plant coffee trees on the mound, true? So the people can drink coffee. But what will the people eat?"

"Mmm. Beans. Rice?"

"Where will they get it?"

"From here." He pointed to the model of the market, where Santo shopped.

"That can be true. But some people do not have money to buy beans. What will *they* do?"

"I don't know."

"Well, maybe if they planted beans on the hill here, maybe they would not need to buy the beans at the store, true?"

"Yes. Can I have the string?"

"Yes. Here."

Paco took it and began tying two tiny sticks together, as he had tied several others to make the various upright figures that stood among the houses and buildings, as tall as the buildings themselves. In a few minutes he completed the figure and leaned it against a building that was made of broken bricks, different than the rest of the mud houses.

"Now, who's that?"

"He's a guard."

"Oh. Is that the guardhouse?"

"Mm, hmm."

"Oh."

Enrique leaned over from his squatting position. With a finger cocked under his thumb, he flicked the guard stick-figure right where the face would be. The figure flipped over the town and bounced off a wall of the work shed.

"Why did you do that?" demanded the boy.

"Why? Well, because..." and Enrique looked down, "because he had just beat up this poor guy here." The blue-eyed Latin took one of the other stick figures and lay it down on the ground. "Here. This guy. Some poor farmer, and the guard fellow just finished beating him up."

"Why?"

"Why? Well, no reason, I suppose. Doesn't like farmers."

"That is mean," said the boy.

"Mm, hmm," mumbled the worker.

They both looked at the tiny town for a moment; the boy sitting on the ground, the man over him, squatting. Paco reached over and picked up the guard figure, stood it up in the middle of the street that ran by the newly formed mound. He grasped the farmer figure from the dirt, lifted it up, and slammed its legs against the guard stickman, knocking it over the mound. This got a laugh from Enrique, one that rocked the man back and forth. The boy joined in, and they both

A Fire in the Earth

laughed and giggled. Then Paco did it again and again for the blue-eyed worker.

$$\approx$$

Romilia never heard this laughter. The ranch house remained far enough away from the brickyard that she never had to listen to the giggles of her son as he laughed along with the workmen. Being the good *patrona*, she returned to her responsibilities. The guest list for the following evening held forty-one names.

Patricio left home with only one message, "I will be late tonight." He gave no reason. She did not ask for one. Nor did she ask if the boy would stay for the party or remain with him. That argument proved futile.

"We will miss you tonight. Perhaps you will arrive in time to see someone."

She spent her afternoon in preparation, and that night entertained on her own, skipping from guest to guest, asking for drink requests. The young Schonenberg arrived with another bought woman attached to him. Again he brought a bottled gift, and handed it over to the *patrona* while tripping drunkenly throughout the party. At times he used the English that Paco had taught him years previous on his date, "I eet sheet, jyu ar a hor."

A North American named Harold, who spoke Spanish, pulled Schonenberg to the side. "I am really surprised how long you've gotten away with saying that..."

Schonenberg, though in a stupor, brought Harold together with Romilia. "This fellow speaks excellent Castilian, Romi. You two should, should...." He stumbled away, seeking a place of prostrate refuge. The two watched him with slight embarrassment, smiling to each other to break it.

They talked. Harold had come with a business companion. "I am with the telephone company," he explained.

"Oh! You are the one responsible for that wonderful machine!"

They spoke of several subjects, which led them to sit on a couch while the rest of the party cheerfully waited on itself. He did most of the speaking, as she had hoped. Harold had come into the country recently, having signed a four-year contract. "This is my missionary work," he chuckled.

They talked for a long while. Yet they hunted for topics, feeding the conversation in order to stay together. She asked him what he did with the phone company. He gave a disparaging answer, some tedious office job, keeping up with where the telephone poles go, nothing exciting to explain. She acted as if she were fascinated. He asked from what part of the country did she come. She answered quickly, saying that she was but a country girl, which made him laugh.

"Then do you go to the capital much?" asked Harold.

"Oh, no. Rarely. I would like to go more often."

"Yes, that would be good. You know, they will inaugurate your new president next week. Too bad you cannot come for that." Harold sipped his drink, looking for other things to say.

"And you have a son?" he asked, happy to find a new topic. "How old is he? Seven? He is ready for school. Where will he go?" His voice showed some interest.

"Oh, I do not know. My husband and I, we have not talked about it."

"You don't seem to have any good schools here," he commented, then pensively, "Have you thought about sending him to the capital? There are many schools there. In fact, my partner sends his boys to the Jesuits. Fine school, from what he tells me. And of course he would be safe there. They have their own guards."

Romilia cocked her head slightly, confused somewhat by what he said, unsure if it was because of the periodic mistakes in his Spanish. "Excuse me? Guards?"

"Well, yes, they have a few. But no one is going to attack the school, so they don't need too many. But everybody is getting them, you know. I even hired two for my home, since I will be here a few years. Must keep up with the times, you know." He smiled. "I was surprised to see that you do not have any guards here. But I suppose, out here in the country, it's not so necessary, not as many workers around...."

"Yes. What is the name of that school?"

A Fire in the Earth

"The Academy of the Society of Jesus. If you think about sending your boy there, talk with Mario, my partner. Then," he smiled invitingly, "you would have a reason to come to the capital, to visit your son. And if you ever need a place to stay, know that my door is always open."

She smiled for a long moment, then fished, "Ah, yes. For my husband and myself."

Harold busied himself writing his address on a small card taken from his wallet, then pressed it into her palm while holding the back of her fingers with his other hand. "I will leave that to you."

᠕᠕
᠕᠕

Paco heard them arguing. Supposedly he was asleep. It was impossible to rest, with them yelling as if they stood on opposite sides of their bed, a barricade that kept them from striking each other. The fighting circled around two subjects: buying guards for the home and sending Paco to school in the capital. They did not stick to the subjects. They reached for other tactics, other crude, obtuse weapons to hurl at each other—teaching the boy English, how she could treat the cooks better since they have been his close friends for a long time, taking the boy to that dirty brickhouse practically every day; and as to the guards, how we need them to keep us protected from those filthy attackers that you let the boy play around every day.

Paco stared up at the dark ceiling. He could see no attackers, could not remember anyone hurting anyone else at the brickyard. Everyone worked, everyone smiled, talked with him, laughed with him. No one turned angry or sad. He heard his father echo the same thought as he yelled, "That is stupid, Romilia, no one is holding an uprising in the brickhouse. And you know why, don't you? Because they do not have any reason to."

"Then why are they blowing up all over the country? You told me yourself, you read more and more about it every day in the papers, in Sonsonate, in the capital, practically everywhere, they are trying to kill people, our people! It was said that they tried to kill the new president last week, and he, with only a few days in office—"

165

"Yes," answered Patricio, "cutting his term in half."

"Do not try to be funny. What about all those riots you read about?"

"Those are people who are instigating it. It is some outside influence, some political group, getting people all riled up..." Paco tried to understand the rest of what his father said. But the walls were of sturdy stucco, and he was using words that the boy had never heard. Paco heard a retort from his mother, "But what if those instigators come here? What if they get everyone angry here?"

His father tried to calm her down, explaining, "They will not come here. They won't. The people are happy here. They won't rise up."

The argument was momentarily settled. It seemed that peace had been achieved in the upper room. Then the subject of sending Paco to the capital for schooling came up again. His father bolted and burst angrily. Paco thought this would certainly succeed in shutting his mother up. It did not. She boomed almost as strongly as her mate, until they rocked back and forth, and the haphazard tide of anger and distress shook the child so much that he turned away to close his eyes and escaped into sleep.

He awoke to future plans. Before he had time to finish breakfast, his bags had been packed and had been placed in the back of the carriage. It would appear this way to him years later, whenever he looked back to that time. The heated argument and the sudden move to the capital seemed so connected to his mind that he didn't remember the days between them. All three of them piled into the carriage. Paco was asked to wave to the cooks, which he had been told to kiss goodbye moments before. Santo had a stream of tears running down her cheeks. Paco felt a clutch in his stomach. What kind of place was he being taken to? he wondered.

To a large and majestic site. The city, which he had heard about from the gringos, from his mother, at times from his father, stood among the mountains as if trying to compete with them. "Here is where you are going to live, Francisco!" his mother gleamed.

A Fire in the Earth

Brick enclosed them on both sides as they rode through one of the main streets. The capital stared at him from every angle, then ignored him. It ignored everyone; it ignored itself. Gringos walked by, wearing derby hats, laughing and smoking. A drunk fell into the street. A guard came by and pushed the man with the heel of his boot to the curb. Hundreds of women walked about with fruit, tortillas, pies, bread, meat, sugar, all balanced on their heads or placed next to where they sat, waiting to be sold. His mother pointed up, showing him the tall steeple of the cathedral. "They say the altar is made of gold, Francisco. Real gold!" His father rebutted her statement, dampening her enthusiasm. She snapped back, and the cab turned silent.

They entered into an area where a large building stood. It was built of bricks, much like those he had seen every day in El Comienzo. Boys his age ran everywhere, all with the same clothes on. The cathedral that he had previously looked upon stood nearby. Priests, wearing black gowns and small white collars, silently moved here and there. One greeted his parents and patted him on the head. In that same moment, Paco suddenly found himself turned around and held by a black-dressed stranger, his back pressed against a gown that reached all the way to the ground. Two large, soft but heavy hands fell upon his shoulders.

"We will take care of him. He will learn all that is necessary."

Paco heard the voice above him bridging over to his parents, as if he were in some cavity of childhood. The boy could barely understand the curate. The latter spoke as if he had cotton in his mouth.

"We want to say goodbye to him," said Patricio.

"Of course. I will be waiting there," answered the smiling priest. Paco was pulled over to one side with his mother and father. Romilia doted over him a moment, straightening his little string tie, combing back his hair, trying to knock down a cowlick. She talked. He did not hear. His father stood above her, waiting for her to finish, his hands in his pockets. After trying to touch up his appearance, and changing nothing, Romilia stood up. Patricio took her place, squatting at eye-level with the boy. He did not look Paco straight in the eye, but stared like an angry animal at the school building. He spoke in English, "Speak to me in gringo. Listen, if you do not like it here, if you just

167

hate it, get hold of me. I will come to carry you home. Watch out for these priests. They are strange. If you need me, call."

"How? Uncle Antonio, should I call on him?"

"No, do not call on him, not my brother. You do not need to call on him at all. Never. See that building down the street?" He motioned to the one with a large sign hanging off it.

"Yes."

Suddenly Patricio spoke in Spanish, saying clearly so as to throw his wife off, "Tendrás que estudiar bien duro, como no." *You will have to study very hard, of course,* then back in English, "For your mother's sake. Okay, that building is a telegraph building. It has no telephone, but it has a telegraph operator. Ask them to send a telegram to me, and send it in English. Just say five words to them: 'I want to come home.' Say it again and again, and they will send it. Then I will come and get you." He put an end to the English conversation, sensing his wife behind him. Patricio patted the child on the back, rubbed his hair with his calloused palm, mussed the cowlick. The parents walked down the yard, back to their carriage where Diego waited on them. The priest, again standing behind Paco, waved at them with a smile. Paco could barely hear his mother demanding to know what his father had said to him. When the carriage pulled away, the priest dropped his voice to the boy,

"Well, it is time to learn something. Come with me."

Paco grabbed the large chest with his belongings. They entered the building, suddenly stepping into darkness. That bright, busy yard of dust, rock and brick where he had played almost every day of his life slammed away into the distance with the closing of the door behind him. In the dark hallway, crosses loomed over him, with crying, bloody, dead men affixed to them. They were all the same man, white like a gringo, with long brown hair and beards. They all stared down, moaning silence, blaming him for something.

"Who is that?" Paco asked, pointing to the crucifix.

"What? Who is that? You do not know your Savior, Christ our Lord?" The tall priest with the creamy olive skin and lisping accent grabbed the boy's arm as if to jerk him quickly and more closely to the

A Fire in the Earth

truth. "You have a lot to learn, boy. Thank God they finally brought you here."

〜〜〜
〜〜〜

In the seven weeks he was there, Paco learned quickly how to survive. It was an environment where time was of the essence, one in which the hours of each day were chopped into disciplinary pieces of moments. Quiet time dwelt in the sanctuary, a time of silence and prayer. Talking time fell to the playgrounds, moments of play, of precarious danger. That was how he would always remember it. That third time, classroom time, did not concern him, as he did very well. He learned, he soaked up education with little effort. The skills of mathematics, Spanish, writing and reading came quickly, and he became adroit in all categories. The English class bored him to exhaustion at times, as his father had catapulted him far beyond what any student would want to do with the language. Even the teacher, Sister María Jacinta, came short of Paco's abilities, to her chagrin. She soon learned to never call upon him, for he would give not only the answer, but also a whole paragraph of English that she could not understand. Her English accent fell below the mark, perhaps just a step above his own mother's skills. Thus he sat for that hour, his mind slumped over in his skull, as Sister Jacinta and his classmates struggled over some three-word phrases, "Ay pley ausid. Jyu pley en haus. Ay eet fud."

The classrooms did not concern him. He took from what they gave and placed the knowledge deep in his head, becoming as familiar with it as with the English language. The other times, the sanctuary or playground, kept his fears alive. The playground meant confrontation and pain in all forms. The sanctuary, the daily mass, meant something for which he had no definition. The sanctuary stood for everything that mouths professed, things, ideas never carried out by anyone, not even himself. There they stood, and kneeled, and sat, listening listlessly, hands folded together, looking up at the back of the priest who was also the school principal, the tall man who stood facing the altar, mumbling inaudible words that were neither Spanish nor English. In the sanctuary everyone turned silent, staring, professing to strive for something never heard about on the playgrounds. Then there was that box that everyone was forced to walk into weekly, to tell of their sins, tell of all their sins. Paco listened to the whispered conversations of the boys around him as they all waited in line for the confessional to open for them. In their whispers they traded wrongdoings, one for the other, good ideas of appropriate sinning—that I stole a pencil, I lied to my friend, I cursed. For the older boys in line, the ones who could accomplish it, the whispers were different: I touched myself twice, I touched myself once this week, Father. Paco never understood that one. He touched himself many times, and he had seen others touch themselves. Once he had a bad itch on his neck in class, where a mosquito had bitten him. He had scratched throughout class, like a dog tearing into a flea. No one had said a word about it, no one had protested. Why, always in this line, did the older boys talk of touching themselves as a sin?

"I will say three times. I touched myself three times."

"Three? No way, friend. I never go farther than two a week."

"Last week Carlos confessed to seventeen times."

"Fuck, he's crazy! Father Martinez would have jumped through the screen and cut his prick off!..."

The silence dwelt in the sanctuary like a dying grandmother. It was a safe time at least, where no threats were raised. On the playground, daily intimidations by word and fist always awaited him. Older boys laughed at him, called him a fucking peasant because of his country accent. They punched him in the stomach and sides and sometimes his face, and scolded him with laughter when they heard him mumbling in English. "Hey, Colónez, what are you, a gringo or a fucking *labriego*?" The teen-agers laughed and pushed him to the ground, being three or four years older than he, with just enough developed muscle to rule the world.

Sometimes others his age arrived after an attack and helped him to this feet. Hoping that the older ones were not watching, they patted the dust off Paco's back, brushed off his little tie, and asked him what shape he was in.

"Yes, thanks. I am fine. Those *sons of bitches*."

A Fire in the Earth

"What?" one asked, not understanding the sudden burst into English.

"Sons of bitches. *Hijos de putas.*"

The others tried to say it over again, giggling as they tried. The levity broke a small crack in the wasteland of the playground, as if suddenly there were a slight reason to exist. One boy named Juancito exclaimed, "Hey Paco, teach us some of those words. Once again, how do you say it?"

"Son of a bitch."

They laughed, then repeated after him. Soon, after practice and coaxing their new teacher, they said it quickly and adroitly.

"How do you say *pendejo*?"

"Uhhmm. That is difficult. I have never heard my father say that in English. It must be something like, well, let's see, *huevos* in English is eggs, and *pelo* is hair. *Hair eggs* is the closest I can get, or *hair around the dick*, I am not sure."

They all repeated it, hair eggs, hair dick, and laughed at their endeavors.

"Now, how do you say *capullo*?"

"Oh, that is easy. I have heard Papá say it many times. *Dickhead.*"

They moaned with laughs, and their laughter and repetitions echoed through the playground into the hallways, where others began to laugh and to practice, until they all said these new, wondrous words correctly. At times they crowded around Paco, consulting him on how to say the phrases, asking him to teach them more. He did. Some of the words he just made up, as he could not think of an English equivalent. The phrases echoed away, like sound, impossible to detain. The older boys caught a word, and soon they asked the new student for his council, then slapped him on the back in a show of acceptance.

He felt saved. For the first time in those weeks of attending the school, he walked about the playground and the hallways with candor and safety. They no longer called him the peasant gringo or compared him with the young, weak faggots scuttling about the school. It lasted as long as the crowd of older boys allowed it to, until the day that Mauricio Antonio Sosa turned around to Father Villalobos and called him, in perfectly pronounced English, a prickhead asshole, while Sister María Jacinta—a late vocation who had lived her youth in a secular college where she learned conversational English from some visiting New Yorkers—stood nearby.

The explosion ensued, and the culprit was sought. Like matches touched to torchwood, the flames flickered backwards from boy to boy. Thus the flame of guilt and blame burned and licked back until it found its source, little Paco. Sister Jacinta looked down at the boy in the crowd of little, quiet, angelic faces with ties strapped about their necks. She held back a smile. She had suspected this, but did not want to point her own finger, when she knew how well the others could do that for her. She looked down at the child prodigy who had embarrassed her by correcting her English during class, and poured down upon him the wrath that her order was famous for.

He was ostracized by all the boys, little and big alike, as he had been publicly proclaimed anathema. This was more dangerous than his previous position. Before, he had been merely one of the young ones, upon which the others naturally picked. Now he had fallen to the rank of The Unclean, shunned by teacher and student alike. The few that inhabited this rank clung to one another like young souls entering the walls of a well-groomed Hell. The teachers threatened them with failure, with bad marks, with trips to the principal's office. Students their own age shunned them, not wanting to be near them, fearing to be mistaken for one of them. And the older boys, the teen-agers, they ruled over the Unclean like capricious masters over slaves.

"Hey, Colónez, you *prickhead hair-egg son of a bitch*," Geraldo Castillo addressed Paco.

The teenage Geraldo was born the son of a general of the country's National Guard, a fact which he made sure everyone knew.

The taboo English words sheered across the young teacher of those words, forcing Paco to turn around. Paco stood with two other boys, Unclean like himself. His bladder squeezed inward. He tried to answer firmly, but failed. "Yes?"

Castillo, with two cohorts, approached the quaking little group of boys. "'Yes, *my general*,'" demanded the older one.

"Yes, my General."

A Fire in the Earth

"Correct. You may not be one of my army, boy, but still you call me by my rank."

The other two, standing behind Castillo, held their arms crossed.

"Land on your knees, Colónez."

Slowly Paco did so, and knelt in front of the fourteen-year-old boy. "Good boy. Now, kiss my shoe."

Paco bent down slightly, then held himself over the older boy's foot, staring down at it, as if that slightly dusty stain of leather decided his whole future.

"Come on, fucker, kiss it!"

He leaned over, barely bringing his lips to the expensive shoe when it suddenly ducked under him, caught him under the neck, and flung him backwards. Laughter followed him to the ground.

Barely a breath came from Paco as he grabbed a stone that lay next to where he fell and hurled it at his attacker, slapping it against General Castillo's groin.

At that moment Sister María Martínez shook the large bell with her raised fist, calling all of them into the next class. The students all ran from their recess in the courtyard, except Paco and the small group. They stood in horror at the General, doubled-over in pain and groaning something more obscene than any of them would ever dare. Paco almost cried, stuttering, "I am sorry, I did not mean to...." His words were numbed by the groan of the bent boy.

"Colónez, you die."

The hunched General, with the help of his retinue, stumbled away.

The other two shunned ones, ostracized for whatever reasons, also moved away from Paco, not wanting to be near him. He had committed a sin they all yearned to commit, but one none would dare to attempt. Paco walked alone, in silence, toward the great doorway that swallowed up all the running boys.

Two classes drifted by that afternoon, Spanish and Mathematics. He sat in them as if in death row.

Between classes they walked from one room to the next, and the wounded Castillo passed by, moving in the opposite direction Paco's line of boys was following. A nun, one of the true generals of the hallway, stood above them all, demanding with her silence peace and serenity in the corridor. Paco stared straight ahead. His bladder called out, and almost emptied itself when Castillo walked directly by and whispered "Degollar." Paco swallowed deep. *To slit a throat.* It sank into his abdomen with the weight of the silent hallway and pressed against his bladder. He touched his neck.

They ate, as always, in silence. Afterwards they all marched down to the church and held night prayers, with Father Villalobos leading them in vespers. For Paco, the usually boring half-hour did not last long enough, and he found himself pleading with that once-stranger, God. Soon they all marched to their rooms. The nuns monitored the hallways for an hour after that, making sure that no one escaped the bedrooms. Then lamps were soon extinguished throughout the private school. Doors were closed, locked from the outside. Everyone lay in bed.

Paco stared at the ceiling. The moon fell through the window, throwing a small spot upon the wooden floor. In the opposite bed his roommate, named Adán, also one of the ostracized, breathed peacefully, asleep. Time passed. The moon's beam moved to the right. His bladder, as it had done so many times that day, called out to him. He quietly got out of bed. As usual, the nuns had locked everyone's doors from the outside, according to the rule. He, like all the rest, had learned the art of climbing gracefully and almost silently through the windowpane above the door. He did so, without waking his roommate. He walked down the blackened hallway toward the bathroom, which remained far to the other side of the building in a small corner. He went in and urinated. The stench from the commode revealed that others had already been there, as always, and they had filled up the toilet without flushing, for fear of being heard by one of the half-sleeping nuns. Paco did the same, leaving it to be filled by others throughout the night. He walked back, placing his careful feet on the creak of the wooden floor. The hallway spoke of an omnipotent presence, of threat, that his stalker approached, General Geraldo, waiting around a corner with a long machete, ready to cut Paco's head off. The eight-year old's mind raced with such pictures, painting them with details.

A Fire in the Earth

As he walked back he heard muffled noises, groans of some sort, emanating from another room. He moved in the direction of the sound as if approaching a wild animal. Through the recently opened window above the door he saw the glow of a candle. The mystery made him momentarily forget his fear of the teenager Castillo. His curiosity brought him to the large keyhole of the door. He stared in, and in the shadows he saw movement. He counted five of the large boys milling about, two of them holding the arms of a kneeling, ostracized boy Paco's age. A third teen-ager held tight a necktie, wrapped about the victim's neck. There on the bed sat Castillo, while the strapped head of the victim bobbed up and down over the famous bully's naked skin, over the same muscle which Paco had wounded earlier that day. Castillo groaned slightly as he leaned back, and he whispered threatening, caressing words. Another young boy lay half-hidden, cowering in another bed. The teenage guards held the jerking boy's arms tight, at times pushing his head downward, following the young General's commands. Then came the growled, whispered phrase, "Pull him away soon, I want that gringo bastard Colónez to finish this."

It sent Paco flying down the hall and stumbling up the doorknob with one foot while he pulled himself up to the windowpane and dropped down onto the floor of his bedroom.

"Paco, what are you doing, making so much noise?" asked his roommate Adán, looking over the sheets. Paco said nothing. He breathed heavily and stared out the window at the moon, at the ground below, about fifteen feet down from the bottom of the window. Bushes stood below. He pushed the window open, stuck his head out, quaking with a dry weeping. He paced the room back and forth, stuttering something. Adán could not understand the English. Paco heard footsteps coming down the hallway, and he slithered backwards toward the window. He looked down and let himself fall out of it.

Adán jumped from his bed and looked outside. He called out to his roommate. The words echoed behind him as Paco scrambled from the bush where he landed. Scratched and bleeding, Paco ran out of the prickly foliage, across the street, and disappeared into the shadows.

The gang climbed up into the window and began their descent into the room. Adán stood at the window as he watched the older boys enter, using one another's shoulders with grace, obviously having had done this many times before. They looked about and saw that Paco's bed was empty.

"Where is he?" demanded General Castillo. Adán said nothing, apparently shaking. "Oh. So he got away, out the window. You helped him, true?" Castillo pushed the shunned child to the side as he leaned against the window and looked out at the city street which he seemed to own. He ignored the blubbering cries of the little boy behind him, who pleaded that no, he had not helped Paco, he would never do that. Paco had jumped out.

"That son of a bitch, son of a *bitch*," The general ground out a whisper and jerked himself away from the open window. His build, larger than that of any of the children, stood silent for a moment, a brooding, older shadow that, in the little world of the school, could exercise much control He turned, and in a moment forgot much of his anger, or rather, channeled the rage toward his adolescent pangs. "Well, Adán, you will just have to take his place. We have something for you, something better than fucking Sister Jacinta."

The necktie flew around the little boy's throat.

〰〰

Paco repeated the phrase over and over again to the half-sleeping telegraph operator, "I want to come home, I want to come home."

"Listen, boy, why don't I just say it in Spanish? Just tell me what it means."

"No! It is to my father. Just write it down like it sounds. 'I want to come home.' Please, mister, please." The crying, panting boy drew a raised eyebrow from the telegraph operator.

"What are you doing out here anyway, boy? You should be home in bed."

The child paid him no mind. He gave the operator the home name and address.

"Oh. So you are the son of Mr. Colónez. Yes, I know him. I sent many telegrams for him when he lived here, and still send one out there to your home every once in a while. Very well, son, I will send it.

176

A Fire in the Earth

I will send it." The older man shuffled toward the telegraph key and began tapping.

≈

The confused telegraph operator in El Comienzo wrote all the letters down, listening intently to the beeps coming through the wire. The letters did not follow any expected order. "Oh, for Mr. Colónez." He remembered a conversation with the brickhouse owner, about someday receiving a message in English from his son. He typed out the telegram as best as he could. Then the only Spanish word came over the wire and he quickly typed it out. The last word triggered him. He took the telegram immediately up the hill to the large ranch house and knocked on the door. Around the side of the house a flame flickered, lighting a cigarette. It was Diego, the coachman. He called out in a whisper, "Hey, Luís, what are you doing here, old man?"

"I have a message for the *patrón*. From his son."

"What? At this hour?"

"It's important. I should get it to him now."

In a minute Patricio answered the door, wearing a long thick robe. "Yes, Luís, what is it?"

"A telegram, Mr. Colónez, I did not think it should wait until morning."

Patricio took it, held a candle to the paper, and read the typed note with eyes that were still awakening.

AY WAN TU KUM JOM. EMERGENCIA. PACO.

"It is my first English telegram," the operator spoke proudly, holding his hands behind his back. Patricio took no notice, but called out to his coachman, who, he knew, always stood outside at night smoking, watching the ranch for a few hours before retiring.

"Diego, get the carriage ready. I will be dressed in fifteen minutes. Have it parked out here in front." Patricio turned to enter the house, then brought himself back. "Oh, thank you, Luís. It was very good that you came now." Patricio disappeared into the front room, then came back and put a large bill into the operator's hands. "And your first

177

English telegram, it is very good, an excellent job." He said good night to the thankful worker, and ran upstairs to dress himself.

∿∿

Paco spent the night half-sleeping in a corner of the telegram office, half-looking out the window to watch for his father. At times the old operator said to him something about leaving the school, and that he should have reported the boy back to the nuns, that he would have done it had he not known his father so well. Paco said nothing.

Three hours later the familiar carriage pulled by two horses came around the corner. Paco bolted out of the office to wave Diego down. The father jumped out of the carriage and grabbed his son, who was still clothed in pajamas. The boy burst into English, explaining to his father what had happened, stuttering over the final part, not knowing how to put it to him. It soon became understood, and Patricio's eyes opened wide. The enraged father cursed in both English and Spanish, then turned and explained with acid upon his tongue how the hypocritical school with its priests and nuns who probably fucked one another every night after putting the boys to sleep had made a bunch of hoodlums out of the rich, snotty children so that they would violate little ones like Paco. Diego, as much an iconoclast as his boss, roared into the fury with his own creative words for curates and sisters. The telegraph operator, shocked at this display of irreverence, backed into the office and crossed himself. He shook his head in disbelief at what had ostensibly happened to Paco after hearing Mr. Colónez's translation. He got over his shock as the country *patrón* placed a large bill into his hand.

The carriage pulled away to another side of the city. There they rested the horses for the night, as Diego had run them almost the whole distance between El Comienzo and the capital. Father and son slept inside the carriage. Patricio had asked Diego to sleep with them, that there was enough room. But the driver remained outside, sleeping on the roof of the carriage, as he preferred.

Morning came, and they ate breakfast at an inn while the horses were fed and watered outside. Afterwards Patricio left his frightened

178

A Fire in the Earth

son in the carriage and entered the private school without asking for permission, walked to the upper room that his son had pointed out to him, and collected the boy's belongings. He gave his back to the protesting priests and nuns in the hallway, who cried out to the *patrón*, telling him of his mistake, that his unrefined boy should stay with them, as they could teach him the true, Christian doctrine that he so lacked. Their protests fell upon him like cold, fluffed ash from a distant volcano. He slammed shut the carriage door and ordered Diego to move on, leaving the curates out in the schoolyard.

The excitement rang in Paco's head like a cymbal. He looked up at his father. Patricio smiled slightly and put his arm around the boy's shoulders. The child, exhausted, had slept little that night. He fell under his father's arm. He could barely dream. The city's morning noises bashed against the carriage. He glanced up. His father appeared to him as a great knight who had ridden valiantly into the city in those black hours of morning. Now he nestled under the arm of that courageous man who silently wrapped warm muscle around his shoulders, holding him to his chest. The school drifted away. It fell and folded and was tucked into the recesses of childhood, not to be opened until much later, when life offered him more experience, more situations from which to formulate a distant truth. Sleep wrenched away that reality, those priests, those nuns, and the teenage General Castillo. Sleep, that other reality, was good to him, and it was but a moment, for soon he awoke and looked out the window of the carriage. They were still in the city, that place that his mother always sought out. He could tell by the large buildings surrounding their coach, by the thousand people walking by them, by some old woman who stuck a wrinkled, blue arm out of a wrapped, stained dress, shaking skeletal, groping fingers at passersby.

♒

Romilia looked out her window. It was late morning, the time when she usually awoke, always after the day had long begun. Late nights were her best time. There was no need to show her face to the morning, to the workers who populated the world. This morning she

179

was dressed in black, her mourning dress. She had asked Cristina to bring her coffee and some sweet breads. The kitchen maid had done so, and had set them upon the small table next to Romilia's chair. Romilia never looked at her, but nodded with a whisper, "Thank you Cristina." With that, she sent the young woman from the room. The maid knew to close the door. This was one day, all the maids knew, that the *patrona* was not to be confronted. Not that they ever confronted her. But on this day, they hoped, prayed, to not even see her. It was the day of the boy's birth, eight years ago, a day that everyone still questioned, like some old game of serious trivia. From that day forward, she had carried out this small ritual of sitting in this chair, looking out the window, ordering coffee and cakes. From here she looked out toward the distant cemetery and watched one of the maids, the one she had paid to perform this service, placing flowers upon the grave, eight-years old today. She watched that distant hill with eyes that scarcely blinked. The maid at the gravesite bent down to pray. She remained in that position like a statue of the Virgin, holding her enwrapped hands to her face, with a shawl draped over her hair and shoulders. Romilia watched, with no sense of either respect or disrespect. She turned away for a moment, searching for something. In the drawer of an end table she found some of Patricio's cigarettes, and lit one with a wooden match, a commodity from the States that was difficult to obtain. She smoked defiantly, blowing out the puffs of aromatic tobacco that had been cultivated for men's use only. Her eyes closed from the rush. She opened them again to observe the woman at the grave who thumbed a rosary through her fingertips. Romilia smoked, watching the little maid's body that never looked up, that never moved. The girl kneeled out of respect for the dead, frozen by the fear that the woman watching from the distant ranch house would push her against the grave if she ever dared to look up.

The prayers were sincere. Her contemplative fervor could not be matched, Romilia noticed that when she hired her. This same maid, whose name Romilia had forgotten, had performed this duty the past three anniversaries. Romilia hoped to keep her, for she was very good. The maid never moved, not when the carriage pulled up to the house nor when Patricio and Paco stepped out of it. The praying woman did flinch, however, when the *patrona* slammed open the bedroom window and screamed, "What the fuck is he doing here?"

♒

Father Mateo was hired as a tutor for Paco, and would fill that position until he died, in Paco's early teenage years. Paco's days followed a schedule: In the mornings he studied under the priest in the den of the ranch house. In the afternoons, after lunch and siesta, Paco left his books which he could easily read, and joined the workers. They slapped him on the back and greeted him, teasing him back into their friendships. He rarely saw his mother, except at night, when, with his father, the three came together to eat supper. She slept during class time, and remained at the ranch while he played at the brickhouse. There was no need to be with her, except for that one time during the day, the dinner hour. He played daily, worked daily, spoke with his father in English. Patricio had given him the English dictionary and grammar with which he had taught himself so many years before, and Paco worked through it with ease and with his father's tutoring during lunch hours. He played and studied, and life unfolded in peace and hard work as El Comienzo welcomed the *patrón's* son back into their midst.

♒

"You have not come out to visit me."

Romilia smiled, embarrassed at the statement. She responded as if the entrapment pleased her. "I have not had the opportunity...and my son, he is no longer in school there."

Harold, the businessman from the telephone company, showed surprise at this, asking why. She explained quickly, with no facts, as if it were of no importance.

"Well," Harold leaned over to her as the rest of the invited party mulled about the house, entertaining themselves, "someday we will just have to get together, you and I." He drank from his glass, but it

181

did not interrupt his blue eyes from staring into her pupils, round and shiny like black pearls.

"Yes, perhaps we can someday." She smiled back.

Chapter Seven

In his eighth year a word echoed around Paco wherever he turned. *Milagro*, a miracle had come about in their midst. That was what the maids claimed. It had to be. He knew what that meant, something awesome, something incredible. He had heard the word used many times during those daily masses at the private school, that an event had happened, Christ had performed wonders for the sick, the dead, the hungry. Paco waited for the event to occur, waited to hear more, to find out what it was. No one said anything to him, and he had to burst out one morning to the head cook, "Doña Santo, what miracle?"

"What miracle?" The cook looked down with her large, white eyes. "Boy... well, you see, it is like this... it is always a miracle when someone is born, true?"

"Who is going to be born?"

"Well, your mother, she is expecting.... Do you remember when Cristina gave birth about three years ago? Your mother is about to do the same."

"But I have heard people say that Mamá and Papá cannot have children."

"Oh, uhmmm... how can that be true, when she had you?"

"Oh. Yes." The boy looked ahead, searching for a question. "So will there be a baby soon?"

"Oh, yes, soon," Santo chuckled. "You will have a little brother. Or sister."

"Oh." The curious boy asked no more questions. A strange sense of the forbidden distanced him from the intimate things the news might carry. He said little else about it. He asked nothing of his mother, even though she grew larger and moved more slowly when approaching the supper table. Life did not change completely with the expected newcomer. Paco hid behind his food, eating with his head down, especially when his parents began arguing once again over how she should not drink; that she was expecting; that she should be more responsible. Then the riposte—that she should not be told what to do; that it was only a glass of wine; that she knew what she was doing, having been pregnant before, and she had not killed *this one* (pointing to Paco), nor was it her fault that the very first one had died.

"That was because I did not let you drink when Paco was in you!" shouted Patricio.

"That has nothing to do with—"

His backhand smashing against her glass of wine killed her words. The explosion of wet shards showered to the floor, leaving a stain on the back wall. Romilia left the table and walked to the stairs. She did not cry. Paco's mother never wept.

Soon he never saw his mother. She did not come down for dinner. Cristina took food up to her bedroom. Patricio and Paco ate alone. It was a joyous month for the boy, a time when the silence of the meal did not seem threatening, when they both ate and said little, when the father spoke of profound things. He seemed so secure, that large man Paco looked up to if he wanted to see his eyes. In these days of the pregnancy, Patricio seemed to have become stronger. He demonstrated his force with such actions as smashing a full glass of wine, a necessary show of power. Together, father and son spoke only English. In this last month of pregnancy, during supper, Patricio placed his fork down on his plate, chewed down the food, swallowed some coffee or *refresco*. Then he spoke, seemingly forgetting his dinner, as he leaned on his elbows and intertwined his fingers, creating an image for the boy: His father was the hero who had rescued him from the scholastic pit of Hell in the capital city, the warrior suddenly turned thinker, making him Man Complete. Those words, those essential phrases, fell in the boy's ears like the whispering wind that runs through a silent cave. Such soliloquies began with small things, such as when Paco used an English word erroneously, and Patricio corrected him.

"Enrique has a lot of power. This afternoon I saw him lift a whole stack of bricks by himself and move it to one side."

A Fire in the Earth

"Power? No, no, no. You mean 'strength.' 'Enrique has a lot of strength.' Not power. You see?" The boy did not see. His father explained, differentiating the concepts. This was the beginning of the whispered wind.

"Power, Paco, real power, does not depend on guns or strength, on how much you can lift, how much you can carry in a wheelbarrow. That is strength, but it is not power. Power is to be able to speak like we are speaking now. In English. Do you see? Strength, to pick up weight." He took his side of the table and lifted it slowly, slightly from where he sat. Then he placed its legs back on the floor. "But power is to go back and forth between two different languages, *para hablar así, sin titubear, y de repente intercambiando entre los dos*, to interchange, like this. *Al saber, conocer, entendiendo todo lo que se dice*, to really know the language, understanding everything someone says, that is power. You can do so much with it. Education, that is power. Power of the mind. It makes the world move, men who can attain it make the world move. It. And *you* will achieve much with it. Those asses of that school in the capital, they harassed you because they do not have that power, and they do not want you to know how powerful it can be. They were jealous, and probably even frightened. They did not want you to know that you were much more powerful than they. But you will know, and you will use it."

"How?"

Patricio sipped the pineapple drink. "Well, someday you will go away to school. Not yet. Not for a long time. And not to some religious shithole school like in the capital. But someday you will go to a good school, perhaps in another country, in a place like Mexico where they have good schools, where there are others like you who can speak English. And perhaps you can go to the United States, maybe even live there. You will make money, no doubt. That will be no problem. That is how I made money, by talking with the gringo tongue. But that, my friend, is only part of it. The other part is important to know: Do not forget that *strength* is necessary, too. Enrique, who can pick up all those bricks, he is a strong man. And those same strong hands can come in the night and snap your neck in two. What good is power in your head if you don't have strength in your neck? But Enrique will not use his strength that way if you use your power in the correct way."

Paco did not hear what followed, for he had a difficult time imagining Enrique's hands coming in to strangle him. He looked with surprise at this father for making such a statement.

"There are strong people growing angry in the country right now, Paco, and they are using their strength. But if you use your power correctly, that will never happen to you. Do you ever see it happening here? Never. Because the workers are treated well here, and that keeps them happy. They eat daily, they make decent money, and if they can do that, they will have no reason to be angry." Patricio looked straight at the boy, saw that he was confused. He made a final statement to clear it all. "Paco, treat them well and be their friend. Use your power to help them. Then they will never turn against you."

"You mean like Enrique?"

"Yes. Like Enrique. We are friends with him, like we are with all the men who work at the factory."

"Then why do they not eat here with us, or have parties with us, like those people from the capital, or from the United States?"

Patricio laughed. Quickly his smile vanished. "Those are your mother's friends. They are not mine."

Paco held silent for a moment, then asked, "Papá, why do the workers call you *patrón*? Enrique told me that everyone in town calls you *patrón*. Do you own El Comienzo?"

"No. No. I do not own it. I do not own the people." Patricio spoke in a cynical tone. The boy felt it, though he could not as yet define it. "The Schonenberg family owns it. But they call me *patrón* because, well, because they do not know what else to call me. It is just the way that they are." Patricio answered gruffly, as if the boy had sunk his shovel of questions into soft dirt. "I am the one they see. They never see Schonenberg; he never comes here. Since they see me all the time, they call me *patrón*."

"Then why do they not call you friend?"

"Why? Well, because it is different. They could not…they could not get accustomed to that."

A Fire in the Earth

Such conversations continued during that month of Romilia's absence. Paco hoped for it to never end. Yet he would always remember how it did. These were the last discourses of such calibre that Paco would remember, ones abruptly interrupted by the stream of curses that screamed out of the upper room. Truth tolled through the house, that it was time, time for the birth. Every one of the maids bolted up the stairs. Patricio also ran up, smiling; Paco would remember that final smile for the rest of his life. His father would never be the same once he took the hallway down to the master bedroom. The *patrón's* demise was momentarily put off by the hired doctor who cut through the small crowd and asked for towels and water, boiling water. He then closed the door behind him.

〰〰

Patricio was not the first to see the newborn. Somehow the maids, Santo, and Cristina made their way past the door before the *patrón* could. The women, giggling slightly, entered one by one, each with an excuse, "Well, Mrs. Colónez may need me in there. Another woman, you know." They left Patricio and his son in the hallway. Patricio laughed incredulously, yet allowed them to play their game.

When the maids left the room, they did not look at him, but rather turned away and walked down the hall. Santo left the room and tried to do the same, but her boss stopped her. "Santo. May I go in now?"

"What? Oh, yes, of course. I...I suppose you can."

"Are you all right?"

"Oh, yes. Fine. The *patrona*, she is very tired."

"And the girl?" Patricio smiled, putting his hand to the bedroom door.

"The girl. She's, she's lovely. You are very blessed to have her as a daughter."

They said nothing more. Again he chuckled, unsure, looking at his friend of many years who suddenly excused herself and took the hall to the stairs.

Patricio entered the bedroom. Upon first seeing the newborn, a hot wave rushed through him, as if Death changed his mind at the last

187

minute, seeing that Patricio was not quite ready for the taking. Patricio's heart scrambled in his chest, seeking refuge.

Romilia, who held the infant to her breast, had seen his expression. She seemed prepared for this. She saw in his eyes a man on a distant cliff, ready to topple over beneath the weight of a great shame. It was then that she spoke.

"Well, she certainly has your eyes."

Patricio looked down in that moment, waiting for the tiny being to open her eyes, to give him proof. She did open them, though barely. The fatigue from being born still held her. They were brown, dark as roasted beans, and they shone like a ray of earth-light through that other brilliance of her skin, that creamy white, vague skin.

"See? She is lovely. Right, Patricio?" The spent mother displayed no sign of doubt, no guilt, only affection and wholeness, expecting him to feel the same, and nothing else.

The silent blatancy pricked him, with the child spread over his wife's bare chest like the moon sleeping on a rich, ploughed field awaiting to be sowed. Romilia still spoke, confronting the issue in a convoluted fashion.

"She does have such lovely, creamy skin. That *must* come from your side, since you are a bit lighter than I. Perhaps from your grandfather..." She left it with a cooing toward the babe.

"Yes. Yes, from my side." A leap of faith into the vagueness, ignoring the dangers. The child was much lighter than anyone in his lineage that he could remember. His faith tried to calm memory, as if halting a galloping horse, only to be trampled.

"Yes. Certainly not very Indian," Romilia smiled, obviously pleased. "Your side has helped in securing her happiness."

"What?" Her statement interrupted a gray spell.

"Well, she is such a beautiful baby. She will be a beautiful woman."

"*You* are beautiful," he stated in a flattering defense.

"Oh, thank you, Patricio," she chuckled, "but not like she will be, with such a color." Romilia spoke of the light skin as if it were suddenly safe ground, as if she had solved everything and there were no need for further questions. She had never been happier. This cream-skinned child born from her body had awakened in Romilia a smile the moment she first saw her. She had looked through her pain and seen the doctor touching the head of the newborn, a fragile white animal digging out from a mound of dark, moist soil. "She is like a white rose on the land," said Romilia. The analogy, coming from his wife, reflected a poetic callousness, oblivious to any present pain. "Please, let us name her Rosa."

A smile crumbled over Patricio's face. His mouth spoke in spite of himself, though his throat wanted to close up. "Yes. That is a lovely name."

≋

Paco's father still took him to the brickhouse every day. The boy managed to see his baby sister in the mornings. Rosa demanded that her mother awaken much earlier than usual, and Paco would watch his mother nurse Rosa, casually pulling out a huge breast from her dress and pushing the nipple into the expecting little mouth while both sat in a large rocking chair in the room adjacent to where he studied. He felt vaguely jealous when Rosa was hoisted up to those large, dark breasts, and she closed her eyes with utter contentment. It was from that distance that the boy saw his little sister grow.

In the course of the years, Paco's play at the brickhouse slowly became work. He traded his little wheelbarrow for one that was a regular size. "If you can play with a real wheelbarrow, you are ready to work with one," said his father one day.

At first begrudgingly, the youth began loading bricks with the men in whose shadow he had played all his life. Still, he did not work all day. He studied in the morning with Father Mateo, excelling in every endeavor—in every book he read, every math problem he solved. Then after several years of tutoring the *patrón's* son, the old priest died finally on a late, peaceful Sunday afternoon. They found his body fallen over a wooden table in the rectory, his head resting upon a prayer book. The strangely twisted cigarette that had burned out between his fingers had filled the room with an odor that smelled vaguely familiar to some of the older people who entered the rectory. It

189

awakened in them recollections of childhood, of an old Indian who used to tell crazy stories, but they came from so distant a past that the elders could not place the memory.

~~
~~

Paco reached the age when he was allowed to go down the hill by himself, to take off on Sundays and play in the streets of El Comienzo with other boys. Although the encounters were at first brusk and difficult, he became friends with a small number of kids his age. He owned one thing that they did not have, a soccer ball. This was the key that gained him entrance to the circle of boys who played together on the church grounds every Sunday. The ball was made in Mexico, and sewn out of deep-brown leather. It replaced an old bunch of rags wrapped together with a string they had up to then played with. Paco thought he played well, as his father had taught him the game. Yet the boys of El Comienzo were just as adroit. Once they were accustomed to the feel of the real ball, they ran with it and challenged the owner to keep up. They played for several hours every Sunday, and often on weekdays during the siestas, when much of the town slept. Paco considered acceptance a worthwhile exchange for the use of his ball. For the first time he had friends to play with, people his own age, boys who got as dirty as he did. They became so close that one day he invited them up to his house for lunch.

"You will like Santo," Paco told them as they approached the back of the house, planning to enter through the kitchen. "She is our cook, and makes the best sweet milk."

"You drink sweet milk?" asked Bernardo, a boy one year older than Paco.

"Lots of times. We have cows. Come on in."

They entered, all seven of them, and walked into the clean, white-walled kitchen. The six boys stared and took in the wonders of the things they saw in the cooking quarters—the pots and pans hanging on the walls, the smell of coffee and sweet milk cooking over a fire, and the large, finely-shaped stove with sharp corners and edges, so unlike the sluffing, cracking mud stoves of their own homes.

A Fire in the Earth

"Hello, Doña Santo. May my friends eat with us today? We just finished a soccer game and—"

He did not complete his phrase, for the cook cried out some old, unused Catholic reference to the mother of God. Santo gasped as she turned around and swallowed the boys with her wide, white-eyed stare. "What are all of you doing here?"

With that, Bernardo stepped back, his elbow knocking down a pan that dangled from a nail in a working table, and sent it crashing to the hardwood floor. Stumbling to pick up the frying pan, he stepped on it, kicking it slightly with the side of his foot. The other boys trembled, moving backwards as Santo walked out to, as she announced, talk with the *patrón*.

"We better take off," said Rubén, another boy, who held the soccer ball.

"No. You do not need to leave. Come on, let's go outside until Papá comes."

"But won't he be angry?"

"Who? Papá? No, not at all." The twelve-year-old son of the *patrón* tore a banana from its bunch and peeled it. He offered the others to do the same. Soon they heard the returning footsteps of the *patrón* and the cook. The latter was spewing forth a river of defensive arguments concerning the lack of food, the inability to feed all of El Comienzo, and her own perspective as to the relationship between peoples of different status. It ended with the welcome Patricio extended to the boys. "Hello, fellows. What are you doing today, playing a little soccer?" The boys answered, nodding. "That's great. How about some lunch? I believe we will be eating soon, right, Santo?" She grumbled something somewhere between resignation and disgust. "Good. You boys can clean up some at the fountain. Paco will show you where it is. Then come on back when the dinner bell rings."

The boys said nothing, turned their eyes away with embarrassed smiles. Paco thanked his father and pulled his friends away to show them where to wash. As he turned, Paco barely heard the head cook's furtive words, something about his father contending with the *patrona*.

191

Santo and Patricio walked through the kitchen. "She is not my wife. *You* will have to tell her," the cook grumbled.

"Fine. I will. Just set six more places at our table, please."

"They will eat with the family. Wonderful. Mr. Colónez, I just cannot understand. Why do you insist on this? They can eat with the workers in the annex. There is no shame in that. Why must they eat with you?" Patricio, smiling as if ready to chuckle, simply explained that they were Paco's friends. "Friends, yes. Paco makes friends with the townspeople. None of this is correct, Mr. Colónez. None. I just do not understand how you can allow this sort of...of mixing to occur. It is not good for anyone, for us, for them...." Patricio did not face her, but was still smiling as she spoke, like a child getting away with playing a trick. She turned away from him, one fist resting on her hip, the other stirring some beans. The steam rose up and around her large, fat bosom. "Besides, I do not believe we have enough beans, nor rice, and obviously not enough sweet milk."

"Come now, Santo, you know you throw it away when there is too much, which there inevitably is."

"I do *not* throw food away, Mr. Colónez. You know that." She had turned to him, looking the man in the eye. After stating her emphatic words, she turned back to the beans. "If it were not for my leftover food, our pigs would be nothing but bones."

"Yes. Well, why not feed the leftovers to the boys this time. Perhaps, for once, we can put some fat on them, instead of on the pigs."

Santo did not listen. Instead she rattled onward, a free flow of cavils that rushed by him with no hindrance, until she groped for words without thought, phrases that ignored propriety. "You certainly would not find your brother doing this. Don Antonio knows—" She stopped, for he had wheeled around and had stared at her, as if to warn her, for the sake of friendship, not to speak of his brother. Santo understood. She brought her fist from her waist to her side, her fingers spreading in shame and in sorrow.

Patricio walked out. Santo continued preparing the food. At one point she called out to Cristina, who was working in the annex, preparing lunch for the workers. Santo told her to come soon, as her help would be needed. Then she set the table for the young guests.

A Fire in the Earth

The *patrona* came down the stairs with baby Rosa in her arms, groping for a breast. Romilia's eyes fell upon the dining table, where seven boys, somewhere between clean and soiled, sat with the *patrón*. They all raised their eyes to her as if watching a dark angel dressed in blue descending from God's throne, one who had decided to eat mortal food this day. She stopped on the sixth step and stared. Little Rosa slapped her breast, reminding her to move on down. After finishing her descent, she stopped ten feet short of the nearest boy, Bernardo. She looked from the boys' small brown heads to her husband and uttered, clearly, precisely, "I see we have guests."

"Yes." He smiled.

She breathed in deeply. Again Rosa slapped her breast. Romilia moved to her end of the table, sat, and placed the child in her high-chair.

"Well, we are all here. Shall we eat?" Patricio announced. The boys shot their arms over the table and threw some food on their plates. Suddenly, as if having been struck by the same thought at one time, they realized where they were and almost threw the food back. They turned to one another, then to the famous *patrón* sitting just across from them. He gave them his silent approval, and they reached again. The *patrona* folded her hands together and turned her face to one side.

Heberto, a younger boy, passed his right hand briskly over his abdomen, bowed his head for about five seconds, then crossed himself again, his little arm circling his chest, naval, shoulders. The others did the same. Paco looked at them. "I know what that is. You said grace, true?" he remembered from the weeks at the Jesuit school.

"What? Yes."

"Who told you to do it?"

"Mamá," answered Heberto.

"Oh." Paco, confused, failed to make a connection between the large Jesuit priests and his friends' quiet mothers.

"Paco," interrupted his mother, "I am surprised you did not clean off any today. You are still sweaty from playing."

"Well, I did, a little. But I will bathe later on."

"Oh. Not enough time? Or perhaps not enough water. I am sure your father would not have minded if you and all your friends had jumped all together in the water. God knows you could have swum in the fountain, for all he cares." She smiled.

"Only if I could have jumped in with them." Patricio grinned through a closed mouthful of tortilla.

Words blurted out from one end of the string of boys. "You used to live next to the *Tienda* González, didn't you?" It was Heberto. Romilia turned. He was looking at her.

"I, well, I do not know that store."

"It's down on the first street of the mound."

"Oh. Well, yes, when I was a little girl. And when El Comienzo was much...different."

Heberto shook his head, half-listening, then went back to shoveling down some beans. "Isn't that where the witch lives now?" mumbled one of the other boys. Heberto confirmed the statement. "Papá said to me that she once lived on the other side of town, but then moved into that house, about when we were babies."

"Witch? What witch?" asked Patricio.

Bernardo answered surprised, that someone would actually not know the witch. "She lives next to the González's store. She is married to the devil."

"Yes! And she casts all sorts of spells, too!" another boy cried out.

Another boy joined in, all of them suddenly filling in with stories they all knew about the old woman.

"Culebra is her son. He was born in the rocks. They say he came out of a snake egg."

"Who is Culebra?" asked Paco.

"He is about our age. But we don't play with him. He's as poisonous as a snake, so that is why they call him Culebra."

"You know he beat up my brother, and my brother is eighteen!"

"Yes, well, your brother has the strength of a rabbit."

"Still, I heard that Culebra had killed old man Sosa's biggest cow with his hands."

"I think the witch did that. She hexed the cow. It died the next day. I have heard her speak her hexes, right in the street. And she

194

threw that ghost on Doña Ramírez one day. Remember when she did that?"

"And what happened to Doña Ramírez?" asked Patricio, bemused.

"She went crazy. Can't speak now, just screams every once in a while and beats tortillas into the table. Beats them into dust."

"Oh. I see." He winked at his wife, trying to win her over. She turned her eyes in a different direction.

"Yes. She can do anything with her magic, like when she cursed the Colónez ranch-"

All the boys fell into a crevice of silence, not even chewing. They darted their eyes about. Bernardo fixed his gaze on the gold eagle sitting on a mantle.

"Really?" Patricio tried to dispel the embarrassment and muffle the sudden words of protest from his wife, "What kind of curse?"

"I, uh, I don't know, sir. Nothing really, just like my father says, a bag of lies."

"Well then, I suppose we should be careful, right, my love?" He smiled at Romilia. She stood quickly, snatched the baby girl, and quit the dining room. The boys glanced up at her as she clicked her shoes up the stairway. They remained silent until Patricio brought them around, talking about soccer. He suggested that they should form a team to play other teams from the capital or Sonsonate when they got older, since soccer was a growing sport. The conversation went on for another half-hour on that Sunday afternoon, and the day remained quiet until that evening. When Patricio finally entered his bedroom and flicked a match to a lantern, it ignited the anger of the *patrona*. For many hours into the night Paco heard it, all of it—Those dirty mice of children, infested with everything, why did they eat with us, how could you dare do that, how could you dare?—his mother screamed. His father retorted, flinging other words back, reminding her where she had come from, those same roots, those same homes. The shouting fell upon the bed, the floor. The crying baby controlled the following movements as the mother abandoned the argument and retreated with the girl to another bedroom. Doors slammed, screams followed one another, and the boy, accustomed to it all, fell asleep to that obstreperous violence, recognizing its impotence.

∿
∿

The leather soccer ball bounced over the dirt field, way out of bounds. It was followed by a couple of curses toward Bernardo, that he could have done much better than that.

It bounced over a rock, past a small tree, then halted under the foot of a very large boy.

Culebra looked down at the ball, then toward the boys. They hesitated, then ran, then walked toward him. Whispers were exchanged among them for some seconds. They approached in silence. Paco led them.

"Give me the ball," said Paco.

The large youth stared at him. His hair stood very short, as if shaved carelessly. He was thin, lithe, yet still big. He appeared so huge to them, his neck wider than most of their legs.

"Come on, it is my ball. Give it to me."

Culebra dropped a long arm down, scooped it up, bounced it between his hands. "Nice soccer ball. Looks expensive."

"It is mine."

"I thought as much, rich boy. Take it from me."

Culebra said it as if he had uttered such a demand many times, as if bored with it, yet saying it out of necessity, keeping up with his reputation. Paco tried to take the ball. A fast knee plunged into the boy's abdomen, then a bony fist smacked into his chest, another in the face, and another lightning kick found the groin, punching him much like the soccer ball. He kept Paco in the air, kicking him until, with one final blow, he let him drop face down, billowing dust. Culebra turned around. Again he lifted the ball, cradled it in one arm and walked away.

"Friend, that was not smart," Bernardo mumbled. The boys picked the body up and carried him to a shady grove of mango trees in the church grounds. Once Paco's demanding lungs inhaled a substantial amount of air, he puked, choked on it, vomited again, then balled up as if in a womb, holding his hands over the tenderized scrotum which had disappeared between his legs. Heberto and another boy ran to fetch water. They sprinkled some over his face. They walked about him, like amiable, timid soldiers guarding the remains of a fallen comrade. Roberto pushed a small stone with his bare toes, then kicked it with the side of his arch, like the absent soccer ball. They looked to one another, then looked around. They felt the absence, pondered it deeply. They had grown accustomed to the presence of the leather ball. Now they would have to go back to the bag of old rags, which would prove difficult. "Well, what do you want to do?" asked Rubén.

Paco spat out some spittle, mixed with the remains of his lunch, "Get my ball back."

"Right. You better think about just buying another one."

"Yeah, Paco. That soccer ball is not worth going to the grave, or losing your balls."

"Yeah. Don't worry about it. We can use the old ball, though I think my mom took the rags from it, used them to make my sister a dress—"

"We will get my ball back." Paco spat again. In half an hour he was standing up, and with the help of his friends, he began walking.

Paco tossed them one question after another concerning Culebra—what he did; what he liked to do; when he did things, at night, or in the morning; where did he stay most of the time. They pointed to the house where Culebra lived, an old adobe hut, next to the González's store. "Papá told me that was where your grandmother lived, Paco. The witch lives there now." They scurried away. Paco was full of other questions about his grandmother, questions the boys could not answer. They returned to the subject at hand.

"Paco, he is the son of the witch. You cannot harm him, unless you kill him, I suppose. But that means cutting his heart out and carrying it away from his body, burying it, so he can't find it."

"Then that is what we will do."

"What? You are crazy."

"No, I am not. That is my ball. He has no right to take it!"

Rubén jumped in. "That is right. It is not his to take. We have the right to have it. It is like my father says. It is not right to just take something from somebody, even if a man is following the laws, is stronger than you, or, or whatever."

"Well, if we are to do it, we will need to do it together."

"Yes," said Rubén, imitating his father and the men who visited him at night. "We need to organize, have a plan of some sort."

"I think it would be best at night," said Paco. "There is no one around. It is dark, he cannot see us, and we can surprise—"

"That's not true. Culebra can see at night. Just like a snake."

"What? Well then, if he can see both at night and during the day, we still should do it at night. And there are many of us. He is only one person. He cannot win."

"That is right!" shouted Rubén. "There is power in people, all the people, against the mean and evil one!" Other phrases fell from him, ones which his father had recently learned. "When we organize and take him at night, we can also take all the other things that he has snatched from us, like my water jug, and that time, Bernardo, he took your shirt that your mother had just made for you."

They talked on, formulating different plans, rejecting certain ideas, taking others. It would happen at night, it had to happen that night. To wait for another night, they all silently knew, would be to lose the fervor, to lose the power of enthusiasm. Tonight they would attack, and, as Rubén said, take back what was theirs and redistribute it to all the kids of the town. They would be heroes.

Evening came. Paco sneaked out of his bedroom window to a great malinche tree that stood outside. He crawled over the branches slowly, not as adroitly as he usually did, as his groin still pulsed certain pain. Once on the ground, he scurried down the hill. After making it down the slope, he ran most of the way to the meeting area, at the mango trees next to the church.

The half-moon revealed the six other figures as they huddled, crouched, whispering underneath the green mangoes that hung from the tree. They stirred up their nerve they had felt so strong earlier, but now their courage had dissipated in the uncertainty of night. Paco's presence roused bravery.

The young band scurried off, running first to the mound. They darted about in different directions until they had the old adobe house surrounded, two of them to the side of the González's store, two others toward the back. Paco, Bernardo and Heberto prowled from the mound to one of the windows of the adobe, peering in. The old woman stood inside, working over a fire, the only light in the house. Culebra lay on the floor in a far corner, apparently sleeping. Roberto pulled Paco down and whispered intensely, "It is she! The witch!" His face twisted, losing control. Paco brought his hand to his friend's mouth and silenced him.

The plan began. Paco tossed a small stone through the window. It landed softly on the serape that covered Culebra. The large boy turned, slapping at the pebble as if it were a customary rat. Paco let fly another stone, much harder. Culebra was startled. He looked up, studying the room. A whispered word outside the window brought him to raise himself up and walk to the door. He distinctly heard someone call him *pendejo*. Stupid fucker.

Culebra opened the door and took one step out. Another *Pendejo* beckoned him toward the mound. His ancient mother did not notice, as he was prone to go meandering into the night all his life, supposedly from the time he began to crawl. He stared out, saw a small figure run into the root cellar of the mound. Smiling, he walked quickly toward it, then speeded up into a run as he approached it. He stood above and over the door. As he reached down to grab the handle and pull it open, the rest of the young bodies flew all over him, covering him, thrashing him with one-inch-thick wooden rods. They came down once, then a second time, before Culebra got hold of himself and stood up. He jumped, throwing the six figures various ways.

The sticks dropped to the edge of the mound. He snatched up two. As the half-dazed boys once again stood to attack, Culebra turned the thin clubs towards them. One caught Paco on the side of the head, cutting deep into his ear. Another was thrust into Roberto's stomach, then turned sideways and swung into Heberto's side. The other boys stood by. They had recovered their sticks and held them tight, shaking as they stared up at the figure. Culebra screamed something guttural. They scuttled off in opposite directions.

Culebra again took the door handle and wrenched it open. A shaft of moonlight fell inside and revealed a scampering foot that disappeared into a corner of darkness in the small root cellar.

"Someone called me *pendejo*."

As Culebra took his first step into the hole, a weight fell upon his back. He looked up, saw the face of the boy whose soccer ball he had stolen earlier that day. With the two sticks in one hand, he grabbed Paco by the neck with his free fingers and flung him over his back, tossing the boy into a vine of beans that grew upon the mound. Paco shook his head in time to see the huge figure slip into the mound and slam the cellar door closed.

Paco jumped up, tried to open the door. Somehow Culebra had jammed it. He pulled and jerked, failing miserably, then dropped his jaw and stared at the door as he heard muffled noises coming from inside the mound. Paco banged against the door with his fists over and over again, trying to stop the sounds. The thrashing continued consistently, almost methodically, once and again the wood finding bone.

A guard walked by, grabbed Paco and demanded calmly to know what was going on. Paco stuttered out an answer, pointing at the door. The guard had a cigarette dangling from his mouth. He took one final draw from it, dropped it to the ground while he looked at the cellar door, then smashed the butt thoroughly with his leather boot before knocking. "Hey, Culebra. Open up."

"What?" a low voice answered from inside. The thrashing stopped.

"It's Chungo, the guard. Open up, boy."

"All right."

Three final, cracking whacks succeeded one another, dulled by the earthen walls of the root cellar. In a few seconds the door opened and the large teen-ager walked out. He dropped the makeshift bats at the cellar door. The guard shrilled a whistle into the air. Soon two more guards approached the mound, roused the half-conscious figures on the ground, and marched them toward the police house.

"What's your name, boy?"

"Paco—Francisco Colónez."

"Colónez? You are not the son of Mr. Colónez?"

"Yes, sir, I am."

The guard looked at one of his other colleagues, but the latter shrugged his shoulders. They brought them all to the jail, put the seven boys together, Paco and his five cohorts, and Culebra. The head guard, who had asked Paco his name, ordered, "No, wait, put Culebra into that other cell." He turned back to Paco. "Boy, what will your father think?" Paco said nothing. The guard shook his head, mumbled something to one of the others about hanging out with the lower class, how it will get one into trouble.

"Paco," whispered Roberto, "where is Rubén?"

Paco looked around, then took his eyes to the floor of the cell. "In the root cellar."

"What? He got away?"

"No." Then he dropped his voice to a shamed murmur. "Culebra got him."

"Is he all right?"

"I don't know. I think so. At least he is not in here." All the boys agreed. Being half beat up was better than being in jail, any day.

In half an hour Patricio showed up, sleepy-eyed. He stared at his son through the small cell window, then turned around. "Yes, he is my son. Let him out." The guard automatically obeyed the *patrón*. "Let the others out, too."

"We cannot do that, Mr. Colónez."

"Why not?"

"Because they are hoodlums. They will be held here."

"Until when?"

"Until their parents pay their way out."

Patricio stared at the man as the guard worked at unlocking the large wood door. "What if they cannot pay for it?"

"Well, the boys will have to wait. Or we send them to the camp, in the east."

"How much is it? The bail?"

"Fifty a head."

"Fifty? There is no way anyone here could pay that."

"I am sorry, but that is the law, Mr. Colónez." The guard opened the door and motioned for Paco to leave the cell.

"I will pay it. Let them go."

The guard looked at Patricio with sleepy yet serious eyes. "Mr. Colónez, these are hoodlums. We bring them in practically every night, or others like them. All they do is whip the streets, looking for trouble. It is best to—"

"Then what is my son?"

The guard stumbled a moment, then said, "Well, sir, some children, although brought up correctly, which I do not doubt you have done, still can make mistakes, and when they mix with the wrong crowd...." His voice trailed off, allowing silence to make his point.

"Let them go. I said I will pay."

The guard did so, and the boys trailed out, including Culebra, who slid out of the building in silence. Patricio told them to go home, then added that he expected to see them at his ranch tomorrow morning, as he would have work waiting for them in order to pay off the debt. The boys poured gratitude over him, promised to be there the next day, and ran home.

A guard passed, walking into the police house. He scarcely glanced at the boys as he entered, then said to another guard, "Fuck, you should have heard it."

"What's that?" asked the second man, smiling, waiting for a good story.

"I took that kid to his house; they live on the outskirts and—"

"You took him to the house?"

"Yeah, well, I was on rounds. So anyway, I dropped him there, and you should have heard his mother. Wailed like a fucking donkey." The other guard chuckled. "She tried to pick him up off the floor, looked like fucking Mary holding Jesus under the cross."

"Culebra worked him well?"

"Pile of broken bones."

Paco ran around the corner, stopped, and stared at the chuckling guards.

The following morning the boys showed up at Patricio's door. As he walked to meet them, they timidly asked if they could begin work later that day, because of the church bell calling them. Patricio answered yes, of course, and the boys returned to town.

Patricio entered his house and walked into the den. He stared at the back of his son, who looked out the window, neatly dressed, waiting to go. He seemed held like a statue by the cheap clanging of the old bell in the church below. After a long moment, Patricio, his hands in his pockets, his arm bunching up a riding jacket, quietly said, "We'd better go."

Paco turned and walked to his father. They left out the back to the two horses waiting for them and rode down the hill.

Cristina watched them leave. She asked Santo, "Where are they going?"

"That funeral down the hill."

"Who died?"

"Some *chigüino*, a kid from town. I did not know him. One of the boys who ate here the other day."

"How? Sick?"

"No. The cheese woman Gloria told me he was beat up by some other boy."

"Oh." Cristina crossed herself, then kissed an imaginary rosary in her palm. "Why then did they go?" She motioned to the outside, to the father and son riding off.

Santo sighed heavily while slapping down some tortilla dough. "Because the *patrón*, he does such things. Cannot get it out of his blood, thinks he is responsible for...for something. I do not know."

After the funeral, Patricio and Paco marched to the guard office, and the *patrón* walked straight to the front desk. "Have you found the boy's murderer?"

"No, sir, we have not."

"Why not?"

"Well, Mr. Colónez, we are very busy here, you know, and—"

"You know damn well who killed him. That, that Culebra boy. What will you do with him?"

"Sir, what can we do?"

"Punish him!"

The main official looked over at two guards leaning in chairs against the walls. He motioned them to follow the yelled order. The guards left the building. In a few minutes they came back, with Culebra held between them. He walked into a cell.

"There. Is that all, Mr. Colónez?"

"You freed him last night?"

"Well, yes."

"Why?"

"You had told us to."

"I did not know last night that he had murdered the boy. But you did! You released a murderer!"

"Mr. Colónez, excuse my saying this, but we know what we are doing. He is one of them. Culebra is in here all the time. Whether he is in or out, he is always the same."

Colónez stared at the officer. "Well, now that he has killed someone, what will happen to him?"

"Well, if no one pays any bail, he will stay here until we send him to the camp."

"What? No trial?"

"Trial? Mr. Colónez, we know he is guilty. He will be punished."

"But if someone like his mother could bail him out—"

"Mr. Colónez, do not worry about it. We are the law. We will handle it. Oh, and do not worry about your son, for Culebra will not bother him any longer." The official smiled, as if answering a need of the *patrón's*.

"Officer, I want to see that justice is done, not merely for my son to be safe. He killed someone! Doesn't that mean anything to—"

"Sir, what do you want? If I may speak frankly, you treat these people as if they are your children, then you treat them like, like they are almost your equals. Now you want to throw them in jail forever. Listen, please: We are the law, and we will follow the law, and we will see that Culebra is taken care of, that he is punished. Is that enough for you?"

The angered *patrón* walked out, his son behind him. He mumbled something, but Paco could not hear it. Outside, people watched them walk out of the guard building. Their faces displayed confusion. The story was spreading about how the incident had occurred. They looked at the *patrón* and his son, both of them suddenly an enigma. Paco looked about, then walked closer to his father as if for protection. He almost jumped when a soldier called out their names, "Hey, Mr. Colónez! Is this yours?"

A Fire in the Earth

The two turned around and saw three guards punching the leather soccer ball with their knees, knocking it to one another, laughing at their own maladroit play.

"Come on, fellows, give it to them," said the first officer.

One of the other men kicked the ball to Paco. He caught it with both hands and looked down at it. He looked back up, at the two guards who waved goodbye to him, as if they were his friends.

⁓⁓
⁓⁓

"Well, hello, little man. What have you been up to?"

Whenever his uncle Antonio asked him that question, with a smile smeared over his face, a frog always came to Paco's mind. As far as anyone was concerned, all frogs were poisonous.

"I am fine."

Paco hoped for his father's quick arrival. He was grateful to see Patricio walk in. All three stood in the parlor, casually dressed for a Sunday visit.

"I have something to show the both of you." The older brother led them outside to his coach. Paco's Aunt Gloria and his mother sat in another corner of the parlor, chatting. Once at the carriage, Antonio set his drink down upon the wheelcover and reached under his seat to pull out two new leather holsters.

"These are called Colts, .45 caliber. Brand new. Come, let's try them out."

He handed one to Patricio, the other to Paco. The youth touched the leather casing with fingers that wanted to explore all of it at once. He unbuttoned the flap and pulled the lithe weapon out.

"A beauty, true?" said the uncle. Paco shook his head in silent approval.

"They shoot clean and straight. I have only shot that one." Antonio entered the annex of the house where the workers ate and took four metal cans that had been set upon the wall, cleaned and ready for a multitude of uses such as carrying water or storing dried foods. He placed them on a fence a few yards away. "And they are easy to shoot.

205

You pull this back; it is called the hammer. Each time you want to shoot, pull it back, and that cylinder will move over, see?"

"Where did you get them?" asked Patricio. In his own way, he stood as curious as his son.

"Bennington, that fellow at the phone company. He sold them to me. I really do not need two, and thought you could use one."

"One is mine?"

The older brother confirmed that as he readied one gun and commenced firing. They did not know, due to the explosions from the pistol and the intermittent clicks as they pulled back the hammer, that behind them, in the kitchen, Doña Santo and Cristina had both fallen to the floor with their heads ducked under, not knowing what to think, as these were the first shots to be fired on the Colónez ranch.

With the five bullets spent, Antonio had kicked two cans off the fence, leaving two standing. Paco pulled his fingers out of his ears. He had watched the two cans fly off the fence through squinting eyes. With an anxious silence, he waited to be invited to shoot.

Patricio shot with the other pistol and left one can out of four standing. "Very good," said his brother. "When did you learn to shoot?"

"Just now," Patricio mumbled.

"Now, how about the boy," Antonio said, and handed Paco the weapon.

The youth did as well as his uncle. He smiled, pleased at his first endeavor with a gun.

"Here." Antonio handed Patricio two small boxes. "This should keep you shooting for a while. If you want any more, just let me know. It is good that you have a gun, brother, the way things are going." He gesticulated toward the east, toward nothing. "Romilia tells me you still refuse to have guards. Perhaps this can be your soldier."

It was an obvious attempt on Antonio's part to win Patricio over. Paco watched the gift-giving and saw some ambiguous signs of friendship exchanged. Antonio took the gun from Patricio, pulled a handkerchief from his pocket, and rubbed the instrument down, polishing the supple, steely shaft that pointed upward in cool, smoking potency. He shoved the barrel deep into the perfect fit of the holster, then once again gave the loaded gift to his brother. Paco's father suddenly seemed small, as if he were accepting the gun in humiliation. The boy felt his own heart drop into a cauldron of thick, warm sadness.

He had sensed it before. It always occurred during these visits. Paco's father became suddenly silent, and it was not the quietude of peace or contentment that Patricio wore while milling about the garden in back of the house or working among the employees of the brickyard. This was a cold silence, as if a sickness had come, one that closed off his father's throat. Even such a gift as the new pistol which Paco hoped to shoot many more times could not dispel the enigmatic heaviness that enveloped his uncle, could not bring a happiness into the relationship between the two brothers. Perhaps it was best to leave it, he thought. He reset the metal cans upon the fence, then prepared the gun to aim while father and uncle watched him. He clicked the hammer back, ready to squeeze out, expressing an explosive manhood that he had hitherto not known existed. Doña Santo came running out, screaming, telling them not to shoot, for those were some of her best storage cans. She cried out as if to save a line of loved ones from a firing squad.

Paco had not gone to town in several weeks. El Comienzo stood before him as a judge. There was no danger awaiting him, for the Culebra had been sent away to a national prison far to the east. But Paco did not know how that incident lingered in the minds of the townsfolk. During these months, he had been working more in the brickyard, and although at first unsure, he knew he was still accepted into the workers' rank. He had, in fact, never been rejected. The brickhouse offered escape from that past, from his uncle's insidious phrases concerning the peasants, the workers "who would strangle us if they ever got the chance. That is the risk you take, Patricio, without guards."

The guards. The bulldogs, his father called them. They were the only ones who had forgotten the incident, the death of his young friend. For them Rubén was but a pile of broken bones, something to laugh about. Paco listened to his father and uncle speaking, the latter making long, garrulous statements concerning the well-being of the family, of what was the best thing for their security, what would keep some farmer from coming in and raping Patricio's wife, "for these are the times in which we live, brother." Patricio answered, mumbling a phrase that he had screamed several times at his wife, that he was not going to hire dogs to sit at this door. The uncle sighed as if he was confronting a pitiful situation and poured more whiskey. Meanwhile, Patricio put his new loaded gun into the locked drawer of a reading table.

"Things are better for us, Patricio. Our new president keeps promoting safety for the country's first families. He is the one making it possible for us to have guards. I like him. He is a good man. Already he has been in office four months." Patricio made a comment under his breath about the new president, forgetting his name among the many. "Patricio, face reality, brother. The people are violent, more so than ever before. Even the young form gangs. It is crazy what they do these days. You just better hope that they kill each other first before they try to get you."

A vague statement, trying to be definitive. Paco did not understand what Antonio meant. Perhaps it was just the whiskey. Yet whatever fell from his uncle's thick lips dropped like dead flies brushed off a corpse, and Paco felt them as they hovered over him, reminding him of the burden of guilt that he carried. It was best to escape from the burden, from his uncle's comments.

Paco found refuge in the work of his father's company, in the obstreperous noise of the brickyard, the mucking and drying and cutting that went on all day. They beat against Paco, made him sweat, trying to tell him something, *It was not your fault*, and he sweated it out of himself every day, forcing a forgetfulness, lifting the bricks into the wheelbarrow, carrying them, rolling them to the other side, to a pile of bricks further away, *Do not own the guilt*. Some bricks broke; that was to be expected. They were forgotten, as all was forgotten during those working hours which he craved. Thus he worked more, the young teen-ager who beat his body with the rhythm of their labor. Memory came with nightfall, along with the voices and faces of the guards as they tossed him the soccer ball. They looked like friends, spoke like companions. They laughed like pigs, *Culebra worked him over well? Pile of broken bones!* Those were his friends by birth, by status. The world told him this truth, that they were the companions of

A Fire in the Earth

families such as his, the watchdogs that his mother always wanted to hire to guard their ranch house. She beat this fact in, insisted, until his father finally lashed back, "I'll be fucked if I hire rabid dogs to sit at my door!" This ended the conversation, ended his mother's hope of hiring them. A relief for the boy, because the guards would have meant more distance between himself and the Comenzaños.

It took time. As his mind grew into later adolescence, he tried to sort out all the facts, all the details surrounding Ruben's death, which he tried to forget in the course of the years. In the final analysis, Ruben's death to the people in Paco's class meant no more than killing a cow for its hide or shooting a game bird. The abstract theory that death was something which equalized everyone did not apply here. In this country, not even at death were all people equal. Another lesson for the young man. He carried it with the bricks in his wheelbarrow, trying to dump it into the neat pile of his burdens.

It was in these years that Patricio's brother began to visit more. His presence seemed to poison the very air in the house. Paco entered into the din of one party and heard his parents whispering. "Why did you invite him again?" his father had asked. His mother answered that she had not, that he had arrived on his own. They did not need to refer to the name, for Paco saw him, drinking himself away, laughing along with the other guests.

"Paco, son, how are you?" The smiling uncle approached as if to hand some candies to the boy, though Paco was too old for candies. "Been working hard, I see. Why do you do that? I will talk to Patricio. Just because he acts like a *labriego* does not mean he has to make his boy one." He guffawed, then turned to look for the country *patrón*, who had disappeared. Paco knew where his father was—up in a bedroom, reading a newspaper or a book or writing in his journal. The journals were something that Patricio had always kept. Once Paco had opened the notebook. It was written in English. Something about salary increments and the cutting of line items, nothing which interested the boy. Now, Patricio spent more time with a pen in his hand.

Antonio slapped Paco on the back. It was a strange, unaccustomed event, to see his uncle. It was as if the man had returned from a distant journey and had given himself permission to appear constantly by

Paco's side. The visits and parties forced the *patrón* increasingly into the upper bedroom, as if he was never to come out again. Patricio did come out, however, as everyone else did on the day Antonio arrived in a black-plated, horseless carriage. It quickly crawled up the slope of the hill on its own like a turtle crawling out of a swamp.

"It is called a Model T Flivver, one of those automobiles we have been hearing about." Antonio grinned, a thin, excited laughter leaking between his teeth. "Imagine that, Patricio. This machine is making the whole city turn around!" Antonio spoke about stores where one could buy fuel to make the machine run, and how new roads, the finest of roads, were being built everywhere. "They can match highways in the States!"

Patricio walked around the new brainchild of modern technology, staring at it as if through a fog, at the open seats, the tiny windshield that protected the front seats. He did not see the men who sat in the auto and smiled. Patricio had forgotten protocol for the moment.

Antonio's companions opened the small square doors and piled out. They were a father and son from the Soundy family, and a man from the United States. Antonio introduced them. "I am sure you have heard of Mr. Mario Soundy. This is his son César." César, a youth in his late adolescent years, shook Patricio's hand and tipped his derby to Romilia, touching the brim only slightly. "And I have the pleasure of introducing Mister Frank Jones from New York, a friend of the Soundy family."

Immediately Patricio began speaking to Jones in English, a pleasant surprise for the American, who stumbled wearily through Spanish. Antonio turned to the smiling though perplexed Soundy family. A grumble found its way into his grin. "Hmm, yes, as everyone can see, my brother speaks English." Antonio interrupted the fluent conversation with a grunt. "Yes, well, we were just in the area and thought we would stop in for a moment to show you my new auto. How about a drink?"

They entered the house where the *patrona* showed them to the bar and the parlor, telling them to make themselves at home. Antonio explained the reason for their arrival. "We are here, believe it or not, to do voluntary work. For the country, you see." He smiled.

A Fire in the Earth

"Oh. So you are a missionary now," replied Patricio. Antonio waited for the polite laughter to end.

"No. We are going around the different areas of the country to tell the people of a new holiday that has been established by the government and by the good families such as the Soundys."

He was interrupted by little Rosa, calling for her mother while running through the room where they were drinking. Romilia gently scolded the five-year-old girl in a whisper. Then she held Rosa in her arms, squeezing her as she smiled. All the men looked down in approval, then Antonio continued. "Yes, well, we have a new holiday, and we want everyone to know about it so all can celebrate, and so—"

Paco walked in. He swung the door wide open, then stopped as all eyes turned to him, to his torn, dust and mud-covered work clothes, his sweaty hair plastered against his skull. No one spoke, until his father came to his rescue, in English.

"Son. How was work today?"

"Fine. Lots to do."

"We've got some folks here visiting, even a gentleman from the States. Perhaps you want to join us later?"

"Sure, I will clean up quickly and try to be back before they leave." His smile was nervous. His eyes kept darting away from his mother's stare. He excused himself.

Antonio rolled his eyes while Mario Soundy spoke, "Well, you have quite a working son there, Patricio. And he also speaks English!"

"Yes. He has to sweat for what he earns."

The conversation turned in search of other topics. They talked in roundabout, circular motions; conversations that tagged and tied together from sentence to dropped sentence. The talk never lagged, the words stretched onward, about the country, about the world, hard times and good times in the States, and how the people survived them. "We're a handful of years into this new century," said Jones. Patricio translated for him. "It can be nothing but a prosperous experience, the way technology is leading us." They all agreed, even Patricio, who leaned toward the window and periodically glanced at the self-propelled carriage in front of the house. He said nothing of the auto; but Romilia did, wanting to know about the changes and advancements

211

that had taken place throughout the country. The guests filled her in. They talked about the hundreds of new autos racing up and down the streets, of the stretches of new highways being built all over. And the railroad, that wondrous railroad, how it had changed. "Nothing like the days when you were there, Patricio," spoke Soundy. "Brand new engines, brand new coaches. They're beautiful. Our capital is a model of these Americas. It grows every day, every day. New telephone system, comparable to what they have in the States. And that's because of the new power company we have down here. It is as efficient as anything in New York, right, Mister Jones?" Mr. Jones agreed, stating that for all practical purposes, they had another little United States of America here, right here, in their little country. With that, Antonio's enthusiasm, which had been worked over and mounting like foreplay, climaxed. He burst forth, and ejaculated, "Yes! Yes! Here, is to, the United States, of, America!" he boomed.

They toasted. The men finished their drinks, and they all walked to the automobile. The guests crawled into their machine. Soundy had his son César take the small steel crank at the front of the horseless coach and turn it until the motor cackled into activity. The metal crank flipped out of the youth's hand, slapping against his palm several times before he could grasp it. He yanked the crank out, put it in one hand and tried to nurse both palms, rubbing them together, cursing in a high-pitched voice as he made his way into the car. The auto chugged away. The men waved as they drove down the hill into the small town to complete their work for the day. Patricio and Romilia stood, much like a happy couple, in the front yard, waving and smiling to those who had just departed. The machine crackled around a corner, leaving nothing except the rude noise it made. The *patrona* stared, still wearing a slight smile.

"We must have one of those," she said.

Patricio said nothing, but turned away and walked into the house. He did not see his son above them, staring out of a bedroom window like a shamed animal, checking to see if it was safe to come out.

The automobile sped down the long hill. It made less noise because they were coasting. César Soundy looked out over the hills and volcanoes protruding in the distance. "I never knew there were so many mountains out here. Those volcanoes, do they erupt often?" He had lived in the capital most of his young life, had gone to Spain for his college education. The land surrounding the capital was foreign to him, picturesque, quaint. Someone answered him that no, that the volcanoes, although constantly steaming, had very seldom erupted in recent years. César took off his derby hat, set it on his lap, and wiped a few clean beads of sweat from his forehead. "It certainly is warm up here. The one bad thing about this machine. It has no top to protect us from the sun. You told me that the mountains were cool, Papá."

"Well, April is hot everywhere," his father answered as a way of an excuse.

"How big is this El Comienzo?" the son asked.

"About 800 or a thousand. Very small." Soundy looked ahead and spoke out of a vacuum of thought. "That Paco certainly works like a horse, doesn't he? He looked as dirty as a little *labriego*. Just like his father. They both work hard. Nothing like Antonio." Soundy pretended to whisper. "At the mention of 'work,' Antonio shudders." Soundy laughed to make light of the statement, reached forward from the back seat over the tiny windshield, and slapped the driver on a shoulder. "Better to raise money with a good hand, true? Yes, Antonio knows the weight of poker cards!"

"I do not see why he lets his son work like that," said César. "It is not very, well....becoming."

"No, not at all," Soundy agreed. "But, perhaps it is in the blood."

"How do you mean?"

Soundy spoke in a lower tone, glancing at Antonio who was busy fumbling in English with Jones. "Well, Paco's mother Romilia, she comes from a different stock."

"Yes?"

"Well, she—now this is nothing to talk about just anywhere—she comes from down here."

"Really?"

"Yes. From what I understand, very low. Indian."

"Why I would never had known that," exclaimed the youth. "Except, of course, she is very dark. And her features, I suppose... But she seems very respectable."

"Yes. She is an upright woman, very mannerly. That is why such talk should not fall in just anyone's ear." With that, Soundy stopped the conversation.

Mesmerized by the clacking motor, no one spoke for a few moments. Mister Jones asked in his broken Spanish, "Mr. Soundy, do you think they will accept it here?"

"I have no idea. I do not see why not. How have they done in other areas?"

"In most places, very well," answered Antonio. "The people have joined in on the occasion, have planted several hundred, perhaps a thousand pines. But have you heard about that new group that's formed in the country? Communists, they're called. Supposedly they come from Europe. Very troublesome lot. They plant other ideas in people's heads, and say that what we are doing is some sort of subversive action."

"Subversive? How silly! How are we subversive? We are doing it right out in the open." Soundy tried to light a cigar, though the wind prevented it. He leaned into the little windshield that separated the front and back seats.

"These communists have a way of manipulating people's minds. In Sonsonate—I was there, I have been volunteering for two regions—when we told them the news of the new holiday, the people started jumping up and down and yelling as if they had been waiting on us. We could barely keep them down."

"That was Sonsonate. This is El Comienzo. And as your brother has said before to me, the people are happy here. They are simple. Besides, there are not many people here. They are cut off from everything else in the country. From what I understand, there have been no uprisings here. None at all. They should take it well."

The coach stumbled over small rock, gravel, dust. They drove through the town's main street, scattering chickens and raising curious heads. So occupied were they with dodging cattle, chickens, and oxen, that they barely looked about at their surroundings, except for César, who asked, "Isn't it strange how that mound just sticks up in the middle of the town?"

"Yes," said Antonio. "It is their god."

A Fire in the Earth

"How's that?" Soundy Junior asked.

"I too have heard it called that," Soundy Senior responded. "I cannot remember where, though. Oh, yes, from Schonenberg, just before he sold me this area over here. Something about the people worshipping the hill in the middle of town. I do not know, some Indian belief, I suppose. Anyway, Schonenberg never did anything with the mound, just left it with the people."

"I never knew Schonenberg to have a soft heart!" laughed César.

"Well, I think it was my brother's idea," said Antonio. "He is the one with the soft heart."

They drove to the middle of the village and asked for the mayor's office. There was no office, but they were told to go to the house of Daniel José, who was recognized as the one responsible for the town, since he could read and write. Soundy told Daniel of the reason for their visit. They were here to proclaim a new holiday. Soundy explained that, being an upright man who stood behind the Republic in whatever way he could, he had decided to personally go out to his landholdings and tell the people face to face about the good news of this upcoming holiday. Excited by this news, Daniel excused himself momentarily and went to find a friend who would inform everyone that they had visitors, men from the capital, along with a gringo, who were here to speak to them. Daniel ran back to Soundy and the others and invited them into an inn for some coffee. There Soundy Senior requested the presence of at least four guards at the public meeting. Daniel promised to take care of the matter. While they sipped coffee, the people gathered together in the usual town-meeting place, a small field on the edge of the village next to the first row of coffee trees.

Many people arrived, over one hundred. Campesinos walked in from the fields. Upon seeing the visitors, many of the men, wielding their working machetes, turned back to the fields like rabbits scampering from a predator. Daniel called back as many as he could. As the crowd grew, Soundy turned to his son. "César, I want you to announce it to them." He smiled proudly.

"Me? But...but, Papá, I think since you are the new *patrón*, you should be the one—"

"No, i think it is for you. Someday, you know, you will be the *patrón*. It is time you began taking charge now." He pushed his son up to the front of the crowd, helped him up onto the small wooden box that Daniel had placed on the ground. Soundy stood beside his son, a few feet below him.

"Well…uh…ladies and gentlemen of El Comienzo, we have come here, my father and I, with our friends Antonio Colónez and Mister Frank Jones, from the United States." He paused a moment to let that sink in, that a gringo stood among them. "We come to bring you some good news. We come from your capital to bring some good news about a holiday, a new holiday, in the country." Some of the people smiled at that. Most of them showed nothing except stone faces fixed in a squint before the sun. Several guards milled around and through the crowd. Soundy looked over at them, smiling appreciatively.

One man named Hermes stood close to the box, his arms folded, a squint etched in the wrinkles of his face. He adjusted his hat so as to look up to the youth standing above him.

"This holiday is to be a real fiesta, one which we can all partake in. This is a holiday that not only you can enjoy, but in doing so you will be helping your beloved country. All people are joining in on this, especially those of you who have the opportunity to live out in our glorious fields and valleys." The youth gestured toward the legion of coffee trees, at the sunbaked, crumbling adobes popping about, sepulchers for the living. "Our new holiday is named *La Fiesta de los Arboles*." He rang the title out to the sea of puzzled faces. Some of the farmers looked down, studying the name of the holiday, pondering what "The Party of the Trees" meant. They looked up to the young rich man for an answer.

César slapped his hands together into a cup. "Well, it is a day of trees, people. It is a holiday in which we all will do our part to help beautify our country by planting trees. Each and every one of us will plant a tree."

Hermes, his arms still crossed, spoke out from among the soft buzz of whispers. "Why?"

"Why? Because our land needs trees. The countryside needs more forestation."

A Fire in the Earth

The answer sufficed for a few seconds. The man looked down at the ground, kicked a stone with his foot, then looked up.

"We once had trees. You burned them down."

"I burned—" César pointed to his own chest. "I am not sure I understand," he chortled, stumbling through his ignorance of history.

"When we first started growing coffee, you burned down all the forests," continued Hermes. "You had *us* burn them down."

"Well, my good man, I do not know anything about that. But I do know that there is a shortage, that the railroads need more wood for fuel, and that there is to be a new holiday, on the third of May, and we will be sending out some saplings that have been donated by this fine gentleman, Mister Jones from the United States, and—"

"I remember them coming with gallons of fuel, pouring it all through the woods." Hermes spoke like a rippling river, moving toward a stronger current. He looked out toward the land behind them. "Then they had us do it, going around with torches. We spent days doing that around here. You would have thought that hell had exploded, like we touched off a fire in the earth." Another *campesino* approached, touched the middle-aged man on the shoulder, whispering.

"No, I will not shut up! I do not understand this. No, it has nothing to do with my son!" he shouted into the crowd, refuting a speculation whispered among some women about the boy Rubén, how when he was killed years before, Rubén's father had never been the same. "My son is dead because of that rich shit on the hill, and I know it," he rambled for a moment, the memory of Rubén encircling him like hunger. Antonio said nothing, for he stood at a distance away behind the Soundys. Hermes turned, looked back at the young César who stood above them on the rickety wood box. "Whose idea is this, about these trees? The Government?"

"Well, yes, in a way. There was a committee, made up of some of the families." He added that, hoping to leave an impression.

"Then why do the families not hire people to plant them?"

César faltered. His father spoke for him, a demand in his voice that seemed weary of his son's capitulation. "Because they thought it would be good to allow the people of the whole Republic to help in the

217

development of the country." César stepped down from the hot seat atop the wood box and stood by his father's side.

"Oh. I see. Free labor."

Hermes uttered the statement loudly, making sure that all heard it, *free labor*, something many of them had come to understand, to define, from their own empirical knowledge. The melancholy *campesino* then mumbled something about how the proletariat was always getting fucked over.

Soundy stared at the *campesino*. Both he and the farmer were the same age. Soundy stood with his hands behind his back, his chest out, tall and lighter-skinned than any of the village people. Rubén's father was smaller, his shirt open halfway, showing the bones of his chest.

"My good man," said Soundy, "from what I understand, that is a communist phrase."

The response fell on the street and bounced about the walls of the surrounding houses. The people scampered about, turning as if from an evil vision, tearing away from any association with the dangerous label. They waited for some response from Rubén's father.

"Yes, sir. It is very common nowadays." The impudent *campesino* threw out his words as if he had nothing in life to lose, as if all had died with his son. He went on to ask, "Will there be a penalty for not planting these trees?"

"It will be enforced."

No one spoke, except for the old *campesino* repeating in a mumble, "It will be enforced, yes...."

The crowd stood silent, waiting for the meeting to end, waiting for the rich one who came down from the Unseen to disperse them with his word, like a priest ending mass.

In the dead conversation César faltered slightly. Standing next to his father, he looked even whiter. He swayed back slightly, then collapsed. One of the guards standing behind caught the youth in his fall. Two other guards carried the boy to a large oak nearby, setting him next to a young, fragile coffee tree. "Goodness, the heat," mumbled César. His head tilted back, and he said nothing more. Mister Jones loosened the boy's tie. One of the guards demanded fresh water from a local woman. She came back with a full gourd.

A Fire in the Earth

Rubén's father stared at the scene, at the youth sitting under the tree's branches. People crowded about, staring at the pallid boy lying next to the small coffee tree, both the tree and the youth cowering in the cool of the shade, both fragile and young. Rubén's father muttered something. No one heard him. His eyes turned black, deep as two caves on the side of a weatherbeaten cliff. He stared at the tree and the youth as if they were indistinguishable, and the caves turned blacker with hollowed hatred.

〜〜〜

Two weeks later young César woke to an already warm morning. He looked out the balcony of his house in the capital, a glass of papaya juice in hand. He leaned against the concrete railing, watching one of the menservants dig a hole in the middle of the courtyard.

"Papá," César called back into the house, "what is José doing in the courtyard?"

"He is planting a pine, I believe," came the answer from an office deep in the house behind him. A bit of scented pipe smoke puffed like serenity from the room.

"Oh. Is today the third of May?"

"Yes. Happy Day of the Trees."

"Oh, why thank you, Papá!" the youth exclaimed while sitting on a patio chair and pulling his bathrobe over his crossed knees. César turned and smiled at the servant, who shoved the sapling into the hole and poured water from a bucket around the roots, then scraped rich dirt into it. César watched the planting with pride, looking down over the railing, smiling, sipping, knowing he had played a part in implementing the national holiday.

"Very good, José!"

José looked up, grinned slightly toward the son of the family, who held his glass of papaya juice overhead, toasting the Indian's labor. He let his smile drop into the hole and patted the dirt down.

〜〜〜

Marcos McPeek Villatoro

"Where are you going?"

"Out," he answers. Paco leaves in those waking years.

His mother's questions are an acid that burns the back of his neck. It is time to go. It has been long, too long, since he showed himself in the town, ever since the death that was a subject of mockery for the guards, ever since that trumped-up scene in the great mound which became a mausoleum for the beaten. It is time. His father says nothing. He stares at his son and watches how he is growing. In the privacy of his office the *patrón* drops his head, perhaps with shame, with sadness or fear. He writes a note to himself, to hand out more jobs, to promise more work.

The son does all his chores. He studies. In the late afternoon he is gone, missing the final meal of the day. "He is at a time of growth," the father explains with blunt phrases. "I was the same way." The mother sputters over it while trying to get the daughter to sit still and eat. They never see Paco after the afternoon hours. He returns late. Sometimes he enters through the kitchen door; other nights he climbs the malinche tree and swings into the open bedroom window from the strong, bending branch.

He descends the hill in conscious, furtive motions. Walking down, he stares at the thatched roofs, the adobe, the buildings with the remnants of old roofs caving in, falling under the weight of age. Smoke rises, billows above them, blackening the tile around the holes. He descends, walking onto the streets. There the quaintness and beauty of the little town slowly, methodically dance before him, telling secrets, ones that speak in whispers. Dust crumbles from bullet holes that were dug long ago into adobe walls, tracing a haphazard line across the outer layer of slapped-on mud and clay. This is as far as he can go alone. He keeps looking, searching for a door, a moment, one that will let him leave the street, allow him passage into some darkness that he knew existed. He had witnessed the shadows once before, in the laughing of the old guard who joked about a pile of broken bones left in the mound. Now the shadow hides and remains concealed until he comes again and again, descending, walking, looking. Then the door is open to his steadfastness, to the fact that he keeps coming, that for some reason he continues leaving his hill, leaving that beautiful ranch, the home, the plentiful food. He's coming here, eating this food, drinking only water at meals when it is known that the *patrón's* family always drinks wine with every meal, liquor imported from some country far away. Yet he is here, always here. The door cracks wider. He walks in, sits down. Some old man pours him *guaro* in a clay cup. He downs it, looks about, hands back the empty cup, ready to answer whatever demand covertly confronts him. Soon it is demanded. He sits at a table with the best of them, drinking, talking, and with them, yelling, once they know that yes, they can yell with him, yell at him, about his own. Yet even though they consume *guaro* they always tread carefully, replacing old phrases with stipulations, that, of course, the *patrón* here, Mr. Colónez, he is a good man, if only the others were like him. Once they know how the youth hates his distant neighborsSchonenberg and Soundythey too allow their anger and hatred to ring out, how that son of a bitch Schonenberg pays them shit, breaks up their families, that now my brother has to live out in the fields, out there in those coffee trees, and cannot even get help for his little daughter who is so sick, while that prickhead Schonenberg sits in the capital, drinking his expensive liquor, fucking his wife every night, and she has more children from him, vomiting out more rich shits soaking in the blood of the same family. They talk and yell, and Paco raises his voice with them all, now that he is sixteen, then seventeen; now that he is known as the rich kid who prefers to live with the poor folk.

Their laughter bounces off dull walls, falls half-dead and trickles out the door. Their words follow a woman with a large basket balanced upon her head, the one who brings the goat cheese up the hill to the ranch house every day. She carries the empty basket thankfully through the streets. Her legs bulge with whelps of veins that are ready to burst with old, coagulated blood that has been collecting there for years. She walks to her adobe home, sets her basket down and heaves a heavy breath to the back of the house, to the baby who has been crying for three days. She picks up the naked little body and wipes off the stream of brown that has dripped from his buttocks and which flows over both little legs and stains the straw bed, adding to those old stains that the child has been sleeping in for three days. As she wipes the baby boy off, she turns and curses the older daughter of eight years for not cleaning him earlier, for not doing anything about the crying. She turns upon the screaming baby in her arms, not hearing the pleas of the eight-year old who tries to explain how she had tried all morning, but the baby would not stop shitting water. The cheese woman feeds the baby bean soup again, telling him to take it, prying open the mouth and pouring the soup in so as to put weight back on the little bones, fearing, yelling at the facts of the matter, at the skinniness, at the diarrhea, shuddering, showing her fear with an angry scream. Away from the streets, it is always this way. Drunken husbands on Sunday afternoons fall homeward, one after the other, slobbering, their breaths dripping from their skin, hot rum boiling them dry. Three raid the root cellar, looking for cheese, something to eat, their drunkenness reminding them of the old days when the cellar was always so full of food. They sleep in the cellar's empty coolness until night. The others head home, pulling wives away from children who lie in stacks of hay. They mount, fail, then bring their knuckles down upon the women, for they cannot function as the men they are supposed to be. So the children flee into the streets, escaping the grunts and slaps coming from the corner of their adobes, and make balls out of old rags, tie them together, throw them to one another, hit them with sticks, kick them. For fun they sneak over to the house of old Doña María Ramírez, who had been cursed into insanity by the witch. Doña María, insane as a coyote looking for a mate, sometimes sitting, sometimes standing. The boys stand outside, listening as she yelps and wails and beats her hand against old, dry dough that was once destined to be a tortilla, but was given to her by her daughter-in-law in order to keep the old woman in one place. She stands next to a table, beating the dough with her palm, slapping it in rhythm to her screams. She mumbles noises, prayers, then thrashes the walls with curses which usually rise in tempo every so many minutes. She curses the walls, curses the food, the children, and screams out fervently how the Almighty sent the Virgin Mary down to Hell to clean up the place and the Devil kissed her on the cheek and slapped her buttocks, making poor Mary scream as she rose out of that fire, with that little Devil laughing like a maniac, so there you have it, the children will all die, the children will all die. The little boys outside shudder at her words, speak among themselves, remind themselves of the myths: she had encountered the witch of El Comienzo long ago, sometime during the night, and has been like this ever since. They listen, crouched over into the shade of the adobe's outside corner, until the father of the house, the son of old Doña María Ramírez, comes out once again and chases them away, telling them to be respectful. The children do not hear in Mr. Ramírez's crackling voice the tears of a son. They only run, as boys do everywhere, to find refuge somewhere else. They run toward the cooling fields of coffee. A ramshackled funeral passes them by, and they stop as their mothers have taught them to do. They look to see who it is ("probably an old woman"). It is not. It is a young man, a worker, not completely emaciated. They ask each other questions as to how he died. Perhaps it was the guard, and they say this in the quietest of whispers. The funeral passes. They kick away, play a game of hide-and-seek in the coffee trees. They strip the thin branches and fling the coffee with all their might, stinging the ear of a friend with one of the hard, green beans. They run, they play, they grow, and in the moments of years that follow they change their games and bring other friends out to the coffee trees at night. They lie between the coffee trees on soft ground, here where the guards never care to come, where it is quiet and lonely. They lie and exhaust themselves upon one another, and fall asleep until the moonlight shines directly overhead. Sometimes they run to the river, and splash and play under huge trees that shade the water from moonlight. This happens so many times, as many times as days crawl over into nights, followed by nights that overwhelm the days, swallowing each other, answering to a hunger that not even day, or night, can overwhelm. The pangs of hard-working youth. These same people answer to the call of day, with machete and calloused hands, with baskets holding a bit of produce to be sold to the house on the hilltop or to one another, or to the small number in town who can afford to buy instead of to make do. Hunger comes onto itself, naked and throbbing in the river, among the coffee trees, away from the watching eyes of the guards. Hunger thrashes itself in order to fill its emptiness, and more little, crying hungry mouths are born to the earth. The fields cannot yield food, neither can the hills, for both are covered with coffee trees. So the young drink from the fruit of their womb, and enjoy transitory satiation. Then they awaken, and emptiness cries out to them again, so they look about for answers. They turn and walk the same streets of their little village, walk about that old mound in the middle, covered with patches of beans meant for the whole community. They pick their share of beans, go home, dry them out, then toss them to barely cover the bottom of a pot, and let water boil them into becoming bigger, swelling them to feed the size and multitude of open mouths. The men work, fall into the bars, go past small funerals with little boxes holding tiny, emaciated bodies that have never had the opportunity to live through the other hunger pangs of older youth. There the cheese woman follows the caravan, while her man and all other men fall into glasses, cups of cheap rum sold by outsiders. There he sits, the son of the *patrón*, and there he realizes, *I have never been hungry*. It is cold within him, so very cold, that no hillside, no ranch house could ever again keep him comfortable and satiated, no poetry or prose could ever shield him. He knows, he believes, that truth should not be manipulated by rhetoric or reasoning, that it should be dealt with. *They are suffering, my people, they suffer*. Thus in the eighteenth year of his life he talks intimately with these men. He grows angry alongside them. With these, his brothers, he greets the outsiders, those strangers who come in quietly, at night, speaking in excited whispers. He listens intently to the strangers as they talk about rights and land ownership and common land holdings and the imperialistic threat of capitalism that sucks them dry. In the back of bar rooms they meet, speaking of future hopes and dreams; of putting an end to hunger; of no more dead children, no more oppression of the workers; of land for all, for everyone; of overthrow of the guard, they who are the watchdogs of the Unseen Ones. No one asks where these men come from. The *patrón's* son listens intently. He wants to espouse this doctrine. The meetings come to an end as the one stranger at the window of the bar whispers *They are coming*. The men break up like splintered wood and hide behind cups of rum in the public bar. The guards walk by, staring, searching. They pass by. Paco and his new brothers and the strangers grumble and curse, and in that cursing they are one. They all leave, finding other fruits for the night. There he consummates his marriage to the new ideal. He finds someone who struggles within the cause, an older woman, mother of three. She knows he is new. She takes him to the river, shakes the clothes off his back, and rides him as his feet dip into the water's rush. The youth has little time to admire the moon reflecting off her. Before the day crawls over the night he groans, feeding the hungry with hunger, and it is final, he has become one with them.

Chapter Eight

In her tenth year, Romilia's daughter Rosa learned to wring the necks of two chickens at the same time.

Doña Cristina had not expected it to be a day of teaching. It was a busy afternoon. She had to kill eight chickens for that night, as Romilia was planning a large party that evening, complete with a full dinner for the guests from the capital.

"Doña Cristina, Doña Cristina, may I help?" yelped the girl from the side of the fence.

The old woman, running about the yard behind the fleeing fowl, answered, "What? No, girl, I need to get this done quickly. I do not have time to show you how to do anything now."

"But I want to *help* you."

In the next moment she had jumped over the fence. After much coaxing and pleading from the girl, the aging cook found herself teaching Rosa her art. Rosa grabbed the heads of the chickens as if they were fluffy, squawking doorknobs, then twirled her arms, holding her wrists stiff. The necks crackled like live splinterwood. Rosa dropped the warm bags to the ground, where they flopped, jumped, and spasmed to opposing corners of the chicken yard. Rosa yelped with delight over her achievement.

"Quiet, girl! Dear God, you will get me in hot water yet." The dark Indian woman looked about, afraid of the worst. She imagined the *patrona* standing in the chicken yard, watching with her infamous black eyes. "Now, go on. You've done your work. Go on and find something else to do."

"But, Doña Cristina, there are two more that need to be done." Rosa ran them down, catching them more quickly and adroitly than the cook could ever hope to do. For this she was thankful. The final two chickens flopped about, their heads flipping back and forth like balls on strings. Cristina cringed as Doña Santo screamed out the back door of the kitchen with the appropriate question of "What in the name of God is going on?"

"Don't worry, Doña Santo, I asked if I could do it. I wanted to!" Rosa exclaimed, still giggling at the flopping carcasses.

"What? Child, do not do that anymore. My God. Our fate would be the same as the chickens' if your mother ever found out."

"Then we must say nothing," Rosa said, and brought her hand to her mouth. She smelled the odor of the chickens on her palm and wiped a feather off her dress.

"Rosa, please do me a favor and go look for some other work. If you feel you need to stay busy, go do some sewing. At least your mother approves of that." Santo sighed, watching the young girl skip over the fence with her long dress flipping softly, almost femininely, above the rail, touching only air. "Thank you, child," the old cook said, relief in her voice.

Rosa entered the main working room, where Elisa, a hired seamstress from El Comienzo, was mending dinner napkins. "Hello, Elisa. May I help?"

"Of course. There are the needles and thread. That stack needs to be done. Plenty to keep us both busy."

Rosa sat down and threaded a needle. After some moments of silence, a conversation began. They spoke about preparatory school in the capital, about how active life was there, and how quiet it was here during vacation months.

"There is just nothing to do. Or at least Mother will not let me do anything."

"What is it you want to do?"

"I do not know. Anything." She looked out the window for a moment. "You know what I really want to do? I would like to pick coffee!"

"Hah! I see now why your mother doesn't let you do what you want."

"Why?"

"Because that is not work for you. It is men's work."

"There are women out there, too."

"Well, yes, but not women like you. It is work for *labriegos*. Think about it, Rosa, how absurd that would be."

"I do not care. I just want to do something."

"Well, you just sound bored to me. And believe me, you would be even more bored if you were picking coffee."

"I do not know about that. Look at that out there!" She motioned through the window, down the hills into the fields and *fincas*. "All the world is working in the coffee."

"All the world of *labriegos*. Come now, help me with this. There is plenty here to do."

They mended. Rosa fidgeted as she stitched the worn areas in the cloth. "So who is it that is coming tonight? Mother is worrying over her best dresses, wondering what she should wear, and Santo is putting out the best plates. And all those chickens! I know it is more than just Uncle Antonio and Aunt Gloria."

"Well, I am not sure if they're coming. But I believe some old business associates of your father's are invited to dinner tonight. And a few North Americans. Somebody from the telephone company, and from the railroad."

"Old friends of Father? Or new friends of Mother?"

"Well, child, I do not know what you mean by that." Elisa did not look up at the girl. "All I know is that it is an important evening, and that these napkins need to be mended. Besides, it may be that your mother just wants to throw a pre-Guadalupe party."

"I doubt if Father wants to attend."

"Why do you say that?"

"Well, I think he gets tired of parties. He does not mingle with the guests too much."

"Well, perhaps your father is missing his son."

"It must be. He has not been the same since Paco left, and that's been, gosh, how long? Six months? I miss Paco, too, but, well, I don't know... I would not want to be so sad all the time. Maybe I'm just used to it, since I go away to school, too." She spoke with sudden precocity flashing across her child's face.

"I suppose. But I believe your father is preoccupied. Mexico is so messed up now, if I were your father I would be concerned, too, having a son over there."

"You think Father is scared that Paco will get hurt?" Rosa asked the question quickly.

"I do not know, girl. Perhaps your father is...well, yes, that your brother might be involved in it in some way. I do not know. I am sure he misses him deeply."

"Mother says that the communists have taken over Mexico, and that they are trying to do the same here." Elisa said nothing. "Elisa, do you think that is true?"

"I have heard that being said about Mexico. But I do not think they will take us here."

"Why not?"

"I do not understand all the politics, but I hear that the communists are fighting one another in Mexico. They must be a crazy bunch. And have you seen any communists here? Have you seen anyone attacking anyone else?"

"No. But the paper has something every week now. And when I am in the capital, there is much more news. We have guards around our school buildings now."

"That is for your own safety."

"Mother thinks we should have some here."

"Perhaps she is right." Elisa bit through a string.

"What is a communist anyway, Elisa?"

The seamstress, somewhat weary from the questions, sighed out, "I do not know, they are murderers of sorts from what I have heard. But they are very bad, else we would not have so many guards walking about the streets now."

"Ah! So there *are* communists here! We have more guards in El Comienzo, so there must be communists around." Elisa did not respond. "You know, Paco once told me that the guards are just as bad."

"Paco has his own ideas."

"But my brother is very smart! And he told me things that the Guard did—"

A Fire in the Earth

Romilia walked through the room, coming from the kitchen. The daughter and seamstress became silent.

"Rosa, have you seen your father? Has he come home yet?"

"I suppose he is at the brickhouse, Mother, for I have not seen him."

"No," answered Elisa, "I saw Mr. Colónez in back, talking with some of the hired hands."

"Talking with the hands..." and she muttered something. Then she spoke crisply once more. "He knows he must be ready for this event, that the people arrive within the hour. He never helps me with these things..." She walked through the kitchen, out the back, and searched for him over the hills.

Patricio was talking with one of the workers. "Patricio! We must be getting ready now!" Patricio did not answer. She turned and said to Cristina in the kitchen—the maid's hands bloody from the chickens—"Cristina, go out and tell my husband that if he is not ready within the half-hour, we may as well forget the whole damned event. I *cannot* be expected to do all of this by myself."

The bloody-handed Cristina moved immediately. Santo worked furiously on the other side of the kitchen. Romilia left the room and took herself upstairs.

In a few minutes Patricio was with her. She turned. "What in the hell are you doing? Do you care one fuck that we are to have guests tonight?"

He looked at her, staring as if through thick glass. "Why do you speak like that? Why is it that my wife must curse like some—"

"Like some hired hand; something you seem to find so appealing. Well, I say to you, we do not want to mess up this party tonight, as much as we need to get *it*!"

The "it" rang and echoed in his head. They had argued about this long and loud, for two years now—the automobile which they had the opportunity to buy through one of the gringos that was coming to visit that night. The incessant coveting after all that was new had come between them. There it was, she had reminded him: the most magnificent piece of consumer goods to arrive in the country, and they still had not purchased one. Numerous times throughout the past years that wonderful machine had clacked up to their front door with either his brother Antonio or a gringo at the wheel. The shiny beast's eyes had stared at Patricio and his ranch, looking out of smooth, glinting metal as if to demand respect as the newest babe of modern technology.

Business had become irregular at the brickhouse. The cash flow was not the same. Financial security had become dubious. Patricio was opening his strongbox more often, taking from it most of the time, rarely putting anything in. All this during his son's absence. The boy had learned quickly. Were he here, he would have no doubt frowned on the purchase of the new machine. But Paco was no longer there. Romilia reminded her husband of that fact, though never alluding to her son, never using his name. Somehow, in Paco's absence, she was winning everything.

"I will be ready in half an hour," Patricio said to her, stopping the argument.

She mumbled other caustic phrases, walked out, and slammed the door. He slowly shed his clothes, brought his thinning body to the filled tub, sank himself up to his neck. His newspaper lay aside the tub on top of a stool. After several minutes of soaking he picked it up, staining it with the water that dripped like cooling tears from his hands. He glanced at the headlines, looking, searching for something, a clue, a sign to life of the future, of his son. He skimmed for lines concerning Mexico, but there were none that day. Yet there were other lines. The North had sent more marines to a neighboring country, just a shallow gulf away. Peace was being kept and established over there, no threat of Mexican Bolsheviks invading that land. A special article on the canal, in its seventh year, how it had heaped capital into the central region. Yet it had heaped nothing over his brickhouse. The foreign wave of economic growth somehow sputtered and fell into a trickle by the time it reached this area of the mountains. "There is competition, little brother," Antonio had once said. "Do you realize that three brickhouses have opened throughout the country in the past four years? And that the gringos are now exporting bricks to us? Yes! The gang in the capital, they are buying gringo bricks!" His hearty laughter rolled over Patricio. It seemed ludicrous, mumbled Patricio,

A Fire in the Earth

buying bricks from several thousand miles away when the same type was made in their own backyard. He felt distanced from many things, such as that incredible war that he read so much about, the great war, the honorable war. The North had brought it to a close on several fronts with victory and pride. It was all over except for the myths left in its wake, which would last forever. Myths that would allow for grandiose economic policies such as exporting multicolored bricks of various shapes to a small country such as his; bricks, of all things. He had begun to think of selling, as his brother had suggested, of returning to the railroad business. Could that be possible? He would discuss these matters with him tonight. But to leave El Comienzo, its silence, its remnants of tranquility. He stared at the pool in front of him, at his thin knees. His skin was covered with insect bites. The mosquitoes were hungry these days. He looked down. He touched himself, but he did not respond. He gathered memories and imagination, yet still he did not respond.

He closed his eyes. Many yesterdays surfaced, blocking his sleep: Mexico and its trumped-up revolution, the communists eating away most of the land owned by the Church, keeping the priests from speaking and performing mass. He had heard from others how they would publicly beat the clerics, spit on them, curse at them in the street before lining them up against a bullet-riddled wall. "They do not deserve that," he mumbled to himself, though he was never one to defend the Church. But after getting to know the old priest Mateo, who gave his boy such a sound education, Patricio did not believe the clergy deserved such treatment. The thought suddenly made him weep. Tears, a sign of some inner poison, of certain death. He fought it before it was too late. "Best to die as Mateo did," he mumbled to the water, remembering that simple short story of a life, and of how the townspeople found the old priest slumped over his desk, dead of old age. Months before, when he had heard the bells tolling, Patricio had gone down the hill to be present at the funeral. He quietly reassured those who had received food from him, through Father Mateo, that it would not end. Goods would continue to be distributed, his chauffeur Diego would make the rounds. This was his way of fighting, ever since the boy left. He had given, and he had fought, far too much for his manhood to survive.

Paco had decided early to pursue his studies in Mexico. The universities there, he said to his father, would offer the best. He had protested against going to the United States for college, without giving any reason. But something unspoken had been understood between them. Paco had recognized the reality of the business, of its downward turn, of less bricks leaving the factory, fewer men working. Going to Mexico during a time of great change meant a very cheap education. "See how they are answering the people's needs, Papá? It is the best thing that could happen!" Meeting needs, all the needs; Patricio sensed his own failure. The needs of the workers, as they sifted off the sides of the brickhouse and tumbled down the hill like crumbs off bread, then fell into the hills of coffee, inevitably. His son had seen it happening, had, in his youthful zeal, spoken out against it. "It is occurring everywhere, Papá, all over our countries, I have read about it. Some people are getting richer, but others, they are getting poorer and poorer. The rich, they keep selling out to imperialist countries, the United States, Germany, England. But they keep paying shit to the workers." Patricio had agreed with a silent nod, then calculated how much he was paying his employees. His son had continued talking, some strange, newly-acquired knowledge spurting from him. Paco's words burned his father like a penance for the sin of status. Patricio had listened, then to compensate, he had returned to his brickhouse and raised the salaries of the employees left him, bending over his emptying strongbox. He raised the supply of food that he sent down the hill with Diego, telling Santo to never breathe a word to his wife. Diego took care of distribution, changing the route every week until most all of the Comenzaño families, every so many weeks, received a cornucopia of goods from the passing carriage.

Thus Patricio Colónez endeavored to hold life together in the tightness and security of their mountain. Yet the sides continued to crack.

Then there was the automobile. That wondrous machine which would drive them away from all this. More were arriving into the country. He had read in the papers that they were sweeping Europe, that the world would never be the same. And all those new roads ribboning across the country. They stretched all over the globe as well. "We *must* get one!" Romilia had announced. This was the reason for the party, and the special invitations sent out to the gringos of the telephone and telegraph company, a few to the railroad, and one, though Patricio did not know it, to his brother Antonio, who would be the key.

The gringos were coming. Patricio could still have power, weaving Spanish and English adroitly, and controlling the party. The water turned cool in his tub, as if to tell him *that is not enough; these days, to speak gringo is not enough.* Others were acquiring the power. That bothered him. The language was a precious gem, his final wealth, one that he thought could never be stolen from him. Yet others were learning, and this burnt him more than the automobile, more than his wife's actions, such as when she had extracted the money from the safe. She now held the cash. Somehow she had led him to his safe and had taken money from the box. Now she controlled it, with no questions asked. In the few months since his son had left, monies, gifts, and other materials had somehow disappeared by way of Romilia. He remembered only how much it had been: one thousand colones, the last of the private cash in the strongbox. She now had it. There could have been more, but it had gone to the workers. She had only grumbled, asking for nothing more, as if fearing to break his maudlin spell.

He heard her coming up the stairs. He picked himself up from the water, dried quickly, standing in the tub room naked. She walked in, looked at his thinness, and turned away.

"They will be here soon," she said, and left him alone.

He dressed himself, put on a new cloth tie, so popular these days, and a gift his daughter brought him when she returned from the capital to spend the summer months with them. He walked down the corridor and could hear people talking downstairs. As he turned the corner of the steps, he looked at the decorations, the reds, greens, golds, yellows of Guadalupe and Christmas, and smelled the aroma of chicken basting in wine sauce. People chuckled as they greeted one another. Then he heard his brother's outrageous laugh. He stopped. The ebb and flow of his power changed too quickly. It left scars. This had not happened before, when Paco was present. There had been no questions then, as if the *patrón* and his son could conquer together all doubts. With Paco he felt powerful. In his absence old doors creaked open, exposing doubt. It all tumbled out like bones from a shallow sepulchre. His brother's laughter snaked up the stairs, crawled over Patricio, held him on an old gravebed of memory...of youth and brotherhood, of rage that came down with a boot, always aiming for the boy's pelvis, always striking the most vulnerable point. Patricio coughed, yet the vision clung to him like old sap onto a dying tree.

He straightened his tie, though it did not need straightening. He walked down, looking at all those men, creamy-white except for his laughing brother. His wife smiled, cooed greetings to the people coming through the door. The same voice turned to him after she heard the familiar creak on the stairs. Her voice sifted through the occasion and slammed closed the door of the glass cage that encircled him, "My love, our guests have arrived."

He walked onto the ground floor. His daughter came to kiss him, asked him how his day had been. That lovely ten-year-old daughter, so light and perfect, helped her mother with drinks and smiles. Throughout the rooms, Spanish and English splashed together. He heard nothing except for "Hello, Patricio, old sport, how goes life, how goes the business?" To which he answered with quick phrases and a heavy smile.

His brother spoke with him after commenting on how long it had been since they last saw each other. He talked about economics, how it was becoming a true race, a competition, how "you had better get out of this business, little brother, it will swamp you. No time to play around anymore, not with the big competitors coming in." Antonio had learned some English and was speaking directly with the gringos. "We need to speak it, little brother. It is mandatory. The only way to win." Not very much, but the bigger sibling could survive in a small conversation with the North Americans. Antonio disappeared, falling into a conversation with some of the white-skinned visitors. Rosa approached and placed a drink in Patricio's hand. He followed about, looking for Romilia, then found her with a group of the few women who had arrived. They stood with Gloria, speaking about some show that had just opened in the capital.

"Did you invite Antonio?" asked Patricio.

"Of course."

"Why?"

"Because it has been awhile, more than four months." She stared through him as if to break the glass cage.

"We will get the auto. I told you that," he said, his voice falling under rasped air.

"I know we will. I just want to make sure." Again, her eyes demanded, then she turned away. He walked in another direction, looking at nothing, wondering if he visibly shook.

Frank Jones walked by, the man of the tree saplings, and said many things to Patricio, none of which the local *patrón* heard. From Jones' arm dangled a dark-skinned woman. A glittering dress hung from two straps over her brown shoulders. She wore thick, green eye mascara. She was looking around the party, hunting for prey. Patricio asked her name. "Sofía," she answered. "Can I get a drink somewhere?" Her accent was obviously urban, from the capital. She glanced at Patricio only once, as if disinterested with her own kind. Soon Jones and Sofía walked away, leaving Patricio alone.

"Daddy, are you feeling well?" whispered Rosa.

"What? Oh, well, I feel a little tired, I suppose."

"Perhaps you should lie down for a while, or maybe it is better if you eat, then go rest afterwards." She held his arm and led him away. She touched his hand. "Oh, you have a bit of a fever. You must be getting sick with something. We will be eating in a little bit. Why don't you just go sit down over there for a while?"

She led him to a sofa. Soon a gringo sat next to him. The North American kept talking about politics, which put Patricio in a recessed pool of muddy thoughts.

"But I tell you one thing that is hurting you people, Patricio old boy, and that's all these presidents you keep having." The gringo swallowed deep from his glass. "Jesus Christ, what is it, three this year? You people go through them like new shoes, a pair for every damn season."

Everyone drank, laughed, and smoked, downing the cocktail hour with smiles and laughter over whiskey-covered fruit.

In a flash of a moment Romilia bent toward her brother-in-law. "Go upstairs, please." Antonio looked toward her, but she had already averted her eyes another way. He swallowed from his second glass, and soon did as he was told.

Upstairs he waited in the corridor, looking at some of the paintings, still drinking, swirling the straight whiskey in his glass. Soon she arrived and walked past him. "Come in here." She closed the door quietly after they entered Paco's old bedroom. "You know why I asked you up here?"

"No, not really. But I was not about to pass up the chance." He grinned.

"I want to buy an automobile. A Packard, or that, that, how is it said, *Pears Erro*."

"Oh. A Pierce Arrow. Well then, buy one. But those are two expensive autos. Do you have enough money?"

She looked at him, silent, then slowly sat upon the bed, bringing one arm dramatically behind her to rest upon. "I believe you owe me a favor."

"How is that?"

"I have one-thousand colones. We need that much more to buy a car."

"Why don't you have the other thousand?"

She turned, looked out the window a moment. "That was all Patricio had in the safe. I do not know. I was sure we would have much more, but we do not. So I thought you could give it to me."

Antonio stared down at her. "You know the brickhouse is not doing well. You will never raise enough money, not for such an automobile, not now." He leaned toward her. "And why should I give you the other thousand? How is it I owe you?"

"You know."

"No, I do not."

She stared at him, eyes black with anger, a hatred for being pressured to even have to say it.

"Because you raped me."

A Fire in the Earth

He laughed. She held to him, though with confused eyes. Her legs were still crossed under the long, dark-blue dress, her mouth dropped slightly from his response.

"Woman, that was almost twenty years ago. What are you going to do with that?"

"Tell your brother."

"And what will he do?" She did not answer. "And perhaps he already knows. What does that matter anymore; it is old news."

"Because it may have been known, but it has never been said."

Antonio looked down at her. His thick brown lips wrapped about the edge of his glass methodically.

"Do you want to destroy your brother?" she asked

"Or you your husband?" he raised. "And it is old news, almost twenty years. Twenty years dissolves any threat. If you had wanted something from me, you should not have waited until now. Of course, there were no autos then." He chuckled, disengaging the power of her threat. He turned away from her, lit a cigarette, still talking about the value of an automobile—how it was not worth breaking up a close family such as theirs, how she should not let such material goods get in the way of good judgement.

She did not hear, for she busied herself with finding a thick book from Paco's shelf. Extracting an English dictionary, she brought it down upon the head of the brother-in-law-turned-moralist. It knocked the cigarette from his mouth, which sizzled into his whiskey.

"Bitch!" he yelped. He turned around, grabbed her arms as she raised the book overhead. He pushed her away, back against the bed. "Come on, Romilia, we are too old for this." His breath pushed heavily, sporadically, from the attack.

"Give me the money, you fucker. You owe me that!"

Long moments passed before he stuck out his hand to her. "Do you have the thousand with you? Give it to me. I will take care of it."

"What do you mean give it to you?"

"I said give it...I will double it, do not worry. And I will get the auto for you."

"By when?"

"By, well, by Monday. No, wait—Tuesday."

"You will have the cash then?"

"I will get it, yes. Tonight. I will raise it."

"Tonight? How?..." Then she knew how. "Oh. Do not fuck up," she warned, as if forced to swallow bitter coffee.

"No, I will not 'fuck up.'" mimicking her curses, which grasped back to rural days.

She handed the money over to him. He pushed it into his worn, leather wallet as if it were nothing but paper.

"Now, why did you bring me here with all these gringos?"

"They are connections. I thought you could get one through them, one of those better autos."

"They are all the same, just different shapes. I will use your strategy in a different way. But why all this for a car? You act as if you have not eaten in days—"

"I want an automobile. We must have one here. I hate the thought that we are always the last to get anything new. He always thinks we can do without." She looked away from Antonio, darted her eyes about like some lost disciple. "We are stuck out here in this damn countryside when we could live in the capital; he could work at the railroad as a representative. But no, he wants to live out here, with all those hard workers of his, those workers that his son just admires like God, fucking filthy *labriegos*...."

The conversation dissipated, both of them realizing their absence from the party. Patricio stood outside in the hallway. He left the door of Paco's room after listening to it all, every word, after hearing the flapping sound of money pass from a wife's hand to a brother's, all of it, now stuffed into his pants. Then those words, those realities rose in a fever within him, drove him away from the door and into their own bedroom. There Patricio sat, then stood, then sat again. Sometimes he glanced out the window, clutching his hands into fists as if to snatch the night. For half an hour he paced the master bedroom. He pulled a book out of a drawer, scribbled lines into it, then choked on an escaping rush of tears. Throwing the book into the drawer, he rushed down the corridor, and as he came down the steps he looked for his daughter, the one innocent soul in that gathering, the only bit of kindness he could see in that herd of people. He searched for her, but it seemed she was not there. Yet she was there, serving drinks, handing them up to the adults. It had taken a moment to spot her, for her skin blended in so quickly with that white crowd. There stood the whole world that counted, in his parlor, all white. That was reality, that was truth. There walked his wife, knowing that truth, and trying to take from that world.

Patricio leaned against the banister and walked himself down as if entering a pit. He looked about, said nothing, looked back and forth as he found the separated pair, his wife and his brother on opposite ends of the cocktail hour. He stood alone, feeling his knees crack with pressure. He almost fell into a crevice in the floor that would have allowed him to fall directly into Hell, except for the gringo who slapped him on the back and greeted him, "Well, Pat, how the hell is business?" The English, slamming like a bent tree limb, forced him into safety.

"Oh, fine, fine, we are doing good work here."

"Well, that's good to hear. I understand that the brick industry wasn't doing so well, with all of that competition around. Good to know it's not undercutting you, though I'm not surprised." The man smiled, slapping him again on the back.

"Yes, we do well, just fine.... Listen Charlie, I was wondering, how, how is the railroad?"

"Oh, Pat, you wouldn't believe it! We've gotten so big since you've been there, you wouldn't recognize it. The biggest engines, and now, with the tourists coming in, it's just, just incredible. Just incredible. I...I just can't tell you how amazing, how incredible, it is now!" The white man sipped from the huge glass of sherry. "It's all these new businesses coming down here, Pat. Sears, Rockefeller, I hear that even Singer is sending down some plans to start a company here. It's just booming, just booming."

"Yeah, that is good, Charlie." Patricio swallowed the dry sides of his throat, rubbing them together, coughing up no moisture. "Listen, what's the chance of an old hand coming back and getting rehired there?"

Charlie looked at him, surprised. "You? Oh, Pat, that would be great, just great! You were the best back then, old boy!" Charlie drank a quick swallow. "But I'm afraid, well, the clock's working just perfectly now. I don't think we could promise anything, not at the same level you were, no, not now." Patricio answered him with understanding, quick nods of his head. "Say, you sure you doing all right out here, guy? I had heard that bricks are—"

"Oh, yes, doing fine, very well, thank you. I was just more curious than anything. And, perhaps, an itch for the city again. But then, nothing like the country out here." Patricio smiled suddenly.

"Oh, you know it. Listen, every time I come out here, I feel like I'm relaxing. You've got a gem of a home here, Pat." He pointed with his eyes. "And a gem of a wife, too. And that daughter of yours, if you don't mind me saying, she's gonna be the cat's meow when she gets older!"

"Excuse me? What did you say?"

"The cat's meow. That means, well, that she is very beautiful." Charlie chuckled.

"Oh, yes. The cat's meow... beautiful."

"Gotta keep up with these expressions, friend. They're changing every day. That's the world today. Changing so fast, it's hard to keep up with it!" Charlie excused himself and melted away to a part of the bar.

Patricio bumped from person to person amidst the deluge of smiles and laughter, slaps upon the shoulder, lapping against him, choking him like the tide. The party poured itself over dinner, taking him with it. He ate very little, picking at the delicate slices of chicken with the white sauce poured over it, barely touching the salad, chewing upon bread. He felt sweat lick down his neck and sink into his collar. The dinner passed, the plates were taken away ("Mr. Colónez, are you not hungry?" Santo's worried voice whispered from behind). People sat and talked, drank more, depleting the cabinet of liquor. Laughter and business, talk of the States, comparison of lives here, there, all swirled about him, until it brought him to the floor.

Harold Bennington, the phone company manager, lifted him by the shoulders and brought him to a couch. A woman fanned him. Someone else brought him water. Everyone crowded around him, concerned over their friend, asking what in the world could have happened. His daughter's hand went to his face, announced that he had a fever, no doubt coming down with something. "It's those damned mosquitoes here," said a guest, and explained how the insects were carrying illness, that it was happening to people who visited the countryside, just as bad as Africa.

Someone proposed that they all should leave, give him some rest and quiet. They all agreed, being the good people that they were, ready to accommodate such a sport as Patricio Colónez. They waved goodbye, wishing Merry Christmas to all the family and to one another.

A young blond man handed a wood box to Romilia. "Feliz Navidad," he said to her, and she smiled at the handsome fellow as she took the gift of North American whiskey. Patricio tilted his head to one side toward them. He watched as Harold Bennington approached the younger gringo. "Kiss her on the cheek, son." The youth did so, leaving a glittering smile upon Romilia. Then Harold leaned over and kissed her on the mouth. They smiled to each other before Romilia put her head down in a blush.

Patricio heard the cackle of automobiles start up outside, some cranked, others turned over electrically by chauffeurs, by Guardsmen that stood in the night, waiting for their bosses to come back to the autos so as to escort them on the hour-long drive to the capital. The machines crackled through his fever and sweat. He lifted his head and muttered inaudible words as he watched the crowd leaving through the door. Patricio gazed as Antonio waved his arms to the others, as the corpulent sibling disappeared through the door, carrying a wad of cash. It had all been extracted from the strongbox. Now it was stuffed deep in his brother's pants, in one tight little pile.

♒

Gloria Colónez had gone to bed in a loud huff. This was nothing novel. She had huffed all through their marriage, especially when Antonio pulled out the deck of cards, while friends and associates sat down to shuffle and deal the night hours away. Gloria walked down the corridor of their house in the capital. She passed the paintings that he had won at cards, walked by the furniture bought with gambling money, and glanced at all the mirrors which they had acquired from another poker player, a man who owned a mirror company nearby.

"Well, gentlemen, shall we play?" Antonio invited the men with the English phrase that he had learned to pronounce perfectly.

Young Gregory Bennington, the son of Harold Bennington, spoke, "Sounds good, Antonio, but not too many hands for me tonight. After that meal at your brother's, I can only handle a little. That certainly is a lovely place out there. What is your brother's name again, Tony? Oh yeah, Patricio. He speaks real good English. And you say he was head of the railroad company at one time?"

"Well, he was the manager."

"Hhm. I never heard of him, never heard of him. Back in the good old days, when the railroad was just getting started, huh?" The young blond Bennington stuck a cigar between thin lips, lit it, and poured smoke from his mouth like a youth trying to act older. He and the other North Americans loosened their tiny bow ties just slightly, enough to unbutton their shirts. "Okay, toss them babies out."

"Hey, Frank, you playing?" Harold Bennington yelled back toward an upper room of Antonio's house.

"Leave him there," said Charlie, the fourth player.

"Yes," smiled Antonio, "let him have his *puta*."

"His what?"

"His *puta*, his woman, or bitch."

"Oh, he brought her here?" asked Charlie. "Nice little gift you set him up with, Tony, old boy. She from here? Better watch out, he'll want to take her back to the States with him."

"If he wants to, I am sure we can arrange that," said the only native at the table, smiling. "We are a generous people, especially to our northern friends." He slurred out placations, his mind and body still content with the alcohol from the party.

"Hey, Frank, close the door up there. We don't want to hear your animal imitations." The door slammed shut. The men laughed and shared cigars with one another, lit them up from the young blond man's stogie. Harold Bennington displayed a large glass flask. "Hey,

Tony, you'll love this stuff. We call it White Lightning. So strong it's illegal."

"I hear it is *all* illegal in your country," Antonio said with a grin, holding the glass up as Bennington poured.

"Yeah, hell, those asshole preachers pretending to be statesmen. Hey, where did you get that from, Harold?" asked Charlie.

"From Joe. Where else? The same stuff my boy gave to Romilia tonight."

"Oh, God, Joe, yeah. Watch out, Antonio, that stuff will kick you through the window. That's just like they say about Catholics like Joe. Where you find one Catholic, you'll find a fifth."

Antonio swallowed the alcohol, then squinted his face from the burn. They guffawed. He took another. They all snatched small glasses. Their cigar smoke swirled into the lowered overhead lamp, billowed up, and ran along the ceiling to the stairs. It could not penetrate the upper room. It collected in a pocket of air at the head of the stairs, between the laughter and the tossed cards downstairs and the movements on the other side of the door. The smoke thickened between caressing and losing, winning and exhausting the more sensitive parts of a man, his mind, his zeal for the hunt. In that upper room Sofía moved as she had been taught, running one hand under a belt, the other into a back pocket. Downstairs dollar bills and colones fell like dead leaves through stale air, falling under the blatant, shadow-making light of the overhead lamp. Cards slipped under cufflinks; a dark hand unbuttoned a crisp, starched shirt. Another dark, fat hand ran fingers over the bills below, scraped them over to one side of the table, smiling, speaking broken English, "Well, perhaps the beginning of a good night, true?" Yet other cards slipped and were stored away, with concern feigned by white-skinned worriers. The movements slipped through the night, chiffon sluffing off a smooth, dark thigh. Bills slapped against the table; a wallet slipped from a thin hand and plopped against the floor. Aces and Queens slipped out of cufflinked sleeves like lithe weaponry. The hands moved quickly, running over the cards like youth touching for the first time, the excitement of winning over a gringo. Yet as the native groped for the money on the table, the hand was stopped by the announcement of three Kings, which beats your two pair, a hand as quick as the one upstairs which found the groping fingers of a native who searched for an open wallet under the bed. The cool white hand snatched that brown wrist and brought it back, holding it, chuckling low at the sly girl, then slipped her tiny wrist into a belt loop and tied it to a metal rod of the headboard, meeting her other wrist, then wrapped a sock about her open mouth like a horse's bit. *You shouldn't move too quickly* whispered the voice of the gringos as they moved over the one tied to the game, and began stripping away. *What else can you lose, my friend?* And they began whipping with Kings, with Aces and Hearts and Jacks and suspenders lashed over a dark breast. It was never said, but it was heard by all, we will teach you, we will show you, you will learn who are the masters, the proprietors of winning, the owners of the game. Sweat poured down a fattened face, burning with the illegal drink of the northerners. Many things were lost and gained, colones, dollars, then that statue, that lovely mirror over there, this fine mahogany table, then one of the horses out back, one of those beautiful beasts, *I will take the dark-brown mare.* The night drained itself quickly. One had to move, to act, or be swallowed by it, moving until wrapped and tied in the entanglement of the night itself, strapped into the game. All movement was impeded by the mistake, by the sound of the dropped wallet, the anxious grab of cards, the mistake of ever playing. The night had to end, and the foreigners, they always wanted a grand finale. That young one, the blond man, sober and dry, with his tie still neat though slightly loosened, dropped upon the table the promise of fifteen shares of his own stock in the telegraph company which his father had given him, right there, *there on the table friend, match it, match that one*, so the native did, with a brick factory out in the country. The cigar smoke found an opening through the crack underneath the door. The smoke entered the dark upper room as the only witness to the angry shadow of the foreigner forcing her thighs apart like a wishbone and dropping his weight upon a pinned, whimpering loser.

"Well, boy, what are you going to do with a brickhouse?"

"I don't know. Does this make me the *patrón* of that village out there?" The young, blond Gregory Bennington laughed as he recounted his money. "Tony, old boy, you can get me the lease before tomorrow, can't you? We leave by midday."

"Hey, boy, you aren't going to really take that, are you?" Old Charlie glanced over to Antonio as he spoke to Gregory. Antonio glanced about through storm-weary eyes. His head dropped down, looking spent and shrivelled in alcohol and sudden reality. "I mean, come on, that brickhouse belongs to his brother. Patricio lives there."

"Well, that's too bad, but that's the way the cards fell, right, Tony? He put it on the table; he must have some right to it." Gregory, appearing to be a kid with a candy cigar stub sticking from his smooth face, leaned over the table. "That's what it means to win and lose. If you play the game, gotta expect to lose sometimes."

"Yeah, but come on, son," contested Harold Bennington, "a brickhouse? What the hell you going to do with a brickhouse in this country? You'll never see it again. Come on, forget about this last deal. It was just a game—"

"A game that I *won*! And I'll be expecting that lease tomorrow morning. Goddamn, I can't believe you guys, feeling guilty for something. How the fuck you ever get money, huh? I'm sorry, Dad, but it's not right to get soft. These people know what the stakes are. If they want to play our game, then they gotta learn to take the punches." The boy again leaned into the table, sticking his thumb toward Antonio as he spoke about 'these people.' He sat back, relit his cigar, and looked about the room. "Really, Dad, I can't believe you," he calmly ended.

The two older North Americans sat with their chins in their chests, almost to the edge of sleep, their concern dissipating, as it had to be, for they had played such a game many times. Antonio groped away from the table and reached toward his telephone. Before reaching it, he fell to a basket and vomited. Moonlight punched through a window and fell onto the phone as Antonio grabbed it, the midnight light tapping against the window, reminding everyone of the time, even Frank Jones from upstairs, who doggedly strapped himself back into his clothes.

Marcos McPeek Villatoro

The clanging of the telephone clashes through the sweaty, feverish pitch of dream, of nightmare, of the boy Paco walking among the mountains, working with a *labriego*, bending down, using mattock and machete against the earth in order to cultivate it, sweating as he has done at the brickyard, then looking up to his father *Dad, we must change things, we must change them.* How was he speaking? Whose words were those? Always coming back from El Comienzo with those notions of helping everyone, of changing things around society, all the countries, the world. What is that? *I help people*, he answers his son. *I am good to my workers, you know that, Paco.* But the boy walks away, disappointed, walks down the hill into the town where there is an *alboroto*, an uprising of anger and hostility toward the store owners, just as he had read in the papers every other day, the people getting drunk and fighting, or instigated by all those communists from Mexico, from Russia. Bolsheviks, that's the problem, he reads about it all over in the papers. Is it coming this way? Like a daytime thief, obstreperous, demanding. He stares at the uprising, at the dust kicked up from raised fists and gunshots. *Will it accept me, reject me?* And yet to look the other way, toward his ranch house and its small farm, then beyond that, toward the capital. They too have left him. Not so much rejecting him, but they left him out here in the woods, in the country, with a failing factory. Failing, because those from among the Unseen looked elsewhere, looked for bricks from other companies, from the very rich up North, where everything has at least a spoonful of gold poured into each batch, even the bricks. Leaving him behind, looking elsewhere. He turns back to the small town, which has always called him their *patrón*, their owner, and they have loved him as such. Yet he knows that he will be the target when the *alborotos* come, for he is the one that they can see, a representative of the Unseen. There will be his son at the front of the line, coming toward him, telling him to change things, to change everything. There the bells ring against him, clanging, demanding to be answered. He does. Sweat stains the wood of the receiver as he leans against it, hearing his brother's gruff voice through a long night, then seeing Antonio standing before him, there in front of the ranch, looking at him with those eyes of nothingness. There he stands, the same man who breaks his manhood with an angry kick, who leaves him doubled over, then goes to find his wife, Romilia. There she enters, that strange contra-

246

**diction of darkness; for white always meant superior, whether
in cheese, in sugar, the paint upon the walls. Yet she somehow
defies that, and she has broken the prejudice of two brothers,
for they both covet her. Only one gives seed, and brother Antonio leaves his own bedroom while the *alboroto* approaches
with his son. There the voice crackles through the telephone
receiver, through sweat and fever of a dying manhood. The
message is delivered, it is all gone, brother, all gone, my name
still on the papers of the brickhouse, but I will take care of
you, come to me, you who are weary and feverish, do not
worry, you will be fine, taken care of.**

An open bottle of North American whiskey stood silently upon the
kitchen table, its handsome wood box next to it. In the adjacent room,
which led to the front door, a pistol holster dangled from a rocking
chair. Moonlight shone through the window and fell upon its leather,
displaying to the empty, silent room the words "Colt .45 U.S.A." Outside, below a hill that faced the opposite way from El Comienzo, where
a few trees protruded and fresh grass grew, a shot cracked the air,
then the night swallowed it.

〜〜〜
〜〜〜

The Comenzaños rang the tinny church bell all day, as if it were
their only gift. Under the bell another rhythm sounded, of metal
pounding metal into dressed timber, of a sweating carpenter putting
all his talents into making the best coffin possible. They all knew that,
with this, there would be change. Other things would end: the food,
perhaps even the jobs. They did not make their presence known at the
gravesite, for that could never be possible. Rather, they waited, and
listened as the workers from the ranch house, the maids and
farmhands, told of how small the funeral had been, what few people
came from the capital. "They buried him not ten feet from where they
found him," reported Enrique, with mist collecting around reddened
eye sockets. "They almost did not let me stand there, but I told them
how long I had worked for the *patrón*. I had a right. A *right*." He said
nothing of the present guards, as if it mattered little. Others did, how-

ever, telling the Comenzaños how the soldiers hovered about the visitors from the capital like armed guardian angels.

Enrique told them about Santo and quiet Cristina, how they both wept over the grave as if he had been their grandchild who had died. "Yes," he muttered, "they made up for *her* lack of tears."

"And the boy came home. There he was, a pure man now. Paco arrived some time before the funeral. He had hitchhiked. I saw him. He jumped off the truck when he saw me." It was the only time that Enrique smiled while relating the tale.

"The first thing he wanted was to see his father. He asked me, but I could not tell him how, I could not. We do not know, we are not sure..." Enrique muttered the story of how he had taken Paco to the barn where the body had been placed, where the carpenter had helped a ranch hand with moving it so that the carpenter could take measurements. Paco had stared at the cleaned body, at the two-day old gash on the left side of the head.

Paco had not turned around to the approaching motorcar. Enrique had, and watched a man dressed in black and red, with white encircling his neck, step out through the auto door that had been opened by the chauffeur. Enrique had said nothing, but had stood by Paco, waiting for the latter to react, to question. Paco had done neither, not until hearing the Castilian voice of the monsignor speaking with the *patrona*, to whom Paco had yet to present himself.

"I am sorry, Mrs. Colónez, but it is just a case of what is right. I first had heard it was murder, but some of your workers were speaking while I came around the corner, and I definitely heard them mention suicide. If so, well, Mrs. Colónez, it will just not be possible to bury him under the auspices of the Holy Church...."

It was then that Paco had turned. He watched as the *patrona* and the monsignor approached. His mother argued with a restrained, cutting voice that it had not been suicide, that one of the workers had obviously murdered her husband, and that the monsignor had a duty, as a man of God, to give him a proper burial. She had glanced ahead, had seen her son, and had silenced herself. Neither had moved toward the other. In a final moment her formality had taken hold.

"Monsignor, I would like to present to you Francisco, my son."

A Fire in the Earth

In a slow approach the monsignor had raised his wilted hand to the youth for his ring to be kissed. Paco had not followed custom. The cleric had brought his hand down like a whipped pet.

"Francisco has been studying abroad," she had said.

"Really? Where?" But the cleric had feigned no interest. Paco had answered, "In Mexico. At a state-run university."

Something then had shrivelled under the priest's black gown. "Oh. In Mexico." He had at that moment mustered angry defiance carried in a shaking voice. "No doubt you have remained ignorant of Holy Mother Church."

"On the contrary, I have learned a great deal about it."

The cleric then had stumbled through a change in conversation, saying how regretful he was over the man's death. He spoke through a raised kerchief to his nose and took a step back from the body, which had more than challenged everyone's visceral strength. They had already waited more than usual.

"Since his demise is such a mystery, well, as you can see, the Church must act carefully, you understand...."

Immediately Paco, still standing next to the corpse, as if recalcitrant to the odor, had clarified matters by interrupting, "If it is where he is buried that you are concerned about, do not think of burying him in any cemetery. Bury him in his back yard. And do not worry over the prayers. He was not Christian anyway. He was not Catholic, either."

With that, the monsignor had huffed away, mumbling in a high tone something about the lack of respect in such a young, obstinate man.

"I almost laughed, except the *patrona*, she was still there," related Enrique to the Comenzaños gathered about him. "Then she left, chasing after the priest. I guess she won him over, for he buried the *patrón*. And there they buried him, not ten feet from where they found him. And she never cried. She never dropped one tear."

♒

Romilia walked briskly through her ranch house, tore the black veil off her head and dashed it to a hallway chair before entering the

249

kitchen area. "Santo! Where is Rosa? I am sure I saw her come this way."

Santo answered, her baggy eyes not looking up. "No, ma'am, she has not come—"

"Santo, I saw her come this way, no doubt looking for you. Now, dammit, where is she?"

"Mrs. Colónez, I have not seen her. I've been preparing for the lunch all this time—"

"DON'T talk back to me. I know what you have been doing. Is everything prepared?"

"Yes, ma'am," grumbled the cook, who had been ordered to leave the funeral of her boss early in order to prepare food.

"Good. They will all be here any minute." She left the room, met Rosa coming through the front door. "Rosa, there you are. Listen, we are short of hands today, so I need you to invite the guests in and sit them down anywhere here." Romilia motioned to the large den area. Rosa stared at her, exhausted from her tears. "Santo and Cristina will bring out the dishes of food and put them here. It will be slightly informal, I think that is best, true?" she said, talking to the little girl like an adult.

Rosa pulled away and dragged herself into an adjacent room empty of people. Romilia looked at her daughter, who stared down at the table in front of her.

"Rosa, you will help me with this, won't you?"

Rosa still stared, but gave a slight nod of affirmation, her mouth still slightly dropping. Her mother walked away, slipping a small "Good" into the air.

The people arrived, the friends from other cities, and the monsignor. Rosa endeavored to greet them. After ushering a number in, she retired to a bathroom for several minutes. When she came back, her mother was in the receiving room. Romilia shot her daughter a sharp glance before walking into the den with a couple from the city who were trying to console her.

"Romilia, Marina and I want to express our sincerest apologies. We know how hard it must be."

A Fire in the Earth

"Thank you, Raphael. It has been hard, but, we must keep going." She smiled, forcing her smile upon them.

Marina, the businessman's wife, spoke. "You are so strong about it, Romilia. That is good. But you know, it is also good to cry."

"Oh, I have cried, Marina. I have cried. Do not worry. Please, may I get them to fix a drink for you? And there are small sandwiches coming soon. I will check. Please, if you will excuse me." Standing up quickly, she left the den.

Upstairs she opened Paco's door without knocking. The youth lay on his bed, his shirt unbuttoned. He stared at the ceiling. He turned and glared at her, at her disrespect for his privacy.

"Come downstairs."

"No."

"We have guests."

"They are hypocrites."

"Do not start that. This is no time for your fucking ideas! They are your father's friends."

"They did not care for him. They knew him; they made deals with him. They did not care."

"Then who did?" Her words snipped. "Your beloved *labriegos* who clung to the edge of the property? I think not. We have guests, and you damned well better treat them with respect." She slammed the door which she had held throughout the conversation and stood in the hall a moment before moving back downstairs.

More people came in, rummaging around in small, grumbling groups of three and four, dodging family members until forced by decency and protocol to say something. Several men gathered in small groups to drink and mumble about their businesses in the city, to make small deals, the funeral lunch becoming their own business meal. They talked about the loss, the gamble. They all knew. To kill himself seemed so out of character, Patricio being such a man of the world. Yet others had done the same. Antonio entered the house. They became silent. The brother walked about like a lone soldier through a battlefield at the end of the battle. He looked for a drink. His niece put one in his hand, smiling half-heartedly at him. She knew nothing.

251

Antonio dodged his sister-in-law, losing her in the small, mumbling crowd.

Several times during that early afternoon, Rosa looked up from her mourning and saw her mother smiling, at times laughing, with another person who politely chuckled along with her. She seemed to be telling jokes. There the *patrona* went, blindly sucking life from a party that lacked levity. Rosa retreated to her bedroom.

Romilia forced the continuance of the luncheon, but the crowd began to dissipate soon after it had formed. Half the people remained, talking with her, trying to console one who did not seem to seek consolation.

"Please, we want you to know we are here to help if you need us, Romilia. We may live in Sonsonate, but we can be here quickly if necessary."

"Thank you, Hugo, that is good to know. Perhaps, then, I may not need you for consolation, but how about if I need you to help us eat a large turkey meal? We have two running about in the back. Would you please come for that, too?" she smiled.

"Oh, yes, of course." The gentleman politely returned the smile.

Hugo's wife spoke up, standing beside him. "And also, Romilia, please know that we can help in whatever way, especially because of the brickhouse, and your home. If you ever need any help, you know, financially, we would be glad to be of service." She had finished her sentence as her husband pulled at her to leave.

"Financially. Yes, well, of course. But I do not think that will be necessary. And, I am sorry, but what did you mean by the brickhouse, and, and my home?"

"Oh, the loss...I mean—"

"I think my wife does not understand the situation, Romilia, and thus cannot speak upon it too thoroughly."

"I am afraid I do not understand the situation either, Hugo. What do you mean the brickhouse in trouble? Is there something wrong there?"

"I think you should talk with your brother-in-law, Romilia. It is not our position to speak. We must go now. Please, I reiterate what my wife has just said, if you need help with anything, we will try our best. Come, Sara."

Romilia showed them to the door, shutting it behind them and removing her smile as she stared at the floor before her. She turned, looked back at the dissipating party. Few people drank, not wanting to spend the time downing a round. One man held a glass, as usual. Antonio. She approached him.

"Antonio? Oh, excuse me, I did not mean to interrupt. I was wondering, could you please tell me how the brickhouse is faring? You know, your brother never told me about the business. I seem to have heard that something is troubling it. Could tell me what this rumor is all about?"

"Perhaps we should talk later."

"No, I think we should speak now."

With some hesitation, he excused himself from the other guest, and followed her to a side room.

The door closed behind them. She circled him without looking into his eyes, then stood in front of him. "First, I want to say I have changed my mind about the auto. Give me back my money, please."

Antonio breathed out heavily. "I cannot do that now."

"Well, if you do not have it with you, please get it back to me as soon as possible. But about this rumor, something about the brickhouse, and Sara said something about this, this house, my home. I would appreciate it if you would tell me, since I suppose I will be handling the business now, although I cannot find a single one of his papers anywhere, though I have not been to the office to look...."

Antonio walked to the window while she spoke, looked down at a procession of women in the village who were carrying an image of the Blessed Virgin, celebrating the Feast of Guadalupe, when centuries before the Blessed Mother had appeared to an Indian. They turned a corner. The peeling, chipped statue, perfect in the distance, disappeared with them. A fattened pig strolled behind them.

Antonio turned and looked toward Romilia who had stopped talking. She waited, staring at him with eyes that hunted down reality, wondering if this time, the hunted were much larger than she.

Marcos McPeek Villatoro

Several moments later the door to the side room opened. Many more guests had left. Antonio found his wife Gloria, and saw themselves to the door. "Wait for me in the auto. I must stop by the brick-house office," he whispered to her. In the next few minutes the final mourners escaped through the front door. Shiny, black automobiles crackled to attention and kicked dust behind them, leaving the ranch in an estranged silence.

"Rosa? Rosa, could you please come down here a minute? Oh, there you are. I was wondering where you have been. Listen, there are a great many of these pupusas left. Do you think we should save them? I was thinking about giving them to Elisa for her to take to her family in town. She has done so much work with the sewing, especially all those napkins. I am sure they could eat them quickly; she has enough brothers. There is also some uncut fruit here—some oranges, bananas—I think I will give them to her, too. Perhaps a Christmas gift, or for Guadalupe. I believe they will appreciate it, true?"

Her daughter, standing on the stairs, looked down at her. She agreed confusedly, with words that mumbled and fell like pebbles kicked off an eroding cliff.

"Good. I will take care of that. I would like to surprise Elisa with it." The *patrona* smiled and walked away, disappearing behind the door of the empty kitchen.

Rosa remained there, her hands resting upon the railing of the balcony. She looked down at the empty space where her mother had been standing and talking—her mother, older, yet still very lovely, perfect in distance. Rosa kept staring until everything fell out of focus, until the rug, the shining tile floor, the paintings, melted together.

The shattering of glass against a wall stunned Rosa back into clarity. Another shattering sound came from the kitchen, then another followed, then another, and another one yet.

The girl ran down the steps and into the kitchen. In one corner she saw the remains of an old ceramic pot, a room away from where it usually set. In another corner she saw her mother kneeling over a pile of glass shards, the remains of a crystal bowl. Rosa expected tears and heaving. She was ready to push through her own childish fears so as to give comfort to her mother. But as her mother turned, the girl saw only crimson dripping from the older woman's hands, sliding down the large shards which she wrapped tight in her palms. The woman's bunned hair had become partially undone, and a lock of hair fell over a dry, wide-open eye, partly covering over her gritting teeth. The face turned and stared at the girl, as if to shatter her as well.

Rosa turned and ran from the kitchen. In the hallway, where she fell onto the stairs and into her own tears, she felt an inhuman groan that shook the walls.

Part Two

Prologue

It was a poetic time for her. The old witch could not have asked for more. The sun, deep orange as it fell behind her, warmed her shoulders. She was thankful for this, especially in these final weak moments as she walked, almost stumbled, toward the cemetery of the little town.

She shoved her staff as best as she could into soft earth, leaned on it, and looked about. There were many more crosses than before. The wood monuments, colored in blues and pinks and whites, protruded from the ground. Some leaned to one side, while others stood more erect, the elements not yet having had a chance to work on them. She stared at them through wet, wrinkled eyes, moist from age, from the inability to take the sun as she had for so many years, all those years. No one, not even herself, knew how old she was. In some of the villagers' minds, 300 years. She had never refuted it.

She staggered toward one specific grave. The old cross planted decades ago had little left to show the earth. Both of its arms had almost rotted away and broken off, leaving only the stipe shoved into the ground, and at that, leaning to one side. She walked toward the grave quickly, as if fearing that she would not make it. Once she reached the site, she stopped, breathed heavily, coughed like an old dog riddled with cancer and tumors, then spat upon the ground just aside the grave. She spoke to Don Pablo.

"You old Indian. Got there long before I did, eh?" She smiled. Her head shook slightly from a guttural chuckle.

"Well, I always wondered whose god would die first, whose would make it. Looks like neither one, although I thought mine had a chance. Everybody believed." She coughed again, then worked the red mucus through the crack that was her mouth, past her lips and upon the earth. "No. Nothing at all like this new one that is coming. It will take everything. Every little thing. And it is coming quickly." She glanced back to the town, watched for a moment a lone Guardsman strolling on the outskirts, smoking a cigarette. "Yes. Quicker than the Devil.

"But all you wanted was your earth, old Indian. I do not blame you, I suppose."

The wind blew strong enough to push dead banana leaves across the earth. Such was the season, the latter weeks of summer, when all remained half-fresh, though without any more rainfall. The gusts flopped and shoved the banana leaves across graves, slapped them around the stumps of old crosses, tumbled them past and over that heap of bones barely wrapped in wrinkled skin, which had fallen atop the forgotten grave. Soon the heap began its first stages of melting into the soil.

A distant black angel lifted itself into the wind and floated toward the scene, ready to help with the process.

Chapter One

Paco sat next to the grave, his legs wrapped in his arms and pulled to his chest. He looked out over the meadows. On various occasions his eyes turned back to the grave, as if to make sure it had not left him.

In these first quiet days after his father's death, Paco spent three mornings sitting at the gravesite. No one dwelled upon the private land. The farmhands who had handled the pastoral responsibilities had been sent down the hill. The two milkmaids had gone with them. The house maids had also departed, looking for work in nearby towns. Doña Santo and Doña Cristina waited to the last, and left together, back to the capital. Santo had lingered about the home, cleaning, finding chores to do, as if searching in all the dusted items or under her well-used pots and pans for any remnant, perhaps a shredded cloth of the *patrón's* soul, anything to keep her there, to bring him back. She had cleaned everything, but found nothing.

Upon the small headstone only the dead man's name, along with his birth and death dates, had been scratched. Before they left, the farmhands had taken water from a nearby stream and had sprinkled it upon the fresh dirt of the grave. Tiny, strong weeds had broken through. The next rainy season would promise thick grass.

On this, his third day of visiting the grave, Paco looked behind the stone and saw a pile of well-placed rocks on the growing edge of woodland. It was the tiny grave of his failed predecessor, the dead firstborn. Paco looked down in speculation. Then he smiled, as if to laugh at some personal theory.

Over thirty days had passed since his father's death. None of the family had celebrated the first-month anniversary, though his mother continued to wear black. A quiet gathering had taken place among the

Comenzaños. Paco had participated peripherally. It did not last long. The guards had broken it up, fearing the possibility of some public uproar. During the service the Comenzaños had praised their deceased *patrón* as a man of goodness and courage, and they had recollected all the stories concerning him and his generosity. Among them, certain truths could be spoken, ones that could not be said anywhere else, concerning position, status, all the years that the *patrón* had fed them. In this reunion Paco had learned some things about his father, and he had laughed and grinned and lowered his head with respect together with the villagers. The praise had almost become a way of placating him, and he had begun to wonder if the whole ritual was for his benefit, if it would have been different had he not come. The guards had given him little time to speculate. They crashed into the room where the mourners were gathered and demanded that they disperse. In doing so, they gave him reason to stop speculating and to realize that in dispersing the people, the guards demonstrated their fear over the thriving of a cause.

Strength, however, broke down as he sat next to his father's grave.

"I do not understand," he said on the third day. The words surprised him, for he did not mean to speak. He looked about. It was safe. Yet to talk to the dead meant to relinquish the intellect, to abandon oneself to emotion. "Why, why did you do it?" His hand tried to rub the tears into his skin. "There is no reason, none at all, for a man to do that. Not now, not in these days..."

Suddenly Paco regained the recalcitrant person he had made out of himself in the early days of manhood. He pushed the tears and the emotions back within a remote area of his mind. He left the grave quickly, as if he were betraying something or someone. He did not come back, not even on the day of his departure.

Paco would not return to Mexico, because of the abrupt change in his family's finances. Though he remained in El Comienzo for a while, Paco saw little of his mother. After selling various pieces of furniture from her house to individuals in the village who could afford them, she took the cash to the capital in order to fight it out with her brother-in-law in the national courts. She was gone for two weeks. She returned, spent a day in the ranch house, looking through old notebooks left by the dead *patrón*, with her eleven-year-old daughter by her side, reading everything aloud. Twice she tried to enter the office of the brick-house, but could not, as the three guards standing post, although apologizing, did not allow her to go in. After that day of sporadic research, Romilia slept for one night in the master bedroom of the ranch, and the next morning tossed a small handful of colones to the coachman, who drove her by way of public transport back to the capital. In four days she returned, wearing the same dress that she had on when she left. She slept one final evening in the bedroom. After that, the guards came to inform her that one Gregory Bennington now had possession of this land and these buildings, and that she and her family must abandon them immediately.

Paco found them a home, paid the rent with money that would have gone to his schooling and travelling expenses. He had slept in much worse than the little house in El Comienzo, though he knew his sister had not, and his mother, not in a long time. Yet it was clean, safe, with a good, solid door, three rooms, and an unleaking roof of cool, clay tiles. It belonged to González, the man who owned the store down below. González rented it to Paco for a reasonable price. He paid for the first six months. That gave his mother and daughter time to search about for work.

Paco stayed with them that summer and worked in the coffee fields. In January, the busiest month of coffee season, he worked like a fury to fill his basket as many times as possible a day. With the increasing weight, the wicker basket bumped against his waist and the banana-leaf cord cut into his neck. When the basket was full, he poured the red fruit into a waiting sack as a soldier standing nearby watched. Then he returned to the trees. The soldiers were new to the area, though he had heard that guards had been placed in almost all the coffee plantations. "The campesinos, they work harder with a soldier standing over them," he had heard two *patrones* whispering to each other at his father's funeral. So true. The workers tore off everything from the tree limbs, sometimes even the shrivelled beans atop the tree that had seen too much sun. This they would mix with the ripe fruit at the bottom of their baskets. Paco picked and filled, and at the end of a week he took his handful of colones home, added them to the pile of colones in the drawer of one of the few furniture pieces that they had kept from the ranch house. He handed it all over to his mother, then, before leaving, asked for a small portion for his travelling expenses.

At first they protested. His sister, especially. She wept, pleading with him to stay with them. Yet he knew that he was another mouth for them to feed. Once he saw that both his mother and sister were working, and that they could bring in a modest income, he made his decision.

Romilia crossed her arms, standing before him. "Yes? And where do you plan to go? Mexico, to follow ideas, I suppose."

"No. I plan to go farther South. Or maybe North."

"How will you live?"

"I can work wherever I go. I can also teach English. That is a power that money can buy." He grinned. "I can send you whatever I make, except for my living expenses."

"Will we see much of you?" asked Rosa. He looked down at her. She was growing rapidly. Her birthday had passed recently. It seemed to him that a lovely woman was quickly emerging from the fragility of childhood.

"I am sure I will come to haunt you again." But his voice made no promises, as if to say that it was not on his agenda. "Come. Let's go visit Don Enrique together. Then I must go."

He grabbed his sister's hand, and they walked down the road to Enrique's house, which stood on the southeast side of the mound. Their old friend stood in his doorway, an almost full bottle of rum at his feet. Enrique's Sunday afternoon was just beginning.

"You leave us on a Sunday? Son, lousy time to begin travelling. No traffic anywhere."

"Well, I enjoy walking."

"Then you will have a very enjoyable day." Enrique did not move, only smiled from his leaning position. "So, where will you find your first adventure?"

"I will go to the ocean first. Then I will head east."

A Fire in the Earth

"East? How far east shall you go?" Enrique grinned, as if he knew. A little boy with almond eyes stood behind Enrique. He peered at Rosa, then turned away when she saw him. "Come here, Edmundo," Enrique gently whispered to his son while still listening to Paco.

"Oh, I will make it to the gulf. Then we'll see from there. Maybe I'll go into the belly of the northern beast. Make a little money for mother and this one." He pointed with his lips toward Rosa, who was busy spying on little Edmundo.

"Yes. I thought as much." The older man broke into an uncontrollable grin, displaying a friendly envy. "But will you come back to us someday, boy?"

"I do not know. It is difficult to plan that far in advance."

Enrique handed him the bottle and spoke while Paco drank from it. "Well, we need you here. It's difficult to say how tough life will become." He motioned to a distant guard, strolling around a corner down the block from them.

All this time Rosa had stood quietly, patiently, holding her brother's hand. Then she released it in order to catch the eye of the young Edmundo, who had shut himself into his shyness. Failing to regain his attention, she returned to Paco's hand and placed her tiny fingers into his palm. She listened, but it was difficult, for the men spoke in soft nuances and vague phrases that left her confused as to what and whom they referred to. Yet their half-statements fell from the lips of the two friends with ease, as if they had practiced for a long time.

Soon they said goodbye with a long handshake. Enrique gently twitched Rosa's nose, told her to take care of her mother while her big brother was gone. She smiled at the friendly old man, waved to him as they turned a corner on their way back to the house. She seemed content for the moment, as if she had forgotten that her brother would leave soon. When she saw her mother working in their small adobe kitchen, and placing Paco's packed bag upon a chair next to the door, memory returned quickly to the girl's thoughts, quivered through her chin, and pushed a tear from her eyes. The next moments proved nebulous for Rosa. She only felt things—the touch, the strong, warm embrace as Paco bent down and hugged her; the whispered goodbye that brushed against her ear like a caress.

Marcos McPeek Villatoro

He tried the same with his mother, but Romilia only took her crossed arms apart and patted him slightly on the back with closed fingers. "I will keep in touch," he said to her. She made no reply. She said nothing while standing at the door, watching him walk away with his small knapsack slung over a shoulder. He wore simple work clothes, a thick white shirt, old, faded blue pants, boots that his father had bought him when he was still a teen-ager. In recent years he had refused to wear anything else. He wore the same clothes for his father's funeral, standing out like a strange anomaly among all the well-dressed women and men who wore ties and skirts from the States. Romilia knew this was his way making a statement: that what he wore became a symbol of who he had become.

"Hhmph. At least now he is not lying," Romilia muttered.

She returned to her kitchen while he was still on the front road. While cleaning the formal dishware that she had saved from her previous life, she glanced out the glassless window to her right and watched her son walk up the hill in front of the ranch house and onto the main highway. She stared at the ranch as he passed it. A streak of painful lightning shot through her face.

∿∿
∿∿

"Do you smell that? Do you smell what is reeking all over the country, that sweet, sickening smell of rotting coffee beans? Do you know what makes it smell like that, why it is rotting so much? Do you know what is really rotting? Promises! Nothing but fucking promises from your government, a bag of lies that they have been feeding us for the past fifty years. They tell us to let it rot now, leave the coffee alone, because the prices are not good on the world market. So we starve to death. I'm here to ask you, *what are you going to do about it?*"

The crowd of Comenzaño men responded to the simply dressed demagogue standing before them, "We will fight. We will fight for our rights, for our land." They stamped their feet upon the dirt floor of the adobe room, stomping with the force of hunger, of anger, as if to stamp it out now, right now.

266

A Fire in the Earth

It was difficult for them to keep quiet when they left the back room of Eduardo's, the first of two bars established in El Comienzo. The other place, informally named The Other Place, stood two blocks over to the east. The Other Place had never been open to meetings such as this one. Eduardo, however, allowed them to hold their meetings, not realizing how much of a din they would create. Eduardo had worked at the brick factory in his younger years. It was Enrique, his foreman at the time, who had advised him to leave the brickyard and go into business for himself. In less than a year, Eduardo opened his establishment where he served his homemade corn and oat liquor. Later, he hooked up with beer and liquor distributors in the capital. Enrique always reminded the young Eduardo of the piece of advice he gave him long ago, and how it undoubtedly gave the impetus to his successful business. This led invariably to Enrique's request to use Eduardo's big back room for a meeting.

Several meetings were held at the bar, but not all. They knew it was necessary to keep moving them so as to not be discovered. As months passed, the meetings became heated. The young speaker brought in from another town (the name of which no one knew), set them on fire. They broke into small groups to talk about what needed to be done in their little village to bring justice to the workers. Their first goal, all agreed, was the brick factory.

After the *patrón's* death, a man had been sent from elsewhere to manage the business. He barely spoke to the workers, and had explained upon his arrival that the brickhouse now belonged to a certain gringo in the United States, whose name none of the Comenzaños could pronounce. He said that work would continue as usual, and that everyone still had their jobs. With that, he turned and walked to the ranch house, as if that were his home.

The workers realized that the new foreman had not given them his name. It also came upon them that they were making considerably less than with the *patrón*. "When Mr. Colónez was alive, I was receiving five colones more each payday. What is this horseshit pay?" All the others expressed the same angry complaints. The paymaster, a fellow Comenzaño, shrugged his shoulders. He pointed back with his thumb

Marcos McPeek Villatoro

to the ranch house, as if to say that the source of the problem now resided there.

During the meetings held in Eduardo's bar, two goals were set by the brickworkers: Their salaries were to be raised to what they were making before, and that bastard of a foreman should come out of the dead *patrón's* ranch house.

Old Enrique became their spokesman. He brought the workers' complaints and petitions to a little man who worked for the new fore-man. The latter, ensconced in the ranch house and representing an Unseen One from the North, did not respond. Again they brought up their complaints and petitions, and still, nothing happened. Their pay remained the same. After a third endeavor, when no response was made, they crowded about the ranch house, demanding that the fore-man come out and face them. He locked the doors. They broke open a window. He ran to the back. They grabbed him and pulled him through the window, picked him up and carried him on their shoulders and arms, down the hill and to the river, passing a number of guards along the way who did nothing, as they had not been paid to take care of this unknown foreman. After depositing the foreman in the river and pelting him with handfuls of rotting coffee beans torn from nearby trees, the huddle of men walked through the streets and were greeted by mass approval. Children stood on bald areas of the mound, laugh-ing and signalling to other kids who stood below them, many of them bragging that their fathers played a part in the deposition. Edmundo, Enrique's son, now a teen-ager, ran down the mound, passed a guard, and hugged his father with love and pride.

In the course of the welcomed diversion, no one noticed an old woman who shuffled by. She walked the streets as if they were vague-ly familiar to her. She stared at the groups of people, then turned away, confused. The majority of the crowd moved toward Eduardo's bar, ready to celebrate by giving the proprietor some business. The elderly woman moved in the opposite direction, toward the door of the old root cellar in the bottom of the mound.

It appeared that the cellar had been abandoned several years ago. The wood had rotted on the edges, rust coated the door handle which dangled off one nail. Around the door, where the large stones protruded as a wall, weeds and wildflowers pushed forward. She moved to push the door open, but decided against it. She knew that the weight of the door would be too much for her. She looked up to one side of the mound. Bean vines dried by the summer heat lay scattered, stripped of their seeds. Soon they would be uprooted and burned. She stared at the gnarled remnants of what once was nourishment as if waiting for the beans to resurrect. This would be as much a miracle as her returning to this town.

Silvia Córdoba Montenegro had been away from El Comienzo for a generation. Death, though she had prayed for it often, had refused to take her. She had heard that Death had taken her husband, sent away long before to a prison-plantation. She thanked God for that. She had had no contact with her grandchildren. They had been torn away from her and placed in an orphanage. A handful of years before, the authorities had released her because the prison cells were overcrowded. No need to keep an old lady here, they had mumbled while turning the key. They had no idea what crime she had committed until someone tossed the reason, "Vagrancy." An illegal practice of a time long ago. Plantations and fincas had been filled with people guilty of the vague, unlawful practice of vagrancy. It was as if more than half the population of the country was guilty of sloth. It was proclaimed for a number of years that to be lazy at a time of economic revolution was the greatest of sins. The guilty parties, when physically able, were put to work on the large farms; if unable, in small jails. Sometimes they were forgotten and set free.

Silvia had drifted after the release, looking for her husband, for Death, and finding neither. She traveled to nearby eastern cities, finding no relations there. Life said plainly that nothing existed for her outside of El Comienzo, that, outside that little village, she had no existence, no story. Yet it was her own history that had kept her away from El Comienzo, ever since the day she was blamed for the death of the *patrón's* unborn son. Since then, she had quit the practice of midwifery. Now, as she returned to her hometown, she hoped that after three decades she no longer remained on the pages of anyone's memory.

Talking with people on the streets, Silvia asked about a woman named Amanda Velásquez Hernández. One old fellow told her that she had died several years ago. Silvia asked other questions, then listened as the townspeople discussed Doña Amanda's death in connection to what they called "The Great Fall," something that evoked bitter smiles.

"What was that? The fall?" she asked.

"It was the fall of the family up the hill. Well, of course, they no longer live up there. The Colónez family. You say you are from here, old woman? Well then you must know something about them." But she did not. Her informant sketched for her the story of what had occurred a handful of years previously. She listened intently, and as the story ended, she lowered her head as if in prayer, or perhaps sorrow. Silvia thanked the man and his companions. They watched her shuffling away from them mumbling about her when she slowly turned a corner.

Silvia looked for the woman, knowing the danger implicit in the encounter. Perhaps she would meet her death there. She smiled. She looked about at the strange faces, the new buildings that were already aging. Those structures served as the tombstones of former neighbors, friends, now buried beneath a layer of earth, as deep as her own memory. As to the children, many had also escaped beneath that earth, unable to win their battle with hunger. Now other children took their places. They ran around, playing strange games, yelling and laughing and crying when they skinned their knees. The old woman asked one of the little ones, "Boy. Tell me, where does Doña Romilia Colónez live?"

"Dirty Lips lives up there." The boy pointed up the street at a little, modest house in the corner.

"Dirty Lips? Why is she called that?"

The boy looked about to his friends for assistance, then answered, "Because she curses so much. They say she curses at everything." He ran off, following his friends.

Old Silvia, with lowered eyes, began climbing the hill. At times her gaze darted upward, as if to check her final destination.

A Fire in the Earth

At the house in the corner, a woman stirred the trough of goat-milk curd with a wooden stick shaped like a paddle. She sloshed the cream-colored curd against the wooden sides of the trough, spilling a few droplets to the ground. The cheese cloth, spotted with holes and torn from use, floated in a small vat of water adjacent to the trough. The woman took it and wrung it out, then spread it over the curd, helping it to smooth out over the thickness. She wiped her hands onto her soiled apron, all the time looking down at the trough, watching it settle for a moment. Some women walked by and greeted her. She did not respond. Again she wiped those hands—gray, hardworking hands. On a dilapidated table behind the woman sat a large block of goat cheese. She turned to it and commenced cutting it into half blocks, then quarter blocks, and even smaller pieces. They were ready to be wrapped in wide banana leaves and taken to market. There was still much work to do. The cheese in the trough still needed to set, to age long enough before it was moved to the cutting table. She said nothing. She worked. Others walked by. She never spoke, as if conversation were meaningless, as if she knew some other language, one she had used most of her life in speaking to others, never with them. Yet now they were her peers, no longer her servants. She slammed the knife through the cheese. Youth had taught her the art of forgetting. Now, with age, memory revolted against her. Memory was something to be screamed away. The knife dashed echoless against the old wood table. She wrapped the cheese, tied small strings about the individual packets, and placed them in a large basket.

Romilia had kept some things. An old mahogany chair, thick with upholstery, now sat in one corner of the well-kept adobe house. To one side stood a nicely carved oak table. Hanging from a rusting nail, an intricately shaped mirror displayed the other side of the house, the adobe brick, red, dark and damp. In the desk she kept her belongings—hidden money that she had saved from the days of the Fall. She rested in the chair during the late evenings, when all the cheese was made, when the deals had been settled with the goat herdsmen from the surrounding countryside. She never used the mirror. She had demanded from a neighbor that he hang it up high so that no one could use it, not even her tall daughter Rosa.

The elderly visitor came to this home. "Hello. Good afternoon," the old woman said. Romilia made no response. "Excuse me, may I buy some cheese?"

"What? No, I do not sell it here. Wait to buy it at the store, down the street."

The ancient woman turned in the direction in which Romilia had pointed and looked down toward the market, where both of them once lived, long ago. "You would send me all the way down there in order to buy cheese, when I could buy it here?" She released the slightest grin.

"That is the way everyone does it. I do not see why you should do any different."

"Well, perhaps you would see why, if you looked at me."

Romilia turned and stared at the old woman, saying nothing.

Silvia said, "I am very old. It has taken me practically all morning to come up here. Please let me buy some cheese. I am very hungry."

Romilia sighed angrily, turned and searched about in the basket of new cheese. She pulled out a newly wrapped block. The old woman, wrapped deep in her shawl, searched about her ragged clothes, ostensibly looking for money. She asked the price. "Twelve centavos," answered the cheesemaker. The ancient one kept searching, looking in her clothes, in the old sack that she held beside her.

"I...I have very little money," she mumbled.

"What? You have no money? Ay, fuck, then why do you come here?"

"I was told of the cheese, and I was hungry—"

Another gusty breath interrupted her. The cheesemaker turned away, snatching the block from the counter as she disappeared into a back room. Soon she returned. She tossed the wrapped cheese back into its basket and held the other hand out, holding a tortilla with crumbled goat cheese and beans piled upon it. "Here. Now go."

"May I sit here to rest a moment?" The old woman pointed to a chair in the corner.

"What? I do not care."

The old woman thanked her graciously, turned away, and headed to the small, homestrung seat.

A Fire in the Earth

Romilia continued her work. At times she glanced up, as if hoping that the old one had left. She had not. She still sat in the chair, chewing over the food delicately. Romilia kept on working. Silence never bothered her, until someone else entered it. "Where do you come from, old one?"

"Oh, here, there. I have lived much time in the east. But I was born in the old city."

"The old city? So was I," Romilia responded, something to be proud of.

"Oh, really? Funny, you do not look that old."

"I was born just as it died, or so they told me."

"True? Perhaps we may have encountered each other."

"Well, I would not have remembered."

Silvia sat back, took a bite from the food, slowly chewed it and swallowed. "I remember that night. Horrible, just horrible, to see your city fall to the earth like that. And it happens so much, with the earth trembling and all. Perhaps they are correct, that there is a fire beneath us, true? But we lived on from that one; we survived. We just walked out and started our own town."

"Yes? Which town was that?"

"Oh, uh, a town, well, a little village really, farther up in the mountains."

"We did the same thing here. They told me how they started this town right after the earthquake. They did not go with the rest of the city, those who went to build the new capital. They saw this mound here," Romilia pointed with her lips toward the open door, "and decided to be on their own. My family came with them. How I wish they had gone the other way!"

"You wanted to live in the capital?"

"Yes, God, yes, that would have been good. To live there would mean everything."

"Oh." The old woman picked slowly at the tortilla, adroitly scooping the beans and cheese together with a torn-off piece of the corn meal bread, not spilling a single bean. "Would you have been better off in the capital? Would you have been rich, perhaps?"

"Rich? Hah! Yes, I would have been. I am sure I would have been. Somehow."

"How could you have been rich if you were born poor?"

"Well, it is possible." She turned to the old woman with direct eyes. "How would you know if I were born poor?"

"Well, I look about here. You are not rich now. So I say, why would you have been rich when born poor? You have a very nice place here, yes, but it is not exactly a mansion, not like, well, not like that huge house on the hill up there, where some rich guy obviously lives. And besides, what is it to be rich?"

"What is it? I can certainly tell you that. It is to be happy. I know, lady. I once was rich. I was the rich one who once lived in that big ranch up on the hill. Up there, yes, that was my ranch, it was. That is where I lived, I—" Then it was enough, too much. She turned away from the old one and found something to do behind her counter.

Still eating the tortilla and beans, Silvia spoke softly, "I know what it is to be rich."

"Yes? What is that?" Romilia did not look at her, but found more work.

Silvia held up the handful of food and smiled. "This is to be rich."

The cheesemaker turned around, with her hands on her hips. "Well, good. Then we are all wealthy."

"Ah, that is very true."

No words fell between them for several moments. With hesitancy the stranger asked, "Do you have children?"

"Yes. Two."

"Oh. Boys, girls?"

"One boy, one girl. Both grown now, a man and a woman." Romilia kept working, letting the old woman ask questions, as if out of some sense of mandatory respect towards the elderly.

"Where are they now?"

"My girl is still here with me. She has a job at the bakery now, down the street. The boy, I have no idea. Whipping the streets of some other country. I am not sure. Do you have children?"

"Yes. They are all gone. I know not where. Children do that, you know."

"Yes. I know."

"As they must, I suppose. Children must find their own riches and poverty. I know I have found mine." She smiled again. Smiles kept coming to her, almost uncontrollably.

"You are so happy?"

"Well, yes."

Romilia peered at her. "Why?"

The old woman hesitated a moment, then slowly raised up the disappearing handful of food. "Because, because I am rich now. Thanks to you."

Romilia smiled, then laughed a moment, shaking her head. She continued with her work. "It is nothing."

"No. Not for nothing. For something. Please know, it was for something."

"What is that?" asked Romilia, confused, with a hint of impatience.

"Ah, forgive me, I am old." She stood up slowly from the rickety chair, held on to her cane, and walked toward the door. "I am old and ramble like old folks do. But I am thankful for this time, for the food, for you to listen to an old woman with many sins." She smiled, but did not laugh. "Take care. God bless you."

"You too, old one. May it go well with you."

"Thank you, child."

Romilia watched her as she shuffled away, down the hill, as if she had a destination. The cheesemaker smiled. The old woman calling her "child" reached back to a vague, long-ago moment, touching the familiar.

As the sun set, Silvia circled the dirt mound several times, as many times as her elderly pace allowed. Some men on doorsteps watched, chuckling to themselves, wondering what the crazy old one was up to.

As night fell upon the mountaintops, she slightly lifted one leg to the base of the mound, taking the first step of a climb, and her hand, brown and cracked as mud on a wind-hot, April day, reached for the mound, touching with a finality the last bit of moisture in a clod of soil.

Marcos McPeek Villatoro

The next day the sun greeted her, breathless as she lay upon the mound, her face pressed against the dry limbs of the bean vines. A few of the townspeople gathered around, found her halfway up the hill, as if she had been moving toward something, seeking something that only she knew about. Her face smiled slightly. Many speculated that she had found what she was looking for. They whispered to one another, asking who she was, no one being able to answer.

They took her and buried her in a shallow grave. One old farmer made a quick, simple cross and planted it above the site. They packed the earth tight so no animals could wander about and take from it, then secured the body with large rocks placed atop it. Only a handful of people attended the informal service, as there was no priest in the town anymore, not since Father Mateo had died. Yet the dead were not forgotten, though their names had been. The rumor whispered about that she had been from El Comienzo from years passed, but no one could remember, not without a name. Several women rubbed their beads together, praying for the stranger, clicking her soul on to an ostensibly better land than theirs.

Chapter Two

No man in the world was happier than Joaquín Reyes.

Joaquín Reyes was so happy that he had ordered a Mercedes Benz Supercharged SS Sportscar imported for him all the way from Germany in order to celebrate his joy. He drove the new dream vehicle at a fast clip, slashing through the plains and mountains of the country, using these brand new highways for all that they were worth. He drove everywhere, from Santa Ana to San Miguel, with a woman whose name escaped him wrapped about him in various positions, tying him in happiness, reminding him constantly of the ecstacy that he practically was drowning in.

Joaquín was in his mid-twenties. He was in fine shape, tall, thin, with skin like that of a white man who has tanned himself most his life. Youth still allowed him to drink and eat whatever he desired. His broad smile grew wider as he left the confines of the city. It was much better to travel out here, far from the capital. In the city the guards and the police had a habit of stopping him. Even they were taken aback by his driving. Again and again they had told him, "Please, Mr. Reyes, slow down, you are too dangerous at that speed, you know that these fast autos are the number one killer, even in the States...." He nodded them away and headed for the country, with the high-pitched, smooth clicks slapping against the metal walls of the new motor. It was the best running vehicle of its time, sleek like the era. He drove from town to town, laughing, drinking whiskey while steering, smoking and popping the elixirs of levity with which he now shifted into third. He and his eighteen-year-old companion sped over various hills and valleys, with nothing to look for, paying no attention to the numerous smoking volcanoes that had helped make the country so popular with tourists. Into those mountains they entered. They circled the valleys and hills which forced them to slow down a few kilometers. Suddenly they reached the edge of the bowl which encircled El Comienzo. He pulled over and stopped the engine.

Joaquín opened the little round door, laughing as he pulled the arms of the lovely, giggling lady away from him. He pushed her back into the leather upholstery, grabbed her tube dress with a pinch before jumping out. "Wait a minute," he cooed, "hold on, I have got to pee." Placing his drink below the seat, he walked to the bowl's edge and urinated toward the village. He faced the town with a young, bright smile.

"Hey, look at that over there," he called back to his friend. "Baby, come here."

She jumped from the car and walked to his side. "What is it?"

"That house over there, above the village." Joaquín walked about, gazing left and right at the landscape. Then his eyes always fell back to the house. The woman became quickly bored and chewed her fingernails.

"Yes?"

"It is beautiful!" He kept his eyes on it, studied the view while placing his hands on his hips. He turned toward all the scenery, as if realizing something slightly profound. "Just look how lovely it is here. Do you know the name of this town?" She did not. They kept looking out. "I just cannot believe how beautiful it is out here. I mean, it is just so impressive. Let's go over there."

She protested mildly, as they had no one with them for protection in this strange village. Soon, however, he had her in the auto and drove them over to the empty ranch house.

In the distance it stood in perfection. Closeness displayed the chips and cracks of the years of abandonment. Joaquín parked directly in front of the house. A few people below, in the shallow of the bowl, looked up from their homes, gazing at the incredible machine that had driven up to the old ranch.

Only one person walked about the ranch house. He was an elderly indigenous man, a head shorter than the two strangers. The wealthy visitors could not see him, for he stood silently by the large malinche trees that grew next to the house. A pile of tied sugar cane dropped from his fatigued shoulders. Joaquín and Josefina approached the front door, knocked, then called out for someone. They called again, then a third time. Finally the old man timidly answered, "No one here."

The woman clambered upon Joaquín, straddling his legs. Joaquín turned toward the voice, so quickly that his New York riding cap flipped off. "Joaquín," she whispered with a withheld screech, "it is an Indian!"

"Calm down, it is all right, just, let me do the talking."

"Joaquín, we have no guard—"

"Just do not worry." Joaquín took one step, hesitated, then took it back as if it were an irrational move. "What, what are you doing here, old man?"

"I come to town. I go to sell cane, some sugar cane from mountain—" The Indian shuffled his naked feet together, back and forth. He stood like a rabbit held by the stare of a fox.

The "fox" pushed his mate aside and behind him. He stood tall, fabricating strength. "Why are you sneaking around this house?" The old one did not answer until the same repeated question shook something from him, *"Why are you sneaking around here?"*

"The shortest way, it is, my village, out there in the mountains, it...."

"What did he say?" asked the young woman.

"I don't know. Probably speaking one of those shit languages. But I do not think he can hurt us. I believe I could overpower him if I needed to."

"Oh, Joaquín." An exhilarant breath pushed over her sudden smile. This gave him the courage to do what he knew needed to be done. Mustering up all of his being, he began to approach the Indian.

The old man was chewing some dried leaves. He coughed heavy tuberculosis sputum from caged lungs. He rested against the bundled cane, wiping his hands upon the old, fading shirt. His face was turned away from the two youths, and he shuffled his feet again as the man approached.

Joaquín walked with premeditated steps, staring at the old man all the way. The Indian did not move, which frustrated the youth.

Joaquín expected some physical response from him, for he had heard that Indians, by nature, attacked without cause or reason. The fact that this one did not follow suit ran like ice up Joaquín's back, and when it touched his neck he shouted out, "Hey!"

"Huh?" The Indian turned quickly. His little farming machete, tied around the waistline with a thin banana-leaf string, bounced against his thigh. The sight of the rusted old blade moved Joaquín. He jumped back, then fumbled in his coat pocket for ten full seconds before pulling out a tiny palm pistol. The woman screamed. The Indian jumped. Joaquín waved the little weapon.

"Do not even move, you fucker!"

"What, what?"

"My God, shit, Joaquín, he has a machete!"

"Calm down, I can see that! What are you doing with that weapon?"

"What weapon, what? I have no—do you mean this?" He lifted the familiar blade still tied to his waist.

"Drop that fucking knife, killer!" Two shots burst out, the only two in the tiny pistol, both of which darted far past the farmer. The old man turned and ran, leaving his tied sugar cane behind as he disappeared around a corner of the ranch house.

Joaquín jumped and turned every way around him, pointing his empty gun to corners, trees, a shed, the house, a rock, the shed again, waiting for the dark one to show his face. After several jumps he stood erect and smoothed his slicked hair back over his skull.

"I, I think he is gone."

"Oh, Joaquín, he was so frightful, oh...but you, you took care of him...oh Joaquín." She embraced him. He kissed her neck twice, then pulled her away slightly.

Joaquín caught his breath. "Come. Let's go inside."

After many words he persuaded her. In a few minutes they found a window that stood low enough to look into. Though others were locked, this window had been broken open. With some work he pushed it up slightly, just enough for them to be able to slip through. He climbed in, then, with some difficulty, pulled her in. They stood in a den, musty and damp with years. They walked about, into the kitchen

A Fire in the Earth

which also stood empty, then up the steps toward the bedrooms. Two beds still remained, old and simple, but any other furniture was gone.

He wrestled her to one of the beds, and she laughed as he quickly unbuttoned the dress, bought for her at a store called Macy's in the North, all the way down, grabbing her breasts as if to squeeze juice from them. He kissed her up and down with the over-zealous grunts of a valiant knight who had just scared off a great enemy. He zipped down the slide fastener of his white riding pants, pulling it down slowly, as he knew how that novelty excited her (as she had once said, "to be at your manliness in just one *zip!*"). He covered her with himself, as if caring little about protection, as if all could be taken care of later with a douche, a wad of money, or a quick goodbye. Nothing mattered, which was the beauty of youth in this era. They laughed and touched and kissed and wetted in the emptiness of the house, in the smell of moisture and cold mustiness and mold and rat turds dropped in abundance over the floor of the little, dark bedroom.

Outside the old man had returned. He walked on the balls of his naked feet in order to approach the dropped pile of sugar cane. He had left the small work machete leaning against the malinche tree so it would not bump against him and cause a racket. He stopped and sucked in a breath as he heard a metal click snapping the air from just above him.

"Do not move."

He did not.

"Tell me, Indian, whose house is this?"

The elderly man did not turn around, but stared away, his large eyes leaning upon El Comienzo. "I do not know, sir. I do not know at all. I, I have heard that it belongs to some gringo, but—"

"Gringo? A North American? Who could that be?" he wondered aloud, as if forgetting the old man.

"It did belong to Mr. Colónez, God rest his soul. But he is dead, and it all went to some gringo."

"Colónez. That sounds familiar, but there are a hundred Colónez families in the world. What is the name of this village?"

"El Comienzo."

"El Comienzo? How quaint. Right out of some Bible story I suppose. Well, thank you, Indian. For your help, I would like to repay you. Turn around."

The elderly man obeyed. Joaquín raised the gun up higher, ostensibly aiming it directly at the old man's head, and pulled the trigger. Nothing happened save the click. Again the Indian ran off, leaving his sugar cane to sit under the peals of young, rich laughter.

"I am the Director of the Singer Corporation for all of the Republic." With that introduction, Joaquín Reyes demanded from the operator to talk with Mr. Antonio Colónez that very moment. The operator tried several times before a line became available. He turned to Mr. Reyes with the news that Antonio Colónez, he regretted to say, could not talk with anyone at the moment, as he was dead, had been dead for four months. Perhaps, asked the operator, there was someone else Mr. Reyes would like to talk with.

Joaquín paid the bill to the man on the other side of the counter. "He is dead," he repeated to the woman, who had waited at the door of the telephone office. "How lousy. But I do not give up that easily." Again Joaquín entered the office, had the operator ring the number of his lawyer in the capital. Joaquín made a lunch appointment with the lawyer for the next day.

The woman persuaded him to get in the car so that they could leave the village and return to the capital, "Where we will be among our own," she said. She slid a glance right and left upon the street. They left the town, kicking dust over it. They returned to the capital, where a party awaited them at a friend's home in the north end. They danced and drank as the stars tipped out from their empty glasses, until he had told and retold his story of how he had saved them both from a violent Indian.

He awoke in a strange bed, alone, with his clothes strewn all through the room and down a hallway. Upon the floor rested his wallet, empty of all colones and dollars he had been carrying. He leaned over the edge of the bed and picked it up, but did not check it. He had played this scene many times. "The bitch," he grumbled through a dry mouth, then turned over and fell asleep again.

The lawyer, named Francisco, called several places looking for his client, and finally found him in the north-end home where the party had been held. He reminded the young man of their appointment. They decided to met at Joaquín's house in an hour, where he explained to Francisco his fortuitous finding of the country house.

"First of all, I do not want Mamá and Papá to know about this. They would just get upset. But I want to live out there."

"What? You are crazy. What do you want to do, living out there in the country? And on a ranch? You know nothing of farming."

"Oh, that does not matter, no. You should see it, Francisco!" The young man leaned back in his chair, placing his fingers gently upon his face. "It is just beautiful out there, it really is. Yes. I want it. Let's buy it, my friend."

They parted from each other, Francisco with the promise that within the week he would have as much information as possible about the ranch house.

When they reconvened, Francisco came with a story. "Well, you will not be buying it from Antonio Colónez, for certain."

"I realize that. Difficult to buy from a dead man. But who had hold on it? Some gringo, from what I hear."

"Well, not exactly." Francisco took from his satchel two sets of papers and a book, along with his notes.

"What is all this?" asked Joaquín.

"These are articles that I procured from Antonio Colónez's office. Interesting, the people in his office could not have cared less about what I was doing there. This paper is a copy of the title of land ownership. This one is a Last Will and Testament of the man who lived in the ranch house, Antonio's brother Patricio. And this is a diary. Patricio's."

"Yes? What about it?" Joaquín lit a cigarette.

"Well, these things say who you can buy the land from. Actually, who you could have bought the land from beforehand, even before Antonio Colónez died. You see, Antonio never owned the ranch house, though he did have some stake in a brickhouse which the brother ran.

And the gringo, named Gregory Bennington, never owned the ranch either. No, the owner of the ranch is, and has always been, since the time of Patricio's death, a woman named Romilia Colónez."

"Who is she, a sister?"

"No. A wife. To Patricio. It is a vague story, but this is what seems to have happened. From what I picked up in his office, Antonio gambled everything, and made money that way. One night it all came crashing down on him, or rather on his brother, because Antonio gambled Patricio's brickhouse away."

"I suppose that is the factory that I saw near the ranch yesterday."

"I imagine. That belonged to Patricio, the brother. But he lost it because of Antonio's gambling habits. So anyway, this woman Romilia decided to fight for the brickhouse, but she had lost it, since Antonio, who had his name on the property rights, had already signed it away to the gringo. According to the people in the office, the woman Romilia had fought for everything, but gained nothing. So all she has is the ranch."

"Oh. Where do we find her?"

"At the ranch, I suppose."

"No. It is abandoned. No one has lived there for years."

"Probably she moved away, to another city. I suppose we can find her. But you will need to carry these papers. This one, the title of land ownership, has Antonio and Patricio's names, which of course Antonio lost to Bennington. It is not so necessary. But this paper, Patricio's Last Will and Testament, shows Romilia as the owner. I am sure she has her own copy." He showed Joaquín the paper, which was very short, and which stated "All to Romilia Colónez, my wife" in a curt clause. "This, I suppose, you should return to her, since it was her husband's diary. Strange, that his brother had it."

Joaquín paid little attention to the details of negotiation. "When did Patricio die?"

"About six, seven years ago. Shot his brains out with a pistol." Francisco went on, explaining the story about the loss, the tragedy of having the name of a brother who was a gambler on one's ownership papers. "Not a smart move, especially with a brother like that. I would not have trusted him with anything." He told a second story, of Antonio's own demise, just after a successful night of card playing with other North American friends. They had challenged Antonio to play a drinking game called "Stuff," to put it all down, all in one long drink, a whole fifth of the best liquor made in the Kentucky hills. Antonio had thrown the bottle back, his neck stretching the few inches that it could, like a turtle flinging a stick over its shell. He had consumed over half of it, choking as he brought the bottle down. He graciously had thanked the men for the pleasurable challenge. Fifteen minutes later, walking out of the bar for a breath of fresh air, he had collapsed into a deep gutter of Colonia Campestre, a very lovely part of town. His face was soon covered in his own vomit. He had drowned to death.

"Goodness, such a sad story. Now, where can I get in touch with this woman, her name again. . ?"

"Romilia Colónez. Probably the best thing is to return to El Comienzo. People there can tell you. Then you can meet her, see if she is interested in selling it. Perhaps, since she does not live in it, she would be open to selling. But from what I understand, she loved that place. Most of this journal is in English, but there is some Spanish. At one point he wrote something like, well, here it is, right here. 'She loves this house more than she does me.'"

"Hhm. How much is it worth?"

"I do not know. Depends upon the size. According to the will, it has about forty acres. With a ranch house and other buildings, around twenty or twenty-five thousand colones."

"Oh. Yes, I think I can manage that." The interested buyer smiled.

The speeding roar enveloped them so quickly that the nearby Comenzaños had little time to hide from an ostensible attack. Then they saw that it was the sleek Mercedes that had kicked up the April dust. Questions and rumors began circulating, especially when they saw where the incredible auto was parked.

Romilia cursed aloud as she covered her newest cheese, not realizing at the moment that the automobile had stopped in front of her adobe house. The young man looked about the house, at the hard mud walls, then stepped in. Romilia coughed and let out two curses. She demanded an answer as to why this stranger had entered her home without permission, but stopped when she looked through the settling dust and saw his fashionable clothes. "Yes? May I help you?"

"I do not think so. I am looking for Romilia Colónez."

"I am she."

"Who? You?"

She walked from the other side of the counter to the front, placed her hand out before her in an unforgotten, practiced fashion. "Yes, I am Mrs. Romilia Colónez, at your service." He took the extended hand with clumsy, confused fingers, and quickly dropped them.

"You are the one who used to live up there? In that ranch house?"

"Yes."

"Oh, well..." He mustered up from his confusion some sense of negotiation. "I was wondering...well...I want to buy it from you."

"What?"

"I want to buy your ranch house."

She stood perfectly still. Her hand went to a table that stood in the middle of the small room. She looked at him, then slowly asked, "I do not believe I know your name."

He answered defensively, as if there was no reason to identify himself to her, a woman of the working class stature. "Joaquín Reyes."

"Ah. Very pleased to meet you. Now, why in the world would you want to come all the way out here to El Comienzo just to buy some country ranch house?" She smiled.

"If you need to know, I like the area. The ranch is very lovely. So I want to buy it." He spoke like a youth, one accustomed to having his Christmas list filled. She smiled in appreciation.

"And what makes you think it is for sale?"

"Well, no one lives in it. It looks like it has been abandoned for years. And since it is yours, and you do not live in it, I thought you would want to sell it."

"Yes. Yes, it is mine. And yes, I might be interested in selling it. I am sorry that you cannot see it, however, because, well, because—"

A Fire in the Earth

"I have seen it already. I want to buy it. How much is it worth to you?"

It took some endeavor to force back a gleeful smile, but she tried on a face of serious business. "Six-thousand colones."

He grinned, saying nothing for a long moment, then offered, "I'll give you four."

"Hhm. I am sorry, but it is worth more. I must stay with six."

They debated like two people buying a chair or a table. Several moments passed, an extended period of time that seemed comfortable for them both. Then they found the price, 5,400 colones for the house and property.

"Fine. I will be back tomorrow with the money and my lawyer." He quickly shook her hand and was gone. The Mercedes pulled out of the dusty road and skidded onto the main highway, then left the town with a distant roar.

Money and a lawyer. The latter shot through her, a laceration of truth and fear, that the lawyer, no doubt a sharp, intelligent man, much more so than this money-packed kid, would find out the truth. A lawyer would discover that she had snatched at an opportunity to take this man's money for something no longer her own. She turned back to her cheese trough.

Money. Fifty-four hundred colones. An opportunity, given over by a life that had slung her about on a tenacious string, slapping her back and forth just before she could see the edge of some irredeemable cliff. Yet somehow she had never seen that edge, the one from which her husband had stumbled off. That would not happen to her, she swore that with her silence, even though she had been tossed out of that ranch house, the tabernacle of her life, and had been kicked about on the floor of the earth. No matter, for now the string had been pulled in the other direction, and hope was within reach. With the money, she could leave this house, buy some land, move into another home, some-thing better, more spacious and accommodating than this adobe tomb which her son had insisted upon. Fifty-four hundred colones would drag her up into a higher status, pull her out of the bowl of this vil-lage, away from those who passed by her home asking for handouts, for a tortilla with just a morsel of beans. It had gotten around, the day that she had helped out some strange woman who had walked through town, giving her a tortilla with beans and cheese, a whole meal, free of charge. From then on others had walked by, tucking away fear of her anger and caustic words, squirming through in order to receive something to eat. Fifty-four hundred would take her away from that.

She wrapped her cheese. The thought of the man, his youth and beauty and wealth, told her what she had believed in all these years, that, yes, the ranch house was hers, as it always had been. More important, Reyes believed it. Romilia's sureness became almost indestructible as her daughter Rosa walked through the door after her day of work at the bakery. "Hello, Mamá," she said, kissing Romilia on the cheek. She walked with the posture taught her by her mother while still a child, straight and tall and so very light, that white rose of Romilia's hope.

"Rosa. Tomorrow, I want you here. Explain to Doña Marta that you are needed at home. We are having guests, and I want you to wear that red dress that hangs over the back bed. Press it tonight; get it ready for tomorrow." The girl questioned as to what guests, who would visit them, who was so important that it was necessary to wear such a dress from the past.

"Someone wants to buy the house." It was not necessary to explain which house. She began to tell her all—of the young man, the fifty-four hundred colones, of him coming back tomorrow with the cash, "Yes, with *cash*, girl!" While she spoke, a smile bloomed over the mother's face, and from that bud of happiness a river, excited and continuous, rushed out, a flash flood running through town, collecting the debris of a past life. It rushed over the daughter, washing her onto a strange, unknown shore.

"Mother, we can't sell the house. It is not ours."

"You *cannot* say that! It is ours as it has always been!" Romilia turned away. "Taken away from us without our knowing it, by that rich ox of a brother-in-law living on bags of riches in the capital right now as we sit in this shack! He has tried to make us the forgotten ones! That was his idea, I know!" She put her head down, as if to cry. As her daughter approached to offer comfort, she recoiled, a touched serpent. "We will have that money. We do not have the house, the land, all snatched away.... We will have that money. And you will go along with this, you will act assured that it is ours tomorrow, or you will just be silent. Rosa! We will be paid for our suffering. I will be damned if I let this pass us by. Fuck it that we sit in the filth of this village and rot forever."

Their afternoon changed to evening. That night, in the darkness of their home, Rosa heard that rich voice which hovered about the candles, whispering out of desire, memory, those words which she had not heard in several years. The voice of experience, of how to speak correctly, those phrases, to say them over and over again, "How do you do. Very pleased to meet you. May I offer you something to drink? We have little, but something refreshing, please sit down, please, sit down." Practiced, spoken in a whisper while washing dishes, mending the dress, or resting in bed, phrases never used down here in this village, that never needed to be used, but pulled out like an old uniform from a chest. Placed back on, it fit, they fit, all those words. They fit the curve of her mouth still so perfectly. She said them in the same lovely way. Those years had not taken them away from her, not those precious words that represented her existence.

〰〰

Joaquín and Francisco arrived at the cheesemaker's home the following midday. Romilia greeted them in her finest. She had cleaned the house all morning, had concocted fresh fruit drinks and had left them in the coolest shade of the building. Little candies that she had ordered, some cakes that she had bought, sat upon an old plate from their past life. She smiled and talked carefully, introduced her daughter, Rosa Colónez y Velásquez, and while she spent many words on the lawyer, who unfolded a portrait of numbers of the past six months, Joaquín kept his eyes upon Rosa. The latter periodically glanced toward him, then turned away to stare at an upper corner. She had been stared at before, by the men of the village. She had learned to walk on, to ignore. This man's stare, however, seemed different. Perhaps it was the blood that pumped through them, or his head wavering back and forth like a soccer ball that had rolled into a ditch. His previous night's levities had yet to wear off. Romilia and the lawyer spoke amiably. She asked Francisco questions concerning various families that she had known in her earlier life, and she conversed with the smiling attorney as if she still kept in touch with those people. Joaquín turned his head from Rosa to Romilia, and suddenly blurted out from the woven chair where he was hunched,

"You her daughter? You are so white. How the hell you come from an Indian?"

It brought down a sledgehammer of silence. Everyone looked about different ways, including Joaquín. Francisco cleared his throat, then began with the business.

The story spilled out upon the small table before them, in that little pile of papers that the lawyer had organized the day before, of names, places, of boundary markings down to the final meter, stretching toward the south hill, all the way to the east, to the edge of the land of the brick factory. He explained that there would be no need to worry about the percentage of payments on the acreage, since it would be in cash—she smiled almost uncontrollably at that—yes, he repeated, cash for it all, "not good for the market, you know, since credits and percentage on payments always keeps the economy progressing toward the bigger banks in the States, keeping us in the best competitive bracket, especially at seven percent on the dollar. But then, I know Mr. Reyes, he likes his deals in cash." He talked on, barely touching upon that problematic tragedy of the gambling, which he glossed over with a quick condolence. Then he explained how it would not affect this deal. Then those other names, how they had changed over, all had changed, and now, "all you need to do is sign this, right here." She heard little of it, the confusion. Fear kept her from responding, questioning, knowing something incorrect would fall from her lips, that the lawyer would have known she did not really own it. Her signature, however, he wanted her signature, and she could do that. She had learned it from her late husband, how to sign her name. He had taught her in the earlier years of their marriage, writing it over and over again so that she could see what she looked like in print. It had been something prestigious, a must for a woman of her status, and she signed it proudly. All the while the lawyer spoke, telling her of all the

A Fire in the Earth

complexities, but how it all worked out, and this piece of paper that she now signed took care of it all, as she had signed it all over, and they were so happy to do business with her. The lawyer reminded his client to pull out the cash and hand over the fifty-four hundred colones.

"By the way, Mrs. Colónez, I want to say that I am sorry about the death of your brother-in-law," mentioned Francisco.

"What? My brother-in-law? Antonio?"

"Yes. You did know that, did you not? Oh, you did not...I am sorry, I did not mean to shock you..."

"No. I knew nothing about it. How did he die?"

"Well, it was an accident, I believe. His heart."

"Hhmph. Well, I should do something, I suppose, for Gloria, his wife...I cannot believe no one told me."

"Perhaps some miscommunication. But it is good that you knew about your land. I had heard, well, I was not sure whether or not you knew, how much Antonio had told you..." The lawyer stumbled, looking for the correct words concerning mourning and the financial loss of the disheartening gambling situation. "But you certainly had a very intelligent husband, Mrs. Colónez. It is good that he left all of it in your name in his will, so even if you did lose the brickhouse, you still had—"

"What?"

"Your husband, it was good that—"

"You have a copy of Patricio's will?"

"Well, yes. The original, actually."

"From where?"

"Well, from the files of your brother-in-law."

"May I see it?"

He showed it to her, and although she could not read it, she looked for those familiar words, Patricio Colónez, those which she had learned to read. There they were, in the jumble of hieroglyphics that she looked over as if staring at a foreign palimpsest. There too she saw her own name.

"Antonio had this?"

"Yes. It seems to be the original, so I supposed that you had the copy."

"I, we had looked all over for this. No one knew where it was. Antonio had told me that he did not know."

"Well, whatever the case, it was good that you already knew about your ownership," responded Francisco, smiling, knowing that the transaction had been made in a courteous, fine manner. "By the way, Mrs. Colónez, why did you move out? It is such a lovely home."

In the following moments the guests found themselves leaving very quickly. Joaquín, who had stared at Rosa all through the meeting, threw a handsome smile at the young woman as he and Francisco boarded the Mercedes. The grin fell upon her like wire mesh. Rosa tried to shake it off, as she was very busy holding her aging mother who had doubled over from some inner jolt of pain.

Chapter Three

A large truck, most undoubtedly from the capital, pulled through El Comienzo. It entered from the southwest. From its bed dangled a few hitchhikers, holding on with hands and feet pushed through the wood railings of the grated walls. There was no room inside the bed, which was stuffed with pine and oak tree saplings. The hitchhikers tried to name the little trees during the trip, but could not, as they had never seen these kinds before. They guessed that the saplings were probably a gift from the North, for the Holiday of Trees was almost upon them.

The truck coasted down the hill into town. It turned right at the corner, just in front of the mound, then passed the house of the town carpenter. The carpenter, named Leonardo, waved. He stared at the railings of the truck, since he, a week previous, had helped the driver renail several dilapidated planks back upon the bed of the vehicle.

As it circled the mound the truck slowed, looking for a certain road to take to a well-known diner. At a turn it passed a lone man, walking in the opposite direction. The driver waved, but the individual made no response. He only looked at the truck as it passed by him and stared at its contents, ignoring the hitchhikers as they randomly sluffed off the side of the vehicle.

Hermes Alarcía held his eyes upon the tree saplings, then turned his head to other tiny trees that had been planted along the roadside last year. They had not grown one finger's worth, had burnt up during the dry season from lack of rain. Trees of a northern, foreign land could not adapt to such tropical climates. He did not bother to shake his head. It was all so ludicrous that he saw no point to it.

Hermes was walking home from an afternoon of work, though no doubt the morning still dwelt in his head like a sickness. Earlier he, his wife Marta, his daughter Lupe and his only living son Pedro had gone out to visit the grave of their oldest child Rubén, who had been murdered by a youth named Culebra in the root cellar of the mound several years previous. Marta had dressed in black, as customary. Lupe had followed suit. The boy Pedro, who was four years old when the incident occurred, had worn his best suit of working clothes, which his mother had cleaned and pressed the previous day. Early that morning they had all walked together in silence to the graveyard that stood east of their home. Marta had strung wild roses around a circle made out of a stiff vine, and had placed the crown of flowers upon the arms of the cross that marked the grave where Ruben's broken bones lay. They had prayed the rosary, with Marta leading it. Afterwards they had walked home, beginning their working day.

Sometimes Hermes could remember who he was, what kind of man he had been when his first boy was alive. Glimpses came to him like sunlight spraying behind thick September clouds, a shaft of memory about rights and justice and working for the good of the whole community. Those had been fervent years. He had worked a great deal with the incipient moments of the cause that many others had, since then, joined. Sometimes he remembered that fervor. Then something would change, the wind would blow, or the smell of rain in the air would make him forget everything. He would turn his head toward the cemetery to see a child of ten jumping from one grave to another. The boy played soccer with an invisible ball. Periodically he bent over a grave and tried to coax up another resident of the earth to play with him. Through the many seasons Hermes watched this, stopping his work to stare as the boy pulled another child from the dirt—the one who died of diarrhea; the baby girl, the one with the dirty blonde hair and crossed eyes who had passed away last month. They all played together, the various children and an occasional adult who would finally, after much coercion, come up from the ground and join them. Such sights were as rain falling upon the thick dust of a dying season, and they could not be hindered by memories concerning what type of a man he had been some years before. Best, he knew, to forget, and watch the dead children play.

A Fire in the Earth

Hermes walked home, his day of cultivating newly planted coffee trees finished. After the large truck passed by, and its odor of burnt oil and dust dissipated, he smelt the warmth of new sweet bread. It was Tuesday. His wife Marta was busy baking bread which would be sold tonight in their bakery. This, the major portion of their income, meant that he and the family would be busy, putting out the bread, selling it all before nightfall. This also meant that the new helper would be there, the hired hand, Rosa Colónez. Colónez. He blew out a burdened breath, as if weary of so many memories.

♒

"Sergio is not just any teen-ager. I want you to know that right now. He is a serious fellow, and thinks a great deal about many things. You should hear him at night, the way he talks, he uses such words. He will be a great man someday, I believe that. He talks to me so seriously when we are together. He has such things to say!" Lupe's pride spoke of her man while working with Rosa in the bakery.

"So is that what you two do at the river," responded Rosa, "talk all night. Goodness, how boring. I think I would find at least a few other things to do." Lupe slapped her friend on the arm. "Ay! Careful! You will make me drop this bread, and then we both will be in hot oil with your mother."

Lupe's mother, Doña Marta, stood at the dome-shaped, clay oven, pushing the coals deeper. The two girls stood with the stacks of shaped bread, all in various trays, waiting for Marta's word to bring them on.

"So I take it that you and Edmundo have many things to talk about while at the river?" asked Lupe.

"Oh, we find things to...talk about." They both giggled until Marta interrupted them.

"All right, girls, stop your chatter and bring me some bread."

As they carried the bread to Marta, Hermes walked in. He greeted them quickly, then put himself to work carrying the trays. A number of children gathered at the front door, all of them holding baskets of various sizes. "Later on, kids, later on. It is not ready yet. There will be plenty, just come back later, when the sun sets." Hermes shut the

295

front door then returned to helping the women. "Where is Pedro?" he asked.

"I suppose he's out working with the carpenter, where he always is at this hour," answered Marta. Her frustrated response reflected how many times she had answered that question in the course of their marriage, and how tired she was of it. Marta was a quiet woman, yet firm about her work, her baking, and her ability to keep account of how much they made from the bakery. Though Marta's capacity for joy was partly lost since the murder of her first boy, she still managed to smile from time to time during a normal day. She laughed with her daughter and Rosa while shaping the dough into loaves. Though life, work, and the loss of her son had aged her, her smile still made her lovely. She also allowed their son Pedro to grow up, giving him more freedom to walk through the world than did his father Hermes.

"Are those other two still working over there?"

"I have no idea, Hermes."

Hermes handed her two trays of bread and looked at her as she placed them both on a large wooden paddle. She slid the trays into the clay dome. He turned to find where the two girls were. They stood in the back of the kitchen, stacking trays. He turned back to his wife. "I wish he would find work somewhere else." Marta said nothing, as she had heard the arguments before, several times, since 'those other two' had begun working with Leonardo, the carpenter.

In that moment old Enrique walked by. He turned as if to walk into the bakery, then heard the clash of trays falling upon one another. He knew this was not a good time. It was questionable if any time was good for him to stop in the bakery, as Hermes cared little for Enrique's company. For Hermes, Enrique was as popular as 'the other two' at Leonardo's shop.

Enrique moved on, and walked to the carpenter's home to sit awhile before the sun set. He walked around the mound and to the south. He approached in silence an ongoing conversation that was going on between Leonardo and three young men: Edmundo Lazo, Enrique's son; Sergio González, whose father owned a large store on the west side of the mound; and Pedro Alarcía, Hermes' boy.

A Fire in the Earth

Edmundo was still as shy as in the days of his childhood, when he would hide from Rosa while Enrique spoke with Paco, Rosa's older brother. Edmundo now worked on finishing the lid to a coffin. He smiled a great deal, as if pushing through constant timidity.

Sergio was much taller than Edmundo, and rarely smiled. A serious demeanor always shadowed his face, as if he were constantly thinking of worldly problems, ones which he needed to solve. His father was the proprietor of the biggest store in town. Sergio always brought a handful of small candies imported from the capital to the carpenter's shop.

Pedro Alarcía was the youngest of them all. He spoke little, as he did not have the vocabulary that his older companions somehow possessed. He listened intently. At times he glanced out the open window to see if his father Hermes, who disapproved of his boy's presence here, was leaving the bakery and coming up the road.

Their conversation deadened as they heard the easy knocking on the door. Once they saw who it was, the three smiled with an air of relief. They all shook hands. "What are you carrying between your paws, old man?" asked the carpenter.

"I do nothing wrong. I am but a poor, ignorant farmer."

"Yeah, right. Have a seat, comrade."

Leonardo's wife made some coffee and brought it from the back of the shop. The conversation resumed quickly, as all the men, except for young Pedro, knew the subject matter well. Pedro stood and worked, planing a board, listening intently to their fervent, intellectual statements. They talked about the state of life, the incidents of a previous meeting, the number of guards present in town, and what they as citizens, as patriots, had to do. Sergio and Edmundo leaned against the half-finished coffin. "Papá," asked Edmundo, "when will we begin to take this to the mountains?" He grinned, a wide-eyed boy ready to play a man's game.

Enrique smiled. "The best time is now, I say. Best, that is, to be in the mountains rather than here. Safer there, when you are speaking about the guards. But here, well, I am careful these days on how I talk, how I walk. There are many more ears than before. And it is because of what happens on the hill."

They all agreed. Something was occurring up on the hill, on the abandoned ranch house, though they were not sure what. They had heard the din of construction for several weeks, and had seen in a glance a large framework encircling one corner of the site. One day a man, no doubt a newly hired foreman, had arrived at Leonardo's shop and had asked him if he would be interested in working as a professional carpenter on the new project. Leonardo had declined the offer, saying that he had enough work to do already, since he was the only carpenter in town. The man, somewhat annoyed by the refusal, left Leonardo, telling him nothing of the project. Since the work on the hill had begun, more guards had come into town. Whenever the new owner of the ranch happened by, which very rarely occurred, more guards appeared on the streets. The connection was easy to make.

Enrique continued. "I would not be too concerned with going out and 'preaching the gospel' right now. The mountains will be set on fire soon enough. You two boys should be thinking more about other important matters, such as your women, who are baking bread now." Enrique's gringo-bestowed blue eyes twinkled bright upon Sergio and Edmundo, as if hoping the friendly warning would be respected.

To that, Edmundo smiled with embarrassment, but Sergio made no move to change his serious demeanor. "Why do we wait?" asked the latter. "The more guards that come, the more reason there is to organize, to prepare."

"Yes, but if you do too much organizing now, or if you are too loud about it, someday you will not wake up to organize anymore. You have to be easy about it now, boy. Listen to what our comrades say when they speak with us. They tell us to follow tactics and to be—"

"I know what our comrades say. They say to get ready now because it is becoming worse; the fucking landowners are squeezing the life out of our people. We should be doing something now."

Young Pedro kept his eyes on the speakers, fascinated, so much so that his hands had planed far too deeply into the board and he stood in a pile of long, thin, useless chips.

Sergio's serious anger roused an enthusiasm in Edmundo. "Yes Papá. Sergio is right. We should prepare more now. Look, do you see what Leonardo has us make all day? Coffins, no bigger than this one, just for the children out in the fields. We have to act now."

Enrique looked at them both and saw that they waited for some response from him, being one of the local leaders of the cause. "Yes. I do not disagree. Only, we must be careful. Sly, in a sense. You understand what I mean, right, Leonardo?" The quiet Leonardo nodded in affirmation. "You boys are no longer boys. You are men, and you are active men. That is good, for we need men such as you. And that is why we do not want to lose you so early in the struggle."

The two young friends, invulnerable in their age, brushed the concern aside with more debate on the struggle itself, about what they had been taught in the meetings by the intellectuals who came and spoke with them.

While they talked, someone walked by, an old man with a bundle of sugar cane tied upon his back. Leonardo waved to him. The Indian waved back, balancing the huge load with his other arm.

"Who is that?" asked Enrique.

"Some Indian from nearby. I do not know his name."

"I think he does a lot of trade at the bakery. He trades his cane for some bread. I see him sometimes when I am over there," said Sergio.

"I wonder if the bread is ready," pondered Enrique aloud.

"I do not know if it is ready, but I am," said his son.

Pedro, for the first time, spoke up. "Oh, yes, it is almost ready and...oh, I told Mamá I would help her this afternoon. May I leave, Don Leonardo?" The carpenter shook his head, giving his consent, and the boy ran off.

"Best he leave, before he shaves all my wood into kindling," said Leonardo.

Enrique called his son. "Well, Edmundo, why don't we go out for something sweet. But not necessarily bread. As I said, you and Sergio should spend more time with those girls."

In the next few minutes all four men decided to take some of the afternoon for rest, and walked together to the bakery, where they hoped some fresh coffee and bread would be ready.

A significant amount of the population gathered around the door of the bakery, most of them children who had been sent by their mothers to buy basketfuls of bread. Enrique watched the old Indian who had passed them by earlier. The old man rested against the pile of sugar cane he had dropped by his side. Hovering over the children and the women stood Hermes, smiling at them all, telling the little ones to wait their turn. Upon seeing the Indian, Hermes grinned even wider, then told the children to make a path for the weary traveler who had come a long way carrying a large load.

"Will we receive such a welcome?" asked Sergio sarcastically, knowing the answer.

"I doubt it. You know how he is," answered Edmundo.

"Do not be too rough on Don Hermes, boys," said Leonardo. "He has seen too many things in his life, and has lost a great deal."

Enrique added, "Yes. He has reason for his bitterness. But I only wish, well, if he could just separate his bitterness from the needs of the people. Life sometimes weighs heavier on some than on others. But we are paying customers. He will not turn us away. He is a gentleman. Come now."

The four gently pushed their way through the crowd of children and found the small area of the bakery where some chairs and two tables stood. When Hermes came from the back of the building, he turned to the four men and, without smiling, spoke to them with some congeniality. "Gentlemen, what can I get you?" They ordered coffee and four pieces of bread. In a few minutes he brought what they ordered, then turned away. Enrique watched Hermes as the latter entered the back room. Hermes had smiled again. Enrique knew that Hermes was speaking with the Indian.

Edmundo and Sergio looked about and whispered to each other about how they could get in the back room to see the two young ladies. "Perhaps," said Enrique, "you should carry sugar cane in from the countryside. That could be your ticket to the back room."

"Come on," Sergio suddenly said to Edmundo, and he got up from his chair. Edmundo followed as his friend approached the door to the back room, then stopped next to a post and looked in. There sat the Alarcía family—Hermes, Marta, Lupe, and Pedro. Rosa Colónez was also standing, and sitting down upon a tall stool was the Indian who smiled as he talked in broken Spanish with Hermes. The conversation ended when the two young men came to the door. Looks were exchanged: Lupe smiled modestly at her lover Sergio. Rosa beamed brightly toward Edmundo. Pedro smiled with nervous excitement, mixed with a good deal of anxiety, noticing the presence of his friends in the kitchen. Hermes only looked at the boys, then he quietly asked, "Yes? How may I serve you?"

With some hesitation, Sergio spoke. "Don Hermes, I was wondering, well, if you need anything from my father's store. A new load of flour has just arrived, and I wanted to make sure that you received your amount before it was all sold. I can have it brought to you tomorrow. I can bring it myself, if you like."

The master of the house answered slowly, "Yes. I could use some. How much do we need, Marta, two bags? Yes, two bags. But I can get it, you do not need to—"

"It is no bother, not at all, for me to bring it."

"And I can help him, Papá. I will help Sergio tomorrow." Pedro stood in readiness, as if it were necessary.

Hermes answered, avoiding a confrontation in front of so many people. "Ask your father to hold two bags for me. Thank you, Sergio."

Sergio would not leave the post, waiting for something else to occur. Nothing did. He still felt captured by the moment, until Hermes, who had gone back to speaking with the Indian visitor, turned once again to the two youths. "Thank you, gentlemen."

Edmundo turned, pulling at Sergio to follow him. The latter responded, and returned with Edmundo to their little table. "He hates me," said Sergio.

"I wouldn't disagree."

I do not understand him," Sergio mumbled. "I have heard about his past, and I know it is difficult. But still, why do we get blamed?"

"Keep working on it, boy. Slowly," responded Enrique. "If you persist, you will soften him. Old men like ourselves are known to crumble. And perhaps you will go all the way someday and be that man's son-in-law."

"Yeah, sure. If he knew that his daughter and I are now—"

"I said he may be old and soft, but not stupid. You think he does not know? Boy, you are blind!"

301

Marcos McPeek Villatoro

"Now, now, Enrique, blind with love," said Leonardo. "You suffered from the same disease once yourself." He stood up and walked to the counter to pay the bill. Marta came to the counter rather than Hermes. She looked over at the table as if to remind herself of what they ate, then quoted a price. Leonardo already had the exact amount ready for her. Again she looked over at the table, waiting, saying nothing. Sergio happened to turn around, and she cast a motherly smile at him before turning back to the kitchen.

"Perhaps she will be your saving grace, boy," said Enrique. The four men left the little bakery. Enrique turned to his son. "And maybe you too will have good luck with the deposed princess." The shy Edmundo only smiled in humiliation. "Of course, you would have to confront Queen Doña Romilia before trying."

〰〰

"But, what do you all talk about during those meetings?"

Pedro Alarcía followed Sergio, who walked back to a rear room of his father's establishment where provisions from other towns were stored. He unlocked the door, pulled the hinge back, never looking at Pedro. He asked, "How is it you got to come here today, that your father let you?"

Pedro smiled. "My mother. She reasoned with Papá, told him that he had too much work to do, and that she needed the flour today. So it made sense that I come get it, since I am her helper."

Sergio then turned to him, almost grinning. He looked into the storage room and walked to where the flour was stored. "Well, we talk of many things in the meetings. Why do you need to know?"

"Because, because I want to help. I want to be a part of it."

"I don't think your father wants that."

"Do not let him bother you, Sergio. He has many things in his head. You know he has not been the same since my brother died. Listen, I am almost a man; I am old enough. I am eleven years old; I am a man. I want to be a part."

Sergio worked with the bags. He glanced up through the window in the bin, looked to see if anyone approached. He turned to the

302

younger boy, who stood like a puppy waiting for food. "Do you know anything at all about the meetings?"

"I have heard, from others who also wish to join, my friends, they think, well, they have heard that visitors come, that they are, communists and—"

"Quiet...careful, shit...what else do you hear?"

Pedro looked out the window too, then whispered, "Is it true? Are they really?" He asked with a tone of hope.

Sergio sighed out a weight of air. "We never use that word, understand? We are talking about too many other things to be concerned about labels. We talk about helping people, especially the poor out in the mountains, those who are starving to death because landowners have sucked away all the land, and the rest of us who have to live in fear because of the rabid dogs who run around our country now, who have been hired as watchdogs for the rich, and how we need to change that, we need to take the land away from the rich ones and give it back to those who really need it." Sergio stopped himself, ceasing his enthusiasm for the moment, and looked out the window again. "That is what we speak about. That is what is important."

"Yes. Yes! I want to be a part of that, Sergio. How, how will we bring all that about?"

Sergio lifted up one large cloth bag of flour and dropped it onto the younger man's shoulders. He took the other one and closed the door to the bin after they stepped out. "Come. We have time to talk."

Both of them walked out onto the street. The store that Sergio's father owned stood on the far side of town from the bakery. When they reached the west end of the mound, where the old, abandoned root cellar stood, they dropped the bags to rest on the cellar's steps. Again Sergio began, "There are many plans being made, but no one is sure of which one to take. Some people say to wait, wait, that the time will come soon enough. But others, we are ready to do it now, and...and that is why I think we should play the soccer game over on the field behind the church instead of near the cemetery. There we will have smoother ground."

"What?"

Sergio barely motioned with his eyes to the approaching guard. Pedro turned around, sucked in air, then regained a youthful composure. The guard passed, barely nodded to them, and went on.

"You have to learn how to talk, Pedro. To talk and not to talk. Else you will lose your balls." Sergio pulled two rolled cigarettes from a pocket, handed one to Pedro, lit them both.

"Where did you get these?"

"The benefits of having a father who owns a store." He puffed then spoke again, "Listen, you have to be ready to drop whatever words you are saying whenever one of them approaches. Or if someone you are not sure of approaches. It is a dangerous time, according to comrade Enrique. We are careful where we have our meetings these days, and we have made them smaller, easier to dissolve and scatter if the moment comes. No more yelling in the meetings, like before. That is why I think we have to act now."

Pedro stared at Sergio with the youngest of eyes, desiring to grow old. "What do you think we should do?"

Sergio puffed out, "Begin the revolution."

The word slammed and rang in Pedro's ears like a gong calling people to arm themselves. The word that had come to his mind many times; to hear someone speak it with such consciousness!

"So, are you with us, boy?"

Pedro, squinting because the morning sun was behind Sergio, pulled the cigarette from his mouth. It dropped from his twitching fingers. He clutched at it in the dirt, burning his finger. Pedro could barely keep his heartbeat from bursting over his tongue. "Yes. Of course I am."

The moment broke when Lupe and Rosa approached.

"Well, there you two are. We were wondering if you were going to show up, and here you sit, taking a siesta in the morning." Lupe smiled down at the two teen-agers, holding her lips specifically toward Sergio, and paying no attention at all to her brother.

"We were just coming your way." Sergio grinned toward his lover.

"Fine. We will be there later. We have to buy some cheese."

A Fire in the Earth

"Oh. Tell your mother that I send my love, Rosa," said Pedro. All four of them laughed, even Rosa, knowing that no one sent love to Doña Romilia.

After only a few moments of light conversation, the two young women went their way, leaving the mound. They walked up the southern hill toward Doña Romilia's house. The two young men, with sacks on shoulders, took the flour to the bakery.

"God, he is so good-looking!" Lupe whispered in a high voice. Rosa giggled and looked over at her friend. Lupe's long hair covered much of the side of her face and disguised her slightly protruding upper teeth. Yet her teeth did not matter. Lupe could carry herself in a way that not only spoke of sex, but smelled of it. Whenever she whispered about the subject, the odor grew stronger, more intense, and brought her friend into a whirl of giggles and embarrassment. Lupe continued, "And you should see Sergio at night, in the river. ¡Ay Dios!"

"I am sure you have found him something to behold."

"Oh, and what he does, he is always just, so intense about it all..." Lupe wrapped her arms together in a dramatic movement, then slowly moved her cat eyes to the side to catch her friend's stare. "But then, I usually can loosen him up."

Laughing, sometimes pushing each other, they made it to Rosa's house where Romilia stood, cutting the cheese that was almost ready to be taken to the González's store. "Hello, Mamá," Rosa kissed her on the cheek. Romilia continued working. "I see it is about ready."

"Good morning, Doña Romilia. How are you this morning?" Lupe asked from the door.

"As well as can be expected. How much cheese does your mother want?"

"A small basketful. She is not selling as much as usual."

"I suppose there is something wrong with the cheese. Well, too bad. The shits on the street will have to live with it."

"No, Doña Romilia, it is just that people tend to buy it at the store rather than at a bakery."

"Here it is. Now go. Take two bundles to González, girl. I have many things to do here. I do not have time to be messing with two girls."

They left, as if accustomed to the words. But Romilia had rushed them off more bruskly than usual. Something was distressing her. It was the ache that came from up the hill, the pounding of hammer on wood, on nails, the lumber cut and falling to the ground, the lining up, the measurements, the white paint slapped against the side. The construction had been going on for weeks. She waited for it to end, but it never did. It continued as if to create the future by the destruction of the past. Yet the past was not completely obliterated. She could still see her old home, though the wall to the east now stretched into a corner. Many windows had been added. The building was growing steadily, as if to create something more perfect than the perfection that already existed.

"Once again, your mother is in a wonderful mood," said Lupe.

"Yes, well, she is more tense these days. It is so obvious because of what they are doing to the ranch house."

The familiar moaning emanating near the street corner stopped them both. Lupe and Rosa moved to the other side of the road with heads bowed low and no words spoken as they passed by the house of the yelping, crazy Doña María Ramírez, who continued to beat against the smoothed-out wood of the table and utter her sporadic curses concerning Mary, the Mother of God, and her blasphemous relationships here on earth and in hell. Lupe crossed herself twice. Rosa only kept her head down, staring at the ground. They remained silent until the bellowing was far enough behind them.

"I wonder what they are going to do with the ranch house," pondered Lupe aloud. Rosa did not know. "Do you know what I have heard? I heard that they were going to make a hotel out of it!"

"What? Where did you hear that?"

"Well, I was not sure whether or not to say anything in front of your mother. Carmen told me yesterday."

They dropped off the cheese at the González's market, chatted with the proprietor for a few minutes, then returned to the bakery.

"A hotel. What in the world is he going to do with a hotel?" Rosa asked of no one. They continued their conversation while kneading the cream-colored dough destined to become the afternoon sweet bread for the town. Lupe smiled, then fell into giggling. She covered her pro-

A Fire in the Earth

truding teeth with the palm of her hand while looking around the room. Rosa raised her eyes. "What is so funny?"

Lupe looked about for her mother, who was not present. She whispered over the table, "Perhaps Edmundo will invite you up to the hotel some evening." She giggled again, unable to control it.

"And why is that so laughable?"

"Well, perhaps he will be ready by then. You never tell me what he does at the river. Perhaps he is just waiting for the hotel to be built."

As an answer, Rosa tore off a wad of dough and slung it at Lupe, slapping her in the left breast. Lupe tried to do the same, but missed Rosa. They stopped suddenly, still giggling, realizing they were slinging about Doña Marta's income.

"So, has he asked you yet?"

"Asked me what?"

"Oh, come on, Rosa, don't act so naive. I am always telling you about our trips to the river. I even make up some stories just to get you to talk about yourself, but you never tell me anything. How do you expect me to continue on like that?"

Rosa smiled. "Well, he is not waiting for the hotel to open, know that right now. His are as ripe as Sergio's or anyone else's. But also know that he is not getting too far with me yet. That will have to wait."

"Goodness, you are such a strong one. To think you can stop a boy during his heated years."

"I can stop him. We must wait. It is not correct for us to go laying together so early; we have not been seeing each other for very long."

"Yes, well, I believe you two should see more of each other, and I know the perfect place to do it. The river. Goodness, girl, I tell you, you can see a lot there."

Again Rosa smiled. "We go to the river. But I am careful as to what he sees. And touches."

The poor young Edmundo tried with all his mind to understand this perspective, but the rest of him never came to terms with it. He never forced himself upon Rosa, which was to his credit, and which left him to chew at his little moustache until nothing clung to his upper lip but the tufts. He brought her to the edge of the river in those lovely nights when other couples lay upon the banks. Yet he could not be free to do as he wished. She never allowed it, and dammed his hands which flowed into her dress. "We must wait, we must wait." He listened, respected her, then went home to find other means of release. They spoke of marriage while on the river bank, a future together, believing it to be the best way. They spoke all night, the only couple on the river who carried on a conversation, and others reminded them of this with sudden hisses, like a hundred loving snakes hiding in nearby bushes. They whispered about a life together. She still had reservations, and told them to Lupe. "He is such a sweet and good young man," she confessed, "but I do not know. I just want to wait."

"If you wait too long, he will burst, or will find someone else to let go with."

"If that is the case, then he best start looking elsewhere right now."

"What? Come on, Rosa, what do you expect from a man?"

"Nothing but respect and love, my friend," she said while looking up from the kneading table.

Rosa said the same words to Edmundo whenever they were alone together, and he promised them both, promised every bit of love and respect that he was capable of. "Rosa, I love you. I want to marry you. We are old enough. I'm eighteen; you're sixteen. We're more than old enough."

"Yes, old enough. But what will we do for money? For a home?"

"Oh, that is no problem. I am working now, under my father at the brickhouse. I make money. And in the beginning, well, we can live with my father, yes! He would not mind. There is that back room where I sleep. We could live there, just, you know, until we make enough money to be on our own. We can do it, Rosa!"

Rosa reported the news to her friend, who laughed and squealed with excitement. "Ooh, I knew it would happen! So move in together."

"We must wait to be married."

"What? Girl, you will be waiting until your grandchildren are picking coffee, for that is the next time a priest will come to town. Do not worry about that. If you want to get married, then you are married." She paused, then added, "You just, of course, will have to tell your mother."

That fact, like cold ash dropped by the shovelful on a fire, quelled the excitement. That evening Rosa returned quietly to the river to meet her lover so as to bring up this issue. But Edmundo burned with the happiness, thinking she was close to giving in. At first he said nothing, kissed her, then whispered of their newfound joy, that some-day soon she would be his wife, the mother of his children. He could sense that in their half-phrased conversations, their limited, promis-ing touches, their lips pressed in a fire that flickered along with all the other flames upon the river banks, something was about to erupt. Rosa did not mention her mother to him. She decided to face Romilia alone.

On the day of that final decision, when she had practiced several times over in her mind what should be said to her mother, Rosa approached the cheese trough. She looked at the cheesemaker. As Rosa was about to raise the subject, fear closed her throat. She cleared it again to speak. It was too late. Romilia tossed down the dry rag she was using to wipe her hands and spoke to the girl first.

"I want to talk to you. Come."

Rosa followed her. From under her bed Romilia pulled out a box, and while opening it she spoke directly and concisely to her daughter. "The building that they are constructing on the hill, it is true, it is a hotel. It will open someday soon. I want you to go there and find a job."

"What? Mamá, find a job there? What could I do at the ranch house?"

"It is no longer a ranch house. Go and ask for a job at the hotel. There will be jobs. I too will go. But I want you to go and apply, for I believe that you will receive a good position there."

"But Mamá, I have a job now, and I make decent money at the bakery."

"You will make better money at the hotel. Many other women will go to find work. I suggest you go soon, when there are no crowds. And wear this." She pulled the contents of the package out and displayed to her daughter a type of dress which she had never seen before.

"Where did you get this... thing?"

"It is the style they wear in the States. I had it ordered from the capital. It is the latest fashion."

Rosa held it up and dangled the spaghetti straps over her arms.

"It is nothing but a tube."

"Put it on."

Reluctantly she did, then stepped back into a dark corner. Her mother coaxed her to turn around. When she did, Romilia smiled, seeing her daughter's creamy beauty properly displayed.

That evening Romilia took Rosa, dressed in her new clothes, up the hill. The sun set quickly; night came upon them as they approached the front door of the old ranch house that stood before pieces of cut wood and planks scattered over the front yard, the dregs of the new construction. A woman answered the door, obviously a maid. Romilia spoke for them both. "Yes, my daughter has an appointment with Mr. Reyes." The maid seemed to understand this, as if preliminary organization had been done. She opened wide the door for both women, but Romilia did not enter. "You go now, Rosa, I will go later. I do not want to mess up your opportunity."

"What? Mamá, I cannot stay here; it is night. I, I will come back to speak to him tomorrow—"

"No, you will stay here and find a job. He is expecting you. Ah, here he comes. Good night." Romilia walked away from the door after she spied the tall Joaquín Reyes coming from around the familiar corner of that old ranch house turned hotel. The understanding maid closed the door to the departing mother, leaving the fashionably dressed daughter in the enclosed building.

Rosa returned several hours later, running through the night air like a skipped stone over tumultuous waters. The tube dress clung to her protectively. It was not torn, and seemingly had not left her body. Rosa had kept every small inch of its cloth upon her. She looked at her mother sitting in a rocking chair. With contempt that seemed unnatural for such a young person, she announced, "No! He did not touch me! And he will not touch me. No one will touch me like that, not until I am married, and I will not be manipulated like that again!"

She wept. Her mother stood above, her arms crossed over her chest.

A Fire in the Earth

"What happened? What did you say? What did *he* say?"

"I tell you what he said! I told him just what I told you, that no man will ever touch me until he is my husband, and that he, Joaquín Reyes, may as well leave such thoughts behind him right now, for I am to marry another man!" She spat out the dramatics, the anger, making every word count.

"What do you mean? What fucking nonsense are you talking about?"

The daughter reluctantly spoke. "I said that he can forget it, for I will marry Edmundo Lazo very soon. We have planned it for a long time. He is the man I love. So, so I will not be manipulated by Mr. Reyes. Nor by you, Mamá!"

"You told all this to him? You fucking stupid idiot!—"

But Romilia had passed on her irascible nature to her daughter. Rosa, as if with a newfound weapon, slung the arguments back at her mother. They screamed without bothering to listen to each other's arguments.

That night Rosa told Edmundo what had happened. There were tears, recriminations, reassurances. The two lovers spoke as if the thought of a life commitment were the only thing that matter. That night she gave more of herself. Clothed only by the moonlight, Rosa came to him like the fringes of dreams that he had created and stored away. She touched him with love and gentleness, and gave him pleasure with her breasts, her fingers, touching his root desire with both. Such was she as a new lover. She almost wept, for then she understood it all, began to believe that she did love this man, one who pleaded for commitment, one whom she hardly knew. She believed in love, it had to be real, they were to marry.

The next day all this shattered about her when they found Edmundo dead, a neat slit running from the ear to the collarbone, his penis cut and shoved between his lips like a wet root. Rosa wept as if she had really loved him; she moaned with the gentle touch that she had given him the previous night.

The old church bell tolled. No one had ever seen this sort of death before. People gathered, strength coming from their numbers. Fear dwelled there also, as rumors wove tight around the wails, gossip tied with information that came to the Comenzaños in newspapers that drifted through the little town. The few who could read learned about the dangerous people of their time, those who stirred riots, who threatened the interests of the country. Such information scrolled down the pages like barrels of truth aimed upon the people's widening eyes. Such data encircled this dead boy, one of their own, who, someone said, had plotted to take over the government and make them all something they were not. *That is why he is dead. That is the reason.*

Enrique stood over the grave. He had a surviving child next to him, a woman named Regina. She held her own child, Enrique's only grandchild, next to her. The tiny girl, named Consuelo, watched her grandfather as he allowed tears to roll down his wrinkled cheek and fall into the grave.

At the cemetery others stood with the surviving family: Sergio, Pedro, Leonardo the carpenter, Lupe, Rosa to the other side, with their families behind them and the confused townspeople encircling them all. Enrique felt nothing but the dull throb of the church bells. Sergio and Pedro leaned toward Don Leonardo as if in search of safety, for they could feel others staring at them, as if the crowd was telling them between the ringing of the bell, We know you are here; we know you. They stood aside the family, heads lowered as if pondering. One of their own had been killed by the protectors of a vague, systematic enemy. Standing like Christ pondering the death of John the Baptist, they suddenly understood that their town was small, and it spoke of everything in clear whispers. Others who belonged to their cause, who met in hidden rooms, had already scattered, taking heed of the warning. All of them afterwards would refrain from meeting in the back rooms of bars, and remain silent to see if there were other signs that would come to speak to them of life's new dangers.

Chapter Four

Four months passed before a tremendous, black wrought iron gate encircled the new hotel. It had been constructed with future buildings in mind. There was ample space between the hotel and the fence. For the first four weeks the workers cut the trench, making sure it was deep enough to hold the spikes of the fence in place. Then the laborers constructed the tall concrete pillars, which came in sections and had to be stacked piece by piece until they reached twenty feet up into the sky. Then the magnificent metal shafts themselves, those long, lithe spears, thirty feet tall, had been strung together with other pieces of welded metal, ten spears to a section, four inches between each spear. The fence stretched far to the east of the hotel, stopping a few hundred feet before the brickhouse yard. One day a pig came by and stuck its head between two of the rods. It's skull got stuck between them, and it panicked while three guards ran toward it, trying to chase it away.

The men were ordered to construct a second, smaller fence to the west of the hotel. Where both fences joined together there were two gates, one that opened to the hotel, the other to the flat, vacant area beyond the second fence. At this point they formed a cage. More men were hired from town to work in the area within the second iron fence. From these men, their wives learned that the new *patrón* of the land, Don Joaquín Reyes, was having his own private home built within this second circle.

"His balls must be made of gold." Sergio González spoke as he took a tiny package of cigarette tobacco from his father's store. Pedro stood beside him. Sergio kept mumbling about the owner of the hotel, the new construction, the money that Reyes must own. "And that fucking fence all around the place. Other rich bastards build a wall, not a fence. What is he trying to prove with that damn fence?"

313

Marcos McPeek Villatoro

"I have heard that it is for protection," said Pedro. "The workers talk; they say that they are putting the same wrought iron all over, on all the windows of the hotel, and on that house, too. But they put the fence so that Reyes could see the countryside."

"Making his own cage to live in."

"They said that he was going to build it all along, but when Edmundo was killed, well, the workers think it scared the *patrón*. He came out yelling at them to work faster—"

Sergio looked harshly at Pedro, putting an end to the idle comments. He finally glanced in another direction and mumbled, "Let's go. Leonardo is waiting." They walked out of the store.

Sergio did not speak until they were alone on the street. "You know fucking well who killed Edmundo." He grabbed Pedro's arm and hissed into his ear. "Everyone knows who killed—"

"Wait. Be quiet." Pedro, out of a sense of survival, brought his clutching friend into the confines of the carpenter shop, where Leonardo stood. The carpenter looked up and asked what was going on.

At first neither said anything. When Sergio turned around, disgust on his face, Pedro answered Leonardo, "It is about Edmundo, about, what happened."

"Oh. Yes. What about it?"

"Sergio was talking about—"

"I was just telling the truth. You know who killed Edmundo, true, Leonardo? Everyone knows who killed him."

Leonardo breathed out heavily, then told Pedro to shut the front door as if he knew what the other boy was about to say. "Yes, what you say may be true. Everyone may know. But why does no one say anything?" Neither boy answered. "Because it would get them killed. If you said what you want to say, and you took it to court, you would lose, because who are you? Nothing but a young worker. And who is he? A rich man. You have no proof about what you want to say, no proof at all. Besides, not everyone believes as you do, about who the murderer is. You know how people felt about Edmundo."

"I know that Edmundo's name is shit now, because of the lies printed in the newspapers, because of what Don Enrique has done in the past when he stood up for everyone's rights in this town, when

314

everyone felt he was a local hero, and now he is a 'communist' and no one will talk with him on the streets. What the hell is going on, Leonardo? What has happened to truth?" Leonardo followed him around the carpenter shop, trying to quiet him down, to help him, to keep him from saying too many things. "No, I can't shut up. I have been quiet too long, ever since Edmundo died. Everything has changed; how can we continue like this? Two weeks since his death, and it seems like everyone has disbanded and all the people in town have turned against us. We have had no meetings, no movement...."

"Sergio, I promise you, nothing has died. It is just that, the men, the comrades, they are keeping their heads low temporarily. They have not lost their fervor to fight, not at all. This, Sergio," the older man pointed outward, perhaps to the cemetery, or to the area where they found the boy's dead body, "this will not weaken us. It will strengthen us. You have to believe that. Otherwise..." He lifted up his hands.

"Otherwise you will end up just like my father," Pedro stated. Sergio turned around to his friend, then turned away, as if he were angry and confused by it all. "It is true. My father was lost to the cause because my brother was killed by some guy called Culebra. That ruined Dad. We could be lost, too, because of this murder. Or we could be strengthened."

"Then why is no one doing anything?"

"They will, Sergio. *We* will, but we have to wait awhile."

"Wait, fuck..." Sergio turned to a window and lit a cigarette. Slowly Pedro turned to the work that awaited him. Leonardo did the same. After completely finishing his cigarette, Sergio turned to his work.

The men scraped, hammered, and sawed for a long while. After some time, Leonardo embarked upon another conversation. "Hey, have either or you two seen much of Rosa?" Both answered negatively. "I have not seen her since the funeral, and wondered how she was doing."

"It seems she's not doing much, except working at the bakery. But Lupe tells me that she is not doing well. Rarely speaks, just does her work."

"Hhm. Perhaps you two could go see her, see how she is doing." They did not respond. "Come on, why not? Afraid to get by Doña Romilia? Boys, if you expect to fight someday, you better take hold of these little battles first."

$$\approx$$

"Rosa, you have a guest."

Her mother's voice did not move her. She sat in the darkest corner of the neat, perpetually clean adobe house, staring at nothing. From the corner of her eye she barely saw the dark, tall shadow in the doorway.

"Rosa?" the shadow spoke, taking off his hat, slowly approaching her. "Rosa, how are you? May I see you a moment?" The shadow sat next to her. In the darkness she looked at Joaquín's smile. "I have come to offer my condolences, and also, my apologies. I am sorry, very sorry, to hear about your friend. Such a tragedy. I know that it is very difficult." Joaquín waited, pausing courteously. Romilia set a cup of coffee before him. He thanked her, then continued speaking to Rosa while Romilia moved back to the front door. "I also want to apologize for our...our encounter of a few weeks ago. You know, when we were together at my home—your old home. I must say, I was not a gentleman, not at all. But please, I think you can understand. Well...Rosa, you are a very beautiful woman; it is no wonder, no wonder at all." Joaquín smiled again, almost shyly, and let the silence of his shadow speak for a moment. "I ask for your forgiveness, though perhaps I do not deserve it."

She barely turned to him. Her eyes lost none of the dark traces of her mourning. He turned away from her, looked down at the floor momentarily and continued speaking. "Yes, this has all been very difficult, and, well, it just sickens me—the pain I know that you are in. That is why I have decided to do something which I wish to tell you about, only because, well, I want you to know." He leaned toward her and spoke. Romilia, who busied herself with sweeping the leaves and loose dust from the dirt floor of the front porch area, stopped, leaned to rest, and bent her ear slightly. Still she could not hear, but she turned and saw the face of her daughter, which had brightened somewhat, though still without a smile. But the *patrón* smiled, responding to Rosa's reaction. Something had been accomplished.

"Now, that is just between you and me. We must not let such information out. Well, I best leave. I am sure you have many things to think about. If you need anything, you can come to me, Rosa. Now, until another time." He stood, tipped his cap to her as he placed it on his head, and walked toward the door where Romilia stood.

Sergio and Pedro walked up the street. They dodged the sun, walking under the awnings of all the buildings that lined the road.

"Why do we go to her house?" asked Pedro. "We could have waited until tomorrow, when she is with my mother, making bread."

"It is good to go now. Leonardo is right. We need to see how Rosa is doing—" Sergio stopped himself as his eyes fell upon the barely dusted sports car that stood just outside the Colónez home. Slowly, both approached until they stood before it. Its two lights stared at them with a grid of metal teeth in between. They stood in silence until a voice above and behind them spoke.

"What are you doing here? Get away from that auto."

It was Romilia, speaking from her doorway, her arms crossed. She had made the same statement many times, keeping the street children away from the vehicle, shooing them like flies. She spoke more harshly to the two teen-agers.

"Is there a problem?" The question emerged from the darkness of the house. Sergio turned in time to see the tall figure of the *patrón*, who suddenly stood beside Romilia. The *patrón* smiled at the two young men. He stepped down, crossed over, leaned against the car with three fingers. "Nice auto. Is it yours?" Joaquín asked Pedro, who had taken a step back. Pedro muttered a negative response. "Good answer. No. It is not yours. It is mine." He entered the vehicle, adjusted his cap. "Perhaps if you work hard and save your pesos, you can get one someday."

The engine ignited, an expert hand pushed the lever into gear, and the soft voice spoke while he held his eyes directly upon Sergio. "You boys should go home."

Marcos Mcpeek Villatoro

The tiny rocks kicked up by the auto cut into Sergio's ankles. Sergio released a stream of hissed curses. Both he and Pedro turned to enter the Colónez house. But the door had been closed. Both boys could hear the dull clack of board against wood as the house bolted itself against the day.

∿
∿

Pedro watched Rosa work as they all placed the bread to be sold upon the cabinet shelves. It was customary for no one to speak during this time, as they were much too busy to carry on a conversation. Rosa, however, had been quiet all afternoon. "She is so silent these days, I do not know what to do," Pedro had heard his older sister say to their mother Marta early one morning. Marta had told Lupe to not be concerned, that it was natural after Edmundo's death. Lupe had gone on to explain to her mother that she understood that, but that Rosa's strange silence went beyond mourning. "It is as if she is thinking deeply about something. I am not sure." Marta had another interpretation, that this was natural, for death makes people think.

They sold all the bread before nightfall. Rosa asked if she could leave immediately after selling that evening, as she wanted to visit the cemetery. When she left, Pedro waited a few minutes then followed behind. He ambled into the graveyard as if by chance. Rosa was on her knees, praying a rosary, with her head bowed before the recent grave. Pedro said nothing, waiting until she finished. He was surprised to see her holding a rosary. He had never known Rosa to be a very pious woman.

As she sat back and leaned against a tree stump, he approached her. He sat next to her. She did not move, as if she had sensed his presence all along, ever since they both left the bakery.

"Did you finish?" he asked. She nodded. "You know, I have not prayed the rosary in so long, I wonder if I remember it at all."

"A long time for me, too. I am surprised I remember as much as I do. This is not even my rosary. It belongs to mother, though she doesn't use it either.

"It looks old."

318

A Fire in the Earth

"It is. It belonged to my grandmother. Look, there is also a lock of hair, which belonged to my mother's great grandfather."

"Oh. Why did they do that?" he asked, but she did not know. They both sat for what seemed like a long time. Pedro, looking for conversation, asked, "So do you hear from your brother much?"

"Paco? No, he rarely writes us. We got a note from him a few months ago. He said he was doing fine, but little else. He does send money from time to time."

"Oh. I have heard so many good things about him."

"He is a good man. But it has been five, six years now...." She drifted into silence, one which tried to separate them. He opted for a more direct approach.

"You know, uh, this new *patrón* here, Mr. Reyes, he, he must be, must be pretty rich, eh?" It fell out like dropped eggs.

At first she said nothing. She stared ahead, then suddenly turned her eyes toward Pedro. "May I tell you something?" Pedro quickly answered affirmatively. "Do you realize that the police are doing absolutely nothing about Edmundo, about finding his murderer? Yes, that is true, at least until now. Joaquín Reyes told me that he himself has decided to begin a thorough investigation into the murder. He told me that the guard will do nothing until you demand it from them, and the police, they are nothing anyway. So he has demanded a full investigation." Pedro heard very little of the rest, and his mouth dropped open. She continued talking about how good that was, how she appreciated it, but that it could not bring Edmundo back, of course, but still, that she was very thankful. She also went on to say that she was not sure as to how many times she could come to the cemetery and visit his grave, as she felt it was doing her no good, that Edmundo was being taken care of now, so perhaps she should stay away from this place, which did nothing but sadden her. "This may be a terrible thing to say, but, well, we still have to go on living, true?" She looked straight into Pedro's eyes.

Thus her pondering became a decision. Rosa no longer returned to the grave. She worked at the bakery, listened and smiled as Lupe told stories. Yet she rarely laughed, and Lupe finally stopped telling jokes. An interminable distance, a space of experience, had wedged itself between their friendship. Rosa worked as hard as ever, especially on the days when they sold bread. But she did not stay around to drink coffee with the first pieces of fresh bread, after the rest was sold, not even when the Indian stopped by, which had always been a time to sit, rest, and visit. Now she declined, and went home immediately after all the work was done.

"What is ailing the young one?" the old Indian asked on one such occasion. No one answered at first, until finally Pedro told the tale in one sentence. "A friend of hers, a boyfriend, he died. He was murdered." Hermes glanced over at his son, as if wishing he had not made that final statement.

"Oh, that is so bad," responded the Indian. "That is sad. What happened?"

"Some drunk killed him in the fields," said Hermes. With that, the air in the kitchen turned thick with silence, and all felt it except the Indian, who knew no more about the subject. It seemed that the matter would drop, with no more words, no more explanations, until Pedro, who had stared deeply toward his father after the statement, left and walked out into the street. He walked hard, his hands contracting into fists by his sides. He did not turn around, not even when his father called out his name. Hermes was gaining on him with a rapid pace until his hand pressed against Pedro's shoulder. "Son, you must be careful. Please, Pedro, stop, stop right now, listen to me."

"Why did you say what you just did?"

"Because that is what I know, that is what everyone says. Pedro, I do not want you leaving the house at night anymore, do you hear me? I do not want you out whipping the streets. Now is not a good time to—"

"I am not out whipping the streets. I am a man, and I will do what is right." He tore himself away from his father's grip, turned and walked away again. Hermes stood alone, with a sickness of memory and loss enveloping him. His wife Marta stood at the opening of their home in her silence, with an impotent, closed hand to her mouth.

A Fire in the Earth

"I do not know what to do," spoke Pedro to Sergio. They sat alone in a back room of the store. Sergio fixed his friend a cigarette as Pedro paced back and forth, telling him of what happened. "Is everybody saying things like that?"

"It was either a drunk or a robber, according to many people."

"What are we going to do? Have you talked with anyone from the meetings? What do they say?"

"I have talked with some, yes. They are keeping low, just like Leonardo said."

"But for how long? This is crazy, all this waiting."

"That is what I have been telling you, comrade. And that is why I say we get to work."

"How?"

"Preparing. Arming ourselves. Getting ready to fight. There are others in the meetings who feel the same."

"Who are they? Why is it I never see them? When can I get into these meetings? I want to see who these men are, see if they really exist!"

"They exist. Come on, Pedro, trust me." Pedro turned away. He walked to the window, looked out at the rising moon. They smoked. Neither spoke for a long while.

"You know what I wish?" mused Pedro. "I wish Paco Colónez were here. I have heard about him, some stories here and there. My father hates him. Well, he does not like to talk about him, ever since Rubén died. But Enrique has talked about him; I heard him telling stories to Leonardo about Paco. You know that he can speak English? That is incredible. I wish I could speak English."

Sergio, who had leaned back against some sacks of produce, closed his eyes, still smoking. He muttered something about why one would want to learn the tongue of the fucking gringos. "Well, I do not know. It would be good just to have that education. And you could use it, certainly. You know, they say Paco is in the States now. Learning from the real comrades."

"Sure. Right up there in the beast's lap. Why isn't he here, where we need him? We have enough things to fight for here, but he is out running around with gringos. I do not understand that."

"He will return someday. Enrique has said so."

"Right. When we are all dead of starvation. Or with our throats cut open."

"Poor Enrique. He looks as if he has aged ten years in a month. And hardly anyone speaks to him; no one stops by his house, not even Rosa. I thought she would visit a lot, but I have never seen her there. That is strange, for she is usually one to care for everyone's pains. And you know, she probably believes it was a drunk, too, because she thinks that Reyes is going to do something about it, have an investigation and—"

"What?" Sergio raised his head from the sacks.

"Yes, she told me that yesterday. We were at the cemetery, and she said that Reyes promised her a full investigation into the murder."

Sergio sat only long enough to mutter, "That lying son of a bitch." Then he was up and walking out the door, with Pedro behind him.

"What are you going to do?"

"Talk with Rosa. If she believes the shit he gave her, then we have to straighten her out."

They marched out, around the mound, up the street that led to the house of the cheesemaker. They said little. Pedro asked once what Sergio had in mind to say. "Just the truth." They turned the corner and walked to the third house on the left. There stood Doña Romilia, leaning against the post of the door. Sergio greeted her. "Hello. Where is Rosa? I need to speak with her."

"She is not here. What do you want?"

"It is very important. You are sure she is not here?" With that, Sergio stepped up the rock steps and walked through the door. People on the street stopped, turned, amazed at the youth's disrespect for traditional courtesy. Many, after seeing who it was, turned away.

"What are you doing? I could have you arrested!"

Sergio did not respond. He called out Rosa's name four times before returning to the door where he looked up and saw, above them all, the sleek black automobile driving away, entering the road that connected with the highway. In the passenger's seat sat the young woman, with long hair billowing out from under a kerchief like black fire. She wore no black, but had donned a white dress that reflected the light of day.

"Get out of here, you young shit! I could have you hauled away, do you know that? *I could report your name!*"

∿∿
∿∿

A formality soon fell into place. One afternoon as Rosa worked down at the bakery, an expensive car—not the Mercedes—drove in front of the Colónez house, and a man of tremendous size approached the closed door. Romilia answered the knock, then fell back a step with a muttered "Jesus Christ" to no one. She looked at the figure, saw that the well-dressed man wore a valet suit and a chauffeur's hat, much more modern than in the days when she was accustomed to seeing such hats. The most striking aspect about him, however, was his skin. Romilia had heard of the people called Negro, had known that they lived in nearby countries along the Caribbean shoreline. This was her first time to meet one.

"Yes, how can I help you?" she asked.

"I have been sent by Mr. Reyes." The voice growled a mellifluous formality, a leopard calmly walking the streets, secure in its strength and beauty. "He is in need of a cheesemaker at the hotel. Mr. Reyes requests that you come to work for his establishment."

She muttered about for some scarce moments, then quickly accepted the job. As the valet left, she called out to him, "By the way, what is your name?"

"They call me Sheriff, Mrs. Colónez."

"Oh. Sheriff. Yes. Pleased to meet you." She smiled, studying him and his thick, accented Spanish.

He smiled back and drove away.

She snatched at the job. Her enthusiasm took her up the hill, where the enthusiasm quickly died. Romilia entered that old kitchen, filled with new people, new maids, unknown faces. They, not knowing her, as they had been transported from the capital, greeted her as maid to maid and showed her where she was to work, in a shed separated from the hotel. It was a shed once used by the carpenters during construction.

They showed her where the goats were kept, along with the milk cows and other animals, far in the back, in and behind the old barn, in the pen next to that gravestone of the old *patrón*. They took her there, and while they talked on and on about who would milk the goats and gather the curd, Romilia glanced every other second at that old gravestone, now encapsulated in thick grass. This was her first visit.

"The men, they will bring the milk to me, correct? I will not have to come here to get it, true?" The maidservants said yes, it was probably best that way, as the buckets of milk were quite heavy to carry.

Romilia worked every day at the new hotel. Everyone kept busy preparing for the grand opening that was scheduled the following month. She asked the maids if there would be a great turnout, and they all responded that yes, of course, it would be majestic. "But why out here? Why is he building a hotel out here, so far away from the capital, or any other city?"

"Because of the tourists," explained one of the cooks. "These new roads, they are bringing tourists way out here, from the United States, Mexico, Europe. The tourists are good business!"

"But why do tourists want to come out here?"

"Oh, to get away from the city. They just love our country, always talking about our 'culture.' They will buy just about anything we make. And if you say that an Indian made it, ooh! It will go for twice as much money."

Another maid spoke as they all stood in the kitchen. "Yes, so if tourists are travelling through the country, say, from the capital to San Miguel, they can stop here overnight, just to rest, walk around the peaceful area, to be more refreshed for the next day of travel. It is the newest thing. It's happening all over the country."

As renovation ended, the construction workers gathered leftover wood and metal and hauled it away. Other men continued to labor in the smaller fenced-in circle. Rock had been placed for a foundation, concrete had been brought in from the capital, and the first pieces of frame had been nailed and bolted together. Romilia stared at the construction: It was a new home, large enough to take in more than a bachelor, built for a family, for children. As the new building threw another long shadow upon the hillsides that surrounded the village below them, Romilia grinned, almost laughing. She watched the new *patrón*, Joaquín Reyes, drive down the hill in that incredible machine of his and stop the motor in front of her adobe house. From there he and her daughter raced away, perhaps to the capital, perhaps to some other town nearby, San Miguel, Usulután, away from here. The new house, said the laborers, would be finished soon.

Came the day of the grand opening, and automobiles lined up through the late morning in front of the new hotel. The workers ran every which way, serving food, cutting and dicing more vegetables, bringing out drinks of imported liquors and wines, beers from Europe, and that wonderful, illegal elixir from the States, made by some famous Catholic fellow up there who played the stock market like it was his own game that he could pack up and take home if he wished. He could not come to the party, but he sent his best wishes and a hope for a prosperous future for the hotel.

The guests drank and laughed, talked and rubbed shoulders, touched and danced like nothing Romilia had ever seen. She stared through the serving hole between the kitchen and the main dining hall to watch them. They were all young. She knew none of the faces. Children, perhaps, of her old crowd. Their party moved differently than her old gatherings. The women, it was true, they *did* wear such dresses as the one that she had bought for her daughter Rosa, those skimpy tubes of cloth that hugged everything around those little bodies, the straps that fell every few seconds over a naked shoulder. And the hair, all tied up, curled, or cut so very short, almost like a man's. The women smoked cigarettes alongside their mates. A new recorder had been brought in for the grand opening, and music such that she had never heard sung through the machine. English words, she could tell from remembering how her dead husband once spoke. These were squeaky women's voices pitching high notes everywhere. The women in the room jumped upon tables and danced, kicked their legs sideways and jerked their heads downward. The men joined them, knocked their knees together and wove their arms from leg to leg like clumsy noodles. They grabbed the women and flipped them about while still on the table, tapping and skipping over the rich, finished wood. All these young bodies, many of them brown like herself, but also several that were white, talked both Spanish and English. They laughed together, fell down and crawled away together to upstairs bedrooms. Each time she passed by the open service hole, Romilia stopped and looked again, amazed at the loudness and blatancy of these children. She passed and watched all night until he entered the room, Joaquín Reyes, and in one arm he carried the hand of her daughter Rosa, dressed like all of them, wearing makeup. Yet she only smiled, and spoke very little, as if trying to hide from the noise, the drinks, the laughter. The beauty of her skin carried her through the crowd, for she was as light as the next mestizo in the room. Mother looked at daughter up and down, as if thankful that the handful of years in the village had not scarred this angelic beauty. She stared at Rosa with a victorious grin, a vicarious smile that placed herself in that dress and in the arm of that handsome man, with all the people watching her. The new, young *patrón* politely asked for silence, as he had an announcement to make, that the lovely lady Rosa Colónez, whom they had all had the privilege of meeting, "is to become my wife, and we will be moving into our new home on the other side of the hill."

The crowd applauded with acceptance, knowing her, knowing her stock. Long before introducing her, Joaquín had told them all that she was of the Colónez family, one of those moderately wealthy families that had worked so very hard for their prestige, and that Rosa, who had suffered through the deaths of her mother and father several years before, had been living with relatives in Mexico all that time.

Having affirmed her past, he could now celebrate his present. "And so, of course, you are all invited to our wedding, which will be celebrated by the Archbishop next month in the cathedral."

〰〰

In the month of their wedding and honeymoon, the parties at the hotel stopped. Business came to town, travelling from one end of the country to the other. People stopped for one or two days, spent their time sitting and drinking in a den or the new smoking room, rode

A Fire in the Earth

horses behind the hotel where the fields sat empty for a few acres before running into the iron fence. Many gentlemen were escorted to the brick factory to see its process, interested in it by their want for trivia, that this was the origin of some of the buildings which they owned in the capital. Sometimes people went down into the town, but it was the rare, daring man who did so, and he never went alone. For the rest, the village was beautiful in the distance. Romilia had heard many guests say that several times, how lovely, how quaint, this little village. They spoke in sibilant voices while standing upon a balcony or looking sideways out a window. The people could always view the town, in spite of the tall wrought iron. So different from the thick walls around the homes in the capital. This protection did not obstruct the view at all. One visitor, some popular writer from the States, called it "An emotional distancing, one in which the abstractions of reality become shaped and hewn into iron, to be appreciated by the eye, unsoiled by the skin, yes." All agreed with vague nods of the head, then sipped from their glasses while looking out the windows. For them, the Reyes hotel was a comfortable setting for any weary traveler.

The newlyweds were to return on the 25th of the month, but they were six days late. When they did arrive, husband and wife ate alone. They had supper in the quiet of an upstairs sitting room. They ate fresh seawater cod. It had been packed in ice from a machine—a new piece of technology that had arrived in the port town of La Libertad. "Yes! I must get one of those!" Joaquín exclaimed as he chewed the delicate meat. "It is incredible what science produces these days. Do you like the fish, Rosa?"

"Yes, very much. Thank you."

"'Thank you?'" he laughed. "What is this thanking me? Come now, we have talked about this before. Would you like some more?" He served her more fish from the covered dish. "I do not understand where you get your formality, dear wife. Yet they liked that in you in the States, true?" He chuckled. "I think they liked more than that, too. They saw how beautiful the wife of Joaquín Reyes is."

She smiled back to him, almost with a formal shyness. She said very little in response to his talk. They both felt weary from the long drive from Guatemala City that day, where they had left the automobile during their train ride to the States. He finished his meal, leaned over the small table. "Well, it has been a month, and still, you are so very beautiful to me."

"Perhaps we will be lucky." She smiled. "Only several hundred more months left."

He laughed, left his chair, fell to his knees, and brought his hands up to her evening blouse. Slowly unbuttoning each silver-white button, he spoke in heavy breaths. "I must say, dear Rosa, you are the most beautiful woman in the country."

"Hhm. In the country. As long as we are here, we are fine. Will you say that in the years ahead?"

"Hah! Well now, let us not think of those years. Now is much more important. Ah, yes, this is why I find you so beautiful." He pulled at the creamy fullness concealed by her bra, undid the cloth, brought his hands over her skin, brought his eyes closer to the perfumed flesh.

She touched him, smoothed down his hair which glistened with some expensive oils bought in the States. She looked down at him, as a mother watches a gentle baby nurse. She let him take her, and turned with his movements. His touch and gaze worked together methodically, as they had all during their honeymoon. He moved like a practiced man, something to be expected. They touched and felt and loved in the silence of that sitting room, where electric lights flickered reflections upon cut glass and silver bowls that waited to be cleaned by maids' hands. So far away from some river that she once knew, where insects screamed as if in protest of the night, with other lovers surrounding her, panting quick-fire love in moss and gravel and coffee trees. So far away. Somehow memory dissipated through a strange form of reason, and she forgot everything as they finished. He turned on his side upon the sitting room couch and fell asleep for a time. In minutes he awoke, and took her, both of them still naked, from the sitting room into the adjacent master bedroom where they slept these evenings while waiting for their home to be built. They pulled a thin bedsheet over themselves. Only the moon reflected light from the carpeting.

She did not sleep. She stared at his naked, light-brown back, that thin, almost delicate tall man. His skin showed no callouses, no evidence of hard work, like that other man. And he did not have the odor, nothing here had the odor, not the walls, the kitchen, not the maids. She rubbed his back, and in his sleep he rolled over to her, placed his head upon her naked pelvis under the sheet. She pushed her arms under the linen and caressed his neck, his hair, touching his gentleness. She moved toward sleep with a smile, with a sense that she had done the right thing. She had taken the correct steps, and it had not been altogether painful. She had acted well. Especially concerning her mother, now back in the rebuilt ranch house, the one petition Rosa had made of him before their marriage. She believed her actions to have been for the good of all. They had even helped her, for his gentleness told her that she had been wrong in her previous judgements about him. He was truly sorry for that first night, months ago, when he had molested her. Yet he was a man, like all others. One had to be understanding about such things. She understood this and believed in it, believed that she had taken the right actions, and perhaps had been rewarded with a good husband.

〜〜
〜〜

"Yes, Mamá, it was an incredible trip. The United States, there is nothing like that country."

They began speaking while standing in the kitchen with the other workers rushing about them, doing their jobs for the weekend guests. It was too busy there, so Rosa asked one of the cooks for two cups of coffee to be served upstairs in an unoccupied room. The cook, turning incredulously to her colleague Romilia, slowly nodded and followed orders.

Mother and daughter walked to the private room. Rosa spoke about what they had seen, all about the city of New York, with its monuments, its city trains, and the incredible bridge called Brooklyn that looked more like a long building. "It is fascinating, so long! Longer than El Comienzo!" Romilia could not believe it at first, but then said something pertaining to the gringos, how they can do or make anything they want.

"There are automobiles everywhere, and the buildings, they are so tall!"

"What about the people? Who did you meet?"

"Well, they were nice people. Very rich, oooh, rich!" She said it twice, as if to please. "But they were, well, they were nice, yes." She stopped a moment, then began again quickly as if to hinder embarrassment. "Oh, Mamá, I wished that you had been there with us! I know you would have enjoyed it all."

The cook entered and placed the coffee on the little table.

"María," asked Rosa, "is there not any more sweet bread?"

María looked down at the sitting *patrona*, then glanced at the cheesemaker. "You want bread, too?"

Rosa chuckled. "Well of course. Like the poorest campesino would ask."

"Yes. I will get you bread. I, forgot...." She turned and walked out.

"She forgot like I forget to piss," said Romilia.

"Mamá! It is just that, well, they are not accustomed to—" but Romilia waved her off with a firm hand. María returned, left the bread, and skittered away.

"Well, tell me about the wedding," requested Romilia, knowing that it had to be asked. Though she was the mother of the bride, she had not been invited. She did not ask why. She knew. Yet it was necessary to ask the question, to step on that stone.

The daughter stumbled at first, until she realized that it was a sincere question, a move, perhaps an attempt at reconciliation on her mother's part. She talked about Joaquín's family. Romilia asked for details of the event, the decorations, the food. The Reyes family had hired professional decorators to prepare the large ballroom. Their wedding was like no other she had ever seen, not like the ones in El Comienzo. "It was much more, well, formal." The bishop of the capital led the ceremonies, as he was a close friend of the Reyes family. "Joaquín has a large family. His mother and father, they were there, well, yes, they were there, but not all his family could come, not everyone could make it." She faltered, then began the story again. "But his sisters were there; he has three of them. One of them is named Necira. She is nice, but, well, a little bit crazy if you ask me. She stuck to

330

A Fire in the Earth

every man at the reception. And she carried a book around all the time, even during the ceremony. I do not know what it was. Can you believe that? You will probably meet her. She kept on telling me how she would like to come out and visit our 'quaint little town.'"

"Tell me, what did you get? What things did you buy in the States?"

"Well, he bought many clothes for me. Joaquín insisted on this. He said that I had practically nothing to wear. I do not know; I think I had enough. We also bought him some clothes. He bought bottles of that liquor, you know, the clear stuff. It is very popular in the States. He bought other gadgets; I do not know what they are. He called them 'inventions.'" She stopped, leaned over, ready to emphasize. "Mamá, he is really a good man. I do love him." She smiled, letting go of a precious secret to her mother as if handing her a gift.

"Good. What do you mean 'inventions?'"

"What? Oh, I do not know. I did not pay much attention to them...."

"That does not matter, I probably would not know what to do with them anyway. I see that the house is almost finished for you to move into. When will you begin living in it? Next week?"

"I do not know. Perhaps." Rosa stared at her mother and forced the gift over. "Yes, Mamá, he is a good man. I do love him."

"Oh. Well, yes, that is good; I am happy for you. I thought he was a solid man the moment I met him. I suppose that is good, that you love him." She smiled quickly.

"Yes, I like to think it is a blessing to love your husband."

Her exasperated words scattered into some wide, unnamed fear as the *patrón* opened the door and entered what up to then had been their private room.

"What are you two doing in here?"

"We are just talking, Joaquín. I was telling Mother of our trip to—"

"This is not your area." Joaquín looked straight at Romilia. "You have no right to be in here, sitting and drinking my coffee as if you were part of the family. You have your place and you know it." He stared down at the older woman, who was slowly placing down the cup of coffee upon its saucer.

"Joaquín, you have no right to speak to her that way—"

"Woman, I have every right in the world." He turned once again to his mother-in-law, continuing in a slow tone. "Get out of this room and to your work, or you will lose this precious gem that you think you have regained."

The order given, Romilia stood, walked between the married couple to the door, ignoring her daughter's angry pleas. "It is fine, do not worry, girl." In the hallway she turned around. "By the way, I am happy for your blessing that we talked about." She closed the door behind her.

Rosa barely heard the abrupt and harsh scolding that her husband suddenly threw upon her. She turned and stared at him during those moments of blatant wrath. She sighed as he kept yelling, preaching, about honor, family, appearances. She dropped her head as if it were a heavy, strange object upon her neck. "Do you understand?" he demanded upon his finish. She nodded affirmation. He left after kissing her on the forehead. Then she lay down and tried to ignore some deep nausea that followed her to sleep.

A few weeks after they moved into the new house, everyone knew about Rosa's pregnancy. So very quick, it entered their marriage as a welcomed blessing. Soon she began to show. Joaquín thought it necessary to bring someone in to care for her. "For now, I think a family member would be best. We will worry about a doctor later. You know, my little sister has wanted to come out here and visit. Perhaps she could come out now, watch you, help you with, well, with whatever."

"Necira?"

"Yes. Don't you think that would be good?"

Rosa raised an eyebrow. "What does she know about babies?"

"What does she have to know? There are no babies here yet. And besides, it is more just to keep you company during the day. I will still

A Fire in the Earth

have to make my trips to San Miguel and the capital every week, so it would be good to have someone here with you. And I trust my sister."

Rosa looked down to her supper as he talked about his trips. "Will you leave many times?"

"What? Well, every week, just for three or four days. You know I must do that, Rosa. We have already discussed this. The new operation is just being built in San Miguel, and I have to be there while it is in progress. Singer is just growing and growing!" He smiled, stretching out his arms, proud of the company that he managed. "To keep this Republic thriving like it is, I have to do my share. But do not worry, my love, you will not be left alone. I will call Necira now. I think she will be thrilled."

As he stood to call, Rosa stared at the blank chair that he left. Necira's young face smiled from the seat, as did memories of the wedding. She sipped her coffee. The sweet black swirl chased away the wedding night. Rosa tried one more time. "But Necira has to attend school, true?"

He chuckled slightly. "Rosa, it is January. She is on vacation now. Yes. I need to speak to the capital, please. The family of Alberto Luis Reyes. Yes, thank you."

Rosa sighed heavily as he talked to his father, then to his little sister, sometimes yelling into the mouthpiece as the connection faded in and out. "Necira," she whispered to herself. She sipped her coffee, made from the first beans of the harvest. She thought of her wedding day, dressing with the other women, his sisters. They cooed all around her, laughed and giggled as they had helped her with her veil. Little Necira, sixteen, had told Rosa constantly how lovely she was. "Oh, how did my brother *find* you? I did not know such lovely brides came from the countryside! My brother will have no reason at all to go shopping anywhere else!" Blatant and childish, that was Necira, and it came through the telephone wires as Joaquín giggled at his young sister's antics, at whatever she said to him.

♒

333

"Oooh, Rosa, you look so *good* in your pregnancy! She looks good, right, brother? Oh, I think so, I really do, oh, I look so forward to *being* with you for a while!" Her thin, cream-skinned arms wrapped around Rosa's neck, hugged her tight. The corner of the book which she held pressed into the space between Rosa's shoulder blades. Necira's arms released her and dangled beside her petite body as she explored her new surroundings. Necira's head turned back and forth, examining everything as if deciding which one to steal. "A *quaint* house you have here, brother. Just lovely! Where would you like my baggage to go?" Joaquín took Necira's suitcases, since there was no manservant near-by, and the only housemaid was too small and too old to carry them.

Necira walked into the large sitting room of the house. Olga, the elderly maid, who had been recruited by Rosa from the hotel kitchen, brought them coffee and sweet bread. "Thank you. Now what is your name? Olga? Oh, yes, fine, fine. She is very good, no? Where did you find her, Rosa?"

"I did not find her anywhere. She was working in the kitchen at the hotel. The head cook wanted to get rid of her, as she is older. So I asked her to come over here."

"How good of you. You are good to your workers, true? I think that is good, to be that way. But sometimes I have no patience, but then again, perhaps my servants are not as good as yours, true?" She smiled.

Rosa said nothing, returned no smile. She did not mind the silence, which seemed to be breaking Necira. The latter held the book out. "Rosa, do you like to read? This is a novel from an author in Venezuela. Oh, it is so good. I think I have read every book that this man has written, and he writes *so much*! I bet I read a new one of his every month. And imagine, they keep coming out, month after month! And, oh, the stories. This one is about a woman who is from some city, and she goes out into the countryside to visit her father's farm, and she meets this dark, handsome *labriego*." Necira almost whispered the word, and the taboo wrought out from her a giggle. "Oh, it is such a story. I will let you read it when I am finished."

"I do not read such books."

"Oh? Why not?"

A Fire in the Earth

"I have enough to do keeping up with reality."

Again they were silent. Necira flipped through the book, barely scanning it. She glanced about the room as if looking for solace from so much quietude. Suddenly she stood. "Well, how long have you lived here now? Joaquín told me that the house has just been completed recently, true?"

"Yes."

"Hhm. It is a lovely house. It looks like something my brother would want, something he would demand." She walked toward a window. "I must admit that I was surprised when he came in one day and said to us all that he had decided to live out in the countryside. We just could not believe it. 'What will you do out there?' Mother had asked him. He just said that he liked it, that there was something about it. I have heard that the countryside has a way of taming a person, you know, making one a calmer man. God knows, Joaquín could use some of that!" On that she turned back to her sister-in-law, smiled, waiting for a reaction. She received only a reflective grin from a gentle, assured face. Rosa sat back on the couch, letting her head rest on her hand. She politely continued to listen to her new in-law.

"But, of course, with such a lovely wife, perhaps even pregnancy will not send him away." Then Necira saw something rise in the *patrona*. The girl quickly defended herself with softer words, knowing that the harsher ones had already plunged. "Just like all men, you know, men everywhere just have that driving force that we must put up with."

At that moment Joaquín called to Necira in order to show her the upstairs quarters. The girl excused herself from the sitting room. Rosa stared at her, her head still leaning on her hand, while the guest climbed up the steps.

In a few minutes both brother and sister came back into the sitting room. "Necira has enough belongings to stay with us forever. I did not know you were moving in with us." He barely turned to his sister.

"Oh, come on, brother, it is just a couple of suitcases! But I must say that I think I could get accustomed to such a life. It is so beautiful out here, quiet and peaceful."

335

"It is a different way of life," said Rosa, "than the one you are accustomed to."

"Oh? How is that?"

"Here, one must work."

"Work? I work, dear sister! I have plenty of things to do at home. I am accustomed to labor."

"Oh. Well, good. I am glad to hear that." Rosa continued sitting while she looked up at her husband and his sister. "By the way, how does chicken sound for tonight, Necira?"

"That would be lovely. What time is dinner?"

"Before the sun sets. About 5:00. If you want, you could take a rest until then. And if you like, you can come down to the kitchen to help prepare the meal. You can see how we do it country-style."

"Oh. Well, yes, I would like to do that. I must admit, I am tired from the trip. But yes, I will help with dinner. When do you want me to come down?"

"Do not worry about the time. I will wake you up."

♒

The two hens had never encountered such a stealthy attacker. When they strutted around the corner of the henhouse, two arms catapulted toward their heads and snatched them both around their necks, choking them. Their sharp, tiny tongues flickered out of their beaks as the pregnant woman trotted toward the house, stood below a certain bedroom window, and held the animals up to the open pane. They spat out clucks and contorted violently in the grip.

"Oh Necira, Necira! It's time to prepare supper!"

As the half-sleeping head lifted up to the windowpane, Rosa, in practiced fashion, wrung the necks in opposite directions like wet, feathered doorknobs until the bodies flipped upward through those final guttural screams, then plopped to the ground and flopped away. They encircled the pregnant woman with a twisted dance that followed the irregular music of cackling death.

"Oh, my God! What are you *doing*? How can you do that?"

A Fire in the Earth

"Why, I am preparing supper. You said that you like chicken. Here they are. You can have the job of plucking them if you like. Olga already has the water boiling."

Necira watched open-mouthed as Rosa took the leaping sacks of animals to a seasoned stump and dropped a hatchet upon necks that dangled like old rubber. With the wooden thud, blood spurt from the skin like a little water hose. Necira's head disappeared from the window.

"Necira? Where did you go? Do you want to help?" She looked into the window, but the girl did not answer. Rosa picked up the carcasses and held them for a moment, waiting for the girl to appear again to see the dripping bags in her hands. She did not. Rosa turned to the back porch where Olga, the maid, stood. She was leaning against the post of the front porch with her own cackling head flipped back. Rosa joined the old woman's laughter and entered the porch with the two dripping hens. "Perhaps you could help me, Olga? I suppose we should clean these up before serving them. Some of these city folks have a delicate constitution."

$$\approx$$

"I understand that you prepared dinner tonight," mumbled Joaquín as he crawled into bed.

"Me? No, I did not prepare dinner. I only killed it."

"That is what I meant. Now I understand why she did not eat any of the meat. She told me later she watched you wring their necks."

"Why should that turn her away? Every chicken she has eaten, its neck has been wrung, or every piece of meat has come from a cow with its head knocked in with a sledgehammer and its throat slit open."

"Why do you speak like this? And why did you kill those chickens when Olga could have done it?"

"Olga is too old to run them down, Joaquín. She needs some help, so I helped her."

"If it comes that the *patrona* must help kill the animals, then it is time to hire some maid who is faster, and younger."

337

Marcos McPeek Villatoro

"We will *not* do that. I am the *patrona* of this house, and I know how well Olga works. And as *patrona*, I will help as much as I need to."

He sat up on his elbows, somewhat speechless at her recalcitrance, then looked down at her pregnancy as if it were the reason.

"Yes, but kill the livestock? Should I give you a sledgehammer so you can help the men with the cattle?" She said nothing. He looked back at her, trying to see her face in the darkness of the bedroom. He lay in the bed, then mumbled sharply, "I will not have my woman wringing chickens' necks."

In the long moment that followed, as he gave in to the first stages of sleep, he heard, "Then you will not have a woman."

He demanded a clarification, but nothing came.

≈

There were few jobs open at the brick factory, except when someone was hurt and had to be let off. Another man was always waiting to take his place. These "casualty jobs" often came about. The brick factory had enough accidents to keep much of the El Comienzo men working at least temporarily. Such was the case when the foreman of many years, old blue-eyed Enrique Lazo, came too close to one of the old, loud machines while he pushed a wheelbarrow of bricks one hot April afternoon, and the backswing of the brickloader kicked him from behind. He tripped, and the rusted wheel of the barrow turned sharply and sent the weight of the bricks down. One of the handles pinned and snapped Enrique's left ankle.

It ended a long career. He went home, and never worked with bricks again. He rarely walked anywhere. Old friends who cared nothing about Enrique's politics said they saw him amble only to the gravesite of his son Edmundo, where he would sit in the shade of a mango tree for hours at a time.

The line of the unemployed shortened one notch that day. A seasoned worker became foreman, and someone new was hired to enter the ranks of the workers. He was a young man, obviously accustomed to such work, one who could do twice over Enrique's work. He had

A Fire in the Earth

come from out of town. The replacement stood taller than his fellow brick workers, lifted double the amount of bricks than the average man, and carried them with little strain or complaint. He worked methodically, almost like a machine that never needed refueling, better than any rusting apparatus in the factory responsible for taking jobs from other men. The others called him *baboso*, the dumb one, for he seemed slow in thought and words. But they deemed his work incredible, and that was all that mattered.

Most of the time he carried bricks to waiting trucks. He seemed satisfied with that, though at times a foreman told him to get inside the factory building and help with the loading and unloading of wood blocks off the bricklines. He obeyed without any hint of complaint or relief. He did all his work, everything which was demanded of him.

None of the workers knew who was their master. The story had come and gone about the Colónez brothers, now both dead, how one of them had gambled away everything that the younger sibling had owned, losing it all to some gringo that none of them had ever met. Now they had no *patrón*, not even Joaquín Reyes, who seemed to have no interest at all in the brick factory. There was no *patrón* for them, no one to focus the blame or the responsibility, or any of their anger or fear over the loss of such a good, honest man as Enrique Lazo. Something missing; it seemed almost empty, though they knew that usually 'patrón' meant the Lord, and not necessary a benevolent one. *Patrones* of the past had been whimsical ones, gods who bought and sold the heavens and the earth, who at times mixed with mortals such as Romilia Colónez and her daughter Rosa. Obviously the gods found something titillating in this lineage of women.

For their own sake, the brick workers had no *patrón* of their own to turn to or turn away from, to fear or to beg from. Yet a *patrón must* have existed, for they still existed and they received money, though much less than before. They wanted to believe it was a blessing not to have a *patrón*, to see no bossman except for Reyes who, they had heard, paid shit wages at his hotel. Just as well that he did not own them. They speculated, but they remained as ignorant as this young, healthy worker, the new fellow who called himself Culebra. As time passed, and as thousands of bricks were formed, baked, and sent away in rickety trucks, the workers asked few questions concerning their ownership, as if too weak to do so. They became almost as silent as this new hired hand.

$$\text{\textasciitilde\textasciitilde\textasciitilde}$$

During Rosa's first pregnancy Romilia moved quickly, knowing how important that first life was for her. She confronted Joaquín in the hotel kitchen, called him in the expected manner, "Mr. Reyes, I need to talk with you about a very important matter." She motioned for him to follow her outside. He said nothing. After a moment's hesitation he followed, still eating some sweet bread snatched from the kitchen. He listened, watching her with preset eyes. They stood in the grass of the back lot, several feet away from the wrought iron fence that towered behind them. "As you know, it is nearing time for the birth."

"If you mean my wife, yes. I think I know a little something about that."

"You need a midwife."

"No, I do not. That has been taken care of."

"What? You have a midwife already?"

"No, something better, if you must know. A doctor from the capital, a friend of the family's, he will come in when she's ready."

"What? You will have some stranger catch your child? Someone who does not even know my daughter?"

"Doña Romilia," he spoke, forcing a respect for the older woman, "my wife will be taken care of. The doctor is an educated man, not some woman who has happened to catch four or five babies in her life. So you see, my wife will be in professional hands, and not in the hands of some *labriega*."

"I did not propose for a *labriega* to catch my grandchild. I propose that I be the midwife."

"You?" He chuckled, his arms crossing. "And what are you?"

"What am I? I am Romilia Velásquez de Colónez, the *mother* of the *patrona* of this land, the one who has the right to catch my daughter's baby!"

A Fire in the Earth

Her shouts silenced them both. He looked about, not wanting the other servants to see him in such a conversation with one of their own. Yet they did see, all of them, and they carried it among themselves like a fabulous jewel.

His voice turned furtive. His arms crossed, uncrossed, then crossed again. "Listen to me. You seem to forget that I am the *patrón* here. You are one of my workers. You are lucky to work here."

"And *you* are lucky to have married my daughter, one of the prosperous Colónez's, who lost both her parents years ago and had been living in Mexico until she met you."

He stared at her, said nothing, looking into her eyes to find out how she knew of his old lie. It was a small town, he knew that. His eyes darted anger like sparks off burning softwood. He turned it to his own benefit. "Yes. yes, of course, you of all people should know exactly what my position is. You see, as well as I do, how it has to be that way, how that story must be believed." He chuckled, as if winning, laughing away an embarrassment that was not deserved: he, the *patrón*, ashamed before a *labriega*.

She responded, "But the problem for you is that I am not dead yet." She looked into his fire, added quickly and with defense, "and I will not be as long as you are married to my daughter."

Again they said nothing, but looked at each other with understanding. They knew each other with an enigmatic intimacy, one based on position, of stepping on stones up a hill of status, of knowing where one stood, on whose head one danced in order to remain on a particular stone, or how to climb up higher. A farmhand walked by, burdened by two pails of milk. Joaquín broke the impasse first. "Looks like work comes your way." He referred to the farmhand. "Thank you for your offer, Doña Romilia, but we have the situation taken care of. The doctor will be here when the time comes." Joaquín tipped his hat, then quickly broke away and walked toward his house. He called out to his valet Sheriff, well dressed and ever-ready, to bring his car to the front of the house. The *patrón* wanted to leave in twenty minutes. Romilia watched as the *patrón* walked to the gate that separated the private home from the hotel. A guard opened the gate for him, closed it

341

again, and stood quietly by. Joaquín disappeared into the house. Romilia turned away. The farmhand followed her to the cheese shed.

Joaquín left for business meetings in San Miguel. These trips had become customary. Every week he left on Wednesday and returned on Friday or Saturday. It was the only way the manager of the Singer company could run the factories throughout the Republic while still living in the countryside. Earlier in the pregnancy Rosa went with him. He enjoyed it, but she found it boring. During those four days she always longed to return to El Comienzo. After his meetings Joaquín had always taken Rosa around the cities, had showed her the various sights and had treated her to expensive restaurants, which did not exist in El Comienzo. Still, she had always felt removed from the nest.

Later in the pregnancy, when travelling became difficult, she remained at home. This served both their needs. She preferred her home, staying and working around the house with the maids with whom she had a happy rapport. He travelled without fear of hurting her in her pregnancy during the long trips, and with the freedom of thrashing about with other women—slim women with the unprotruding stomachs of those gringa models in advertisements that met him in his hotel room and exhausted his youth almost every night of those long business days.

≈

The birth came about just as Romilia wanted. She looked out the window of her adobe house, staring at the torrent of rain as if it were a gift from a god that knew only of her needs. She watched the hillside melt away, its mud clogging and drifting down trenches and crevices. No lightning this day, only silent rain, and clouds that clung together, unwilling to separate for several more hours. It had been raining for days, and all traffic to and from the town had temporarily ceased. Gossip in El Comienzo let her know that Rosa was in labor. Romilia waited, watching the rain beat calmly against the withering land.

≈

A Fire in the Earth

"A lousy time to be fucking around with a lame cow," spat out the hotel worker, Juan de Dios by name, who tried to coax the animal out of the torrents. The other two workers with him heaved and panted, pushing against the cow's flank, prodding it with a short stick. One of the cow's legs had broken when it fell earlier into a mud bog. The animal stood, lame yet recalcitrant, as if it knew the fate that awaited in the barn ahead of them.

"What will we do with all this meat?" asked one of the other two.

"I'd like to take the bones and shove them up his ass," replied Juan de Dios, pointing with a jerk of his head toward the *patrón's* house.

"Well, she will be a decent animal to eat," said the third, somewhat sarcastically, knowing how rich the meat would be. "Maybe we can take thin slices...."

"I will be happy slipping away with the fat, being the simple man that I am. It makes good fried beans."

"Yes? And if the *patrón* finds out?"

"He will not find out. He is busy pulling out his baby."

"Oh? Is he doing it?"

"I am sure. The doctor will not be coming. The road is washed out just a few miles out. No way in or out of here. *Move*, you big bitch!"

"So you think we can slip away with some thin slices?" asked Marcos.

"Why not? Don't we deserve it? Isn't that right, Aldo, don't we deserve it?" Aldo agreed with a rain-soaked smile, barely looking up at his friend Juan de Dios. "Of course we deserve it! Just like our comrades say, we deserve everything equally. And we will get it someday."

"Careful, man."

"What? The cow will fink on us? Why should we be so afraid? They will kill us? The way we are now, the rain will drown me before the Guardia can cut me. It is like they say, Marcos, we will get nowhere if we hide in our fear. They told us that last meeting. We must prepare ourselves."

"Well, we best prepare this cow first, or it will rot on us," responded Marcos, not being himself a man of politics nor of movements, and trying to evade the topic. Slowly they approached the barn, where a burning lantern beckoned.

Behind them a tall, lanky figure burst from the front door of the private, wood house and tumbled toward the protecting wrought iron. He screamed at the gatekeeper to open it and let him out. As the servant followed orders, the *patrón* fell through the gate and ran down a mud-covered hill. Slipping as he descended into the little village, Joaquín arrived at the doorstep of the adobe house and fell upon it, yelling her name, "Romilia, Romilia."

Two minutes later she answered the door.

"What is the matter with you?"

"Quickly, Doña Romilia, she...Rosa...she is dying...."

"What? What are you saying? How do you know?"

"The screams, she is screaming in pain...it is too much, please come, help her."

"Where is your doctor?" She asked as if she did not know, while both the blessing and the curse of the rain fell upon him. She let him stand outside her house. He explained, the road, the mud, and her screaming, her dying.

"I will need a place to stay in the hotel if I am to be the midwife. And I mean for a while. Midwifery is hard work, you know."

He promised that; he promised anything, everything. She tossed on a large coat to cover herself and tromped outside behind him. She could hold herself better in the mud than he.

Several minutes later they approached the gate. He gave an order in a broken voice. They entered the area and disappeared into the house. Romilia gazed at the beauty of the house as Joaquín slipped about, shedding his coat. She then barked demands to him, "Start a fire, it is cold in here. Get some boiling water, and make me some coffee before I die of a fever." She went upstairs, walked past the old maid Olga, who stood at the bottom of the steps, her fingers held to her mouth as if eating fear and ignorance by the handful.

When Romilia opened the bedroom door, the wailing filled the hallway. The door closed again, and by the time Olga went back upstairs Rosa's crying had diminished. The old maid heard pants, heavy breaths, and a low, warm whisper. "Do not worry, I am your mother, I am here, I will not leave you, do not worry." The screams recurred in minute rhythms, but with more control, with a sense of purpose.

〜〜〜
〜〜〜

The rain thrashed against the barn, but did not beat against the men who had shoved the thin machete under the cow's left foreleg and pricked its heart. The animal's bellows broke through the rain, then settled into quiet death throes. They built a fire under a huge container of water and used their knives against the skin of the carcass, flaying slowly, methodically. "Shit, what time is it?" asked Juan de Dios.

"Very late, after midnight I am sure."

"What a time for this baby to break a leg," said Juan de Dios. The others cut and sliced the carcass with little thought. His calloused hands dressed the steaming meat and bone. Juan de Dios was exhausted. His eyes were sunken in deep, wrinkled bags. At times he placed the palm of his hand over the stubble of his face to rub himself into wakefulness, smearing mucus from the animal upon his chin. "Worth it, I suppose. Look at this hide. You think he will let us keep it?"

"You know the *patrón*," said Marcos. "He probably does not realize that a cow has a hide."

"True. Nor intestines. My woman could cook these up with some pepper and onions, fry them in its own fat. Very rich."

In the course of the night the rain abated. By the time the light of day came it was but a drizzle, coating the muddy world with one last soaking slap of water. About the time the servants began to stir with the morning chores, the back door of the grand house swung open and the owner fell out into the mud, laughing, throwing a smile toward the guard that stood at the gate between the private house and the hotel. He laughed at the guard, who only smiled respectfully. The *patrón* offered the soldier a swallow from the bottle which he swung around. The guard took it, then opened the gate as Joaquín had ordered. His yelps and laughter woke the three men who leaned against the corners of the barn, the cow behind them in neat piles. Juan de Dios lifted his

345

hat up and peered through his caked eyes at the *patrón*, who danced in front of him several feet away.

Joaquín turned to the barn and saw the men. "Hey! You boys! I have a son! My first son, I have a son!" He laughed again, a guttural, young laugh, and wandered toward them. They automatically stood. As he approached them he shoved the bottle of smoke-colored rum toward their faces. The sober farmers looked at one another, then Juan de Dios took the bottle. The three took small swallows from it. They all stared at the bottle, tasted the liquor in their mouths, experiencing the cheapest sense of being honored by their master.

"Do you want to know his name?" he asked. They nodded. "Jesús. Jesús Reyes y Colónez. That is what we call my son." He giggled, slapped each of them on their shoulders, offered his handshake, then wandered away. Standing in the mud, he lost some of his laughter and dropped his jaw as if ready to regurgitate.

"Jesús. Just right," mumbled Juan de Dios. "Jesus Christ. the son of God."

The other men laughed only slightly, as they saw that their friend found no humor in his pun. They turned around to the newly slaughtered meat behind them, knowing they still had work to do. They had to carry it to a cooler area before it would be sold to lines of people in town. More money for the *patrón*. A token of coins, really. He would not notice the weight of more riches, nor the lack of one cow. Yet he would still sell it, all for the going price. For now it was morning, time for coffee, perhaps some bread at the bakery. They decided that the meat could stay there for an hour or so, and each grabbed some fat from the animal to take down to their families. Juan de Dios snatched a fistful of cut meat that he had sliced a few hours previous, and shoved it into his shirt, hoping the guard at the gate would not notice. They walked out of the barn, barely glancing toward the *patrón's* private house. They took no notice of the woman standing at the second-floor window, that older Doña who looked out with a bundle of cloth and new flesh in her arms, the first baby she had ever caught. Romilia gently patted the bundle while staring down at the lovely, rain-soaked view of El Comienzo in the distance.

Chapter Five

Lupe had become more involved. From the time the *patrón* Joaquín Reyes had begun the courtship of Rosa Colónez, Lupe had followed her own lover to the depths of his political beliefs. Sergio had a way of speaking about the Cause even when they were down at the river. At first she grew tired of this. As time passed, however, and Sergio introduced her to some of the people he worked with, Lupe found merit in his beliefs. Soon she was participating out of her own volition. While Sergio was attending some planning session with the outsiders who never showed their faces in the light of day (and who held meetings that she was not invited to attend), Lupe gave to what had quietly been known as "the movement" in her own way.

She had made a duty of doing charity work outside of her work at the bakery. Her mother Marta never complained about giving her a small basketful of bread for Lupe to take to people who worked on the outskirts of town, in the coffee fields. She worried, however, about her daughter walking out alone, even in the afternoons when it was still light. Marta asked Pedro to accompany his sister whenever she could. He grudgingly assumed this responsibility. For his part, Pedro was rarely asked to attend the night meetings either. Sergio had explained to him that it was for older men, that he was the representative of the youth in the movement. "Don't worry, Pedro, your time will come."

"But when?"

"When you're older. And when your old man lets you out of his sight."

The remark cut slightly, yet Pedro did not respond, knowing his older friend spoke the truth. He found some meaning in being with Lupe in the coffee fields. Charity work allowed them to meet people much poorer than themselves. The poverty they saw moved them, and

Lupe began to persuade her boyfriend to take a few sacks of food from his father's store for some of the people she was helping.

Sergio frowned upon this work. He told them that charity was the enemy of the movement, as it did nothing but ease the suffering of the poor for a brief moment rather than organize them in their pain.

"That's nonsense. How is anybody going to organize if they're too weak to even stand up?"

"Lupe, you're just prolonging their suffering. They won't get anywhere if you keep feeding them."

"Feeding them? I am feeding nobody! I carry a basket of bread to a couple of families in the coffee fields. And I like getting to know them. Besides, I'm only asking that you give me a few sacks of beans, just little ones. And maybe some rice."

"Rice, too? My father will rip my ass off with his belt. God, girl, you sound like some missioner."

"Yeah, I bet you'd like that if I joined the convent." She packed the bread into the basket without looking at him. "You spend all your time in meetings with some big shots who come from the capital. But do you ever see the people that you're supposedly trying to save?"

It was rare for him to stutter through a response. Pedro stood to the side while the two lovers bickered. He was waiting for Lupe to pack the bread. Their parents were not present. This conversation would never happen if either their mother or father had been there. Sergio would not show himself around the over-protective Hermes. Pedro stood at the door, as if to keep a watch for his mother and father.

Sergio left, mumbling a promise that he would dig up some food from his father's inventory. Pedro watched his friend walk down the street. He then turned to his sister. "You know, that was pretty cheap."

"I don't know what you're talking about."

"Oh, yes, you do. You threatened him with the convent thing."

"Oh. That." She smiled toward the basket that she filled. "Seems like religion *does* have an effect on people. Even if you're in 'the movement.'" She whispered the phrase with obvious sarcasm.

A Fire in the Earth

The three teen-agers walked into the coffee fields together. Lupe smiled all the way and held her lover's hand. The visits to the poor people in the fields had become important to her, and this was the first time that Sergio went with her. It was also the first time that she brought real food. She had always been nervous to ask Sergio for such a favor. After so many trips into the fields, however, she could not hold back.

They first stopped at one adobe house that held a family of six. Sergio watched as his lover greeted them comfortably, sitting down with them and talking like they were friends. He stood quietly, uneasy, watching a scene that he had never witnessed before. He had never been poor in his life. His father had always owned a store, as long as he could remember. Back in the capital, when Sergio was just a toddler, his father made enough money to make the move to the countryside possible. Sergio shifted his weight from one foot to the other, waiting for an opportune moment to speak, one which never came, as he did not know what to say. The rhetoric of the meetings that he had faithfully attended obstructed his ability to carry on a regular conversation.

Lupe helped him out. She said to the mother of the family, "We brought you some food, Mrs. Vargas. My boyfriend here thought you may need some."

Mrs. Vargas, a woman in her thirties, with a baby girl suckling at her breast, opened her mouth in surprise. She took the small sack in gratitude. "Thank you, uh, thank you, yes...." She looked at Lupe, barely glanced at the tall Sergio who stood before her. Pedro squatted to the side, playing with a couple of the older children.

Lupe felt the woman's hesitation. Mrs. Vargas, the mother of six, was usually much more garrulous. Lupe's visits were for her an opportunity to speak adult language, a respite from yelling throughout the day at her offspring. Now she said nothing. "Is there something wrong, Doña Jova?"

"What? Oh, no, not at all, it's just that, well...I know a family that lives about a kilometer from here. Over on the other side of that hill. I think, well, I think they are in real need of some beans. They have only one child, and it's really sick now." Mrs. Vargas looked down at the two sacks of beans and rice. "My husband, he's younger, and pretty healthy. He's working hard, bringing in over twenty baskets of coffee a day. We're not getting rich off it, mind you...but we're better off than some." She looked again at the bags and turned embarrassed at her seeming inability to receive a gift. "This is very kind of you," she muttered. "This will help us through."

"It is our pleasure, think nothing of it," said Lupe.

"That family, where did you say they live?" asked Sergio.

"Over across that hill, past the creek."

"Perhaps we should go meet them," Sergio's voice turned resolute.

"Oh, I think they would appreciate that," said Mrs. Vargas, suddenly smiling. "Yes, they would like that very much."

∿∿
∿∿

She was expendable, and she held her expendable baby in emaciated arms. She once had lovely, almond eyes, now puffed with tears and hollow with days of little food. Though she was very dark, her child was turning gray, and not even the setting orange sun, with all its brilliance, could cast rosy tones upon its skin, not with those tiny worms dripping from its nostrils, not with his bleeding intestine protruding from his anus.

The three young people approached. Lupe walked one step in front of the boys. A man, obviously the head of the wretched household, walked out. He greeted them before they could reach the earth and wood building. The man wore no shirt, only a pair of worn pants of indefinable color. He walked toward them hesitantly, not knowing whether to welcome them, to send them away from the shame of his lot, or to ask them for help. He stumbled forward. The two young men, Sergio and Pedro, smiled and shook his hand. Lupe stood by as the men exchanged formalities. She looked around, and saw through the large cracks in the wall the woman cradling her baby. Lupe could hear her weeping. When the men finished exchanging introductions, they all stopped and turned silent.

"What is the matter?" asked Lupe, pointing toward the woman.

A Fire in the Earth

Her brother and boyfriend gruffly spat out some loose phrases about not having the right to butt in on these people's private life. The father, however, ignored their cliché formalities. "Our baby, he is very sick." His smile melted. He walked ahead of them, said something to his wife in another, more intimate tongue, then turned to the surprised guests and gestured them in with nervous arms. Restraint and courtesies vanished when the young people saw the mother and child. The woman gently knocked the worms away from the babe's mouth and nose, waiting for others to appear. Sergio looked about at the house, the walls that washed away a bit more with each wet season, the thatched banana tree leaves of the roof, the fire pit in the middle of the room, the dirt floor moist from the child's diarrhea, the absence of food, of any sort of produce, and the woman, knocking away the ceaseless worms that peered out of her child's nostrils, pulling them out one by one in a final act of a mother's devotion. She looked up at the healthy young people.

"Please, help us, heal him...."

Sergio stood, his eyes and mouth open and empty of any concept or ideology. He could not move. Lupe bent down toward the mother so as to touch the child. Her brother Pedro turned, and a rush of wind pushed through his lungs as he ran outside and looked away. Sergio turned too, running past the father to retrieve his friend, leaving Lupe to lean down and speak to the mother.

"We will bring help," she said. "We will be back."

Lupe stood, said goodbye to the father and mother, and again promised their return while walking out the door. The father stood at the doorway, called out to them in thankfulness, explaining quickly that this was their third child, this was the third time. The mother behind him wept, confused over the sudden appearance of these three healthy envoys from a distant and unattainable humanity.

∿∿
∿∿

"We will get them food. They have nothing to eat out there. I do not know what kind of medicine to give them, but this can help." Lupe spoke as she arranged the cloth sack of collected foods.

They were in Enrique's home. They had visited him to pour out the suffering they had just encountered.

Enrique had said little, listening to their young fervor. From their limited experience they had taken action. Sergio took more food from his father's store. Pedro removed more bread from the bakery. Lupe found goat's milk at another store. They all returned to Enrique's house. The old man watched them silently, his blue eyes with less sparkle than before, since the days of his son's murder. Finally he asked them, "How many homes did you visit?"

"Pedro answered, "It's way on the other side of the hill."

"Only one? There are ten other adobes behind that one, and twenty more behind those. You did not visit any others?"

"Well, no. We did not have time," said Sergio. "But we should get this food out to that family quickly. They need it."

"As do the ten and twenty families behind them. You go to the next house, which is about a kilometer away from that one, and you'll find another baby dying. How do you plan to help them? And that one family, do you expect to keep them fed from now on? How do you plan to—"

"Look, old man, we're doing the best we can!" yelled Sergio. It shut Enrique up, though it did not keep him from staring at the youth. "How can you expect us to do everything? We can do just what we can do. We cannot...cannot feed everyone out there. We would need more help, don't you see..." His words ended, obviously ashamed from reprimanding an old man.

Enrique overlooked the incident. "Quite true, boy, quite true. You cannot do it all alone. Perhaps you should look around, see if you can find any other resources, other people who have money and are willing to share it. Someone who is willing to help the poor." At that point he lowered his head over the walking staff that he leaned on and stopped speaking.

The three looked at one another, for inspiration had come to them at the same time: Lupe whispered, "Rosa."

"Hey! Where are you going?" asked Sergio.

"To talk with Rosa."

"How will you do that?" She did not answer, as she was gone.

A Fire in the Earth

An hour later Lupe returned, smiling. "I believe we will receive some help in the future. We'll see. For now, let's get this food out there before nightfall."

They began walking. On their way out of town Lupe explained what she had done. "I just sent word through Doña Olga's niece. Olga works for Rosa. I said that I wanted to talk with Rosa, that it was very important, and perhaps we could get together soon."

They walked away and out of town. They had to cross over one hill covered in coffee and pine trees, a thick area that shielded them from El Comienzo. For a few minutes, while hiking through the wooded area, they played a quick hide-and-seek game in which Sergio dropped his serious demeanor and chased after Lupe while her brother Pedro rested under the shade of a tree. They resumed walking, laughing at one another, happy with their endeavors. They grew excited, as they knew that they were participating, finally, in an intimate part of some movement, in the actions of the Cause that they had heard discussed among clandestine friends. Though none of them said it, it was a strange time to be young. Yet it was the only youth they knew of; there was nothing else to compare it with. They knew they were doing a good deed, helping those less fortunate than they. With that knowledge they ran over a small hill to the adobe that they had visited the previous evening. They ran all the way at a full run, with bags of food in hand, sacks of hope and life that they carried as carefully. They did not stop until they caught a glimpse of the father. He was kneeling, and pushing dirt by hand into a recently dug, shallow hole. Behind the man sat the woman, empty-armed, sniffling under the thin shade of the house.

Lupe ran, squatted next to her. Then she took the woman in an embrace. Sergio and Pedro moved toward the man, who raised his head from the grave, showing the wrinkled cave of his wet eyes. They stood beside him, not knowing how to show their sympathy. A bony dog wandered by. It sniffed about, then approached the grave, hoping for a meal. The father picked up a rock and threw it at the animal. The dog rushed away, but did not go very far, as it too was weak from lack of food.

353

Sergio forced out a breath. He turned to Pedro, asked for the sacks of food, took both sacks and went into the hut. He placed them next to the fire pit in the center of the dirt floor. He returned to the grave, where the three men stood in silence. Sergio turned slightly to the man to address him, then stuttered, "I am sorry, please, tell me your name again."

"Zelayo. I am called Zelayo Orcona."

"Zelayo, yes, I am sorry. We are here, Zelayo, because we want to talk with you about some things which we believe may be important to you."

Lupe looked up and straight at her boyfriend. Her eyes glared, as if to shout down his ideology, to scream *Not now, not now.*

♒

Romilia's new room in one corner of the hotel looked out toward both the Reyes family's private house and the town of El Comienzo. She had moved in three days after the little one named Jesús was born. During those days she had stayed at the private home, much to the sobering dismay of the *patrón*. She gave only one reason: the new mother needed the constant care of a midwife for those first few days. Romilia had remained in the bedroom with her daughter all that time, letting no one in except Joaquín, and he was allowed only a few minutes with his wife and child. Sometimes he stood outside the door, pecking on it easily, as he had been told not to wake the baby. The old, demanding hiss of a careful midwife questioned, "What is it?" to which he could offer very little in response, except that these were his wife, his child, and he would like to see them. The hiss told him to come back later, as both were sleeping. Sometimes the cry of the baby contradicted her, to which the hiss formed into a bellow, "*See what you have done!*"

Romilia continued to make goat cheese. It had kept her alive during those years after her disaster. Now in the hotel, she had to make much more cheese to feed all the guests, plus all the new guards brought in from the capital. The hotel paid her well for this. The goats supplied her with enough milk to make more cheese than what the

A Fire in the Earth

hotel bought. She sold the excess in El Comienzo. Thus her income grew. She saved it all, not spending it on anyone, not even herself.

After baby Jesús was born, three shifts of guards watched over the Reyes' compound. One stood in front of the private home. Another was placed between the hotel and the home. Two more stood before the hotel's gate, overlooking the little town. Additionally, guards could be hired for the day by visitors and tourists who wished to have someone by their side. But those came from El Comienzo.

The guards were a special breed. Everyone knew that they had been bought by the Reyes family. They spoke like men, but they seemed removed from humanity. They walked in distance and in solitude, slamming down silence upon any conversation they happened to pass. Romilia knew they were human, however. They ate her cheese. She watched as they dropped the rifles off their backs, leaned them against a wooden pole in her shed, and demanded calmly, as any man would, that she give them some cheese. After eating a tortilla with cheese in three bites, they would walk away.

"Thank you," one guard would always say. His skin was as smooth as new leather. The rifle and bullet cartridge dangled from his shoulders. He would fall silent as he joined his companions. They would walk away to resume patrol.

One older guard, Ricardo by name, wasn't silent, nor did he leave immediately after demanding cheese from the midwife.

"Old woman, you make the best cheese. I always know to bring my tortilla to you," he once told her, the first time they met.

"Yes. The tortilla that you snatched from Doña Ménchez."

"Come on! I did not snatch it! She gave it to me."

"In the same way that I 'give' you my cheese." She spoke without looking at him and kept working her curd of goat milk in the trough, with her hands caked in whey. "And by the way, my name is Doña Romilia. Not old woman." She told him with some trepidation, knowing his position. But she said it. Ricardo respected it.

Romilia's shed was always cool, shaded by the clay tile of the roof. Ricardo made the building one of his daily haunts in order to escape the sun. Late every morning he sat the paunchy forty-seven years of his body upon a wooden stool in the far corner. He chewed on his tortilla and cheese, with cooling coffee in a ceramic cup.

"Well, Doña Romilia, when will you be a midwife again?"

"I am a midwife. And soon, I believe."

"A midwife catching her daughter's babies. I have always heard that is bad luck."

"It does not seem to have brought bad luck to me." For the first time he saw her smile. It disappeared quickly.

"I must say that I do not understand you. Here your daughter is the *patrona*, and you are a goat-cheese maker. I heard that you used to live here, long ago. I mean, that this was all yours. Is that true?"

She spoke with a force that pulled her out of hesitation, "Yes, I lived here before."

"I heard that you were pretty rich in your day."

His words buffed against her like sand on a wound that was just about to heal. "Yes, you could say that."

"What happened?"

"It was lost."

"Lost? How's that?"

"If you must know, mister..." She stood erect, ready to deliver him everything. "It was all gambled away by my fucking brother-in-law who now is melting like a fat candle in Hell!"

Ricardo's back met the pole behind him. His eyes widened and his mouth dropped. "You are the Colónez woman, the old *patrona* of this place? Hah! I have heard of you! And look where you are again! Back in your old home. Or at least living under it. That is incredible, just fucking incredible..."

"I will tell you something fucking incredible. Get off my fucking stool now before I shoot you off it with your own gun, go on, *get out!*" She grabbed his rifle that had been leaning against her cool oven and tossed it at him, then chased the laughing guard out of the shed with her whey-soaked mixing paddle.

Days later, he returned, sat in his same place, and carefully told her how good the cheese tasted. He mentioned nothing of the previous conversation. "You know, I like it out here. I'm glad they transferred me here. It is very quiet, not like Sonsonate. Oooh, what a noisy city.

A Fire in the Earth

Of course my woman, she is not accustomed to the country. But here it is better for kids, you know. The country, the people are better out here, they treat you better. A good... What do you call it? A good environment, that is it."

"I always wanted to live in the capital," muttered Romilia.

"Nah. Better out here. Everything is better. Even the guard. I should know. It is different in the capital. I have lived there, I know. The guard, they're all so young. And all that training now. Yes, it's different...." He looked out the door of the shed. "My son is in training. I never thought he would follow his father's footsteps. He tells me that they bring in specialists from other countries to train our boys, special men from the marines, you know, like the gringos in Nicaragua."

"What is your son's name?"

"Francisco."

"Ah. That's my son, too."

"Yes? Well...yes, Francisco." He held out the name slowly. "He is very young. He came home to visit once, about two months ago. I don't know. He was always such a loud kid, you know? Enjoyed playing outside, screamed just for the hell of it." Ricardo smiled, motioned his arms up, symbolizing a playful child. Then he crossed his arms while shaking his head. "He is so quiet now, much too quiet. He has changed. I do not know." He looked out the door again, stared at the heating day. "Yes, it is very different. They train them so differently than in my day. Well, times change, I suppose, true? It is kind of crazy. Of course, I see more of those young soldiers out here, too. They are sending them everywhere. Well, I am glad that I am here." He turned back to her, threw her a half-smile.

She looked at him for a moment while leaning against her trough. "How many kids do you have?"

"Seven. Three of my own and four 'natural,'" he chuckled proudly, using the euphemism for 'illegitimate.'

"Hhm. The odds are against you; more outside of marriage than inside."

"Aay, God first. He understands, I believe. Hey, children, they are a blessing, true? Blessings from God. And I have helped them all, don't

357

worry about that. Most of them are grown now. And two of my four 'naturals' have gone to college, along with the three from my wife."

"Oh. Very good." She bobbed her head slowly, her eyebrows raised with a smile.

"Thank you. I am proud of them." Ricardo brushed cheese crumbs off his hands and lit a cigarette. Romilia turned to her stone *comal*, still hot from cooking tortillas. One of her calloused fingers turned sideways as she cleaned the side of the huge stove and singed a spot on her skin. "Shit!" she burst out, and pushed the finger onto her lips, where her tongue danced against it.

Old Ricardo chuckled. "What's the problem, friend, not accustomed to cooking?" She told him to shut his mouth. He laughed again, then fell to a smiling, respectful silence. After a safe, long moment that allowed for her finger to begin throbbing, he asked, "How many children have you? One boy named Francisco..."

"I have two. One boy, one girl. You know my girl."

"Yes. My boss's wife, the secret of the whole world. Where is your boy?"

She sloshed her cheese trough, slopping some whey to the sides. "I am not sure. Somewhere in the States."

"The States? What is he doing there?"

"I don't know. Studying, I suppose. He speaks English."

"Really? What is he studying?"

"I have no idea, old man. I have not heard from him in years." Romilia kept her eyes on her work.

"You sound like you miss him."

"No, I do not. He is out there, doing what he wants. I am here. This is my domain, where I should be."

"Your domain. Right. Standing here in your goat-cheese shed, owning the world." He grumbled a laugh.

It did not matter. She was in place and intended to remain there. Her daughter's fertility fed her hopes.

Soon, during Jesús' second year of life, Rosa announced that she once again was expecting. Romilia moved back over to the private home. This time a room was set up for her, just down the hallway from the master bedroom. Joaquín cared little for this arrangement and

358

allowed his resentment to show. Yet he was up against tradition and reputation, for all the world knew how good a midwife Romilia was; that she had been able to come in at the last minute and catch little Jesús during a thunderous rainstorm. Thus came the second child, with no problems. He was named Juan, and came to be known as Juancito. Now, with the reputation of two successful births, there was nothing to stop her, not even the routine visits of Joaquín's sister Necira.

"Oh! So *you* are the midwife that I have heard so much about," said the young woman with a squeal that tapered off to a low, questioning tone. "Yes, the one who caught both of my nephews. Rosa must have a great deal of confidence in you."

"Yes," answered the midwife, "you could say she trusts me like a mother." She finished cleaning the baby and walked out of the room, looking for the *patrona* in order to hand the baby over to her. Little Jesús followed, tailing behind Romilia, hoping to be picked up by her. "Wait little one, I will be with you in a minute. Let me give your brother over to your mother." Romilia disappeared around a corner of the hallway. The boy, left alone, began crying.

"Oh, come here little one," said Necira, cooing to the two-year old. "You don't need one of the house workers taking care of you when you've got Auntie Necira!"

Jesús turned around, looked at her through tear-filled eyes, then screamed and ran down the hallway.

"Hhmph. Little shit," she mumbled.

She went out looking for Joaquín, hoping her brother would soon return from his weekly visits to the city. That afternoon he did, and she approached him before anyone else could.

"Hello, brother, so good to see you." They kissed. He put his arm around her as they walked to the house. Sheriff followed behind, carrying a suitcase. "I was wondering, Joaquín, you know the midwife. Must she stay in the house all the time?"

Joaquín mumbled something that ended with, "I would prefer that she did not."

"Then why not send her back to her other work? Doesn't she also make cheese? I am here; I could help sister Rosa with the children. That way it will not be so...you know, crowded in the house."

He looked down at her, smiled, and kissed her on the forehead. "You know, that is a wonderful idea."

That evening Romilia was sent back to the cheese shed. Rosa said nothing. She only stared at her husband, who used the argument that since Necira was here, there was no need for a midwife. "You will get plenty of work from her, my dear."

Necira smiled, as if appreciating the thought that she was needed. "Yes, sister, I can help in whatever way you think I should. I can help feed the little ones, or change their clothes, or whatever. Just show me what to do, Rosa!"

Rosa sighed. She looked down at Juancito, cradled in her arms. "Well, you can't feed Juancito. But he needs changing quite a bit throughout the day. I am sure you will get enough practice with him. In fact, Juancito needs changing now." Rosa looked around for a clean diaper. Olga stood nearby, and went to get more clean clothes.

"Oh, may I try, Rosa? Let me. I can start learning now."

Hesitantly Rosa handed Juancito over to her. Necira took him, placed him upon a table that had a towel spread over it. "This is easy, I am sure. Here, let me see. You may want to help me with the pins, but other than that...yes, there. Oh my, he was, very wet, yes." She held the diaper by the tips of her thumb and forefinger and dropped it into the maid's waiting hand. "Yes, now we take a clean one, correct? Oh, wipe him off first, I see, yes, such a cute little boy, yes! You are just a lovely little one, your skin is so light, just like the skin of your father, yes, I can tell you are a true Reyes by that lovely skin of yours, yes! You will be a fine and handsome man someday, oh, look at your smile, just look...aaaaaaayyyyyyyyiiiiiiiiSHIT! SHIT! SHIT!"

The other two women turned to her, their eyes wide and almost frightened from the change. They approached her with caution, then watched as Necira clawed at her face.

"He pissed on me! He pissed on me!" She was spitting onto the diaper.

A Fire in the Earth

"What were you doing, kissing his stomach?" asked Rosa, holding her sister-in-law's flapping arm to keep her from swinging at the baby. She looked at Olga while listening to the fragmented reply—that no, that she was standing over him, and that the little shit pissed on her from a distance; that he meant to, he wanted to. Necira tore her arm away and ran out of the room. She slammed the door of the guest bedroom. They would not see her until dinner. There they would somehow be civil. For the moment, the *patrona* walked to the crib to finish the job and muttered to the smiling, giggling baby what a special boy he was.

♒

"I hear you have been an excellent child today, Juancito," muttered Romilia as she picked him up from the crib. She had been invited back once again and quickly settled into work.

Rosa walked in and greeted her mother.

"Where is Necira?" asked Romilia.

"In her room. I believe she is reading one of her novels again."

"Good. We are all better off when she stays in her land of fantasy."

Thus Romilia's life was spent between the Reyes' home and the hotel. She tried as best she could to avoid seeing the *patrón*, which was easy, since he stayed away from home three or four days every week. She quickly learned his habits, how he spent his time while at home, when he left, when he usually returned. His business trips became longer. He took four days more often than he did three, and sometimes had to be away for a whole week at a time. When he was home, Joaquín slept late, not showing his face outside his bedroom until mid-morning. He spent his days in a slow manner, dressing, eating very little for lunch, then ambling over to the hotel in order to see who happened to be there. During the day and into the night he could be seen having a drink in the bar of the hotel with some friend or acquaintance from the capital. He was always looking for reasons to have a party. He remained in the hotel until late at night and on into the early morning hours, and walked home in a stupor of laughter and sadness. Sometimes he stopped at the gate that opened to his house

361

and sat to talk with the guard. From her upper room of the hotel Romilia watched him, and could hear what he said in those late nights. She knew that talking with the guard at the gate kept him away, for brief moments, from the protected domesticity.

From the distance of her upper window, Romilia came to know Joaquín well. The years moved rapidly, though no one could see their passing, not even Romilia, who was well into the sixth decade of her life. Yet the movement of time revealed itself to her, in the change of the seasons, or in the growth of a grandchild who was suddenly able to walk and speak and inspect with fresh curiosity the small worlds of the home and hotel. Time's motion showed itself in other discreet ways, always without warning, revealing its own passage with the simple arrival of a letter from her son.

It had been Paco's third letter. They always arrived three or four months after he had written them. The final letter was sent from a town named Ocotal, Nicaragua.

Only three letters, with a little money inside. But Romilia knew when a letter had arrived. It was then that her daughter, breaking all rules set down by the *patrón*, came to the cheese shed. This time she sat upon the wicker chair in a corner of Romilia's workplace, slightly winded from running. "He wrote to us!"

"Well, don't just sit there breathing hard. Read it to me." Romilia kept working, though at a slower pace. She stopped her chores halfway through the letter.

> To my beloved family: sister Rosa and mother Romilia:
>
> Please accept my greetings when you receive this letter. I hope that you are both happy and in good health. I have heard of your marriage, Rosa, through the usual rumors, for which I congratulate you.
>
> As you can see from the postage on the envelope, I now live in New York, a place where I never thought I would find myself. Yet this is not the United States that you have heard of. The roads are not paved with gold, nor is there money flowing from everybody's pockets. True, this country is not as poor as our own, but it too suffers from the same injustices. The rich man here also steals from the poor one.

A Fire in the Earth

I have learned a great deal since I moved here, but I cannot go into details in this letter. I have met some interesting people, men and women who struggle for justice and the fight of the working man. Do you remember the big war in Europe when I was a boy? These people in New York were some of the many who opposed it, as they knew that such a war pitted working men against one another, while avoiding the real issues that face working men everywhere. These new friends of mine have taken risks in their lives, and are truly an inspiration to me. Perhaps I make little sense in this letter. But I must be vague, in case it does not reach you.

I have learned a great deal. Yet I also feel my heart longing for the old country. I do not know when, but do not be surprised to see me again someday. This is not an empty promise, and I almost hesitate to write it. I suppose I am missing my mother and sister deeply, as well as other friends in El Comienzo. Please rest assured that I am well, and that I am learning many things.

My love and hopes to you both. Please say hello to Don Enrique if you see him. Greetings also to my new brother-in-law, who I am sure is a good and just man. He must be such a man to be married to my sister. Keep well, and know that you are deep in my thoughts.

> With all my love and affection,
> Francisco Colónez y Velásquez
> "Paco."

In the course of the reading, Romilia made several grunting noises because she either did not understand or she disapproved. "You are right to say you make no sense," she muttered near the end.

She continued, "What is all this shit? What is he learning up there? That the rich rob the poor? Where has he seen a rich man rob a poor man? Aay, he is being foolish, the rich *give* jobs to the poor. This town was nothing before your father came here, built that brickhouse, gave the people jobs. And now it is the same. There are jobs. There is work here. Why does he say all this?"

Rosa folded the letter. She listened for a time as her mother criticized, then finally, as Romilia paused for breath, responded. "Well, there are people like this. Right here in El Comienzo, or just on the outskirts. There are people dying from hunger."

363

"How do you know what exists out there? You have never been out there."

"No. No I have not. But some friends have. And they have told me."

"What friends?"

"From El Comienzo."

"What, those kids you used to hang out with? When do you see them?" The sense of being threatened did not go undetected.

"I do not see them. I just hear from them. And I have heard how bad it is in the villages, in the coffee fields."

"Yes, and they would not live that way if they worked. To work as we have worked. That is why we are back here." Romilia pointed to the floor.

"Mamá, you cannot believe that. We are back here through marriage, and so—"

"Are you saying we do not deserve it?"

"No, I am not saying that at all—"

"Fuck if we do not deserve it! It was mine, all along!"

"Yes. I know it was yours. I did not mean—"

"All my life I have worked, keeping us from starvation, making sure that we never fell into that Hellhole of villages behind the town. You would not have wanted that, would you? No, not at all. And so I worked for us both, especially since your brother left to run around in the States. What right did he have to do that? Just a few months after your father's death, and he leaves. What kind of son is that? He cares more for some sick *labriego* than he does his own family."

The daughter interjected, "Mamá, that is not true. He cares for us. He left us most his money. You know he left so as to not be another burden to us, another mouth to feed—"

"He left because he hates me!" The blast forced Rosa to turn her head away. "Yes, he despises me! For what I have done, my life.... Oh yes, leave me here, right, you, too, my daughter." The mother rushed to the door as Rosa walked out into the sunlight. Romilia gave her daughter one final blast. "I have no children who love me! All that I have done, to have brought you back here!"

A Fire in the Earth

∿
∿

Jesús was known by all as "the little man." From the time he was five, he had become a familiar sight to all the workers of both his house and the hotel. It was nothing unusual for the boy to cross the gate that separated the private and public domains of the compound. He did so on this day. The guard smiled at the *patrón's* son as the child asked permission to walk through. Jesús strolled beside the hotel building and headed straight to the shed where the cheesemaker worked. He walked to the door and stared in. The elderly woman had her back to him. He said nothing to call attention, only stared. Suddenly Romilia stopped working, glanced over her shoulder toward the door, as if sensing his presence. Her hands stopped stirring lime into the unground, wet corn. She held the mixing paddle. She took her eyes away from the silent boy, turned her back to him as if to hide, as if it made no difference to her that someone so beloved to her stood nearby. "Hello, boy. What brings you to this side of the fence?"

"I wanted to visit you." The thin, seemingly fragile boy leaned against the doorway post. He pulled one of his feet up to scratch an ankle.

"Really? And why are you not helping your mother to care for Juancito?"

"He is asleep."

"Oh. He sleeps now. Must be quiet in the house." The grandmother picked up the large bowl of corn and moved it to another table.

"What are you doing?"

"I am working to prepare tomorrow's tortillas."

"You have to start the day before?"

"Yes, boy. You did not know that? It takes a lot of time to make them, and a lot of work. Hard work, little Jesús. That is what it takes to live."

He paid no attention to her wisdom. He had a message, and it blurted out of him. "Why do you think Mamá hates you?"

Romilia stopped working. "What? Oh, I see. Your mother sent you here." She stared down at the child, who for a moment said nothing.

"So you are your mother's little messenger?" She said this without anger, but rather showed some gruff affection with the question.

The five-year old stared up at the elderly woman. He had seen a great deal of her in his short life, usually from his bed looking up to her as she wrapped a wrinkled, calloused hand around his forehead to check for fever. Such a brown hand, much darker than his own. He watched as she placed a fist upon her waistline, then leaned against the cool, fireless comal. She appeared ready to feign anger. It was realistic enough for the boy to look down to the ground.

"Where is your mother now? What is she doing?"

"Juancito is a little sick. Mamá is occupied with him, making sure he sleeps."

"When did that come about?"

"This morning."

"Oh. Well, perhaps his grandmother should see him. Where is your father?" Though she already knew, she had Joaquín's schedule memorized. Romilia asked more for the sake of playing a game with him, to confirm her relationship with Jesús. He answered,

"He is gone to work. He left yesterday." His little smile showed her that yes, the boy knew of the silent conspiracy and played right along.

"Go and tell your mother that I will come to the house tonight."

Jesús' lips burst uncontrollably into a smile, showing bright teeth, two missing. He stood there until she raised her opening fist to him and motioned for him to come to her. He did, and she wrapped that dark, brown hand around his head, the nape of his neck, and brought his face to her apron. His tiny breaths captured the smell of goat cheese. It drifted within him and planted several seeds into the fertile ground of the boy's mind. They did not separate for several moments. He did not let go, but rather squeezed her legs together. "Goodness child, you will knock me over. Come." He pulled away, looked up at her, then headed out. He ran to the fence, and she called out to him, "Hey, boy! Tell your mother we will have coffee and bread before sundown." Stopped in his run, he shook his head in two quick nods, then sprinted away again. She chuckled and watched him run, watched as the gate opened and swallowed him, as he sprinted away from her sight, his image flickering in and out between the poles of the great fence.

~~~
~~~

"You do not need to be in my house all the time."

Joaquín looked down at Romilia. He was standing in the shade of the shed's door. He had made it a point to come to this area of the hotel. Normally he never made his presence here.

"I am the midwife. I have a responsibility to be there. I must help take care of the children."

"That is not part of the job. Now you are trying to move in on us, right? Trying to push me out of the picture as much as you can. I will not allow that to happen. There's no way that I—"

"Mr. Reyes, I do not mean that at all. If you feel as if you are 'not in the picture,' then perhaps you should pay attention to where you are most of the time."

"Now listen to me. My life is my life. It is not your concern. I must work; that is how I support this family of mine. So when I leave here, it is because I have to; it is for them, do you understand that? You have no right to criticize my life, woman. You do not have even the right to *think* about it!" As his voice grew into a crescendo, the workers outside—two maids carrying sacks of corn and a *labriego* with a bucket of milk—stopped and looked, once again witnessing how the *patrón* argued with the cheesemaker. Such a sight was never forgotten. Romilia said nothing further. She did not need to. Whenever he was with her, foolishness always seemed to reign over him.

After a long, final stare, he turned away and walked toward the gate. Old Ricardo, the guard, walked up. He had been waiting in the wings of the building until Joaquín took his leave.

"Making headway with the *patrón*, I see." She only replied with a mumble. Without his asking, she plopped some crumbled cheese onto a warm tortilla and handed it to him along with a cup of coffee, as if giving food over to an old husband. He took it, offering no thanks, just like an old husband.

"So what will you do?" asked Ricardo.

"About what? Him? Nothing. I will continue to do my job. He is always gone. Those kids need more than just one adult around them. I will do my job. But I wonder: why is he suddenly so concerned about my presence in the house?"

"Who knows? He's rich; he can afford to be moody. By the way, how are the little ones?"

"They are well, old man."

"I see the older one, Jesús, playing outside a lot. He seems like a good kid. He came up and talked with me the other day. He is pretty smart. How old is he?"

"He's a little over five years. Yes, he is smart. His head is much older than his body. He can already read a little bit. His mother has been teaching him." The old guard shook his head in approval as he chewed over his food. "Yes, he is a special child," she continued. "He calls me *abuelita*." She smiled, thinking of the title, 'Little Grandma.' "Aay! I will miss him if he goes away to school."

"School? That is not for some years, true?"

She grumbled. "The *patrón* wants him to go to a private school, somewhere in the capital." She made herself a tortilla sandwich and poured some coffee. "He does not care for those children. He does nothing but fuck around in other cities, taking care of his business all the time, and God knows what else."

"But that is life, you know. The women raise the children; they are made for that. The men, we raise the money. We work. Besides, why do you complain? He is gone all the time; you get to see the little ones. And that is what you want, right?"

Romilia's smile came forth as if, in her old age, she were too weak to hold it back.

"Yes. That is what I thought." Ricardo grinned.

The cackle of an automobile approached from the west. It clicked through town and drove up the hill toward the hotel, biting into the gravel at the front door of the Reyes' home.

"Who is that?"

Romilia held her answer in for a moment as she looked out to see. Her mouth dropped open slightly in sudden understanding. "That is family. It is Reyes' sister. So that is why he came to warn me...."

A Fire in the Earth

"What is her name?"

"What is she called? Or what do I call her?"

"I am afraid to think of what you call her. Give me her real name."

"They call her Necira." She said it slowly, cocking her head back, imitating the affected young girl.

"I take it you do not care for her."

"She is a bitch."

"Oh. You have proof?"

"It does not take much. This is the reason why the *patrón* came to me. He does not want me around while she is here. Damn! How long will she be around? Seems like she just left here, when she stayed for two weeks during her last vacation." Romilia grinned, and chuckled. "When Juancito gave her a mouthful of piss."

"It is summer now. She could be here a good three months, if she is a student. Why does the *patrón* not want you to be around her?"

She turned and answered, as if explaining the obvious, "Because she does not know I am the grandmother of the little ones."

"Really? Perhaps it is better that way. She is, you know, a Reyes."

"So does that make her shit newly washed?"

"No, not at all. But you know how these things are. Best that they only know you as the cheesemaker."

Romilia leaned against her door, turned slightly and glared at her new friend. Again she turned away, watched as the young woman left the luxury car and walked toward the home. Romilia spoke as if promising something. "They will see that I am much more than that."

$$\text{\Large \symbf{\approx\approx}}$$

The sisters-in-law embraced in formal manner. Necira carried only one thing, an ever-present novel, while a valet took three suitcases to the upstairs bedroom. Rosa glanced at the novel. The cover seemed to be the same cover of the previous book that the girl had brought out here, only with slightly different characters. Even then, the faces appeared the same, with only the hair changed, or the dress, or the position of the love scene.

369

"Oh, sister, it is so good to be back out in the countryside again! I think of this place so often while I am in Antigua. I think it is because, well, because it is out in the country, but there are not as many Indians, true? In Antigua there are so many of them. At least, well, here, I do not see them."

"Yes? And is there something wrong with Indians?"

"Wrong? Well, it is just that they are everywhere, selling their wares, all those clothes. Of course, they are popular with the tourists; I suppose that is how our neighbor Guatemala makes all its money these days. But it is just that, you understand, Rosa, they are so *different.*" She squinted up her nose as if smelling acrid perfume.

"Yes, they are quite different. They must work in order to live."

Necira's plastered smile spoke. "How are you, sister?"

"I am fine. Working hard, raising the little ones."

"That is good. Is Joaquín home?"

"Yes. I suppose you'll find him somewhere at the hotel."

Necira then cut the conversation short and headed toward the hotel. At the gate she smiled at the young guard, chatting with him. The young man pushed the key into the lock, turned it, then slowly, methodically pulled it out while answering her questions of whether or not he remembered her from the last time she had visited here, when they had chatted at this same gate. She walked through. Joaquín stood at the front gate of the hotel, talking with another guard. The soldier stood at ease, his hands behind him, his stance shoulder-length apart, looking out toward the town as the *patrón* chatted.

Necira approached them. At the same time the older, heavier guard and Romilia's friend, Ricardo, turned away from the cheese shed, placed his hat on, and walked out. He saw the *patrón* standing with the hotel guard and decided he should walk over to them in case their conversation pertained to his duties. He was to go on shift that evening. He came closer and then stopped and stood about fifteen feet away, waiting to be recognized.

Necira, however, walked straight up to her brother and stumbled into a greeting. In spite of the distance, Ricardo could hear them. "How are you, brother, what is going on?" Necira was saying.

A Fire in the Earth

"Well, little one, just keeping up with what is happening around our home, it seems some of the natives are getting restless. Good you arrived and got inside before nightfall...."

Soon the *patrón* and his sister left the soldier. Ricardo approached. The guard snapped around and saluted him. Ricardo reciprocated, though not assuming a formal stance, but more in his accustomed way, a lazy hand to his forehead. "Hello, Luis. At ease. What is going on? Anything I should know?"

"There is activity in the countryside, sir. I was informing Mr. Reyes of the possibilities of things becoming volatile."

"Yes? And where did you acquire such information?"

"Through the appropriate channel, sir."

The young guard was one rank below Ricardo. This new generation seemed to follow the letter of the law all the way, even when off duty.

"And what should we do about this 'threat?'"

"We have been ordered to keep our posts and not to fire, as it would give off signals, warning the enemy to flee. Others from among our men are out in the local area. They will handle the situation."

"Oh. So the enemy is near. That is what you are saying. Strange, I have never seen this enemy yet, these communists."

"The enemy is always near, sir." The young guard still stared outward, his eyes focused upon the village below, or perhaps just above the village, as if he saw more than just the town itself, as if he saw some higher, accessible goal. He said no more.

After a few seconds Ricardo thanked him, began to walk away, then casually took his hand to his cap in response to the youth's quick, formal salute.

Ricardo still had some hours before his post began, when he would stand at the gate in front of the hotel. That gate was rarely ever used. Most visitors came through a side entrance, placed nearer the hotel. Ricardo knew the other guards looked down on him because of his age and his anachronistic career. He had not been trained as they had been trained. He knew nothing of the Guardia's new mentality, the contemporary philosophy of a developing civilization, how it endeavored to wipe away any references to an earlier, indigenous society. For this reason Ricardo had not received information about the unrest before the young soldier did. There were new goals for the present day. A guard could look at a town like El Comienzo and see what he had been trained to see. It was this training that would allow a man to rise above the imperfect present.

Ricardo wandered about the hotel, whiling the hours away. It was just as well. Having a fully-dressed soldier walk about the premises lent to a sense of protection for hotel guests spending a day or two in the country. Other guards did the same. He looked about at his comrades, most of them much younger. That one at the gate, Luis, had come from a family in El Comienzo. Pablo, the one in the back around the barn, also was from town. To have a son in the guard was a welcome opportunity for a family, as it meant money, a soldier's salary that would support them—if their son were a good soldier—for the rest of their lives. Some houses down the hill were being rebuilt, with tile floors and an extra bedroom, thanks to the income of those who had sons in the guard. Yet young Luis could stare out toward the town as if it were not there, as if it were not his home. Thinking about it confused the old man, wearying him. It was better for him to find a place to rest under a malinche tree until his time to serve had come.

〰〰
〰〰

Adamancy took Romilia to the locked gate. "Let me through. I have to work tonight." The guard opened the lock, pushed the wrought iron gate wide, and said nothing as she walked past him. She moved, and her face pointed straight ahead. Her eyes, however, darted from tree to tree, from building to building of the private home, watching out for Reyes. She did not see him. Quickly she walked through the side door into the kitchen, like a child running the final steps home through a night filled with ghost stories. Olga stood in the side porch.

"Where is my daughter?" asked Romilia.

"She, uh, she is in the back barn, doing something, I am not sure..."

"Back barn? What is there for her to do?"

"She has some project going on. She has been working on it awhile. I, uh, I am not sure what it is."

"Oh. Where are the little ones?" asked Romilia.

Olga answered that Jesús was on the side lawn and the baby was sound asleep in the next room. At that, a half-cuddled stirring, followed by a practiced scream, then a set of cries of a child waking up to loneliness were heard. Olga moved to quiet the child.

"No, I can do it. Thank you, Olga. If you need help with dinner, I can be in the back with you tonight," said Romilia.

Romilia entered the other room and reached into the depths of the baby crib, picked up the bundle of young life and brought Juancito to her shoulder. She cooed many thin, soft words. Slowly she walked toward the stairs, climbed up them, then entered a bedroom and quietly pushed the door closed.

In a few minutes she heard her daughter's footsteps. Rosa soon entered the room. "Mamá. Olga told me you were here."

"Yes? Is that so surprising?"

"Well, I did not expect you... did, did Joaquín talk with you today?"

"Yes, he did. How have you been, girl?"

"Oh, oh, fine." Rosa pulled toward her mother like finding a hub of strength. As she sat next to her mother and her child, the young *patrona* smiled, as if agreeing with her mother's quiet, subversive actions.

"Where is your sister-in-law?" asked Romilia, with no commitment in her voice.

"Sleeping. She takes long naps."

They sat in silence for a while. Rosa looked at her mother and son, the latter sleeping in a deep peace on the old one's shoulders.

"You perform miracles at times, Mamá."

"Yes? How is that?"

"You get him to sleep so quickly. He is a difficult one at times. It is more a miracle to make Juancito sleep than for Jesus to walk on water."

"Yes, well, Jesus Christ was a man. He could never perform the miracles women do daily. Like all men, he would have worn out by day's end."

The sun cast a red glow over Romilia's face of worked-over stone and seemed to soften it. The final rays of day warmed the sung words and melody falling from unaccustomed lips.

"I have not heard that for so long," said Rosa. "I barely remember you singing it to me."

"I did. The only way to get you to sleep. You were difficult at times yourself."

Romilia kept humming and singing, soft and warm about a mother who worked out in the countryside while her little, dark baby slept in a makeshift crib to the side of the cornfield.

Rosa listened with her hand upon her chin. Only when her mother stopped did she speak. "Maybe you should sing 'light-skinned one.'"

"Well, he is both light and dark. Either way, he is my grandson. He's got some of this old woman's dark blood in him."

Rosa raised her head at this. Her mother's statement seemed a radical movement away from earlier days. Or perhaps it was that the grandmother was happy holding her daughter's fruit, so happy that she did not wish to argue. Rosa decided to prod some more.

"You know, Necira has such a prejudice against Indians, or anyone dark. You should hear her go on about them."

"I do not need to hear her. I can feel it. In her eyes I am Indian. But she is a bitch."

"I suppose, well, I try to understand why she feels the way she does. She has had a different upbringing, you know, and so it is somewhat understandable..."

"She is a bitch."

"Yes, well..."

"That is the family she comes from. I am sure all of them are like that. A bunch of fucking bitches, or sons of bitches."

"Mamá! Why do you curse so? You used to never speak like that, unless you were upset."

"Aay, it is the workers your husband has put me with, you know. They are so kind and gentle and formal in front of all those guests, but when they turn around to work alone it is fucking this and fucking that. You would think they were Mexican."

"That is mostly the men, Mamá. Why is it that you—"

"Now, now, do not correct your mother. Listen, I speak the way I speak. Who gave you angel wings to fly over my shoulders?"

They both sat. Rosa could hear her son's breath as it fell like morning dew upon Romilia's shoulder.

"By the way," asked Romilia, "what is it you are working on in the back barn? Olga mentioned something, but did not explain."

"Oh, it is a small project, though it has gotten bigger recently. I have said little about it, for Joaquín does not know, and I think it is best to keep it that way." To that her mother grunted an approval. "But I have been keeping back some of our produce—just a little, we do not miss it—and we have this project going. Some folks in town, I have it taken to them, and they go out to the villages with it. So it is used up, and—"

"Abuelita! Abuelita!"

Little Jesús' shouts cut his mother's explanation short. Rosa regretted it. She was enjoying the conversation, wanting to share this information with her mother, though she was not sure how Romilia would respond.

Jesús ran toward Romilia, wrapped his arms around her legs, and pressed his face into the pleats of her old dress, as if searching that loving smell of goat-cheese whey.

"Tss, tsss, quiet, boy. Goodness, you scared the shit out of...you frightened the soul out of me, Jesús. Now careful, we don't want to wake up the baby, yes, good." She bent forward, taking care to not bend too far. She looked at her daughter with a raised eyebrow and a slight smile. "They know a good person when they see one."

Romilia handed Juancito to her daughter and told her of her plans to help Olga with the kitchen chores. She walked down the steps, little Jesús stumbling behind her.

Rosa nursed Juancito for a few minutes. The baby had stirred some and was groping for her breast. She sat and sang to him the same song his grandmother had sung to him before. The boy stared up at her as she nursed, as if mesmerized by the strange sounds coming from that friendly, protective face. Afterwards, while Rosa was placing the baby back into his crib, she heard a slight, feminine moan come from around a corner. Rosa turned to her left and saw a thin, light-skinned arm stretch beyond the door in the hallway, as if trying to climb out of the edges of a hole. Soon Necira's head popped around, turned, and called, "Oh, sister! Hello, there you are!"

Rosa placed on a smile while turning around. "Hello Necira. What have you been up to?"

"Oh, nothing much, Rosita. I was just resting in my bedroom. This country air just knocks me out! It will take me the whole three months of my stay to get used to it." She feigned another stretch, turning her thin body slightly to the left, as if Rosa were a man. To the relief of the *patrona*, the girl stopped.

"Sister, I have been wanting to ask you something. I hope you do not mind." She smiled. Her stumbling about for words fell like glass upon stones. "There was something I heard, which I want to talk with you about, find out what you think. Just a few minutes ago I was in my room, and I heard little Jesús. He was jumping about, you know how boys are, just playing and running a bit. Well, he was yelling 'Abuelita, Abuelita!' and acted as if he were searching for someone. So I stopped him and bent down and said, 'Little Jesús, who are you looking for?' Well, he did not say anything at first, he just stared at me. You know, he does not say much to me anyway, almost as if he is scared of me." She chuckled slightly. "You would think he would know me by now. Anyway, he finally said to me, 'Grandmother.' That was it. I told him that his grandmother was in the capital, and I found it strange that he was asking for someone who was not here. Suddenly he said to me that no, she was not in the capital, she was somewhere in the house. Then he took off and ran into the baby's room. Well, I was curious to find out who he was running to, and so I peeked in—I did not want to wake the baby—and there I see little Jesús hugging the midwife's legs. You know, the cheesemaker. I did not know what to think, and I was really confused when I saw you sitting right next to her. I have been pondering it all this time, Rosita, and do not know what to think. Don't you believe it is bad for Jesús, or even Juancito, to think that she is their grandmother? Perhaps you are close to the cheesemaker, because your own mother, well, died when you were so young...but do you think that it is, well, that it is *healthy?*"

Rosa had been placing the baby back in his crib during Necira's story. She crossed her arms and brought one hand up to her chin. "What do you mean healthy, Necira?"

"Well, I should just say that, considering that she is a maid, a goat-cheese maker, well, to have the children associate with her as if she were a family member does not seem fitting for the children, being that they are Reyes, they do have a family name to uphold, you know. Now, I can see how they could easily fall into calling her Grandma, since, well, she is here quite a bit, more than I am accustomed to. I do think I heard Joaquín say he did not want her here all the time." She coughed out to hide her blatancy. "Of course, that is your business. But to call an Indian their grandmother, well, it just seems that it will confuse them. Do you understand me?"

A silence fell between them, one that, for Rosa, was not long enough. Rosa looked at the young woman, looked at her eyes. They were blue, so very blue, cold and dangerous like the clear depths of a calm pond. She remembered that old saying, that shallow waters were noisy and harmless, and that silent, deep waters, seemingly peaceful, could kill. But this did not hold true here, for this girl was so very noisy. The eyes were the only organs that held any depth, and those seemed artificial. They came from somewhere distant, somewhere strange and foreign, as if they had been imported. Somehow those blue crystals had been brought together perhaps beautifully, perhaps strangely, with this light-brown skin standing before her. Rosa still held her hand to her chin, and somehow remained calm before the danger. Her mother now roamed the house after being warned not to. To be honest, to speak frankly at this point, meant certain chaos. Yet those eyes were so distant, so blue. The *patrona* smiled as if welcoming a cheap tumult. She remembered herself, remembered and believed with a clarity and purity that it had been good, so very good, that she had wrung those chickens' necks in front of this girl, in front of those pure blue eyes.

"Yes. I understand you very well, Necira. But the children will not be confused. Why should they be confused by calling their grandmother 'grandma?'"

"What? Excuse me?"

"And to be frank, I do not care for my mother to be referred to as a goat-cheese maker or a maid or an Indian as if you were spitting out the words onto the ground."

"But, I, I...*what*?"

"Now please excuse me, Necira, I have things to do. I must help Doña Olga with dinner, since we are having chicken this evening which I still have yet to kill, and I also want to find Jesús. He should take a nap, unless Mamá can put him to bed. So if you will excuse me..." And with a rush of a shiver that snatched at her spine, Rosa quit the room.

Necira walked out into the hall on the second floor, creating a path of circles. Finally she cried out her brother's name as if calling out to God, and searched the grounds for him in order to inform him of the crisis.

Romilia returned to the nursery to check on Juancito. Jesús followed her. Rosa also entered, and braced herself with the love for her children. She held Juancito, cooed into his ear. The grandmother looked on with her ever-stern smile. Rosa walked to the windows and looked out, the babe still in her arms, slobbering comfortably upon the piece of cloth draped over his mother's shoulder. The midwife gently scolded little Jesús, hushing him. Rosa looked out the window, stared at the evening. Little Juancito suddenly felt the deep, inner tension of his mother, and lifted his head, surprised. Rosa did not see him, for she was staring at the black Mercedes that had pulled over the hill and up to the front gate, coming home after an afternoon drive.

From above, Rosa watched her sister-in-law rush out. She felt the screen door of the house slam over her heart as Necira ran toward her brother. The girl snatched him in order to spout out words to him the *patrona* could not hear because of the distance. Necira and Joaquín moved and spoke like two badly paid actors, tossing the atrocity between themselves, with the *patrón* becoming confused, then enraged. The screen door again closed, as if whacking against Rosa's breast, yet she almost wanted to laugh as she watched them from above. It would come to her soon. But this sort of scene strengthened her defense, told her that what she was to face could be pushed over like the cardboard projections she had seen in circuses, a place where people stuck their heads to have their photos taken. Her husband would be loud and would protest like any man demanding his rights. He would be obstreperous. There was some reason for fear.

Joaquín did not greet his wife. He did not look for her. Evening came, he said nothing. He walked into the bedroom, barely glancing at her, walked by to change into evening clothes, then walked back out and down the stairs.

Again Rosa approached the window, watched as her mother slipped away before Joaquín could see her. She moved away from the house and toward the gate.

The *patrona* walked downstairs to help prepare dinner. She took the live hens and killed them behind the shed, on the other side, away from the house. She brought the dead birds back and helped Olga pluck them. Rosa found refuge in her kitchen work, cutting vegetables and fruit for the old cook. Olga knew it. She understood what was happening without anyone saying a word, and she had warned Romilia to leave.

Rosa helped serve the food to the silent adults sitting at the table, with the noisy children tossing food at each other. She sat down, and Olga brought in the rest, but then skittered away from the room and retreated to the kitchen. Sounds flashed between the eaters, forks clinked onto plates, knives pushed too hard through a chicken breast and skidded across a plate, and a child's heavy hand brought down a glass of milk. At times eyes darted about from one person to another, nervous about making contact. They hid away, looking at the food when caught by other eyes, hid away from the family crisis that hovered above them.

At the end they separated, afraid of one another. Rosa went with the children to prepare them for sleep. Necira skittered to her room where an unread novel awaited her. Her brother walked outside, smoked a cigarette, downed another glass of scotch.

Night demanded some action. Joaquín entered the bedroom where his half-nude wife prepared herself for sleep. She combed out any knots in the long, thick hair that fell like a black waterfall below her shoulderblades. She looked at his standing reflection in the mirror, which stared at her with eyes like a rifle. "What did you say to my sister?"

"Why do you ask? You know."

"I want to hear it from you."

"If you are talking about my mother, I told her that it was fine for the children to call her 'grandma,' for that is what she is."

"You have ruined me!"

She turned to her shaking husband. His threat melted into a mass of anxiety. "What do you mean, I have ruined—?"

"My family will never accept this; they will all die!" His voice collapsed, anger shrinking to fear. He bunched his hands to defend himself from some unseen fate.

"Joaquín, please. Come now. This cannot be the case. It is not that bad. She is my mother, Joaquín. I cannot live with the lie." But he kept muttering to himself, as if ready to cry. He sat down on the bed and brought his fist to his contorting face, that smooth, young head unaccustomed to such a crisis. Finally he did cry. It was a strange sight for her. She sat next to him and smoothed his hair, waiting for him to quiet down.

They spent the rest of the evening confronting the horror that sat upon him like some devil of a nightmare. Truly it was the first crisis in his life, a problem of inexpressible anguish. His family, he told her, would never be the same again. It would be, he moaned, as if someone had died. She smoothed his hair down, wiped his face, wet with tears of mourning.

At first they did not hear the noises outside, not until the final shots came, three rifle rounds that encircled the town. It interrupted their moment. Rosa rushed to the window, yet could see nothing through the night.

One of the guards, the young one named Luis with whom Joaquín had spoken earlier in the day, came to the door and promised them that everything was fine, that the Reyes family need not worry. Those

A Fire in the Earth

warning shots had to be fired. The troublemakers, the communists who had instigated some disturbance, had been found nearby and dealt with.

"What do you mean?" asked Rosa. "Where did the trouble begin?"

"Out in the hills, ma'am. That is where the enemy dwells."

"I heard no shots fired except your own. I heard no battle. What was going on, if there was no battle, no conflict?"

The *patrón* turned toward his wife, surprised at her analytical questioning. He turned to the guard for the answer.

"We caught them in preparation, Mrs. Reyes. Do not worry, no one was hurt." After excusing himself for the interruption, the young guard left them.

"Well, problems come all at once, eh?" said Joaquín with a sigh.

Rosa did not respond. She excused herself for a moment, went to the back of the kitchen to find Olga. The elderly maid sat in her little bedroom, shaking, looking out a small window, with a little candle burning on a table.

"Mrs. Reyes, what were those gunshots? That was a guard at the door?"

"Yes. Do not worry. I believe it is over. Tell me, did the food go out?"

Olga thought for a second, then answered, "Yes, ma'am. I saw it go out, as always, with the produce wagon this evening. It was taken care of, I am sure."

Corn spilled over rocks and wood like the dried entrails of a wounded animal. The flipped wagon displayed a slow-turning, spoked wheel to a half-moon that dropped light upon coffee trees. Some trees rustled with running fear. Humped figures shot about, leaving the scene, heaving out breaths of panic. A cicada screamed as if offering protection. The forms darted through the fields until they found each other. The boy grabbed the girl's arm and pulled her into a scattered woodland. There they waited and listened as heavy boots crushed the earth between the adobe buildings and gloved hands snapped through doors. The hills cried out in sporadic breaths, muffled under by heavy, dull air. The two in the woods waited. At times they whimpered, but sucked it in as if on the edge of a cliff. Young Lupe asked the night in barely controlled rasps of breath, *Where is my brother, my little brother?*

The early morning fog, in all its aesthetic power, failed to cover the raw fear of sleepless people stumbling from their adobes with limp bodies in their arms. It was all so rude, as the fog tried to blanket the wails and pitched voices bursting from the hills. It could not, not with people contending with body fluids and shredded skin. There were the mothers who began their work. There the baker stood, Doña Marta, as they carried her boy in and laid him upon the bread table. Other mothers stood aside her when she collapsed. Behind them Don Hermes turned away from his second dead son and fell against the cold baking oven, again and again.

The quiet baker, Marta, stood again. She took a rag and smoothed down Pedro's forehead as she had done when some useless fever burned into his childhood. She wiped the deep gash that ran from ear to collarbone until it looked almost presentable, then turned the boy's head to the left to close it up. Marta stared at him as he slept, as if waiting for him to awaken. She knew he would. Of course he would, for this was Pedro before her, the little son, idealistic and ready for justice. He would speak to her. She waited patiently, with tears falling from her creviced cheeks to his cold forearm. The other shawled women wept with her, like tears falling from shadows. It took time, but the drops pooled over his arm, and he opened his eyes toward her and spoke so quietly, so full of her holy spirit was he that Marta paid no attention to his throat that barely moved, at the voice muscles that had no trouble speaking through the gashed opening. He said the same words that he had come to know in life, only more softly, how the town of El Comienzo, it had to fight, Mamá, we must feed the poor people, Mamá, out in the coffee hills, we must help them grow strong so they may fight for justice. We are doing nothing wrong, we are just carrying food to those poor folks. Then Pedro stopped speaking, and the women around the bread table all crossed themselves, and continued dressing her son, preparing him for burial.

A Fire in the Earth

Soon they reached the church, where six other bodies—dark-skinned and without coffins—also waited. Many men spent the day in Leonardo's carpenter shop. They made the coffins that were handed over to those Indian families. Mothers had worked well, for the wounds in their children's bodies could barely be seen. Flowers, banana leaves, yucca plants and pine needles had been placed around each open coffin. A crowd gathered about. The farmers and their families ignored the guards that stood at bay about the church, although there were more of them, as had been ordered. The funeral made its way past the loaded barrels, past the mound and moved outside the village to the cemetery. Seven crosses had been cut and carved from pine, three colored white, four painted light blue, as each mother had requested. It was December. The mountains stood deep and lush-green, the color of youth. The people planted the spilled lives. In the hills the people had dared not to pick coffee that day. Nothing was said, not even by the guards. Their night work was done. They felt no need to react to the challenge. They just held their shiny rifles. Yet not to pick coffee was a challenge, a voice trembling in silence, screaming out *fuck you* through a stream of falling tears.

Chapter Six

"Culebra! Get back to work!"

Culebra turned toward the foreman and stared at him for a moment before resuming his duties at the wheelbarrow. He glanced toward the scene which had previously caught his eyes, that of the young woman running out the front door of the Reyes' house. Culebra had heard that her name was Necira. Most of the workers referred to her as the young cunt. She was known to come to town periodically. She was now living here for the season. Necira ran toward the open gate and squealed joy as a Cadillac pulled into the private estate. Culebra could barely hear her shout as another young woman stepped out of the automobile. The vehicle pulled away. The two young women hugged each other like school girls after a long separation. Culebra watched them until Necira grasped one of the visitor's bags. Both disappeared into the house.

"Oh, Necira, it is so good to see you, darling!" squealed the visitor, whose name was Telma.

"You too, dear. My goodness, how long has it been, a month? Yes, school has been out that long. I want you to meet my family here, Telma. Let's see, I think my sister-in-law is around. There is Joaquín outside; he will be glad to see you again. Rosa! Rosa, oh, hello, there you are."

They turned around the corner to the sitting room, where the *patrona* stood at the window, looking out. Necira's voice hoped and demanded a response. "Rosa, I want to introduce to you my friend from school, Telma Curtino." They exchanged greetings. Rosa said very little. The uncomfortable silence compelled Necira to take her friend elsewhere.

"Why is she so sad-looking?" asked Telma.

A Fire in the Earth

"Oh, I do not know. There was something of a blowup in the family a couple of days ago, but it is better now. But then a riot occurred in the village, and she heard that some people were killed. Suddenly she has a heavy lip."

"Oh. Who was killed?"

"Oh, some of the communists. They found them getting everyone riled up. I am not sure; I do not keep up with politics."

"Ah. Well, communists, then."

"Yes. Come. I will show you the hotel. It is a beautiful place."

They walked outside. When they approached Joaquín, Telma sneaked behind him and placed her hands over his eyes. He touched them, smiled and laughed.

"Hhm. Very young hands, very smooth and beautiful. This *must* be some woman named Telma!" She squealed as he turned and hugged her. They chatted for a few minutes, then Necira took her friend through the gate and to the hotel. They walked quickly by the maids and the cooks. Necira pointed out to the various rooms.

"This is the large sitting room. Sometimes Joaquín has the tables taken out of here and they have dancing. This floor is great for the 'half-moon!' Then there are the upstairs bedrooms. There are twelve altogether. Joaquín added on six rooms when he first moved here."

"Is this where you have the parties? Will you have a party soon?"

"Oh, I am sure we will find someone to have an 'orgy' with!"

Romilia walked through a nearby corridor that led to her work place, carrying empty cheese baskets in her arms. It had been a difficult two days. The previous day she had been sent word not to bother to come to the private house. The guard at the gate had been ordered not to let her pass. Within the same hour she had heard of the deaths in town. She could remember young Pedro from the days just before she and Rosa had returned to the hill. Romilia had tested the new rule, telling the guard that Rosa needed her mother, as a friend of hers had died. It did not work.

Now Romilia heard the voices of the young girl, especially the high pitch of the one who had started the trouble the previous evening. Romilia turned, stopped, and listened, standing still like a camouflaged soldier preparing for a second battle.

385

"Before sending out invitations for an orgy, when can *we* have some fun? I mean, come now, Necira, is there anything happening down in that little town?"

"The town? I do not know. I know that they had that riot. I do not think it would be good to go down there now."

"Oh. I was thinking that perhaps, at night...."

"Like we did at school? Take off through the window?" Necira squealed, remembering recent escapades. "Well, after a riot, perhaps it will be quiet. They will not dare to try to do anything for a while, you know how that goes. But the guards, we will not be able to get through without them knowing. And they will tell Joaquín."

"Well, my friend, I will be here for two weeks. I am sure we will figure out something to do."

They walked upstairs, where Necira showed Telma the bedrooms and the upper sitting room. In a few minutes they walked back through the kitchen and out the back door. They meandered with no destination, with only the sense of deep-set friendship that they had promised each other in their two years of college together. They reminisced about their school. "You know, sister, there is only one thing missing there."

"Yes. It is tragic, the lack of men. But you know, young Professor Donaldson is someone to consider."

"Oh, yes. And if well-considered, one could probably make a high grade in his literature class."

They walked about outside, catching up with what each had been doing the past month. With no destination in mind and forgetting the time, they reached the far eastern end of the gate, the corner that stood the farthest from the hotel. Necira had never been here before. She had never needed to come to this corner, which stood closest to the brick factory. The sounds of the factory brought them there. Telma wanted an adventure. "Come on, let's see what is going on. You know how I am about exploring." She pulled her bonnet a bit lower over her forehead and slung her tiny, falling purse back onto her shoulder. They walked up to the tall, unending gate and stared between its wrought iron posts as they approached it. They watched the dust floating over the factory, the noise falling into itself, metal on metal, weighted wood slamming evenly to the ground. Men walked about, old and young, pushing carts, carrying sacks. They stopped at times to rest and to wipe sweat off a forehead with a dusty arm. The edge of the factory had its own small, tilting fence that did nothing except show bystanders where the property ended. It was a steady factory. Compared to those in the capital, or the rest of the work, it was far behind the times. Old machines worked and ground inside, and many pieces of machinery lay scattered around the yard like rusting metal snakeskins. The women stopped when they met their own ubiquitous fence. There they both fell quiet, and stared, looking for nothing. But both pair of eyes fell upon one man who stood back and looked at them.

Culebra stood up. Brick dust fell from him like red snow sluffing off a pile of dirt. He stared like an uncaring animal that spotted movement outside its noisy woodland. The women cocked their heads to one side. Telma lowered her chin in a gesture of learned modesty. At times the girls raised their eyes, knowing when it was correct to do so. Culebra did not play the same game. He did not look around to see if they were staring at anyone or anything else. He looked only at the women, directly, with no intention of turning away his eyes, and he held his ground, as if he were stronger than the gate that protected them. The two girls turned their heads a bit more, looked at each other for safety with a chuckle, an embarrassed laughter, which told them to look again, to see what they had come upon. Perhaps, thought Necira, it was her golden hair. Most assuredly he had never seen such hair before.

The three did not move from their positions, as if unable to turn elsewhere until the harsh words of the foreman fell like a butcher's knife,

"Culebra! Fuck! Back to work!..."

Slowly the three pulled away from one another. The women turned, almost forgetting each other as they took the first step, still glancing back at the figure who returned to his work. They spoke of nothing, as if the silence questioned them and they preferred not to answer. They walked past the hotel, past the kitchen porch, beyond the shed where the cheesemaker stood and worked. There the elderly woman remained in the shadows of her work place, from where she had witnessed the whole scene at the fence.

∿
∿

"So, have you two caught up with each other's gossip?" Big brother Joaquín smiled at his little sister while he crossed his arms. They all sat at the dinner table, waiting for the food to be served. The children fought with each other. Rosa took a fork away from Jesús, who was threatening Juancito with it. She fussed with the fork and with her son longer than necessary, and did not look up from her children to engage herself into the conversation.

"We do not gossip that much!" exclaimed Telma. "We...inform each other about the world."

"That is the word, yes. 'Inform.'" Necira spoke with feigned seriousness that melted into her young laughter.

"Well, with women such as yourselves informing each other about the world, it would be safer to stay out of the world. Don't you find these two simply dangerous, my love?" he turned directly to Rosa, who was still trying to control the fork in Jesús' hand. She stumbled out negative phrases. Her husband stared at her, his arms still crossed, and the leftovers of a smile dangling off his lips. He turned back to his sister and guest.

The food arrived. They ate in silence. Once the children had finished what they wanted to eat and began tossing the rest at each other, Rosa excused herself. Before anyone else said anything, she had taken herself from the table and had commanded the children to follow upstairs, leaving the others behind her whispering questions, "Your wife, is she all right?—" which sent her up the steps more quickly, pulling away from such unconcerned inquiries. She quietly ordered her children into their individual bedrooms. She kissed little Juancito on the head. He cried and yelled from weariness at first, but after a few minutes he fell asleep.

Rosa barely heard the conversations below her in the dining room, glasses clinking delicately against plate edges amidst their laughter. She looked out a window at a reddening dusk. *You stare out windows*

388

A Fire in the Earth

so much, you will break one someday, said an echo of her husband's voice. She leaned against the windowpane. She stared out at the village sitting below her, beyond that iron fence, and followed the fence with her eyes until it came to the gate, just at the edge of her window, to that door which had been closed to the cheesemaker, to that guard who had been commanded to keep vigil against her. In the hotel, where the sun's cool red fell upon the glass window, her mother remained.

Below the town the river washed far to her right. Rosa could not see nor hear it from here, trickling during the summer, rushing through winter, beating upon rock and naked bodies waking early to bathe before a day of toil. It was the haven, where women beat thinning, colorless clothes upon large flat stones chosen by generations of mothers for their work. The river flowed like a memory over a dry, parched brain that had been left in a desert to die. It had died, shrivelled in its own gray mass while sand and wind burned across it. Not many pages of life had passed since this had happened. Rosa had forgotten, and therefore the past had died. There had been hope for her, with her gifts of food for the villagers, with her helping others who were doing something, who were feeding the poor. That had come to an end. There would be no more food, as the fence had tightened and secured itself against what everyone called "the failed uprising." Thus truth smacked against her like cold river water. It splashed upon her baked brain and cracked it into life, then washed it away into memory. She saw that riverbank, those nights, with mosquitoes stinging her ankles as she reached down to slap them off, running her hands down a young thigh as she did so, with moss and stone wedged against her back, it had been so uncomfortable, they had been so clumsy. It had been love, the river had said so. It had been murdered and debased, just as Pedro had been debased two nights before. Rosa remained at the window, imagining the sound of the river. Reality, etched in imagination, told her of her sins and failures, and how she had been rewarded for those sins, with this house, that protective gate that left her imprisoned from her mother.

From outside the door she heard the three speaking. They were walking to their rooms while they chatted. "You will have to come back

Marcos McPeek Villatoro

the second week in February," said Joaquín to Telma. "We will have a *Carnaval* party, much like the Mardi Gras they do in the States. It will be the best!" He still smiled as he opened the bedroom door, but tossed it away as he looked over to Rosa at the window. He closed the door behind him.

"Why the hell are you still crying?"

♒

As Joaquín yelled at his wife, Romilia walked to the hotel's front gate facing town and turned directly to the guard. "Let me out of this fucking jailhouse. Come on, open the gate."

"Who is speaking?"

"The cheesemaker! Let me out."

The guard looked down at the old woman. Slowly, as if to protest, he clinked the key to the large gate and opened it. She shuffled by, her age slowing her walk. "Fucking rabid dog," she muttered, though not loud enough.

She walked down the hill to town, with still enough daylight to keep the way lit and clear. She looked up at the private home as she walked, and barely saw in the upper bedroom the figure of that lovely woman, her daughter. Romilia looked forward and shuffled a bit faster. At times she glanced up. The figure had turned away, then had disappeared. She returned to her regular pace.

Electricity had come to El Comienzo, and a few houses glowed with one light bulb apiece. Most still went without light. As the sun set, fewer children played in the streets. Strung on a single line, electricity lit both of the bars in the town. Romilia went to the first one, known as Eduardo's though it had no sign, no clue, except for the noise of men laughing and dropping empty bottles. There she asked, "The man, Culebra, where is he?"

"Sometimes here, sometimes there, at The Other Place," answered Eduardo. "He's not here now. He may come later. Or he may be there."

She left, walked two streets over to where The Other Place stood. She passed the bakery, glanced at the old Indian who had just left his sugar cane at the establishment. Hermes stood outside with them,

A Fire in the Earth

talking, inviting them to spend the night. The old Indian once again politely refused, saying that he planned to sleep outside the town, near the river, in order to fish early in the morning. "My woman, she said, 'bring fish home,' yes. We do that much these days." Romilia moved on, not wanting to look into the perpetual sadness of Hermes' eyes.

She walked by the mound where a man lay, half unconscious, still holding an empty bottle like a spent penis. At The Other Place men walked in and out, some carrying bottles. She walked in and became one of three women in the bar: one sitting on an old man's lap; the other walking to the back room with a clutching, giggling younger fellow.

Romilia walked up to the main table, did not touch it, but stood a little distance away and asked her question. The bartender, cleaning out a cup, pointed with his lips to a corner of the building. She followed the directions to the sitting man, who drank a beer alone at a small table. Brick dust caked in his sweat. He had obviously just left work.

She walked over to him, and asked if she could sit down. He nodded easily. She looked at his eyes for a moment. They did not glance back at her, but rather looked ahead, somewhat tired from the eleven-hour workday. He was darker than anyone else in the bar. His muscles and flesh were tight. His hair, black as the coming night, clung to his skull. Though some called him an Indian, he had facial features unlike those of the indigenous.

"I am the midwife at the *patrón's* house."

He showed no interest. She looked about, seeing who was looking, checking to see who would gossip on her. She searched for correct words, but there was no graceful way of developing her idea. At this point she had to be blatant. "I know the two women, the ones at the gate. I know them."

He looked over at her. She smiled, a grin that spoke in nuances, one in particular, *I know you, too. You are from here; you kicked the shit out of my boy in childhood.* She smiled, hoping he indeed was the same man, that he had not changed from earlier years.

Romilia spoke of the hotel and the private home, of the women's desire to leave it, to come down into the town and enjoy a night here.

Most undoubtedly, they would need someone to show them around. She said little more than that, as she knew it was not her place. He was young, and so were they, and with that, they would find imaginative means.

∿∿∿

Telma slept more deeply than did Necira. The noise from the brick factory woke the latter at 9:30 that morning. When she awoke she looked out the window at the distant brickhouse, turned to her friend in the opposite bed, then rose. She bathed, dressed, and put on some makeup. Downstairs some coffee waited. Olga poured it, placed two sweet breads upon a plate for her. "Thank you, Olga," she said without thought, not hearing the "at your service" from the humble maid who walked away. Olga returned quietly to the clothes she had been washing before having to fix breakfast for the late-riser. Rosa ironed clothes in the kitchen, taking the irons from the woodburning stove, using them with dexterity and experience. Necira sighed, rolled her sleepy eyes, ate her bread and drank her coffee. Having finished, she walked outside to begin her day.

The guard let her through without question, as always. She walked toward the hotel, consciously ignoring the cheesemaker as she passed the shed. Romilia did the same as she passed. Then Romilia, up to her wrists in curd, looked up and followed the young girl with her eyes. She smiled as Necira strolled out to the far corner of the fence.

Necira stared out, her arms crossed over her breast. She spoke out to the man, "Hello. Good morning."

Culebra turned to her. "Hello." Then he turned back to his stack of bricks that he picked up, two by two. He tossed them onto his arm that acted as a sling, then placed the armload into the wheelbarrow.

"You know, it is so cool here! I am not accustomed to this mountain weather. In the capital it is still warm. It is always warm there."

In spite of the bulk of his strength, he still handled bricks carefully, dropping them onto the rusting metal bed. He turned and stared at her, and before he spoke, his silence rippled through the gate and enwrapped her. He stared as he had the day previous, only she had no friend beside her now, no one with whom to defend herself with an embarrassing smile or a laugh.

"How is it you have gold hair?" he suddenly asked. His voice ground like gravel.

"What? Oh, this?" and she laughed into an escape. "It is dyed, yes, I dyed it at home. It is my new look, as they say in the States. Do you like it?"

"How did you change it?"

"Well, with this stuff called, well, it is a paint of sorts. I do not know how they do it, but they do. People say I look like a North American, since my eyes are blue. You see, I saw this movie, well, it was all in English, but this real handsome fellow fell in love with this woman with hair like this. His name is Valentino. God, what a man. He played this king, or, well, they called him a 'sheik,' which is the same thing, but people said I looked like her, especially with my hair like well, like this, but I do not know...." The cool wind brushed her words away.

Three loads of bricks were placed in sequence far behind him, from a palate to a truck. He spoke again. "Why do you not ever come out of that cage?"

"What? What cage? Oh, this fence. Well, I do not know. My brother, he would not let me. I do not come out of them at home either. Well, of course, to go shopping or to church, I do."

"Come out now."

"What? Oh, right now? Oh, uh, no."

"Why not? You cannot?"

"Well no, well...of course I can; I can come out whenever I want."

"Then come out now. There is the gate, over there. Come on out now." He pointed with half an effort toward the gate behind her. She turned and looked at it, then turned back to him with an unsure smile.

"Why?"

"To show me that you can."

"No. I will not."

"Then you can't." He turned back to his bricks, loaded another armful as she protested his blatancy with words that sluffed off him

393

like brick dust. He interrupted her. "As I said, you can't come over. You are trapped in there. All of you are."

No one had ever spoken to her like this before. In the next minute she found herself, with balled-fist anger, walking to the gate and demanding with a polite smile to the guard to let her through, since she wanted to go out and pick some wildflowers on the other side of the fence, "for my sister-in-law, Mrs. Reyes." At first he resisted in a mannerly, militaristic way, but after telling him that there was nothing to fear, as it was daytime, and nothing ever happened in daylight, he let her through. Walking the length of the fence, she returned to the same place along the wrought iron where she had stood a minute before, only now with the fence behind her. The noise of the brick-house in front of her suddenly seemed more intense.

He turned and looked at her, then dropped his bricks into the barrow. He wiped his hands, speaking while he did so. "That is good. Now, do that tonight."

"Hey, what are you saying? Look, I am here! I can leave whenever I want, see?" She turned to the fence as if to refer to it as evidence. She turned back to him and stared at his back. Her hands went to her waist. "Look, hey, please. What is your name?" He told her without looking back at her. She mumbled it to herself, stuttered, then decided not to ask him his real name, if he had one, or if he knew it. The simple country people, she had heard, knew so very little about the world, and about themselves. "Well, look, Culebra, I am here."

"Good. Come out tonight. I will be at The Other Place, the bar. I will see you there. Only if you can escape your cage." He lifted the filled wheelbarrow and walked away with it toward the factory, leaving her there alone, in a place she had never stood before.

Quickly she rushed back to the gate and asked to be let in. She passed through the second gate, then ran to her brother's house. Joaquín had left that morning on business. Necira woke the sleeping Telma. As her friend tossed off long sleep, Necira told her of the encounter, injecting in the story the excitement of a new novel. Then they planned, talked, and strategized, how to get out, whether or not to do so, then, of course, get out, get out and into the town, find him.

A Fire in the Earth

Joaquín was gone; it would be much easier to do so, to talk the guards into it, as they had done times before in school.

Whenever they encountered Rosa in the hallway, they said little, smiled at each other, and giggled. She said nothing, but continued her daily work, running after a child to change his clothes. They ate dinner with her and the children, then went to the bedroom to talk. Two hours later they returned to make their appearance before everyone went to bed. They made sure the back door remained unlocked. Soon the house fell into darkness.

Some time later, they took a slow walk through the building, down the stairs, into the hallway and kitchen, and out the door. Then it was the same game, outside, just as in college, with the challenge of averting the eyes of the old guard Ricardo, friend of the cheesemaker. Telma did this well. Necira had complimented her on her abilities before, how she took her lovely hose dress and held it up slightly over her knee while talking with the guard. She led him toward the gate, pressed him into his stool, and placed his hand on her inner thigh while moving the other key-holding hand to the wrought iron door and inserting it deeply. One hand moved, not knowing what the other did, leaving everyone safely ignorant. More was promised later, when they returned, and then they were gone.

They found their way to The Other Place and entered, becoming two of the five or six women who stood at the bar. The scattered men all turned to them. The drinkers became silent as their eyes fell upon those foreign dresses that displayed shoulders, that hugged tight around their hips and thighs. The men's weary, sunburnt eyes stared at the anomalies. All knew that these two girls came from the land of the Unseen Ones. Some smiled, knowing exactly why the two had entered such an establishment as theirs: A desire to be among savages, an adventure in the jungle of *labriegos*. They also knew that, if the girls were not careful, they would get what they sought.

Telma moved closer to Necira, who also huddled with her. They looked about, staring out for a protection they suddenly found necessary but absent. Culebra sat in a corner. His were the only eyes not focused on them. Necira walked to him, beckoning her friend to follow. She sat down with a heavy breath of weariness from the long walk down the hill and from the eyes that enveloped them. Then she smiled, as if she had won a victory. "Hello, Culebra." She almost laughed, not needing to say anything more.

He looked up. He did not smile, and said nothing. It was becoming a cliché, this image he created. Necira hoped to break it, to startle him.

Telma looked about, turning her head from side to side as if to watch for groping hands. Necira ordered two beers for them. "Can I get you anything, Culebra?" He shook his head no, drank the last of his rum, and stood up. "Hey, where are you going?"

"My home."

"But we just got here!"

"If you want to come, you can. Unless, of course, you are still in the cage." He had barely turned around to say this, then continued walking.

"Son of a bitch..." Necira turned quickly to her friend, whispered plans to meet her later, close to the gate of the house. Necira stood up, leaving her friend clamoring protests, and disappeared among the men. Telma sat there, leaning her head upon her hand as some of those burnt eyes sat next to her, and breathed upon her rum-dripped propositions.

"Where are you going?" Necira asked him, looking at his large back.

"Where I sleep."

"Where is that?"

He did not answer, but kept walking, keeping two steps ahead of her.

"Look, why do you act this way? I came all the way down into this shithole to see you, and you walk away from me. I do not understand you at all. You are just like some Indian, acting like—" He turned to her at that and stared down at her for a moment. She looked up. Necira could barely see him, as if his dark skin decided to become the night. He walked again, with her at his side. She waited until they had walked about twenty paces before she spoke.

"So, are you from here?"

"Yes."

A Fire in the Earth

"Oh. Your family lives here?"

"No."

"Oh. My family lives here. My brother, you know."

"Yes. I know."

He turned left and walked upon a road that headed away from town, farther away from her brother's hotel.

"Where, where are we going?"

"I am going home."

"Where is your home?"

Culebra pointed to the hill before them that stood on the outskirts of town. Necira could see no building, no adobe house, nothing but the perfect shadow of a cross that stood against a sky filled with stars. She followed his pace, expecting to see a home on the other side of the hill's crest.

They crossed over the hill and down the other side. The cross that she had seen was accompanied by others down on the slope. She turned back and could barely see the few candles flickering in individual homes.

His hand, huge and calloused, clasped her wrist. He pulled her toward the hill of crosses. "Where are we going?" He did not answer. Necira could barely see the outline of his body, except that his walking shadow which stood against the daylight now swallowed the stars before her. She looked around. The various crosses stood around the couple.

"We're, uh, we're in the uh...the cemetery." She stuck a fingernail between her teeth. "I thought we were going to your place." He did not respond. "I think, I think I should leave."

He turned to her. "You left your cage." He began to shed his clothes. He draped them upon the arms of the closest cross.

"I need to leave."

Then she saw something she could not believe. Light glowed from his face, a smile that knifed through the night, which would have appeared beautiful to her had not the laughter followed, then words which spoke as if they had won, "What is your name?"

"Necira."

397

"Necira. Why, Necira, did you come all the way out here, with a poor, filthy *labriego?*"

She did not answer. She looked at him as he stood there, his clothes completely shed, snakeskins hanging from the cross.

"I should go home."

Such were her final words. They were far away from everyone, the town, the young couples on the edge of the river, the guards who walked the sleepy streets. No one walked in the cemetery at night, afraid of disturbing cousins and uncles and babies from the past. Then assuredly there were other creatures, such as the the witch who used to live here and was found years ago fallen dead in a heap over someone's grave, and now, this Culebra, who took the thin, cream-skinned girl by the shoulders and slowly moved her down to the cool grass. She could not scream, though her squeaky pleas were absorbed by the tremendous night above her. One large cross stood over her, just above her head. He pushed her hands toward its base. As he shed her flimsy clothes, the night's stars fell upon her, prickling her full skin.

Her pleas died. Her mouth lay open like a grave, frightened of the shoulders which swallowed the stars above her, then the head of darkness that lowered down and disappeared. She felt bindings snap, like the spine of a new book cracked wide open. She could not see him, could only feel his work as he held her ankles apart like thin tree branches and ate his fill. The night licked like a wind caressing a hilltop, parting the soft leaves of trees. Her fingertips went down and rested in his hair, then massaged his scalp. She felt no need to scream, nor plea, not until a river of blood rushed through her. A breath writhed through her lungs and pushed over her tongue. She lost control of a smile. She half opened her eyes to the stars, toward his head that bobbed below her. Her head moved round and round to all the crosses standing about them like silent observers.

♒

Long after midnight she stumbled up the hillside. She felt nothing. She arrived at the fence, where Telma, pacing, ran toward her. "Where the fuck have you been, Necira! I have waited all—"

A Fire in the Earth

"Shut up, quiet, you will wake someone. The guards...we must get inside."

They walked to the gate together, Telma asking all the way what had happened. Necira explained all with "never mind," and avoided eye contact. Old Ricardo, dozing, jumped up with his rifle in arm. Seeing who it was, he opened the door with a sleepy silence. He muttered to them something about a promise made earlier that night, but Telma brushed it off with a promise of a later date, and left him growling creative names for the girl. They walked to the back of the house, through the unlocked door, sneaked into the kitchen, and quietly made their way upstairs.

In the room, after undressing, they lay in opposite beds. "Necira," a hiss wanting to scream, "what happened to you?"

"Nothing. What happened to you?" .

"I will tell you what happened to me. They almost tore me apart in that bar you left me in! Shit on those *labriegos*. They are nothing but dogs, with stones for balls. I ended up waiting out there, below the gate, for most of the night. What happened to you? Necira?"

"Nothing. I am fine."

Telma muttered other pleas. Necira turned away and stared out her window.

"I do not want to go into town with you again. And I think you should go home tomorrow."

Telma turned and looked at her friend's back. She glanced about at the night that filled the room. It seemed like the dark back of a stranger. Nothing more was said about the adventure. Telma turned and tried to bring about sleep.

The next morning Necira had Telma's bags packed, all in one corner of the room, with a note on top of them. "Your bags are ready. I will see you in school. Necira." Necira's bed was made. She was gone.

The morning moved quickly. Telma took her belongings to the fence, where an automobile awaited her. The chauffeur had already received orders that the guest was to be taken back to the capital.

♒

"Your daughter's sister-in-law makes the wind move with plenty of news."

Ricardo spat out some gristle that his tongue had found in the tortilla and beans. He gulped cooling coffee as if it were meant to be thirst-quenching, and looked at the cheesemaker from his corner stool. She said nothing as she worked.

"It is not just gossip either, friend. I know, since I am the gatekeeper. She is up to something big, that... that... what relation would she be to you?"

"She is nothing to me."

"Well, whatever, she is a part of your daughter's family. She comes practically every night now. At first it was only a couple of nights a week, about every Friday and Saturday it seemed, and you know why, don't you? Because those nights—"

"Those nights are the nights that the *patrón* is gone on business. I know, yes."

"That is correct! That is the truth! He was gone, and she went out to play. Then she began taking the other nights that he was gone. That was in the first days. But now it is practically every night! She just walks up to the fence, says 'Good evening, Ricardo,' then glances at me to open the damn gate."

"She knows your name?"

"Well, yes. I had to tell her. You know, to be polite." His teeth snatched another mouthful. He talked while chewing over the soft food. "I wonder what she is up to?" Crumbs rode the words, gliding across the room to the floor.

"You want me to tell you? How should I know? Am I my bitch's keeper? No. But it seems you are."

"I am not her keeper. I just open the gate."

"Are you not supposed to?"

"Well, there is no rule. I open it whenever they ask me to, any one of them. There is no rule. There is just the gate." He finished the coffee, and his tongue prepared the cavity to receive the tip of a cigarette. "Just the gate. No rules, except, of course, to keep everyone else out." He sucked the cigarette. Inspiration hit with the nicotine. "I heard that she is fucking that snake from over at the brick factory."

A Fire in the Earth

Romilia laughed.

He fixed his eyes on her, but she kept laughing. "You think it is funny? That Culebra—that is his name, you know—he lives down in town. No one knows anything about him, except for now. They say he lives in the graveyard. You believe that? He must be really something, for her to take such chances, and with the *patrón* right over her. They say they do it right in the cemetery!"

"Perhaps you should report it to the *patrón*, old man. Tell him that his sister is fucking a snake."

"Not me. No, no. That is none of my business."

"It well may be your business. You see her every night now; you are getting involved. Before long people will be saying that you are fucking a snake, too. You know how winds carry rumors."

He ignored her and her laughter, a rare, caustic rattle heard in the shed. Too much of it riled him. "Ah, what do you know? Here you are, a cheesemaker, used to be the *patrona* of all this, and you curse like a *labriega*." He glanced at her, hoping the insult had cut, knowing the only test of its poison was in the bellows of her reaction. But Romilia said nothing, only smiled while she cut the cheese that sat upon a flat wooden board. She plopped the cheese upon a tortilla, walked over to Ricardo with a smile, and slapped the fresh food into his unexpecting hand.

"*Labriega, patrona*, cheesemaker, midwife." She dropped the labels off her lips like bones from a chewed-up fish. "All I know is which way life is going." She laughed. He chewed upon the second tortilla, a surprise gift from her, as if she were rewarding him. "Life goes any way it wants," she pronounced. She chuckled some more while looking down at her work. Small laughter fell from her wrinkled face with the mumbled thoughts of a bitch fucking a snake.

♒

Water glasses clinked against plates haphazardly, accidentally, those times when they ought to have come down upon the cushion of cloth that lay over the mahogany dining table. The clicks stopped the silence and said to them all, "It is quiet; it is all too silent." This made

401

them look to one another. The *patrón* glanced over to his wife, who darted her eyes down, who ate, chewing slowly as if to hide behind her eating. The only words said were to the children, or about the children. At one point in the meal, Joaquín glanced over to Juancito, who had dribbled some ground, sweetened corn meal over his chin and had slapped it onto the tablecloth.

"Please, Rosa, that over there." He motioned to it. "Tell him, get that up. Will you get that up, Juancito, you are staining the cloth. Rosa, tell him…" Rosa acted as he stumbled. Little Juan looked up with a stained face at a father who turned away from the staring yellow blotch upon his chin.

When the meal ended, Jesús asked if he could go out and play, as there was still daylight in the air. Juancito vaguely motioned to follow him, but was restrained, except for his screech which had Necira grab the edge of the table. The older boy ran out the kitchen door to the yard that rested under a red glow of an ending day. Rosa looked out the window to watch the child running about, tossing a soft, small ball to old Olga, who rarely caught it. Two guards stood in the far back, on the hotel side of the fence. They walked back and forth, toy soldiers waiting for a game. Rosa excused herself from the table, took the baby from his chair, and carried him upstairs, leaving brother and sister at the table.

Necira placed her palms upon the table to leave, but Joaquín stopped her as she was excusing herself. "Wait, sister, wait. I have had little opportunity to talk with you these past days." He smiled. She looked at his bright teeth as if they were some vague caveat.

"What would you want to talk about, brother?"

"Well, uh, I have been out of town for several days, and have had to make quite a few trips during your summer here. I just wanted to catch up with your life."

"Oh. My life is fine."

"Oh, good, good. Are you enjoying yourself here?"

"Yes, yes, I am."

"Good. I was hoping that you would not be bored. I know how, well, how quiet it can get here. Very quiet in fact. I many times look

402

forward to my business trips to San Miguel and the capital. They
break up the monotony."

"Yes. It is surprising that you live here."

"Oh? How is that?"

"Well, our family never was much for the countryside, Joaquín."
She smiled. "Everyone was surprised that you moved out here."

"Yes, well, so was I, I suppose. It is a different life. Quiet. That is
good."

"You like it?"

"Yes. I suppose I do."

"I suppose you have settled down from your old ways. Rosa must
have some magic, to keep you so quiet and, well, committed." She
smiled once again, a subtle brilliance that wrapped about his thin
arms and held him to his chair and said to him in the aftermath of the
smile, I know, yes, how important those business trips are. I know, my
brother.

"Yes, I have settled down, Necira. I have had to leave those days
behind, as much fun as they were. One must grow up, you know, and
break away from the old ways, and be responsible."

"Yes. I know."

"A person has to be responsible about life, and still have a good
time of course. It is that way here especially, with such a small town,
so few people. You have to be careful what you do and all, or everyone
knows about it."

"Yes? Have you learned this from experience?"

He looked directly at her, weighing his words as he put them out
upon the table. "Well, yes, I have. And recently I have just heard of,
well, the rumors ran by me by chance. Necira, have you been seeing
someone?"

"What? Why?"

"Have you?"

"Have you heard that I have?" She spoke in the old, childish way,
caught, trying to wriggle out with questions.

"Yes, I have. The cooks were saying something about it. I am not
sure. I did not hear everything—"

"What cooks? What did they say?"

"At the hotel, they were talking when I walked through."

"Yes? And what did the bitches say?"

He had been twisting his water glass on the tablecloth, then stopped to answer her. "The cooks said that you have been sleeping with some *labriego*."

The words, falling like crystals upon the soft tablecloth, thumped upon her as a reminder of their family, of their position. He had spoken it with Reyes' force, as they both knew he had the right to.

"And are you going to believe a bunch of women who cook in a hotel?"

"Whether or not I believe it, others will, the whole town will, or already does. So however the rumor began, it must stop."

"So. Did your informers also tell you the name of whoever I was sleeping with?" Her thin body twisted sideways.

"They said something about a snake, his nickname. I do not know. Oh yes: that he sleeps in the cemetery, his home is a gravesite, where his mother died years ago. You see, that's how crazy rumors can get. These country people think up the most insane superstitions." He looked to the side. "I am just concerned about stopping the rumor." With each word he brought his hand down slowly, flat and vertical, like a small soft machete, against the corner of the table. "Necira, I just do not want my little sister's name slung about as if it were mud, do you understand?" He looked up at her, transforming his anger into a plea. In the rushed moment, she stared at him in a different manner, quietly, with a very little, fabricated sigh billowing out of her tiny nose.

"Yes, big brother, you are correct. However such rumors begin, we must stop them, of course." She looked up again, smiled with an apology toward that brother, who had reminded her of everything, of the family, all those Reyes' relations strung between here and the States, how important they were to her.

She was much more careful the following night, walking through the hallways with lighter steps, taking several moments to close the door, to make it appear that it had never moved. She walked around the house stealthily. She wore riding pants made of denim, and in the black of night she looked like a thin, young man. Quickly, she moved toward the gate, looking toward the back of the soldier who walked bordering the fence. With consistent, practiced movements, she approached him. "Good evening, Ricardo. Time to go through."

"That is not possible, ma'am."

"What? Come on, Ricardo, it is time for me to go, I—"

"I have strict orders not to open this door either way."

"Strict orders? From whom?"

He did not look at her, and said nothing. The obvious answer came to her. "What? Oh shit, you will open this fucking gate now, Ricardo, open it now!"

"Miss, quiet, please. He will find out!" Ricardo looked directly at her. "Look, you just cannot go."

"Does Joaquín know?"

Ricardo fumbled with his words, then tossed them to her. "The way he spoke to me, well, he knows something. I am not sure."

"Ah, shit!" she slammed her open hands upon two poles of the iron fence, then hit them twice more as if hoping they were twigs. She yelped several curse words, which made the soldier turn his head away and mutter several phrases of petition to a saint who watched over those in precarious positions. Necira finally turned silent, then leaned her head upon the fence. Her smooth, creamy forehead rested in the narrow space between two poles. The cold of the wrought iron pressed against both sides of her temples. She sighed against the metal.

"It is best this way, Miss Necira. You do not need to go down there. You know it is getting worse these days, people getting killed and all."

He still spoke, spinning reasons, as she walked away. She did not say goodbye. Ricardo shook his head at her as she disappeared into the house. "Such a little bitch," he muttered under his slight moustache. "She will have her own trouble someday."

She took her body up the stairs as if weight had been strapped to her shoulders, perhaps the weight of the fence, of the late hour, or heaviness of the empty absence. She had acquiesced much too quickly. She tried no other tactics, but rather returned to her bedroom. She looked weary, staring absently into the mirror while removing her earrings and placing them upon the cedar cabinet. She did not undress, but rather drifted over to the bed and fell upon it, almost in a faint. She had changed during these weeks with the passion her lover had unleashed within her. It was no longer a novel, but something that had come to life. Such a surprise, to be living a novel in this little town. So much more fun than the extreme boredom of her life, one that had brought her to take on the *labriego's* dare, that had led to her strangely enamored feelings for him. She half-contemplated the discovery while falling upon the bed. She dropped deeply into the cool, flickering memories of stars glowing behind that dark mountain which engulfed her and held her and touched her in unacceptable ways with unacceptable hands. She lay still until early morning, when sunlight caressed her from the window and inner rumbles beat outwardly against her stomach. Then she awoke, stood and ran, and vomited before she reached the bathroom door.

∿
∿

"I do not think it is any cold, Doña Rosa." Olga looked directly at her. The maid dropped her words clearly.

"Then what is it? Should we get a doctor? She seems to be very sick."

"Only in the mornings. And she is also tired. *You* have been sick like this. Twice." Olga raised and lowered her head, spreading the truth.

"Oh." Rosa shook her head. "Yes. Well, we cannot be completely sure about such things. We have to be careful about talking like that."

"Of course," said the maid. "Rumors concerning things like that should never even begin." Olga walked away to the other side of the kitchen to slice onions for the next meal. She looked out the window, saw Carolina, the woman who took care of grinding corn. She wondered when was the last time she and Carolina had rested and chatted together at the fence, and realized it had been a few days.

"Olga, where is Necira now?"

"Resting in her room, I believe. I saw her in the hallway earlier. She told me that she was very tired."

A Fire in the Earth

"Well, yes, I am sure she is. I mean, since she is sick." Rosa left the words behind her, and walked out of the kitchen to the hallway, wondering whether or not to call upon the girl. She walked by Joaquín's empty office. Turning and walking up the stairs, she stepped slowly, quietly, wanting to hear whether or not the young woman slept. No noise came from the upper room. She knocked on the door lightly. A small, weak voice asked who it was. "It is Rosa. Are you all right?" Necira replied vaguely, in almost a whisper, that she would come out later, for she was resting now. Rosa left it at that, and went away to work.

Inside the locked room, Necira stood and looked out her window. She stared at the distant noise of the brickhouse down the road, at the men who walked about like trained, upright animals, carrying sacks upon their backs, loading and unloading barrows of bricks and sand and rock. One stood among them, larger than the rest. At times he stopped his work, stood erect as if to stretch out his weary back. But he was not weary. He looked westward and stared up at that upper bedroom, where she stood, where she placed her palm upon her left breast as if to catch her thumping heart. The house stood tall, and the iron fence did not block their field of view. Nothing stood in their way. It had been four days. In the distance, she could see only his shape. She lowered her hand to touch herself, then turned her eyes quickly to the gate as if to destroy it, as well as the guard.

Though Necira could not hear him, she knew that some foreman had yelled at her lover to get back to work, for he reluctantly turned away and pushed upon a load of bricks. She turned and fell back to her bed, whispering the word "Swoon, swoon..." for several seconds, as it was such the perfect word. Her head rested upon satin, and she fell into memories of that tiny town, of the cool cemetery hill. She fell asleep quickly, for the third time that day.

She did not rise until several hours later. Necira barely remembered slurring out an answer to the knock at her door, when Olga asked her if she would be joining them for dinner. She could not think of dinner. She thought only of darkness. She mumbled out, "No, I am not hungry tonight, thank you." She fell asleep again.

Marcos Mcpeek Villatoro

She did not awaken until night, when all turned dark, and when gunshots stoked the air outside the home, three of them in a row. She took herself to the same window, shaking off the dregs of dream, and watched as lights were thrown in several directions. Guards wandered the grounds, many more than she knew were posted there. They ran back and forth, looking, searching for some culprit, the guilty party who had committed a crime at the gate. Five Guardsmen huddled about, staring at old Ricardo. His head was protruding from the fence, slammed through the narrow space between the bars like an egg pulled through the crack under a door. It had then been twisted completely backwards. Torches were being lit, touching one to another. Necira could see clearly the old body of the man she had talked with several times in the past weeks, his head pulled through the narrow iron fence. She looked out into the overwhelming remains of night that had not been kindled by those brute hands carrying torches. She stared at the dark, at the many stars, and breathed out a sigh, knowing that her lover was out there, the novelistic knight who had tried to save her.

〰〰

The torches turned away and moved out through the gate. It was clear the assassin had come from outside, from the way Ricardo had been killed. They did not even bother the *patrón* on this one. One of their own had been murdered. They were a proud breed. They took their art to the village below, then outward, looking for any action anywhere.

The following morning a sun painted the world deep in crimson, with sprays of white, like tendons of a sinewy god running through the sky. In the little town all awoke to begin another day of existence. There were those who did not make coffee this morning, nor did they eat bread. Those families who knew, who left their adobes and their morning customs sitting on the hillside or out in a coffee field, and went to the woods to seek and to find. Seven Indian families walked onto the dirt paths that ran into the woodland. They remained quiet

408

A Fire in the Earth

as they followed the cool morning that scattered its shards between the branches.

Don Hermes also walked out, searching with the indigenous families. He stopped at the foot of one tree, where a head floated above him. There the face of his old Indian friend, the one who always brought him sugar cane, looked down. The head twisted around within a slight wind, as if searching for its separated body. The eyes told Hermes where to look, beside the large malinche tree where weeds grew tall and where limbs lay upon stone. Hermes read the curse that had been cut into his friends dark-skinned chest, *comunista jodido*. Barely shaking his head, he bent down to perform one final duty for his friend.

Chapter Seven

The moment Joaquín stepped beyond the gate, his valet named Sheriff stood beside him, taller and darker. The two walked away from the private home and toward the brick factory. There was to be an encounter; Joaquín prepared for it. He pulled from a breast pocket a small, gold cigarette case, a gift from an acquaintance in the States. As they walked into the yard of the brick factory, he pulled one of the imported cigarettes from the gilded box, tapped it, and perched it in his mouth while Sheriff walked directly behind the large brickworker named Culebra. Sheriff's metal-tipped boot launched between the worker's legs and embedded deep. Culebra's wheelbarrow fell to one side. He writhed in the dust. He squinted up at the two shadows over him, one with a boot in his abdomen and a pistol to his head. The other stood behind, smoking, waiting.

Believing the *labriego* could hear through the pain, Joaquín weighed out his words. "You raped my sister." He puffed, intentional dramatics floating away with the smoke. "You raped my sister and killed one of my best guards."

The wounded man said nothing, barely glancing up at the small, shadowy figure. This disappointed the *patrón*. "You know I can have you arrested for those charges, true?"

Culebra said nothing. His silence shook the *patrón's* composure. "Listen, I do not know you at all, but I know your kind. I'd have my man blow your nuts off right now except that my sister kept begging that I not do anything to you. But you, fuck, who *are* you?" Joaquín turned away, disgusted and frightened by a strong sense of entrapment. He looked toward his wrought iron fence, searching freedom. "Some prick Indian," he stared at the dark skin of the doubled-over man. No way to hide it. Only, he was much larger than any Indian

Joaquín had ever seen. "Why, why am I plagued with dark-skinned relatives?..." The *patrón* walked back and forth, stuttering sporadic curses. He lost the stature that he had built minutes before, by lighting the imported cigarette, having his valet do the work. Now Sheriff, still pressing the pistol to Culebra's skull, glanced at his boss, waiting for an order.

"Look, what is your name? Your real name? You will not tell me? You will soon, when you come up to marry my sister. You *will* marry her, do you hear? I will get you a job somewhere, perhaps here, in the brickhouse, only, inside the building. I will not have any sister of mine married to a *labriego*. You will marry. I will make the arrangements."

Still the man, slumped over from pain, said nothing. At times his eyes flickered toward the *patrón*.

"Shit on you, mute Indian. I should have your skin flayed."

With that, Joaquín and Sheriff walked away, out of the brickhouse yard towards the hotel's fence.

Culebra picked himself up. No other man helped him. They kept their distance, as they had before. The workers had heard that Culebra was the one who wrung the old Guardsman's neck. No one approached him. Culebra said nothing to them either. He did not ask for help. It had become clear in the past few days that he was not one of them. Neither was he rich, at least, not for the moment. Neither rich nor poor. They questioned if he really was Indian. At times they wondered if he were of this world.

♒

Romilia slammed down the huge hunk of corn dough upon the wooden worktable once, twice, a third time, then picked it up and tossed it between her hands. She dropped it again on the wood, then tore off a chunk and began patting it between the fingers of each hand, molding it until the dough took shape and spread out into a tortilla that she quickly tossed upon the hot comal. She continued the process, covering the comal with six tortillas. While they cooked, she cleaned the flour residue from the stones then covered them in old pieces of cloth cut from a sack. She placed her bowl of lime away, then tossed water upon one area of the wooden table and skimmed it off with the edge of her hand before wiping it down with a rag. The tortillas needed turning. She flipped them, then took a small oil-soaked cloth and pushed upon the tortillas to help steam open the pocket of air inside. She stared at them while they formed, like waking clams on a hot beach. She cocked one hand upon her waist. Soon she flipped the tortillas onto an open towel, then wrapped them in their own warmth, and began the process again.

The *patrón* and his valet walked by, having just left the brick factory. Romilia heard the *patrón* spitting curses about Culebra. She tossed the next batch of tortillas on their other side, then walked to the door of her working area and watched the two men pass by. They entered the hotel. Guards walked through the premises, more of them than before. Romilia ambled back to her comal, turned the tortillas once over again with her fingers, paying no attention to the heat of the comal. Her thickened fingertips scraped across the stone as if they were but other stones, not feeling the heat.

The cheesemaker looked out through a window of her shed. She could barely see a corner of the distant brickyard from her stove. She then glanced toward the empty stool, back to her left. Air pushed out of her lungs as if to rekindle the low fire with her anger. "Foolish old fart," she muttered.

She tore off more dough, formed other tortillas between her fingers. A certain gentleness, born from practice, was necessary to mold the tortillas. She momentarily had lost that, and the flat raw dough ripped between her fingers. She slammed it down, somewhat disgustedly. After molding the failed piece back into the whole of the dough, she began again, blanketing the comal with tortillas. Cheese sat upon a moist wooden beam, waiting to be cut. She took a knife to it. As always, she made much more than was needed for the hotel, for she sold the rest and pocketed the money. It was good business. She saved small, growing amounts of cash, as if she were waiting for a moment that she had planned for. She knew which way life went. Only there was no way of knowing the details, the individual movements that led you to your goal. Then came decisions concerning which dead bodies

A Fire in the Earth

one had to stumble over in order to reach what you wanted to accomplish.

It was midday, but Romilia did not put any cheese on the tortillas, for she was not particularly hungry. She had grown accustomed to eating together with the old guard. Ricardo was always here at this hour, a tortilla piled with goat cheese in his hand.

She lifted the cooked tortillas from the comal to toss them on the towel. Her finger dipped to one side, a soft side, less protected than her calloused fingertips. It singed. She brought the finger to her mouth and held it with her hand, and she almost heard a man's laughter. But her body jerked with the burn and the silence that followed, jolted by the struggle between fate and destiny. It was a lesson: one may create one's destiny; but fate will always surprise you. Fate could take from you your only friend.

∿∿

The time came for Joaquín Reyes' Mardi Gras party.

Joaquín's Mardi Gras was like no other in the country. No one had even heard of the word, only knew that it was the same celebration commonly known as *carnaval*. Three years ago Joaquín was travelling in the States during the days before Lent. He had been invited to sit for half an hour in a Singer corporate meeting to discuss the growth of the company in his little country, and extol how Singer had helped the economy of his country's growing and thriving society.

The meeting had been held in New Orleans. After his half-hour was up, Joaquín had taken to the streets. Once again he became wide-eyed with admiration for the Great Society. The clowns, the masks, the constant eating and drinking tackled him and brought him down to happy knees. He knelt on the floor of a bar in that city, a cat-mask half-strapped to his face and a woman's legs wrapped around his neck, riding him like a laughing mule. He kissed her inner thigh several times, then burst out to a smiling, white colleague who sat above him upon a barstool, "We must have this in my country!"

Marcos Mcpeek Villatoro

Thus he had made a vow in his life, and he believed himself to be a man who kept his vows: As long as he lived, there would be such a Mardi Gras in his Republic.

The first year had been a success. This year was much easier to plan, for he could resort to old invitation lists. He invited all his friends from the capital and all the North Americans who happened to be in the country. He had sent out 150 invitations three weeks previous, and at least one-hundred people would attend. Joaquín had the invitations especially made. Greek masks, "the happy and sad faces," as he had termed them, decorated the top corners of the paper.

Joaquín Reyes and family
cordially invite you to
the second annual
Feast of the Mardi Gras
to be held on the 20th day of February
at 7:00 in the evening.

Please wear any costume you desire,
but by all means, wear a costume!

(Please display this invitation at the gate upon arrival.
It is your entry permit.)

The final request, which had been necessary in the past to keep out the ordinary people, had become a formality in those days. It was unnecessary, considering the capable presence of the guards. Still, their fathers had done it, and there was no harm in continuing the tradition.

"These look marvelous! I am glad we used yellow paper; it looks so joyful!" he had stated to Sheriff. "Make sure they go out today. I would rather you drive into the capital to send them. I have no faith at all in that post office down in the village. There should be 150 invitations in all." Joaquín had walked away.

A half-hour later, after preparing the automobile, Sheriff returned to the yellow envelopes piled upon the entrance-hall table. He noticed that they were not as neatly piled as before, as if someone had knocked the top half slightly to one side. A door shut in the back of the house. Sheriff looked up, but saw no one. Thinking little of it, he col-

414

lected the envelopes in his large hands and shoved them into his small case, then walked out of the hotel in order to mail them that afternoon.

Not even his sister's pregnancy dampened Joaquín's heated excitement. On the day of the party he ran about the hotel, watching the maids as they decorated all the walls, the corners, the windows. He followed them around. "No, not like that, they do it this way, they put the ribbons all across the mantles and hang them from the chandeliers, they cover the tables with sparkles, and the masks, the masks have to all be in one place, next to the door, so when the guests arrive they put on a mask. They cannot enter the party without one!" He had the maids decorate all the different rooms of the hotel, as he knew they would be used, one way or another. As friends from the north were invited, it was important that all was correct, that the festivities fell in proper order.

He worked furiously all day, and did not stop until the phone rang at midday. The head maid answered, and called for the *patrón*. "A Mr. Rubén García calling from Sonsonate, Mr. Reyes."

Joaquín muttered to himself, "García, what would he be calling me for... Hello, Rubén, this is Joaquín. I can hear you fine, yes, go on. How may I serve you?"

"Joaquín! Yes, I just wanted to be sure, you are having your famous party tonight, true?"

"Of course! You can make it, can you not?"

"That is why I call. Though you told me about it last week, I did not receive an invitation. I was not sure if you were ignoring me, old friend."

"You did not receive it? I sent you an invitation, Rubén, I know I did. I am sorry it did not reach you. It is these post offices, you know." He raised his voice as the connection faded. "But, yes, come! Of course you are invited. And do not forget to bring your woman with you. But remember, you must wear a costume!..." His voice climbed an excited note up the scale as he spoke.

Joaquín ran between hotel and private house, making sure arrangements were being made concerning the guests' reservations, whether or not they wanted to stay the evening, and how many planned to be present the next morning for brunch. It was all very exciting. He spent more time in the hotel than his home. In the latter, Joaquín's excitement turned to anger, twisted around him by the mood of the house. There was his sister's pregnancy to deal with. Then there was his wife. Rosa had said so little to him these days, always caring for the two children. She never even made mention of the grand party. "What is the matter with you, Rosa? Do you plan to be at my Mardi Gras?"

"Yes, yes, I will attend."

She sat upon their bed. He paced before her. He had just returned from the hotel, and had kicked into the bedroom vibrant, a child with a new, gigantic toy. In his hand he held two small crowns of plastic jewels and two black eye-masks.

"Then why is it your lips are dragging the the floor? Why is it you are like this? For the past few weeks, even when I come home, you seem depressed. When I leave, you are depressed. What is it with you, my love. What is the matter?"

She studied him for a moment. Slight wrinkles slid down from her forehead between her eyes. "Joaquín, are you not concerned?"

"With what? What do I have to be concerned about?" He spoke as if he had already known, but had filed it away. "There are some difficulties, of course. But, my love, life cannot be all one big sadness, true? We must celebrate, we are human beings, and to celebrate, to have parties, that is important, true?"

"Yes, I know." Her voice drifted like cold ash. He sent his words like a wind.

"Do you believe that?"

"Yes, I said I did. I said it is true. But all these other things, I find it difficult to forget them."

"Such as what?"

She hesitated, as if deciding which one to pick. "Such as your sister."

"That is taken care of!" He spoke with marked clarity. "They will be married soon, and they will live somewhere, perhaps out in Sonsonate, and live happily ever after. And you know, she is ready to marry that man."

A Fire in the Earth

"What if he does not want to marry?"

"Why do you talk like this? Of course they will marry, Jesus Christ, woman, why do you ask such questions?" He turned away from her a moment, still speaking, "always concerned about such matters, problems, weeping over *labriegos....*"

"There is reason."

"What? Reason for what?"

"To worry." She looked at him as if pleading for understanding. "Aren't you concerned? There have been so many deaths—"

"What deaths? Deaths? You speak of death. You mean the Indians? My love..." He bent toward her with sardonic chuckles falling like round pebbles and gently grabbed her shoulders. "My dear, they are the communists. You know that."

She said nothing. She turned her eyes upon his. He smiled, wide-eyed.

"We have to be protected, Rosa. They want to kill us. That is life, and I am sorry to say that we must live like this. Not like in the States, where there are no such problems. The people there never rebel; they never attack other people. I do not know why it is this way here. Perhaps it is because we are smaller, our country. Our people, they are so, damned proud. And they are violent, yes, so violent. That is the problem. Oh, how I wish we lived in the United States. But we do not. We live here, in our country, so we must defend ourselves. You see that, don't you?"

She said nothing.

"It is sad, I know, and so I can see why you are saddened. But, Rosa, do not worry about it. Now, it's time to forget it, to celebrate. Here, take this. This is your mask, your crown. Look, see? We are the king and queen of the party!" He smiled, and quickly donned his mask and headpiece. The plastic jewels crowned his thick black hair, protruding out like dead Christmas ornaments. The black of the mask grabbed the corners of his smile and held them there.

"Rosa, come to my Mardi Gras. Our Mardi Gras." He fell to one knee, his eyelids blinking over the edges of the mask's openings. He kissed her hand then held it as he made the proposal. "There is so much death, I know, yes, I know. But let us celebrate life together, our life, my love." Again he kissed her hand. The affected words fell like drops of ice on her skin. He stood up quickly and stepped toward the door as if heading toward a cause. "In an hour, my love. See you there." He was gone.

She stared at the door that he had just closed. It stood unmoved, stout in its deep-finished wood. Flush with the wall, it completed the perfection of the room. She looked down at her own hands. They were slightly worn from helping Olga. Were they ugly? She did not believe so. She believed in everything that she had done in her life, though many times she felt she had accomplished so very little. Yet she had lived and had helped, and that was good. Now she observed the working of the years upon her hands. "He says he still loves me," she sighed aloud. Then her face frowned upon her own remark, disparaging it.

Upon the bed lay the mask and the crown. She reached down, picked up the mask with her fingertips. She held it up to her face and looked at herself in the mirror, but did not wrap the rubber snap around her head. Behind the cardboard facade, all the weariness of a working woman disappeared, all the pain, all the death down the hill, even the familial maelstrom of a pregnancy. All that disappeared behind the glittering cardboard. It was that easy, that powerful. She lowered the mask. There before her, in her hand, lay her husband. So blatant and true, she whispered to herself dryly, "Yes," and tossed the mask upon the bed where it fell upon the false gems of the crown. She left the room and prepared herself for the evening's festivities.

♒

"You are coming over, correct?" Joaquín stared directly between his sister's shoulderblades.

"Of course, brother, I will be there. Perhaps a few minutes late, you know, it is fashionable...."

"You are not going to become sick or anything like that?"

"No."

"Good. The guests know nothing, and they will know nothing. And they will be very glad to see you. Say nothing of any marriage." He spoke while holding the door with his right hand. He had taken this

A Fire in the Earth

stand several times since the discovery of the pregnancy, a perfect position for him to slam shut the door after he had finished what he wanted to say. This time he followed suit. Necira did not react, as she had become accustomed to it.

"I am going over now, Olga. I will not be back for any supper, as the guests will be arriving in the next hour."

"Shall I have some sent over to you, sir?"

"No, I will grab something to eat over there." He spoke as he briskly walked through and out of the kitchen, donning a formal coat once outside. He walked past his son, who played with a small ball in the back yard. Jesús did not look up to his father. "Son! Jesús, how would you like to come to my party later on tonight?" Joaquín tossed a smile across the yard to the boy. Jesús looked up hesitantly, the ball in his hand. He did not look at his father, but glanced over to one side of the yard. A guard strolled by on the other side.

"What do you say, son? I want my people to know you a little bit more. You have grown much since they last saw you. Yes, I want them to see my offspring!" Joaquín retained the smile, expecting to win something with it. Nothing came. "You can even wear a mask, just like this one!" A dry February wind blew through the distance between them. Joaquín's smile drifted with it. He turned back to the kitchen, called out to Olga to have Jesús come over around eight o'clock. He turned back to the boy, smiled again, then walked on.

The guard at the gate gave out a crisp "Good evening, sir," and smiled. Joaquín greeted him back, walked through the gate, and continued on, paying no attention to the clash of metal as the gate closed again. He looked down to the ground while walking, his hands still shoved deep into his pockets. He mumbled something to himself about not letting anyone or anything ruin his night, as this was the most important evening of the year.

As if regaining some energy, he looked up and pulled his hands out of his pockets. To the west of the hotel stood Romilia. She stared out beyond the fence as if waiting for something. For the moment Joaquín ignored her and continued walking toward the building. In mid-stride he suddenly turned and approached her in twenty paces.

"What are you doing here?" he asked.

"I am just walking around a bit, Mr. Reyes." She looked directly into his eyes.

"You plan to sneak into my home while I am at my party, right, old woman?" She said nothing. "You know that the rule continues. I do not want you in my house, so do not straddle this fence as if you can sneak past it, understand?"

Still she did not speak, but stared at him with hollow eyes. He turned away from her, and she caught his mumbled "Bitch" as he walked toward the hotel.

She had been standing at the fence for over ten minutes. No guards had walked by her, as most of them were busy protecting the hotel and its upcoming party. Romilia had stood unmoving. She had periodically glanced at the stone standing to her left, the grave of the old *patrón*, Patricio Colónez. Not until after the present *patrón* walked away did she see the other little stone, that of her unborn child. A movement pushed inward and through her, decades late. She looked down to the ground, studying, trying to remember. "What had I done…what had I said, when?…"

A baby cried. She looked toward the hotel, and for that instant it was not the hotel but the old ranch, as if some giant had lopped off the additions to the building in order to bring back the past. The cry diminished. There were no babies among the rich guests at the hotel, none that she remembered.

Romilia turned back toward the graves, where grass had sealed the moment between life and death. Her husband's remains, just an arm's length away, broke the seal to become once again that young man who had ridden into town and had slept on their porch, who had given gifts, who had walked among men like a man, worked and sweat and beat the earth for fruit, like a man.

"Yes." Romilia chuckled through those first tears. "It is true, they were correct, your labriegos. You were a good *patrón*." She stared at the building, and again, it was the hotel. Inside the kitchen porch she could see the back of the actual *patrón*, and her tears dried. She turned around to see if anyone was watching. No one was, so she acted out her own piece of wisdom, one that she had once told to old Ricardo, that life goes anywhere it wants. "But then again, you can help it move a certain way. Right, old man?"

Romilia pulled a bright yellow envelope deep from her serape. She tossed it between the iron poles of the fence. The wind just caught it and landed it into some weeds of that deserted field which stretched away from the hotel.

She walked away and approached the gate to the private home.

"Where are you going?" demanded the guard.

"To see my grandchildren."

"Orders against that, direct from Mr. Reyes."

"Oh. Then who will take care of the children while the Reyes are at the big party?"

"I do not know. I only know what I have been ordered. You cannot come through."

She stared at the guard, who did not look down at her. "You must let me through. I am to take care of the children." He said nothing. "Look, boy, do you want to be in hot oil with the *patrona*? Someone must take care of those boys. Would you like to, while I guard the gate?"

He ignored her.

"Fuck it! Boy! Call the *patrona* out here; she will make the decision!" Romilia kept her voice in a high pitch, like an alarm. She glanced periodically toward the kitchen of the home and saw that Olga had witnessed the commotion from the porch, then had disappeared.

Minutes later Rosa walked out to the fence. She had come directly from the bedroom, where the mask and crown still remained. From the back porch she looked at her mother, the first time in several weeks, there, in perfect form, verbally masticating the guard. She smiled, almost laughing through a burst of tears. She rushed to the gate and looked upon her mother a moment before speaking. Romilia barely glanced at Rosa during her attack, and in that glance something was given over.

"What is your name, soldier?" asked Rosa.

"Ramón Torrez Alguilar, ma'am."

"Ramón, please let Doña Romilia through the gate."

"I, I cannot, ma'am. I have orders."

"Yes, well, I have an order for you, too. I need someone to take care of my children while I am at the party."

"Why can't the kitchen maid take care of them, Mrs. Reyes?"

"Olga is too old; she cannot care for the both of them."

The guard said nothing. Both women began talking, one screaming, the other trying to firmly reason with the young Ramón and the gate standing silently between them.

"Boy! Listen! What if one of those kids fell down those steps and broke his neck and died because no one was watching him, or rammed a fork into his eye, or fell into the kitchen fire, do you want all that to be put onto your record?"

Within the minute Ramón jingled keys off his belt.

Once through, mother and daughter walked into the house.

"What do you feed these stupid fucking dogs?"

♒

At the hotel the guests were arriving. Joaquín tried to greet them all, but once the rooms filled, he spent much of his time walking among them. The hired butler remained at the door, collecting people's invitations and handing out masks to those who still showed their faces.

"Joaquín, where is your lovely wife? And your sister, I heard that she is visiting you for the summer, true? You do not have her out picking coffee, do you, old man?" The crowd of men gathered about him guffawed.

"Not at all, no. They will be here in a few minutes. You know the women, it takes them time to prepare."

"Yes, well, I look forward to seeing Necira. It has been many months. She still is not married, true? Good, good. I was hoping for that." Again the men chuckled at the fellow who winked and brought a glass to his lips. Joaquín politely smiled and excused himself. He approached one of the kitchen servants.

"Where is my wife? And my sister? I cannot take care of all this by myself." The maid knew nothing. "Then please send a message over there to have them arrive immediately." His words ground together.

A Fire in the Earth

She bowed slightly and ran to carry out the order. As she approached the gate, the maid saw Necira coming, and she stumbled out the *patrón's* message.

"I am coming, dammit. Do not treat me like a child!" Necira walked by the maid without looking at her and entered the hotel, placing on a mask and a smile as she entered the main den.

The perplexed maid told the guard the message. He called out to Olga, who was throwing handfuls of rice to the chickens in the back yard. "Tell the *patrona* that her husband requests her presence at the party!" His pride and anger burst like buckshot. Olga retreated into the house and told Rosa the message.

∿∿

"Ladies and gentlemen, presenting His Excellency, the Most Reverend Miguel Sanchez y Clavo, Archbishop of the Republic."

Upon this announcement all the guests turned toward the door. The small man walked in, dressed in black and a collar, a large metal crucifix, a gold ring, and a red silk cummerbund wrapped about his stomach. He smiled, somewhat timidly, and walked down the five steps to the main arena of the festival. "Look," spoke one guest dressed as an owl, "The Archbishop came as a holy man." Joaquín giggled, then walked toward the church leader to greet him.

"Your Excellency, so good to see you." Joaquín bent down, quickly pecked the extended gold ring with his lips. "Please come in, and here, here is a mask. You must wear a mask, you know!" The archbishop chuckled as he fumbled with the cardboard piece, hesitated, then slowly placed it over his head. Other guests turned and approved of the new apparel with a cheery applause, and the archbishop laughed along with them as someone placed a drink in his hand.

"Your Excellency, I was not sure if you were coming, so this is indeed a pleasant surprise."

"Well, you know, Joaquín, I have been wanting to come out here for a while." The little man adjusted his mask so it did not interfere with his skull cap. "I do not really know this area of the diocese. Some of my people insist on me going out into the countryside to see how the flock is doing. So now I can say that I did. You do have a lovely place here. Where is your wife?"

"Oh, she will be out in a few minutes. She is tending to the children. Jesús, my first son, will be coming over to visit soon."

"Ah, yes, little Jesús. How old is he now, thirteen? It is about time for him to be confirmed, true?"

"No, uh, he just turned five, Your Excellency."

"Oh. Well then, you have time." He smiled and sipped from his glass.

Another man approached, Douglas by name. He wore fake red hair and his face was painted as a green and white clown. "Hello, Your Excellency, good to see you here." He bent down, kissed the ring that the curate held out. "I just want to tell you, sir, that the paper you put out last month was excellent. Did you read that, Joaquín?"

"Uh, no, I did not. I have not had much time—"

"Wonderfully written, just wonderful. The best piece I have seen written on the times in which we live. What you have done, Your Excellency, all of us must do. By God, communism must be wiped out of this country or it will take over all of our republics."

The Archbishop's face turned slightly red as the other guest spoke, not from any shame, but from the subject matter. "Yes, thank you, Douglas. I must say that when I wrote it, I felt the wrath of God working through me."

"Do you know what he said, Joaquín? The paper says, right there in print, that the threat of communism is not only an evil that will wipe out the good of the democracy that we are trying to build, but also will rot the soul of every person in this country. There will be no freedom, no freedom at all. The communists would take away our religion, our liberties, everything. The archbishop attacked them with fire. Fantastic! Your words, sir, your words were just, just, incredible. Joaquín, you have got to read it. I will send you a copy."

"Yes, thank you, I would very much like to read it."

"Yes," sibilated the high priest, "these are dangerous times we live in. You know, I heard that they had killed a fellow out in Sonsonate last week. Some uprising of the communists, and an innocent man was

A Fire in the Earth

killed. And I tell you, gentlemen," his voice lowered, but did not soften, "our president does nothing about it these days."

"So true, so true!" exclaimed the green clown. "He talks on and on about democracy, freedom, and it is nothing but lies. He is getting soft about the communists. I cannot believe that he allowed them to have a political party! And these reforms he is trying to mandate, ay, he is a problem!" Douglas swallowed deep from his glass, leaving dark green on the rim.

The conversation fell silent as the two men settled into their anger. "Well, my friends." Joaquín cleared his throat. "May I get you anything?" The clown and the archbishop turned to him as if broken from the slight trance, smiled politely and answered that they were fine. Joaquín excused himself to attend to his other guests.

Necira approached. "Your Excellency, so good to see you." She bent down as she spoke. Her lips wrapped slowly about the little hard gem of his ring.

"Ah, dear Necira, how are you? Now who did you come as?" The priest stared up and down at the young woman who wore a dress of white silk and a thin silver eye-mask that matched.

"Why, sir, I came as an angel."

"Really? But where are your wings?"

Necira batted long lashes through the cardboard. "I have none. I am a fallen angel."

Men who had gathered about the archbishop—one cat, one cowboy, the third a soldier—applauded her remark with laughter. The archbishop smiled politely, raised and lowered his face like a high tide that collected in thick waves under his chin.

The soldier standing next to the holy man was not wearing a costume. He was dressed in uniform. He did wear a mask, however, and his thin, bright smile pushed it up off his nose. "Hello," he addressed Necira, "my name is Captain Geraldo Castillo, at your service. And you are?..."

"Necira Carmen Reyes. Pleased to meet you, Captain."

"I apologize, I did not introduce you two," said the Churchman. "Geraldo is to be congratulated. He has moved up the ranks so quickly,

425

and at such a young age. Just last week he was promoted to captain, and I had the honor of blessing the occasion."

"Oh. Congratulations, Captain. How is it you have gone so well so quickly?"

"I do my job. I protect my people." He smiled, and the mask pushed up again.

"You will make the country proud, just as your father, the General, has done all these years. He raised you well, and began doing so early, yes. I remember you in the Jesuit Academy, Geraldo. Already there we could see that you were to be a leader in the country. Why, the other boys used to call him 'General' back then." The archbishop patted Castillo on the shoulder.

"Where are you stationed now, Captain?" asked Necira.

"Nearby. I have been put here, in the Department of Cuzcatlán. So perhaps we will encounter each other again."

"I doubt it. I live in the capital, and am only visiting here."

"Oh. Well, we can hope, true?" At that, everyone smiled.

The archbishop broke the cordial silence with a small whisper in Necira's ear. "By the way, child, I saw your father yesterday. He wanted me to give you this." He reached into a coat pocket and handed her an envelope. "He just wanted to make sure that you were fairing well." The little, round man smiled. He swished his black cassock slightly while looking at her.

"Why, thank you for delivering it." She looked down into the envelope at the wad of money. "Yes, it will come in handy."

"Tell me, child, how are you fairing? Goodness, you are just growing up. Someday some handsome gentleman will take you away from us!" A couple of other guests chuckled. The archbishop glanced at the captain. At that point Joaquín approached, just when Necira began to say, "Yes, well, that may happen much sooner than anyone would ever expect."

"Necira. Glad you could make it, sister."

The archbishop did not notice the *patrón*. "Really, Necira? Will there by wedding bells ringing in my cathedral soon? Oh, I look forward to that day when I can stand before you and your partner in life!"

A Fire in the Earth

Necira barely glanced at her brother, then responded, "Well, someday, perhaps." She excused herself with a final smile and walked away from the laughter and raised eyebrows.

"She is being secretive, Your Excellency," someone said amidst the voices. All the men chuckled, except Joaquín, as they watched her walk away.

♒

Olga delivered the message to Rosa, that it was expected of her to come immediately to the party.

"What is this party for anyway?" asked Romilia.

"It is called a Mardi Gras. Like Carnaval. It means everyone will be more drunk than usual." Rosa sighed angrily, then turned back to her mother and smiled. "It's great to see you in this house again, Mamá." She wept slightly. Her mother's arm drew her near.

From the doorway Jesús watched. It brought a large grin to his face, seeing mother and grandmother like that, holding each other. He did not approach them, as something in his child's mind told him to not interrupt. Baby Juancito gurgled from the crib, then sighed back to sleep. Jesús leaned against the doorway. It seemed the two most precious women in his life were melting together, for which he was most happy, as there had been too long a separation. "It may change soon, girl," he heard his grandmother say. Olga called up the stairs for Jesús to come down, as his father expected him. He left the doorway and walked slowly down the steps.

The two women separated. "Oh, I must find my scarf; it is so windy these days," said Rosa while clearing her nose. Romilia went to the crib and picked up the little one. The women stood, finding something to do with the child, an obvious hesitation for the *patrona* to stay away from the party, to stay here. "Now where is Jesús? He's probably already gone over. Ay, it will be a chore to get him to bed tonight. He will no doubt be at the party longer than he should—"

"What? Where is Jesús?" Romilia turned from the crib and looked directly at her daughter.

Marcos McPeek Villatoro

"I think he is heading over now. Olga said that Joaquín wanted the guests to meet him. Why?"

∿∿
∿∿

At the door of the hotel, the apt butler continued with his work of announcing the arrival of the guests. The most recent visitor walked through, a man, hooded, wearing a thick, dirt-brown serape that cloaked him down to his feet. Leather sandals slapped against his heels as he walked in. The large figure handed over the yellow invitation. The butler took it and smiled up toward the hooded guest in welcome. He turned and looked out to the gathering of knights, princesses, cat faces, owl faces, devils, all clicking glasses together, dancing, and slapping one another on the back. He cleared his throat and announced the name, "Mr. Rubén García, from Sonsonate."

Joaquín turned his masked head around. He smiled at the guest, the one whose invitation had not arrived. "Rubén! I did not expect you so early. Who are you dressed as, a labriego, or a monk?" The guests around him laughed. Joaquín approached the hooded one, holding his plastic crown upon his head with the tips of his fingers, and a third drink held in his other hand. "Where is your lady friend? I had thought—" Once he reached the foot of the five steps that climbed to the front door, his smile and laughter fell to the floor along with the glass of scotch.

∿∿
∿∿

As always, when Jesús walked into the kitchen of the hotel, the cooks stopped and smiled down at him. A couple of them tousled his hair with their fingertips, and one of them handed him a small handful of banana chips that she had just finished frying. "Thank you, Doña Claudia." He chewed on them as he walked through, smelling the various foods that filled the large room along with the sounds of metal on metal, of different condiments sizzling in oil. For a moment he stared at the perfect flames that flickered over the gas stove. The only noises that matched the sounds in the kitchen emanated from the

A Fire in the Earth

main room of the hotel. He walked toward the swinging door, careful
not to fall in the way of the busy cooks. Through the door, more tall
people greeted him, all of them dressed in strange, somewhat frighten-
ing uniforms. A fat, light-skinned cat woman smiled down to him. The
red of her lips smudged the edges of her teeth, and stiff strings protruded from the sides of her nose. Her eyes blinked through black
cardboard. She handed him an eye-mask, which he studied for a
moment before trying to strap it on.

The noises suddenly shut down. A hush fell as heavily upon the
fiesta as the burden of sudden mourning. It lapped over them like a
tide as all the people turned toward the main entrance of the building.
Jesús could see nothing, for the shoulders towered above him. Yet he
had the advantage of being a child, of walking between legs. He did so,
leaving behind the muffled clanging of the workers in the kitchen, and
approached the area which he supposed to be the nucleus of the
silence. He heard small voices, one of them his father's, quivering as if
someone pounded his chest while he talked. Jesús looked down, saw a
small glass toppled to one side with alcohol bleeding from it. "What
are you doing here," said the shaking voice.

The answer came in a strange tone, almost foreign, as if spoken
from under the earth. "You want me to be a part of your family...I
thought I should visit."

At first the boy could not believe that a *labriego* would be in the
hotel until he pushed his face between the legs of a devil and an angel.
There Jesús saw the large man who stared from the deep shadow of a
hood toward his father.

"Get out of my house," retaliated the *patrón*.

The response hissed out of the black hood like venom dripping
from a tongue, ignoring the trembling demand, "How easy it is to enter
the Reyes family. Just fuck one of its whores..."

The few gathered around who were able to hear reacted with a
sudden bustle, including the angel and devil next to whom little Jesús
stood. The men, who knew their place, called upon Joaquín with their
support and anger to defend, to guard the family name. Empowered,
or perhaps forced by the irate voices of his friends, Joaquín acted. He
lunged forward one half-step and pushed his little fist against the wide

429

chest of the tall stranger. The new arrival barely moved. Joaquín stepped back.

Then the cowled man reached deep into the folds of his stained serape and whipped out a silent slice of lightning. When it halted at the stranger's side, the slightest coating of red stained the machete's glint of metal and light. Jesús' father crumpled.

Some good friend of the family, the devil who stood next to Jesús, fell to his knees to pick up the fallen man. He lifted Joaquín until the young *patrón's* abdomen yawned wide open and laughed out dollops of gray and red at the surrounding guests. The sight extracted a long scream from them all. The devil dropped the body and the yawn closed up, losing its symmetry and perfection over loose, wet organs. Jesús opened his mouth wide. A sudden weariness took hold of him. He fell, lost in a sea of scurrying legs. Two arms whipped him away. A shoulder muffled his yelps as the cook ran with him. He awoke in the darkness and safety of some distant corner.

Part Three

Prologue

Laughter burnt off torch flames. The uniformed men who danced about the fires raised machetes above their heads in victory. They walked and jumped around the large malinche tree that stood just outside the northern gate. One howled as he raised a spent bottle. At times they thrust their metal shafts into the mass of flesh that wound and spun like an upset pendulum from a roped branch, the remnants of their conquest.

Behind them all stood their newest leader, the good Captain Castillo, who had left the festivities in the hotel in order to carry out his duties. He gave orders to go out, seek and eliminate, for there had been a murder in the zone over which he was responsible. They followed the call. Others remained around the malinche tree. Bottles tipped high, and the torches and laughter flickered into the disappearing liquid.

Someone stripped the crimson-soaked pants off the dangling figure. There poked the final blast, the erect member of the dead *labriego*, gorged one last time from the pressure of his hanging body. Someone took the machete that had killed the *patrón* at the Mardi Gras Party and caressed the protrusion with the metal edge. Laughter howled upward to a witnessing moon as the blade desecrated the erection and emptied the flesh over the hungry ones running about on the ground.

In other trees, other brown-skinned cadavers floated, yet none of the pack danced under them. Only family members scurried up the trunks and cut the ropes to take the bodies home. They wept as they lowered the cadavers of their children, glancing from time to time at the guards who followed out the new law which said that to bring about justice, it was necessary to go beyond the eye for an eye, to perhaps extract many teeth for one tooth.

Above all this, in the private home, a young woman screamed as family members pulled her into an automobile. Necira's arms flung out of the open window, reaching for the carcass dangling from the malinche tree. Someone forced the window closed, muffling her cries. She was driven back to her home in the city, where she was later held down by loving family members, a father and two brothers who knew better. A medical professional, who was a friend of the family, took an envelope of cash and performed the duty of scraping the dark-skinned shameful fetus from her body. Meanwhile the archbishop went another way. He followed the body of the well-known *patrón* to the family sepulchre. There he performed a liturgy with the utmost respect and reverence. His words boomed from the pulpit that such an atrocity as he had witnessed against a good friend and fellow Christian like Joaquín Reyes must be dealt with, that those in charge must take the reins of this country, that a leader must come forth to establish order. All the families in the pews shook their heads in agreement. Since the archbishop had recognized their problem, they knew something would be done.

At the malinche tree above the little village, in the early morning light, black peace flowed on a river of wind, perched itself upon the hanging carcass of the giant *labriego*, and began its carnivorous duty.

Chapter One

Paco Colónez returned home.

He walked into his town after travelling in other countries for over a decade. Paco lived most of that time in New York, at the feet of some wise man named Reed. He had worked odd jobs to keep alive, as a restaurant waiter, a meat packer, a library assistant. That final job he kept; it gave him access to all sorts of books, both in Spanish and English. When he was not working, he was either reading or spending his evenings in smoky rooms filled with gringo men and a few women, all of whom spoke of the Russian Cause and how they needed to work to bring that cause to this nation. Many of them, especially Mr. Reed, had visited Russia. Paco, however, had never received a formal invitation, and had no funds to make such a trip. Still, he spent his evenings with this group of gringos, polishing his English even more. He had a few Hispanic acquaintances, some Puerto Rican and Cuban teen-agers who invited him out for evenings on the town, in the small corners of the barrios where they had made their homes. He always refused them, preferring to attend the Greenwich Village gatherings. The teen-agers soon quit asking him, recognizing the fact that he had become "gringoized."

The struggle against capitalism became such a daily part of his vocabulary that it was difficult for Paco to speak of any other subject. A few times the intensity of such conversations turned to local action, where he and a few gringos handed out pamphlets to dock workers on the piers. Twice gangs came with clubs to stop their propaganda. Paco received a blow to the shoulder blades, bringing him down to the pier. He was carted to jail, where he spent several nights before someone from the Village came and bailed him out. Paco interpreted the experience through his books and the Village conversations. He knew he was submerging himself more deeply into a proletarian's war against injustice.

It was rare to hear news from home, though the Village did provide snippets of information on the formation of a communist party in his country. When that party was shut down, Paco felt a pain in himself, one that he could not define for several days. He had put great hope in the creation of this fledgling party in his republic, and dreamed that, someday, upon returning, he could work for that party. Considering all his years in New York, seated at the table of the masters of the ideology, perhaps he could even become a leader.

Once Paco heard that the little group had been squelched by the government, he knew how dedicated he was. It was then that he had made the decision to return home.

Packing his belongings in one suitcase, Paco stuck his thumb out on the highway and headed south. Three weeks later, after making it through most of the eastern states, boarding a cargo ship in Miami, boarding another boat in Cuba, and walking through two neighboring countries, Paco stood at the edge of El Comienzo.

Not one vehicle had passed him all day. There was never any traffic during Holy Week. He had walked all morning. An old adobe that looked ready to melt into the ground from the weight of many rainy seasons stood far to the left, dry as compressed ash. Paco approached it, hoping to find water there, as it stood at the opening of a small cove. In an orange tree just in front of the building dangled a dummy, the seasonal decoration. It consisted of an old shirt and pants stuffed with straw, with an old gourd for a head, its features drawn with charcoal. The old hat probably was the father's. Three children ran about the tree, poking at the straw body, laughing and hitting it with a stick. Their parents stood at the door of the adobe, smiling.

"Judas! Judas!" screamed the children.

"Careful, son, don't tear my shirt with that stick..."

Paco walked by the children and toward the door. He and the parents spoke for a few moments before he requested water.

"Carlos, boy! Fetch the man some water."

Carlos ran past the stranger, took the empty water gourd and went off behind the house to the creek that trickled through the hills.

A Fire in the Earth

Paco drank in slow gulps. He thanked them, talked for a few more minutes, then said goodbye. Carlos had returned to the hanging Judas, striking the holiday decoration with a thin stick. Paco walked away. At the road he turned back, stared at the dummy that puked out its dry, grassy innards from various holes in the cloth. He stared at the family and their home. The scene trickled through a mental sieve of well-formed ideas, intellectual beliefs that were universal. The family's situation, their need, also slapped against him. It had been many years, and he had grown accustomed to other ways of living, far different from his old country.

"This is why I have come home," he mumbled, "to change it. To make it right."

An hour later Paco stood before the gate of the great iron fence.

"When in the world did they build this monstrosity?" he mumbled in English.

The guard at the gate was not impressed by what the young, dirty man before him said. Yet he squinted with confusion toward Paco. This wanderer spoke like some professor. And the intellectual vagabond, though feigning good manners, stared at the guard with a silent anger.

"I promise you, the *patrona* of this ranch, Rosa Colónez, she is my sister. Send another guard to ask her, and I am sure that she will verify what I am saying—"

"Her name is not Rosa Colónez."

"Yes, well, I know that she had married, but her name used to be Colónez. Now—"

"Leave this place now, or I will arrest you."

Paco stared directly at the guard. "I am not leaving this gate. I am of this family and I demand to see my sister and my moth—"

"Let him in." The old voice came from behind the guard. "He is my son."

The sun fell red upon the earth. It was turning night. Both guard and vagabond turned toward the voice. They could see only her black figure as she stood between them and the sunset. It was obvious that her arms were severely crossed. The guard stared at her. Life inside the gate had changed drastically during the months of Lent. No one dared to refute Romilia's word.

Paco left the closed gate behind him and approached his mother. Her arms still crossed, she stared down the small slope at him as if waiting for a boy who was coming home after hours. Several feet from her he stopped, lowered his dusty gourd to the ground, and dropped the torn canvas sack from the other shoulder. A few U.S. quarters fell from a hole in the sack. The corner of a book tried to escape through the same opening. He stood before her, with humility that silently begged of her not to look at him that way, as she was still his mother. She said nothing. A brown bird with bright yellow wing tips glided by, snapped at a couple of dry insects just above the guard.

"When was the last time you ate?" she asked.

"I had some fruit this morning. Other than that I—"

"When did you last bathe?"

He failed to respond.

She breathed out a curt sigh that fell over her arms. "Well then, I suppose you found that which you had looked for. Come. There is food in the kitchen. Also a tub."

"I do not need to go there. I just came to visit—"

"You need to eat, dammit." She had already turned around as she spoke. "Come, we will fix you a dinner."

"I do not want to go in there," Paco said, looking at the opulent, now silent hotel.

"Then go into my shed. Over there, the workhouse. There is some cheese there. I will bring you a plate. Yes, it is just as well." She glanced back at his appearance.

Romilia walked away from him and toward the back door of the kitchen. As he ambled to the shed, he looked about and felt the eyes of the guards on him. Without his mother, protection waned. The guards stalked about, some on one side of the fence, some on the other. They walked between small buildings, as if waiting. Paco ducked into the shed.

A Fire in the Earth

After several minutes she entered and placed a full plate on the cooling woodburning stove. "There is more if you want," she muttered.

Paco looked at the mincemeat, the rice and the beans, the three tortillas still steaming, the cut blocks of cheese and the mug of coffee. He approached it like a dog lolling over to a dead animal. Romilia sat down on a bench in a dark corner. She stretched out her feet, stared down at them with half-closed eyes. "These feet are very tired. They will fall off me someday." She looked over at him. He had finished over half the plate.

"So how is the United States?"

"At war." He finally spoke as he chewed.

"At war? I have heard of no war."

"There is one. Between the rich and the poor."

Romilia looked for another topic of conversation. "So why did you come back?"

His ideas and dreams fell between the chewed mincemeat and tortilla crumbs. "I have returned to help free our people from slavery and oppression and starvation."

"Oh. You help the people by starving with them? Wonderful idea. Who is it you are helping, the farmers, the *labriegos*, who?"

"The proletarians."

"The who?"

"All of those people. The farmers, the workers. The ones who keep the country alive and thriving. The ones that the rich take advantage of."

"Oh. And I suppose you too are now a, a..."

"Proletarian."

"Yes. A proletarian. Well, good luck."

"How is Rosa?"

"Still wearing black. It's hardly been two months. I suppose you do know about her dead husband?"

"Yes. I did not know about him. But I heard something in town, just before I came up. I understand he was murdered."

"Yes. By Culebra. You remember him? The one who beat the shit out of you as a kid. Yes, he murdered the *patrón*."

439

"When I asked more about it, nobody in town wanted to talk about the murder."

"No wonder. He was dark skinned, like an Indian. So the guards are keeping their eyes on all Indians. Oh, it has slackened up some. But the dogs still walk with their noses low to the ground these days. You are lucky you approached the gate as closely as you did. And your skin color helps."

"Why is that? Why are there so many guards—"

"Ay, the fuckers keep coming in. I do not know why they send them. The family of that son of a bitch, the ones in the capital, they keep sending them, as if to protect something out here. They have no more family here except for Rosa, and they do not give a damn about her. And their bitch is gone, so I do not know—"

"Wait. Wait a minute. Who are you talking about?"

"What? The Reyes family, Joaquín's relatives. They have not been out here. They think it is a jungle of some sort, and they keep sending the guards in."

"But what, what bitch are you talking about?"

"Oh, Necira. She is gone. Joaquín's sister, the one who lived out here for a while. Such a whore she is. Well, she is gone. Perhaps the guard will go with her someday." Slowly Romilia calmed herself. They both turned silent. She stared out at the falling sun. He finished the plate.

"May I see Rosa tonight?"

"Of course. She is your sister. I think she would like that. She speaks of you often."

The old mother and her son walked toward the other gate. She gave an order to the guard, who immediately let Paco through. "Tell Rosa I will be over later, after I clean the shed. She'll draw you up a bath. And have her put you in the guest room. It's the room in the far corner. There is some stuff in the dresser that I believe is for you."

Paco nodded in acknowledgement to her, though he also looked confused. After being absent for so long, what items could be his?

He stumbled about for a few seconds, glancing at the guard who had fixed his eyes upon him all this time. Then he turned and approached the house. A young woman dressed in black ran out and wrapped her arms tightly around him.

Rosa did not let go for a long time. When she did, she spoke first. "You will spend the night, true?"

"I...I suppose, yes, I will. My God, you've grown up!"

She laughed and brought him to the house. She gave him time to bathe. She had Olga heat up a large pot of water, then Rosa carried it to the tub and left it there for him. He cleaned himself, and a long weariness drained out along with the film of dirt floating atop the water. It had been several days since he had last bathed. Though living in a poor ghetto in New York, Paco still was accustomed to a daily bath.

Paco met his nephews for the first time. He bent over to greet Jesús. The boy looked at him with almond-shaped eyes. Then he respectfully clasped his tiny hands together as if in prayer and put them in the open hands of the new uncle. Paco enveloped the little fingers. "It's a pleasure to meet you, little Jesús." A moment later the boy pulled away and stood beside Rosa. He would say little more to the serious *labriego* whom his mother said was his uncle.

Brother and sister spoke for the rest of the evening. There was much to catch up with.

"What are you going to do, now that you are here?"

"I want to join forces with others, and put an end to these massacres."

She looked down and played with the hem of her dress. "That is good. There is a great deal to do. I do not know what to do, how to end it."

"Will you remain here?" he suddenly asked.

"What? I do not know. I suppose. I have thought of selling the hotel, as it is in my name. But I do not know. Mamá loves the ranch so. Perhaps, though, she could live with me, here. She could be happy here."

At first Paco did not respond to that, though he wanted to. Finally it did break through. "Do you think it is good, to own so much?"

"No. Not at all. That is why I want to sell it. I cannot handle such a business as a hotel. It's too much work. I don't know. I have tried to think about it, but so much has happened, it is difficult to sort out everything…"

He pushed no further. Exhaustion was taking over them both. It was late. They hugged each other at the bottom of the stairs. He again offered his condolences, though he squinted his eyes. He knew they were not heartfelt, but cheap. He had never known the husband, but had heard in town that the dead *patrón* had been a bastard of a man.

"It is good to have you back. I hope that you will stay."

"Yes. I will stay. I am home. I will be around here."

"I know this may seem as if it comes from nowhere," she said, pulling away slightly, "but I have a favor to ask. It is something I want to do with you, please, if you could. I was hoping, would you go to Papá's grave with me tomorrow morning?"

Paco did not respond immediately. He looked down at the floor, then back up at her. "Is that necessary?"

"Well, we never did it back then." She let that sink in. "It would be wonderful if Mamá were to come with us, but I know I cannot expect that." He turned to one side. She pleaded, "Please? Paco, it is Papá."

"We will see. After resting, I will be better able to decide." He added a weak reason, "I—I'm just not much for religious duties."

Rosa showed her brother the corner bedroom, as if Romilia had already made sure that the *patrona* would place her brother there. They said good night. He entered the room. After undressing, he placed his newly washed clothes on top of a dresser, then turned to the dresser that his mother had mentioned. He remembered it from childhood. It was a piece of furniture that once had stood in the master bedroom of the old ranch house. He leaned against it and smiled. "I wonder how many places you have been carted to." He opened the top drawer. Underclothes had been stored there. He wondered if they were from the woman named Necira. The second drawer below it was almost empty, except for some belts and a few ties. Looking at these, he realized that they had been his father's. His smile dried up. He opened the third drawer. It was packed with men's clothes, all of them long out of fashion. Upon the clothes sat three books, side by side, as if they had been placed there for a reason. They were of the same color and make as his own journal, which he always carried, and in which he had written throughout the years. He opened the first one up. It was almost all in English, just like in his own. On the top of the first page was written "Patricio Colónez."

23 of May

I begin this book the first day of coming into this small town. It is called El Comienzo. Small, a few people, hardly anything here. Sleeping on some woman's front porch. Good that it is still dry.

That was all. Blood suddenly pumped through Paco's chest. He flipped through the pages. All the entries were approximately the same length. None of them seemed very long, unlike his own journal entries, which always took him half a night to write. And everything was in English. His hands, moving as if they were suddenly chilled, flipped back to the first page. His eyes read over the foreign language as if they were hungry for some old, needed food, a living father.

28 of June

Finally got an adobe built to live in. They have begun the brickhouse. Perhaps it will be done in six months, maybe less. Antonio signed final papers last week, when I was back in capital. I keep busy with work. Good to be working, away from the city. Good town. Good people.

Romilia Velásquez y Hernández.

His mother's name was followed by nothing else. Paco could not understand that. It seemed his father would have written the name down sooner in order to remember it, for Paco knew that the porch upon which his father had slept was that of his grandmother's. Paco flipped page after page. His father had written at least every two days, and sometimes wrote twice a day. Most of the entries, especially at the beginning, dealt with practicalities, how much wood to buy for the brick yard, when to begin building the ranch. Yet others told much more than that, with very few words.

We will be married in a week. She is a beautiful woman, yet so quiet. We will go to Mexico for vacation. The ranch should be done by then.

I have found a woman here. That is a very good reason to stay.

The men of this town are hard workers. I felt bad today, for we returned from our trip, and I complained to one man that the house was not done. They have done very much work, and I settled down after talking with the man, the foreman of the job. But at first I had yelled at him, and that was a terrible thing to do. They work hard out here in the country, much harder than the fat asses in the capital. Santo has come in from home. I will have her make lunch for the workers, too, so they do not have to use up their own supplies at home. And Santo will keep them fattened up.

Paco found it difficult to distinguish what years the dates referred to, as his father had never recorded the years. It was as if the long dead *patrón* had not meant to keep up with the journal, that he would put it down and never write in it again. But that never happened. Paco read year after year of entries, and paid no attention to the rising half-moon that drifted by his bedroom window.

12 of November

Another Tuesday with Antonio and Gloria. I wish I could put an end to this schedule. Yet Romilia seems to enjoy it. It is good for her; she has few opportunities to be social.

14 of December

Brick sales have gone up 4 colones a load. That is good for business. I can hire more workers soon. Antonio believes I should build on more, put more machinery into the plant. I am not sure about that. No one can run the damn things.

2 of March

For the first time in our years together, she believes that she is pregnant. This makes me most happy. She is a lovely

444

woman, and she seems to shine with the thought of having a
baby.

Paco's father had said little more about the pregnancy, then nothing at all, as if it had never occurred. Paco, however, knew the story, and he did not look for any more entries concerning the stillbirth. He read onward, page after page of business notes, lines about the garden, the workers, a party that his wife had held and Patricio had tried to miss. The entries changed little either in rhythm or in practicalities until Paco came to one about himself.

> I have a son, and he is my son. He is to be called Francisco, or Paco. He is of my flesh, and if such things exist, he will be of my spirit. He will speak English with the same fluency as I speak it. I will give him that, at least.
>
> Amanda died. It was time; she was very old. But I will miss her. She said to keep the food coming, that it will go to the neighbors. I promise that I will, always.

Most all the other entries, one way or another, referred to Paco. The young man saw himself through the mirror of his father. Throughout the rest of the journals, few entries said anything about Romilia. Once Paco was born, the mother was mentioned only in passing, or when she had caused some disruption.

> Paco has grabbed the language with ease. I do nothing but talk to him in English, and already he has uttered several words. He keeps at my side most all the day long.
>
> I can feel her jealous of this. But he is all that I have.
>
> Work goes well. The men are working full days now, which is good for them. They want to work full days. They get along well with Paco. Yesterday Enrique made him a little wheelbarrow. They said Paco will be a worker someday. I said not to tell his mother that.
>
> She wants to send him to school. Perhaps it is a good idea, but I am not so sure. He learns so much here. His English is incredible. I have given him books to read, those that I

have bought in the capital, and he is finished with them
before I can get him another one.

She wants him to go to a Jesuit school. What do these
jodido priests know?

Paco laughed aloud as he read the entry concerning his escape
from the Jesuits,

He is out of there; Paco is back home. He used the
'escape route' that I told him about before we had departed.
He is back with us.

I was wrong about the priests. They can teach one thing
very well: hypocrisy. Filthy hypocrisy.

"Perhaps Papá was a little bit Marxist," Paco muttered to the
empty room. He found himself a corner of the floor to sit in, next to an
electric lamp. He turned page after page. He became committed to the
history contained in the three books, and he, too, began to react to the
written thoughts.

The girl was born today. She named her Rosa. There is
something deeply wrong. Yet I cannot say, I cannot speak, I
do not know. The girl seems different; the baby se parece
seems wrong, different.

It is her skin, I know, it is her skin.

One of the boys in town was killed by a hoodlum. The
boy had been a friend of Paco's. Paco is very silent these
days. I wish I could take that sadness away. But I know it is
his, and he needs to get through it on his own.

Antonio comes around more. I wish he would stay away.
When he is here, I feel like using that gun he gave me on
something. It is as if I want to knock the walls down, but I
know I cannot.

Paco is going to town a great deal. But he is still working
at the plant. He seems to like the hard work. That is good. He
will be a hard worker.

These guards, the police, they make me want to wretch. I
will never have them here, not in my home.

A Fire in the Earth

I see less of him these days. Paco is growing up, I know. He is becoming a man, and a dignified man he will be. He again spends more time in town, with the people. Better than with the rich shits who come here.

I do not want to stand in his way of manhood.

I had to let go of two workers, and I hated myself for it. Enrique was good about it; I think he saw my situation. But he still knows that they need work. So I gave them work at the ranch, though we already have enough hands. They will make much less at the ranch, but it will be something. I can take the money from our box. It will not be missed.

Paco talks much more about school. He certainly is ready for it; I could see him working toward some very high degree. He says he wants to go to Mexico. So far away, but he says he will receive a good education there. I read the newspapers on Mexico. It is different there; things are changing. If he goes there, I hope he is not hurt. But he talks about being with the poor people, wanting to work and live with them. According to Paco, the revolution there has helped so many people. But there is a war going on there. He has said that he would not be near it.

Antonio bought an automobile. It is a fascinating machine. It would be nice to own one, but right now is a bad time to buy. Business is slow, and I have had to take a lot from the box for salaries. I am trying to keep things going with the people in town, too. Diego has continued taking the food down every week. That need has grown.

Patricio had rarely ever referred to the network of food-giving that he had created over the years. Paco searched for other clues, but found few.

He is gone. He said that he hoped to return in a few months, for vacation. Now he is gone. That is good for him. But I feel sick now; I do not know why. It all seems so wrong, there is no one to speak English with, there is no one to talk with.

447

Marcos McPeek Villatoro

The following entry was written in a scrawl,

More men have had to leave the bricks. Enrique is still
there, but it is getting worse. I do not know what to do. I am
almost out de dinero, casi no tengo nada of money. I have
very little.

She is throwing a party tonight. She wants that auto. I
do not blame her; I can see why. I love her, yes. But I do not
know her, not anymore. My brother is here. They are both in
the other room, talking about the past, about that damn car.
I feel I have lost, me perdió a ella, parece que ella quiere a
esta casa más que me quiere a mi. Me siento enfermo, como
con fiebre, no quiero hacer nada. Mi hermano, es la verdad
que me ha quitado todo.

It was the final entry. It had no date at all.

Paco hesitated in closing the book. He looked at the following
blank pages as if in hope that something would appear, more entries,
more life. Nothing.

The red sunlight that fell on his cheek was scarcely warm. An
orchestra of roosters burst over the distance in the town below. He
closed the book, gathered the three volumes together, and held them
to his chest as if carrying a wounded baby.

Downstairs someone began the workday. No doubt Olga, for it was
the innocent, practical sounds of a relit fire, of boiling water and hens
clucking toward scattered rice. Paco pulled a worn serape from his
sack and walked out the bedroom door.

Rosa donned her clothes and brushed her hair. She had already
washed, and was preparing herself quickly in order to help Olga fix
breakfast, to make something special for the newly arrived brother.
She looked out the window. Paco walked across the yard. At the gate
he stopped before the guard. There was an exchange. The guard
responded, then Paco's voice carried on strong, so much so she understood what he had said, a demand, to let him out. The guard obeyed.
Paco walked through and approached the gravestone on the other side
of the fence, where he quickly fell upon his knees.

A Fire in the Earth

Rosa ran through the house. She was out the front door and halfway across the yard when she muttered aloud, "Let me through please," to the confused guard. Nothing mattered, not the guard, not the fence. Neither existed. There were only the wails, as if the older sibling were expulsing a sickness from within. His body fell against the marker, almost knocking it over. He fell upon the fresh flowers that the *labriegos* from town had placed there. It was the only time the local people asked permission to enter the confines of the fence, for they had not forgotten. They were not ones to forget goodness or pain.

Romilia heard the cries from her shed. She placed her work down, as if the weeping was an alarm that she had been expecting. From over the little hill she could see the scene, and saw a fallen journal spread open on the grave. She almost smiled, but her face tightened as a mother looking upon a child that has suddenly seen too much of life in one instant. She had placed the journals in the drawer the previous morning when she had heard that her son had returned. She knew that he would read them, as he was so curious. She had kept the journals—though she could not read them—like keys to a personal history. Her son was the gatekeeper. She had made sure that she had them all, even the one that Joaquín's lawyer had left with her. Romilia knew nothing of the journal's contents, but she knew of that previous life, and had some years to reflect upon them. It was a risk to let the boy see them. It seemed necessary.

Romilia approached the fence. "Open the gate," she demanded of another guard. There was no hesitation. She walked through and approached her children. They were at Patricio's grave, the daughter holding the son as the boy blurted out broken phrases of sorrow. It was in that moment that Romilia's crossed arms unfolded and trembled. Her old fingers opened like new buds and reached out for her family.

〰〰

He remained three days with them. On the third day he went down into town.

449

"It is good to have you back with us," said Rosa. "I hope that you stay."

"I will be here. You will see more of me, or at least, hear about me." Paco smiled. From the front yard of the private home, he looked out for an instant. "What of these guards, Rosa?"

She looked down, as if knowing the problem too well. "They are difficult to remove. Since Joaquín died they have been circling the hotel for security purposes. They are following orders from his family. But we have few people staying in the hotel. Most days we have no one at all. News of Joaquín's murder has gotten around. It makes for bad business. But I want them to leave," she ended, glancing at the guard.

Paco shook his head slightly with some understanding. "They are like a disease, very difficult to get rid of."

She looked at him and asked, "Where will you stay?" knowing that he would never stay here, not for long. The whole estate, every inch of it, burned against his beliefs. "Do you know if you have a place to sleep, to eat?"

"Yes, I believe so. I think Don Enrique will take me in. I will be doing much travelling. But when I am in town, I will be at his house."

They stood side by side for a long moment, saying nothing. She brought her hand to his back, rubbing it. "You are following your ideals. That is good. You do have ideals, true?"

Paco grinned. "You could say that I am religious about some ideas. But God is not one of them."

"Yes, but you can spell out what things you believe in and act upon them. I suppose that is what I lack. Sometimes I wonder if I have acted correctly. I do not know." She turned silent, for it seemed so very big upon her. He put his arm over her shoulder.

Rosa ended the moment, embarrassed over her sudden emotion. "Mamá will be in her shed, as always. The world would have no cheese were it not for her."

They hugged goodbye. Paco walked to the side and back of the hotel, where he found his mother. She had just returned from the kitchen, where she had been ordering maids around, telling them which rooms to clean, which rooms to prepare. There was very little to do, but somehow Romilia kept them busy. When she saw Paco

A Fire in the Earth

approaching, she looked back down to her work while saying, "Well. Ready to go out and save the world from damnation, I see."

"I will try."

"Have you some more clothes in that sack to wear? Good. Wait a minute. I have something else for you before you go." She motioned him to follow. Romilia walked into the hotel, up some stairs to her room. He waited outside. Soon she returned. She handed a black object to him. "Here. This was your grandmother's."

He opened the tiny black pouch and blanched at the small crucifix that dangled out. "This is a rosary."

"I know, you probably will never use it, but you can wear it. Or just keep it with you in your bag. My mother wanted you to have it. She gave it to me before, just before she died. According to your father, she wanted you to have it. There is something else in it, look." She fumbled with it, as if careful to not caress his hands with her fingertips, yet taking the opportunity. "Be careful with this; it came from your great great grandfather." She opened the tattered corn husk leaf carefully, displaying the lock of white hair that reflected the morning sun. "His name was Don Pablo. He died when I was a little girl. He was a crazy old Indian who did not believe in God. Well, he believed in things; he believed in other gods. You know, you have heard Indians talking about the god of the earth and sky and other stuff. For some reason my mother put this lock of hair in with her rosary. Perhaps to remember to pray for his soul, since he did not worship God. But he was a good man, yes, a very good man. He always took care of me when I was sick. Anyway, it is yours. She wanted you to have it." Shoving it into the pouch, she pushed it clumsily back into his fingers. "Take it, do what you want to do with it. I only needed to make sure that you got it."

He mumbled his appreciation, took the pouch, and placed it inside his bag.

"So, will it be another decade or so?" asked Romilia.

"No. I will be around more often. I will be at Don Enrique's. Perhaps I will be able to come up here, but I am not sure about—"

"About what you are going to do. Well, I hope you find it. Maybe you already have. Just be careful out there."

He smiled at her and chuckled. "Yes. 'Out there.' I will be careful." He bent over and tried to hug her. She moved her calloused hands to his sides, patting him slightly. He did not release her. She talked all during the sudden embrace. "Well, you know, it is rough times now, so, just, well shit, watch your ass...but I know, you know what you want to do..."

Finally he broke away, for she had run out of things to say. He smiled down at her.

"Gain some weight," she ended, motioning to his rib cage.

She walked him to the gate. As the guard fiddled and clinked the keys against the metal lock, they stood, silent, looking outward, beyond the bars of the fence. He walked through. Barely turning to see her again, he waved. She raised her arm slowly, then placed it back into the crossed position over her chest. It seemed to him unbreakable, more invulnerable than the iron fence that wrapped around her. Then her voice broke through the fence. It was a strange voice, filtering through an old memory like light through tall trees in a cool morning. She spoke to him in soft, accented English, "Goodbie. Bee cadful."

Again he turned to her. He thought he imagined a smile from her. Then it became true.

"Ay luf jyu."

The voice trickled over him like a baptism. A smile broke over the son's face as he returned the English words.

"I love you, Mamá."

While walking down the hill, he sometimes glanced back. She still stood there. Once he disappeared over a small dip in the road, she returned to her work.

A few vines were wrapped over the mound. They would be burned off soon, to make room for new rows of beans. The dry season puffed dust about him as he sat down. It was the day after Easter, and people moved slowly, coming back to the usual routine after the previous week of festivities. Women walked before him, carrying baskets of eggs and tortillas. A few men stood at doorways, looking out, as if waiting

A Fire in the Earth

for a reason to move and work. Paco scooted back upon the mound, grabbed a handful of its earth, which crumbled brown and dry between his fingers. To his right he barely saw a corner of the door that once protected the inner cellar of the mound. It seemed that it had rested there, dusty and rusting at the hinges, for much time. A memory of death and failure swept through him. He turned his face away with a shudder.

He looked around for his kind.. He knew he would find them, but it would take time. Don Enrique could teach him, once again, how to talk, who to talk to. Then there was the guard. "Get off the mound, move on," said the one as he approached Paco. The young officer had not raised a stick to him. Perhaps that was a good sign.

Paco moved away from the dry-caked mound, down one road that led out of town to the nearby forest and river. Here the buildings separated from one another, became distinct adobes plotted beside the road. A woman, holding her screaming baby in one arm, ran dirty, wet clothes over a perforated rock in the shade of a mango tree. Beside her were three cracked pitchers of water which she had apparently carried from the river. There was work to do everywhere. There was also playing to do, leftover from the past Holy Week. Two houses down, three children ran about a mango tree and slapped sticks against an object hanging from the limbs. Paco approached them, grinning, watching as they slammed branches against the holiday dummy. It was a large representation, twice as big as a man. Paco had never seen such a huge Judas. It's feet scraped the ground with every swing of the rope, while its head still rubbed against the high branches above. The children screeched as they ran about it, slapping it with their hands and sticks.

"Culebra! Culebra!" screamed the children.

Pieces of old cloth and stuffing fell from the dummy's stomach and limbs. Later the mother would gather the stuffing. They were her cleaning rags. Other smaller pieces could be used for patching clothes. Paco walked on. For the moment, nothing occurred to him.

453

Chapter Two

Don Enrique welcomed Paco into his home. The conversations, however, were not what the young man expected. Enrique spoke carefully, avoiding certain words and phrases, ones which had become commonplace for the younger, zealous communist. He had heard through others that the man's son, Edmundo, had been murdered a number of years previously. Paco offered his condolences, yet also spoke of a hope which Don Enrique failed to grasp. All talk of people giving their lives for the Cause, and the motto that you can cut all the flowers down, but you can't stop the spring from coming, seemed to fall by the elder's wayside, words spoken to a sad, deaf man. Paco surmised that it was not so much that Enrique no longer believed, but that he was afraid to believe.

The old man did offer some help. He introduced Paco to Sergio and Lupe, the young couple who had been friends with his son Edmundo. "I believe you all will have many things to talk about." With that, Enrique left them, sat outside in the shade of his tiny lot, and smoked.

Lupe and Sergio glanced toward Paco with some humility and much awe.

"Is it true that you have studied in the States?" blurted out Sergio.

Paco nodded his head in affirmation. The two young lovers crowded toward each other with mumbled phrases of wonder.

"Yes. I studied for several years with the true leaders of the global proletarian movement. It was time to come home and utilize those studies."

They spoke through the afternoon and into the evening.

Regina, Enrique's older daughter, had moved back in with her father soon after Edmundo had been killed. She had brought her little

454

girl Consuelo with her, what was left of a man who came with promises and left very quickly. Though having walked a difficult road in life,
she kept a pleasant smile on her face and a kindness in her eyes. She
spoke little, but listened intently as she served coffee and sweet bread
to Sergio, Lupe, and Paco.

The young communist who had returned home sat before the couple like a teacher before a public hungry for knowledge. He spoke the
hope of the struggle, handed down to him from on high, from those in
New York who had no hesitation in their analysis of the current world
situation. At times Paco's abstract notions lost the young man and
woman, until he would say something about how the people of Greenwich Village drank coffee all through the night until the next morning,
or how Mr. Reed had a growth in his kidneys which caused him to uri-
nate blood while being held in jail for protesting the Great War, all for
the sake of the Cause. Such concrete pictures woke the couple up and
challenged them to give up those things which hindered them from
fighting with their whole being for the sake of the people. These were
long conversations, ones which sometimes frightened Lupe and Sergio,
especially when Paco spoke of the personal sacrifices necessary in
order that all may share in the justice that is to be achieved. "Yes,
nothing must stand in the way of the movement, especially nothing
personal. You two, for instance, must never allow your love relationship to hinder the Cause."

The couple said nothing at first. Finally Lupe spoke up. "What do
you mean, comrade? Sergio and I fight together for the good of the people." She smiled slightly, hoping to soften the texture of the intense
conversation.

"Yes. But your relationship can become so close that you will come
to believe that your love is more important than the proletarian's
struggle. Your personal life must always be secondary. Always."

Lupe said nothing.

Sergio broke the silence by whispering, "It's true, honey, it's true,"
then turned back to Paco, seeking out acceptance from the master.
"What do you think we should do now?" he asked.

"There needs to be organizing in our province. We need to be talking with the people in the villages, telling them that they need to join

the movements of the proletariat. They are hungry and poor, and that must become our first tool of propaganda."

"We have been doing that," responded Sergio with enthusiasm, proving that they indeed had been working. "We have visited the adobes around town. You know that we were feeding many families before our friend Pedro died." Sergio stammered, then fell back on track. "You know, your sister played a part in that."

"I had heard. But of course, we must do more than feed the poor. They know that we are on their side, when we feed them that way. But now we must show them how they must empower themselves, how they must be the movers of this country's future." His voice dropped low, became furtive. "It is time to move directly toward revolution."

The word lit fire in the young people. Someone in authority had said it.

"Yes, yes! Finally we are getting to that!" cried Sergio. "How do we do it, Paco? How do we prepare the people to gather as an army and defend their communal land? How is it that we will arm them?" Questions blurted out of the young man, ones which had accumulated through dozens of conversations held with a handful of others.

Paco chuckled as Sergio pelted him with the questions. "Slow down, son, slow down. It's wonderful to hear your enthusiasm. We will need that energy. Yes, we need to prepare the people. But in many ways the people are already prepared. You see, communism is an ideology that taps into each and every person and absorbs their individuality. No one is a single person anymore. Rather, each one of us is part of the common people. That is why communism is universal. It brings us all together, Russians with Mexicans, Americans with Bolsheviks. And it always begins with the people's struggle. For instance, your question about how we will arm the people." Paco smiled big as he responded. "The people are already armed."

"What? What do you mean?" asked Lupe, obviously puzzled.

"We are all armed." Paco pointed with his lips toward a corner of the room. Leaning upon the wall was Don Enrique's work machete.

"A machete?" asked Sergio.

"Yes. Of course. Everybody has one."

A Fire in the Earth

"But, but, comrade Paco," spoke Lupe, "the enemy, the Guards, they have guns."

"You see, there is where you need to learn the inner ideology of communism." Paco leaned forward, as if ready to hand to the young couple his final secret. "A war is more than just guns. A revolution is more than just bullets. They may have armaments. But we have the *idea*."

The couple remained silent. In the back room, while leaning over a fire, Regina listened intently. Her brows knit together as if to form a question. Beyond her cooking place, outside, old Don Enrique smoked a cigarette and stared listlessly into the day.

〰〰

They began working together. Their days and nights were spent trying to start conversations with certain individuals around El Comienzo, people who were known to be once connected with the now defunct Communist Party. The three received little positive response. Their plan was to preach the same proletarian gospel that Lupe and Sergio had received from Paco. In a couple of weeks a small number of men shook their heads affirmatively, yet darted their eyes about and said nothing. Paco reminded the young couple that it would take time. "We must plant the seed wherever we can. Then it will grow. Don't worry."

Late at night, after full days of spreading across town and finding anyone who seemed the least interested, the team separated, Lupe and Sergio to their homes, and Paco to Enrique's house. Though nothing was said publicly, Paco and Regina slowly began making their way to the same corner of the house. It seemed the natural thing to do. Regina had never taken to another man, not since her husband had left her years earlier. The little girl, Consuelo, had never known her father. Paco, for her, fell neatly into that position, though the girl always called him by name. She became accustomed to watching through half-sleeping eyes the two adults crawl into bed on the other side of the room from her. Sometimes she watched her mother's nude shadow squat upright on the old mattress and move about Paco's

457

stomach. Yet in her heavy sleep, Consuelo paid little attention to the noises that periodically came from the adults' bed.

$$\approx$$

"It's time to move out into the villages," announced Paco.

His decision was made after a month of proselytizing in El Comienzo. A small group had formed in town, one which met with Paco, Lupe, and Sergio regularly. Once it had reached the number of seven men and two women, Paco made the decision to go out to the villages. "That is where we'll find the pure proletariat."

Lupe made only one village trip. When she returned that Sunday evening, her father Hermes was waiting in the kitchen. Marta, her mother, was not present.

"Where have you been?"

"I, I have been out, visiting friends, I—"

"I do not want you out there anymore, understand? I have had enough of this." His voice broke with more fear than rage. "It is bad, dangerous, to be out in the hills."

She hesitated only briefly. "Why so, Papá? They are people; they can be our friends, just like the old Indian from Piricón who used to visit us."

"Used to, yes. But no more." Hermes stood from the stool and approached his daughter. He held an expression that made her step back. "You see what happened to him." His voice hissed low, "Ever since that one murdered the *patrón*, that Culebra, it has gotten worse. Do not be with the Indians, girl, or you will be a target, too!"

She stepped back again and fell into a corner. Hermes had changes so during the years. She had heard others, in the street, referring to her father as if he were insane. Lupe feared being alone with him. She cowered into her bedroom.

"You will not go out there anymore, understand? And you will not see that boy anymore, nor Paco! Do you understand?"

$$\approx$$

458

A Fire in the Earth

The following morning Sergio and Paco hitchhiked on an early truck out of El Comienzo in order to visit a village named Piricón, several hours away. The truck brought them only so far out of town. They walked most of the way. "This is where the old Indian lived, the one who used to visit Don Hermes and give him his sugar cane. He was murdered by the guard."

Most of the women wore old dresses in the Pipil tradition. The reds, greens and blues ran together in various sharp shapes, though the years had worn their brightness. They spoke to one another in Nahuatl rather than Spanish. When Paco and Sergio approached, they fell to Spanish phrases and fewer sentences. The two men arrived as the sun burned directly above them. Paco and Sergio trekked up to one house where several men gathered.

These were not easy trips for them, especially for Paco. Though he lived an austere life in New York, he had grown unaccustomed to being in his own country, in its sudden, humid heat, its jungle climate, the need to walk long distances instead of boarding public transportation. His ghostly figure drew every person's attention in the village. They whispered among one another in Pipil. One woman said to another, "Poor thing. Perhaps we should take him in, fatten him up."

They greeted one another. The women retreated to the shallow kitchens of the houses. One soon returned, brought Sergio and Paco tortillas with beans plopped atop them. They took the tiny cornucopias and sat with the men, and after much time passed in silence, they began talking. In the beginning Paco always tossed out light questions of consequence to the farmers concerning the population of the village, how the community got its name, how long the people had lived there. Then, where did they get their food, how did they like growing the coffee all around them, picking it, handing it over to the trucks that took it away to somewhere where they never saw it again. Some question along the way triggered a complaint from one man.

"They do not let us grow food," he said through a toothless mouth. With that statement, the other Indians looked away, as if to hide in their hats. Paco paid no mind.

"Then how is it that you all have lived, if you have no food?"

459

For a moment they said nothing to him, but mumbled to one another in their own language. Someone answered, "We grow it where we can."

"Do you think that is just," asked Sergio, "that the rich dogs suck your life away?"

The farmers said nothing, as it was too much of a question. Paco reshaped it.

"Do you think you have the right to grow as much food as you need?"

They mumbled a couple of affirmative answers. Suddenly, from around the adobe, one clear and direct voice spoke.

"If we could. But to do so is to have your throat cut open by the guard."

He was an older man. Sergio thought he recognized the Indian, but was not sure. Then he smiled, as it was obvious that this man was related to the old Indian with the sugar cane.

"They murdered my brother."

It was all that Paco needed. The others of the village made room for the old man. With all of them sitting under the shade of an orange tree, Paco began his teachings. "We are here to work with you; we are here to change things." He spoke on, using words from before, yet speaking them as if they were the product of inspiration. At times Sergio tried to break in, but the eloquence and rhythm of the educated and experienced Paco refused to let him intervene. "You people are the heart of our country, the ones raped by every outside force history has known, forced to suffer for being indigenous... Our people are sick of the oppression that has been forced upon us, and the time has come to fight, to take back what is ours, and we are planning to take it back, sometime soon, it is the only way, we have tried other ways, legislation, strikes, protests, legal petitioning to the government that has made us play the game, that tosses out a little bit of law like a strip of mincemeat to a multitude of dogs to chew upon. To take over the government is the only way, and you are the backbone, the root, and you must fight with us for it to succeed. This is your country, your heritage, this is all yours, all these mountains, and you have the right to tear by the roots the cursed coffee trees from the ground and burn them, and plant life-giving corn, beans, and rice. As of now, we have no weapons, not like the Guard." Paco turned toward Sergio, who said nothing, but only stared at him. "But we all have machetes, yes, and thousands of machetes is an army, so hone them and sharpen them, prepare the tools of the earth, the great knives of planting and harvesting, and use them to harvest a new crop of freedom. Work with us, come, follow us, we will lead you out of the land of oppression, lead you back to your land of plenty."

Not everyone understood, as he spoke in Spanish. Yet the people gathered around smiled as the young man, whatever he was saying, certainly had a charisma about him. They did, however, hear what he said about their machetes.

Sergio and Paco returned home that evening. They were too weary to do anything but have a plate of food and fall on their own beds. Thus they had no idea what was happening up on the hill.

The gates of the fence had all swung open. The *patrona* had given a quiet order, that all the guards surrounding and dwelling in the residence must leave immediately, for their services were no longer needed.

The order met with conflict. The commander of the Guard was reluctant, and at one point refused to leave. Yet the mandate had been given, and the Comenzaños looked up and saw the *patrona* standing behind that great fence, pointing outward. Soon the guards filed out with their rifles flung over their shadowy backs. They walked through the gate and down the hill. Outside, their formal line broke like dust upon water, and they slowly scattered from one another.

One final petition came from behind, "Stay away from the town. Go back from where you came."

The guards looked back at her. For a long while they did not move. They did not know how to carry out the order, no longer knowing from where they came or whether they could ever go back.

A day passed. People from town looked up the hill and saw the gates still wide open. No one dared to approach them, except for the few who worked at the hotel or the private home, those who had always been accustomed to ask for permission to enter or leave. Now that was unnecessary. The men who tended the grounds of the home, and the women who cooked and cleaned the hotel, approached the open gates with caution, as if afraid they could suddenly slam closed in their faces. Yet they never did.

"You have heard, haven't you?" Don Enrique spoke to Paco. "The gates are all open."

Paco was pouring coffee. "Gates? What gates?"

"The gates up the hill. Your old home."

"Oh," Paco replied, as if not wanting to be reminded about his roots. "The gates. Really?"

Don Enrique shook his head affirmatively. He puffed on a cigarette, another one that Sergio had given to him. A gray spider the size of a hand crawled over an adobe brick on the wall, just beside the old man. It was the beginning of the wet season, and the great arachnids always came inside with the coming of the rains. Don Enrique slammed the bottom of his fist against it. "You know, such an action is to be respected. She had a lot of courage to do that." He wiped the side of his hand over his pants.

Paco lay down on some straw in a corner, the cup of coffee in his palms. Another spider stood frozen upon the wall below his feet. "Yes, well, if she had *total* courage, she would leave that rich home and come live with us." He slammed his foot against the spider, crunching it to the wall. Outside, rain came down in sheets, and the afternoon had been darkened almost into night by the thick clouds.

"It's clear that you've been gone a long time. You don't even know what that fence means, do you? It was built while you were gone." Enrique puffed on the cigarette, contemplating. "You *have* been gone a long time. You have missed much of the story."

Paco was not listening. He emptied his pockets wearily. The black pouch fell on the floor.

Don Enrique picked it up. "What's this?"

"What? Oh, that. It's a rosary."

"Oh? I never knew you as a believer."

"Only in the Cause. My mother gave me that. She said it was from her mother, who had wanted to give it to me. It's got a lock of one of my ancestors, some Indian, my mother's great grandfather, or somebody like that."

"Oh. Well, for that, it is important. Family is always important."

The old man offered the youth a cigarette. They smoked for some minutes before Enrique spoke again.

"You know, when I was working at the brick factory, you may not believe this, but sometimes I dreamed about living in the ranch. It is a temptation. I can see how people could be tempted to to it. Perhaps some people can live in such places and also not forget the poor. Your father was like that, you know."

"Yes, and he did not forget the poor. He was feeding them, giving them food and money. But he could not continue on like that. Come on, Don Enrique, you do not really believe that a person can live in both places?"

"No, I don't. But, well, I think your sister is trying. Perhaps this is a first step."

"Perhaps."

"Anyway, I think she is to be congratulated for it. You know, maybe someone could show her some appreciation."

"There may be time for that." Paco turned to his side, looked at the old man through the darkness of the house. "Are you saying I should pay her a visit?"

"Like I said, boy, family is important. She and your mother are all you've got."

Paco smiled. "I've got more. I have the Struggle." Don Enrique said nothing, but looked at his young friend intently. "All right, all right, old man. I'll go see them. Soon."

〰〰

Three weeks later Paco kept his word. When he reached the top of the hill he learned that he had to wait his turn at the open gate, for there was a line of women before him. He stood on his toes and looked over their shoulders. There, at one of the barns, stood Rosa. She was helping some of the workers hand out small bags to the women who waited in line. After several minutes she looked up, saw him, and walked quickly to him, smiling. Rosa no longer wore black. She hugged her brother tightly, then pulled him through the line and toward the house.

"You said you would visit! It has been months!"

"Yes, well, I have been busy, I am sorry...."

"No matter. You are here!" she smiled a wide, lovely smile. "Mamá will be happy to see you."

"Is she here?"

"No, no. She is still at the other side, making cheese. She's not as involved in this yet. But I'm working on her." Rosa almost laughed.

"What, what is all this?"

"Oh, you don't know? It is relatively new. All the crops have been harvested from the farm. We have had them stored here. It was usually used for the food at the hotel, you know, when business was going strong there. But now, well, there is not any business at all, no one comes, so, we had to do something with all the produce."

"So what's going on, you're selling it?"

"No, not selling. It has not become completely organized, but, overall, many people are bringing their goods, whatever some of them can bring, and trading. You know, a woven dress for so many pounds of beans or rice or corn. But some people cannot do that; they have nothing to trade, so we just make sure they have some sacks of food. But they end up wanting to help us out in the gardens or the warehouse."

Paco stared. Most of the people were women, but behind the women, men worked in the gardens and with the livestock. The yard of the private home had become a veritable marketplace. It only lacked one thing.

"Is there any money exchanged?" asked Paco.

"No, hardly at all. Nobody has any."

"Rosa, where did you get this idea?" Paco's smile broke into an incredulous laugh.

"Well, I'm not sure. It actually just came to me one morning. We had begun giving out much of this produce earlier, when Joaquín was alive. That was long before you came home. I had to sneak it out to the fields. That was when Pedro and the others, you know.... Well, the hotel now is abandoned. There are only a few maids there, and they will be leaving soon. I am thinking of having them work here at the market, if they want. Of course, the Guard is not here anymore. This wouldn't work with them hanging around. Now, there is other trading going on. Some of the dresses that people have traded for food are being traded for other things. So it keeps on going. I hope it can keep on going. I suppose it will go on as long as they want it to."

People walked around them, carrying bags of food, clothes, ceramic items made of clay, pots and pans, water jugs, woven baskets.

"Rosa, this is wonderful!"

She smiled, happy that he was pleased. "We were wondering when you would come and see us. What brings you here today?"

"Oh, I was talking with Don Enrique, and he reminded me of how busy I've been... and that I've not come up to visit you..."

"Oh. Well then, God bless Don Enrique! Come and have a bite to eat, perhaps over with Mamá. She will not come over here with all this noise."

They walked through the open gate, talking all the way. "What are you going to do with the hotel now?" he asked.

"Mamá and I have talked a little about it. I believe I will put it on the market. Believe it or not, she actually likes the idea. She likes the money part, you know. And she is part of it, since she is family. I had declared that all this is officially hers, too. I did not want the Reyes family coming in and taking it over. I know that sounds cold, but I was following my instincts, and it seemed the best thing to do, to write out a declaration of ownership, that all belonged to Mamá and myself." She talked quickly, trying to be thorough, as was her way. "But if that keeps going on," she pointed back to the market behind them, "we may want to keep the hotel and gardens."

"You will have neither market nor home if you keep giving things away like you do," responded their mother, whom they had just approached. Romilia was eating a tortilla in her kitchen shed when they entered. She looked up at Paco. "Hello. Where have you been?

You would think we threw boiling water on you when you last left us. Made you run off. Still on a diet, I see."

He smiled like an embarrassed child. She poured coffee into three cups while he spoke. "I have been busy, you know, whipping the streets."

"I am sure. Here, the beans are still hot. Have you eaten, girl? Here then. So how is the fight for your prol—prole...thing."

He spoke through a mouthful of beans. "Very well. People are learning what it means to be in charge. It seems to have infected everybody, especially all those people at the free marketplace." He tossed a shoulder toward the direction of the private home.

"You call that a marketplace? I call it a handout. I just cannot understand that, not at all. Do not 'oh Mamá' me, girl, I have worked too hard all my life to think that giving food away is a good thing. They should work for it; they should pay you for it."

"Mamá, you know they are paying for it, what they can. They trade. Many things are exchanged."

"Trading, yes. But what is that? There is no profit in such trading. How do you expect to make any money?"

"That seems to me to be the main idea, Mamá," interjected Paco. "Rosa does not want to make money. It's a market for the people and by the people. Everyone is treated equally."

"Ay." She waved her children off. "I do not see where you get such ideas. Well you, yes, I can see, but my daughter, well, you have always had a soft heart, much like your father. He would approve of something like this. But I have no use for it, not at all." Yet there was no real sting in her voice, as if there stood no belief behind the words of protest. The phrases fell from her mouth because they had to, because she was Romilia Colónez, businesswoman. "You kids must do what you must do, I suppose. But I just call that naive, what is happening over there. It will not last long. The food will run out. The workers will get tired of working for no money and just for food. It looks good now, but it will wear out. I think it is naive."

"I would not call it naive," said Paco.

"Yes, and what would you call it? One of your idea-names, I suppose."

A Fire in the Earth

"Yes. I would call it communism." He smiled. His arms were crossed.

"Wonderful. Get all our throats slit."

They talked of other things, of the hotel, if it could be sold, if there were anyone interested in buying it. Sometimes the conversation fell quiet and they sat in silence, seemingly unbothered by it. Soon the two children left. "Here. Take this to Don Enrique and his family." Romilia handed him a wrapped block of her cheese.

While walking back to the private home, Paco consciously ambled more slowly. "Rosa, there is something I must tell you, for I have a favor to ask of you. You know, I think this is beautiful, what is happening here at your home. It is exactly what should be happening." She smiled, but the smile drifted away, as if sensing something else. "In fact, I hope we will see more of this as time goes on. You know, there *is* hope of that. Things may change soon. All over the country people are organizing; they are raising their voices and machetes together. I think something is going to happen soon, you know, something drastic. The people may erupt, and when they do, major changes will be made. But you are already ahead of those changes. I have a favor to ask of you. My friends, the family I stay with, Don Enrique and Regina and her daughter Consuelo, I am concerned for them. He has been like a second father to me, and he is getting very old. He will, I am sure, not be playing a part in the first movements of this change. I was wondering, when the time comes, could you open your doors to them?" He chuckled slightly at his own accidental pun and glanced at the already open fence.

"Paco, what are you talking about?"

"You know, the changes, obviously the people here know, they are organizing their own market, they know about the changes...you know, revolution." The precious word fell forward, then stumbled like a child in a strange house.

Rosa looked over at all the women trading clothes and food, ceramics, other utensils. She was obviously puzzled. "Paco, I don't think they know anything about this."

"Sure they do. How could they organize like this if they did not?"

"They organized this because they were hungry."

"Yes. That is correct. That is the driving force."

"Yes, but, you seem to be talking about something else. I have heard no one say anything about a revolt."

"It is a part of all this. What you are doing here is a reflection of what is to come. There will be changes in our government; there will be radical moves. And it will benefit all, just as this little market is helping the people here."

Rosa looked at her brother, who seemed animated with a spirit that she was either lacking or did not know existed. She shook her head slightly, then asked, as quietly as he had been speaking, "When will this revolt occur?"

"I am not sure, but it will be soon. The president now, he is very weak. He is not holding up to the pressures from any angle, particularly the right wing affiliates; they are trying to push him over the side. I know that for a fact. And the leftist movements are growing tired of his promises and his failure to honor them. Then others are frustrated over the lousy economy. The colón is not worth a peso now, and, of course, the military and the Guard are doing whatever they want. That is the root of the problem, or the root that is tied to the main root—those who keep such a system alive, the big, imperialist countries, that is what kills us. This administration, I believe, will not last long. Some say the president will be thrown out by the military. And it is the military, the Guard, that I am concerned about. They...you know...have a mind of their own."

Rosa tried to listen to it all, but it seemed distant, foreign, except for his reference to the Guard. She had heard her brother speak like this in earlier years. His speech had a rhythm about it that she could not follow, one which left her groping for understanding. "Yes, well, how is it I can know when to open my doors to Don Enrique?"

"Oh, you will know when it happens. I am afraid that it will not be quiet. It will take some, well, some violence. We have worked through all the other channels. This is the final resort, and we have to take it. It means to snatch out what is ours from the claws of the oppressors, and they will not give it up that easily. We will have to fight. And we will fight, long and hard, for we have the power and the will of the people with us." He stopped for a moment, as if realizing that his fervor

A Fire in the Earth

was carrying him away. "But Don Enrique, he is so old. He will not be able to fight. He has already fought, with his whole life. He has been good to me, Rosa. I just want to make sure he is safe. If you could take care of him here, just when it all happens, I would be very grateful."

She gave him her word. He smiled and put his hand on her shoulder. She reciprocated, not wanting to let him go, to keep him from descending once again into town. Yet she did release him, as if knowing it was necessary. He walked away, turning once to wave at her before walking down into El Comienzo. She watched him until she could watch no more. She stared over the town, silent in its day. Peace seemed to be reigning free, with no stipulations.

Chapter Three

There was a coup in the land.

Though stationed in the Cuxcatlán province for over ten months, Captain Geraldo Castillo had not redeemed himself from the shame he had suffered on that fateful February evening when an Indian sliced the *patrón* Joaquín Reyes in half before the Captain's eyes. Castillo loathed shame. It had occurred few times in his life, but those rare moments had burned deeply into his memory. He remembered once, how his mother had caught him masturbating in the bathroom when he was thirteen. That same year, in school, some hick from the country (in fact, the same region that Captain Castillo was now responsible for) had thrown a stone and crunched his testicles, before all the kids on the playground. That had been a rough year on his manhood. The shame had never been redeemed, as the kid named Paco Colónez had run away. It was such moments that had taught Geraldo Castillo to never let anybody escape.

During these months Captain Castillo had wandered about his new province, making sure that all was safe for his people. Nothing had occurred. At a time of great uproar throughout the country, with protests and strikes and demands shouted publicly upon city streets, his was a quiet, calm department. Still, he had been shamed. At times he had his men pick people up off the roads, bums and winos who littered the walkways of various towns. They followed the usual procedures, just to show that the streets of his towns were clean, that there was no need for alarm, that people could walk in peace and safety.

Then came the coup, and suddenly Captain Castillo came under different leadership. At first he did not know whether this was a blessing or a curse. Under the now-deposed president, his shame over the Reyes incident had not become a political factor. Under the new presi-

470

dent, however, a warning drifted among Castillo's circle. This new leader was of another stock. They called him El Brujo—The Warlock— for his alleged magical powers. The new president did not seem to mind that name; he had, in fact made it an official nickname, and he had it promulgated throughout the land. Magic, everyone said, made possible his entrance into the presidential palace, for no one was really sure how he had arrived there. Some said he had been born out of the pack, from the official watchdogs of the palace, that he arose out of a bloody howl toward a full moon.

Suddenly Captain Geraldo Castillo was no longer Captain. He was an angel. The retinue around El Brujo briefed Castillo as he headed toward the office of the president. He may be busy, they said, with another world; he may be occupied with the spirits. You can't shake those things from him. You are one of his angels, a messenger of the Cuxcatlán Province. He knows that; he knows everything. All of the officers of the land had become angels, and all the angels in the regions were called to the capital to speak with El Brujo, and to receive specific orders from him alone.

Castillo stood before the presidential chair. Though he shivered inside because he was human, Angel Castillo stood frozen.

El Brujo sat in the shadows. Cigarette smoke billowed from a darkened, vague face as he sat there, apparently reading from a letter in his hand. He spoke. His voice slithered out from the shadow and under the smoke. "It is from the welfare department. As their new president, they want me to make a statement about the impoverished barrios of our capital, and no doubt in many areas of the whole nation, how it is affecting the growth of children." He tossed the letter down. "Poverty. Children without food. I suppose that is what they mean. Without food, without clothes. That is what they mean." El Brujo turned and glanced out a window. Angel Castillo wondered if he saw a look of sadness in his eyes, but they again disappeared into the shadows.

"Poverty can be good for children. It is better that a child walk barefoot. Thus they can better receive the beneficial effluvia of the planet, the vibrations of the earth. Plants and animals do not use shoes. Why should children? Poverty, yes, it can be beneficial."

He ended. He did not speak for many minutes, as if he was hypnotized by the power of his prophetic statement. Castillo made no move, though at times his eyes darted about the room. Yet that, too, was disrespectful, and he decided to look directly upon the lower side of the great desk that rose above him. Silence reigned completely.

Questions suddenly fell from the dark desk. Angel Castillo answered them to an appropriate degree of clarity and assurance. When El Brujo asked of the state of security in the Cuxcatlán Province, Angel Castillo answered, "All is well and quiet, sir. There have been no outbreaks of violence against our people in ten months." When El Brujo asked about the incident in February, when a *patrón* was cut in half by some fucking Indian, Angel Castillo answered with the slightest quiver in his voice, "That, regretfully, was truly a tragedy, and yet may the good El Brujo know that the land was purged immediately following that incident, that those who were guilty were liquidated, and peace had come to the earth once again."

"That is good," responded El Brujo, "that is good, for that is what I want for all my people, a purging of the land, a reassurance that all will be well, that our world may be free of this insidious, cancerous growth of communism, that we may burn the infection from us once and for all. How I have dreamed of this, how I have dreamed. To have a cleansing, a final one, to make sure that we are a pure people. That is my hope for the country."

There was silence. Within that moment Angel Castillo dared to share an inspiration.

"Such a deed, good El Brujo, could be done. All of us working together, such a cleansing could happen." He continued talking. As he explained his idea, of how this new communist infection could be cleansed and rinsed off the land, El Brujo listened, and smiled, and smoked a cigarette.

"Yes, that is so good, so good. Perhaps it could be carried out soon, very soon."

Angel Castillo began to speak about details, but El Brujo had no time for that. The angel was sent away and told to wait in his province for further orders. He walked out after a gracious exit, and as he walked through the halls of the presidential palace, Angel Geraldo

A Fire in the Earth

Castillo felt as if he carried something tightly wrapped in his palm. He returned to his province and looked down upon it. He whispered to the countryside, though it could not hear, "You have been my shame, you will be my salvation."

♒

Paco heard the screams coming from Doña Ramírez's house, but he paid no attention to them. They were nothing but echoes of his childhood, of the old crazy woman who had screamed her perversities and had beaten the tortillas into dust for over twenty years. He could not think of her, for he had many things in his mind. He had information, too fresh and warm to keep to himself, and he was running to Don Enrique to tell the old mentor everything.

Paco had just jumped off a truck that he had ridden all the way from the capital. His two days in the city proved successful. "I have talked with the leaders. They are still around, only they have been careful, subversive. So much to say, Don Enrique, but first, one thing: they have set a date. The people are about to explode, Don Enrique! There is no holding them back! We talked a long while, all of us, from the different provinces. We all agreed that it is time. The leaders are afraid of a sporadic insurrection, and it seems that is what we are bordering on. But if that were to happen, there would not be enough strength behind them. It would not come to one big blow, but would be in bits and pieces. If that were to happen, the army could wipe them out. So it is time to—"

"Wait a minute, hold on, boy. Tell me, when is the date?"

Paco smiled, then caught his breath. "January 22."

"What? Paco, that is less than two weeks away—"

"We have to act now. It is the only way. The army will be a step ahead of us if we wait too long."

Enrique was sitting in his favorite old chair. Paco fell to the floor to propose other thoughts to his mentor. "This new president, El Brujo, he is very silent. We are not sure about him. But the day before I arrived in the capital, the guard confiscated almost 3,000 pounds of brochures, pamphlets, papers, all of them from the offices in New

473

York. I was so happy to hear that Greenwich Village was supporting us! But then, to have everything confiscated...I tell you, he is ready to strip away everything that the Party has built up to now. We have to act, and act fast."

With that, Paco excused himself from the presence of the older man, for he had to find Sergio. "We must get the news out, the people are waiting. They will be ready. They only need to know when to act." In a moment he was gone. He left Don Enrique at the old man's doorstep, looking at the street, his face confused. Life suddenly seemed to be moving too quickly for the old man.

Sergio and Paco spent the following several days on the roads around their town, meeting once again with all the people of their territory. They handed over the date, January 22. They spoke of preparation, of being ready to act, that others from El Comienzo would be with them at the moment of the uprising and would instruct the people as to the exact moment when they should strike. They would take the town of El Comienzo and defeat the local guard. From that point, they planned to move onward to all the other little towns, Cojutepeque, San Martín, the towns around Lake Ilopango, until they reached the capital seat. There they would unite with other comrades who would be coming in from every other direction. Then they would take the capital, and the land at that point would be all theirs. Victory then would be theirs.

The men of the settlements nodded their heads in agreement. One man raised his hand to the visitors in recognition of their comradeship and vowed to fight until the death in order to give victory to his people. The old Indian of Piricón shook his head in agreement, though his face did not change. He vowed to take revenge for the death of his younger brother. It was an enthusiastic moment, laced in the blood of the lost ones. Paco looked upon the villagers. He felt ennobled by their presence, as if they were all at the point of being born into a new people.

$$\approx$$

474

A Fire in the Earth

"The spirits, they are floating above us now. Listen, concentrate, else they will flit away. I know, it has happened before. They are above us; they are fucking one another, see? Watch, watch, or they will flit away."

El Brujo held the hand of the Secretary of State to his left and that of the Secretary of Defense to his right. The rest of the circle was composed of all the angels from around the country. The Secretary of State cleared his throat. He turned his head to one side, glanced to his left and right to see if everyone else was obeying El Brujo. They did. Every one of them looked up, searching, especially that particular angel named Castillo, who stared as if he too saw the vision and desired to become part of it. The Secretary of State looked down, embarrassed. "Someone among us is not looking up; someone is not helping," came the master's voice. The Secretary shot his eyes upward.

After forty minutes the seance ended. It seemed to be a success. El Brujo looked about at his men and barely smiled. They were all becoming accustomed to his ways. He spoke.

"We live in an incredible time. Sometimes I wonder if we are living in it, sent down from some higher realm. But we are here, and we should be thankful. We are now the governing body of this country, and we must rule it correctly. There is a great deal going on now. We have been in office only a month, and already we are hearing complaints about our administration, which I suppose is normal. People are going to bitch. This I am not so concerned about. It is the talk in the North that concerns me, yes, the North." He dropped his head back upon the leather upholstered chair. His eyes stared blankly at the ceiling, and his shoulders, laden with the stars of military prestige, fell.

"I have an idea," his mouth said, working alone like living lips on a cadaver. His eyes darted to one side, as if he were watching a departing spirit. "We know that the communists are planning something, and soon. We will be ready for them, no doubt about that. Some things in the future are just too easy to see. Still, I propose that it is time to clean house. You know, the archbishop has called me concerning this. He wanted to make sure that I was not as soft on them as my predecessor. I assured him that in fact I was not. Assurance, that is what all people want." Again, silence, while his eyes stared at the corner of the exiting spirit. El Brujo's fingers lifted slightly in a gesture of goodbye. "You know, the North does not recognize us as a legitimate governing body, just because of a little coup. Well, they will recognize us, they will know who we are. And our own people, they will stand behind us. They are the ones who we must protect. If anything, gentlemen, that is our first responsibility. In fact, I have had a letter written to all the families of the land, so that they may know of our future plans. They will receive the letters within a few days. As leader, that is the least I can do for them. We will clean the country, I assure you. We must clean off these lives so that they may reincarnate and become better lives. Fear not, gentlemen. Fear not to kill a man. It is much greater a sin to kill an ant than a man, for that ant dies and never returns. It dies forever, while a man becomes reincarnated. Remember that, all of you. Remember that when the time comes."

He fell forward slightly, as if drunk from the vision, and remained slumped over for ten full minutes. The men said nothing. They knew to wait. This had happened before, several times. Once he had remained in that position for two and a half hours before reviving. The men, during all that time, had neither moved, nor spoken. Today he was much quicker. Suddenly he raised his head. It was difficult to see him, as no light fell upon his face, only on his messengers. He began, "Now, all of you, tell me everything you know about your province."

One by one, each angel reported. In Sonsonate, the messenger knew of an approximate date planned for an uprising, though he was not sure. He also had the name of the communist in charge of that area. In San Miguel, it seemed that very little was happening, that it would not be an area of much action. Nevertheless, the angel of that province had prepared his troops. Each angel continued, giving as much information as possible. They stopped only when El Brujo suddenly dropped his head back on his chair and swooned. Everyone remained silent, respectful before the presidential vision. It seemed to pass. "Yes, go on. Angel Castillo, give your report," spoke the swivelling head.

"I have heard the same date as the Sonsonate province, January 21 or 22. We are ready. The house of the guard is full and the windows are closed."

A Fire in the Earth

"And have you learned who is in charge of the insurrectionists?"

"Yes sir, I have. I went to school with him."

~~~

Rosa had spent the whole afternoon taking inventory. The common market in her front yard had increased to great proportions through the weeks, so much so that it was necessary for her to keep order. She and Olga ambled through the barn, counting all the bags of corn, rice, beans, finding out how many sets of clothes had been traded. She had decided to import more rice from other cities, as that was their lowest bulk item.

Because of the success of the market, Romilia had put aside any fears concerning what Paco had told her when he last visited. It was mid-evening when she returned home. Romilia had been taking care of the children all afternoon, and though Jesús was awake, he was quickly nodding off. Juancito had already fallen to sleep much earlier. "This market of your keeps you away from the children, more than you realize."

"They're fine, Mother. They have a good grandmother to take care of them." Rosa poured a glass of juice into a cup and sat down to rest.

"How long do you plan to keep this up? Girl, it is becoming bigger than you. I have never seen so many people at a market. And you are not making one peso from it all."

At first Rosa said nothing, then muttered something insignificant about how good it is to keep busy.

Olga walked by and handed Rosa an envelope. "This just came in today, Mrs. Reyes." She walked on to tend to the children, making sure Juancito was sound asleep. Rosa thanked her, dropping the envelope on the couch.

"Have you seen anything of your brother recently? I was wondering when, or if, he would ever come to see us again."

"No. Not since you last saw him." That brought her to look up at her mother, as if to remember everything Paco had told her. "I hope he is all right."

"I am sure he is fine. He has a way of taking care of himself."

"Yes, well..." Rosa's voice trailed off. Without thinking, she opened the letter and commenced reading.

To the Most Esteemed *Reyes* family,

Greetings from the capital seat of this blessed Republic. I send this letter to all of our families in the country, for I desire to grant all of you a safe and blessed year which is before us.

The matter of which I write concerns the tension within our beloved land. As you may know, at times there have been volatile moments among those in the countryside. We all know who is instigating such actions. The World Communist Movement has been trying to reach into the depths of our country, and it is almost at the point of doing so. I, your president, however, have been one step ahead of them. I know of their actions, and of their proposed future events. I send this letter to inform you that there may be some tense moments coming soon, sometime this month. I want all of you to know that everything has been taken care of, that your president and his staff have the situation under control. However, when the time comes, you may want to keep inside your homes, so as to make sure that no one is hurt. I solemnly swear to you, as your president, that before long, this ideological threat to our well-being will be forever wiped off our land.

My salutations go out to all of you and your family members whom we serve...

"Olga! Olga!" Rosa jumped up from the couch, walked quickly to and up the stairs. "Olga, where did this letter come from?"

"It was sent here by Eduardo, the man at the post office. He said that it had come from Mr. Reyes' family in the capital." That was all Rosa heard. She returned downstairs and began explaining to her mother.

"This was not sent to us by the president. Joaquín's father must have sent it."

"Why would he do that?"

"I suppose it is a family gesture. This is all bad. I do not like it. Something is going to happen."

Romilia looked at her daughter, staring as if to search out something. "Where is Paco in all this?"

478

A Fire in the Earth

"I am not sure." Rosa stared down at the letter in her hands, studying it, waiting for some answer to come. She shoved the letter back in the envelope, stuffing it, bending its edges. "I'll be back in a minute." She ran out, looked into the yard where the market had taken place that day. The workhands that labored all day on the property sat under a mango tree in the front yard. There were several of them, and they were singing songs around one lone guitar player and a bottle of homemade liquor. Another small group of people, made up of both men and women, stood around the fence, leaning against it, wooing one another.

Rosa approached the ones with the guitar. "Good evening, gentlemen." They respectfully greeted her back. "I am sorry to bother you, but I have a favor to ask. Could someone please take this letter to the home of Don Enrique Lazo, and see that my brother Paco receives it? He needs to have it as soon as possible."

Pablo, a man in his mid-twenties, took the letter. She thanked him and said good night to all. When she returned to the house, she informed her mother of her actions.

"What do you think will happen?"

"I have no idea." Rosa went to her room. She closed the door, then decided to leave it slightly ajar. She sat down in a chair near a front window. There she let out a heavy breath and tried to relax. It did little good. At times she squirmed from one side of the chair to the other, then sat upright, as if subconsciously remembering an old posture lesson her mother had given her in childhood.

A heavy, full moon stood to the east of the window. By its clean light Rosa could see the whole town below her, soaked in the blue-white glow. She could see and hear the guitar players as they sang a low song just outside her window. The lovers at the fence had left in twos. Now no one leaned against the iron gate.

The moon cast shadows from the fence upon the yard. While she sat in her chair, staring out, the shadows by the fence had moved almost vertically—straight up and down—between the fence and her. She wondered if she had fallen asleep. She opened and closed her eyes a couple of times, squinting. Yes, she had slept, her crusty lids told her that. She looked at the clock to her right. It was approaching midnight. Strange, she thought, to sleep so deeply, but that thought was shoved away when her eyes dropped to the table directly next to her chair where the letter with the names "Reyes" stared at her.

She ran out into the hallway, the letter clutched in her hand. "Olga! Olga what happened?..." Rosa rushed to the bed of the sleeping servant. "Olga, the letter, what is it doing here?"

"Pablo, the boy, he brought it back, Mrs. Reyes. He said that no one was at Don Enrique's house, so he brought it immediately back. He was afraid it would be lost if he did not—" Rosa heard no more.

She ran out the kitchen door, around the large home to the front yard of the private ranch. No one stood there. The guitarist, the singers and lovers were all gone; they had respectfully left the premises for the evening, not wanting to overstay their visit. Rosa stood alone upon the yard. The moon cast the shadow of the fence upon her as if to impale her with the iron rods. She almost ran through the open gate when a low rumble stopped her, a noise that she could feel.

The beat, like the roll of a drum, emanated from the distant mountains. It slapped against her own chest. It was the beat of the earth's own heart. Rosa looked down toward the mound, waiting for something to happen. Nothing did. It began far away, across a man-made border in another country. That heart deep in the mountains vomited a fire in the earth, and quiet volcanoes suddenly retched upward, blazing the moon-glazed sky. A chain of mountains burst alive, until the final one erupted, Mount Joya.

Rosa leaned against the fence in order to hold herself up. She looked at the distant glow of a row of live volcanoes. Though such incidents had occurred before, there existed a distinction, as if there were something so very human about these eruptions.

〜〜
〜〜

"All right, let's go!"

It was Sergio's voice, one that yelled out at the same moment that the volcanoes burst. The earth's signal pushed the several dozen men forward. The moon reflected upon their raised machetes like broken glass in a field of darkness.

A Fire in the Earth

Paco ran with them. It felt strange to carry a machete. He had no callouses on his hands to protect him from the wood handle. Still, he ran with them, as it was time.

They ran in three lines, one behind the other. They scurried over two hills of coffee trees before seeing the few lights of El Comienzo. They knew their destination, and the three lines broke into a loosely strategic order once they reached the edge of the town. The first line was to run around the mound to the west and head up the paths and road to the Guard House. Line two was to run to the east of the mound and take the house from a southeast road. Line three would run way to the west, and take it from behind. Along the way, they were to leave behind on the streets bodies of the individual guards on duty.

The plan was set. The earth had told them, with her final flash, that she stood behind their endeavors. The symbolic eruption could not have been more perfect. Paco smiled. His last thought, just before the machine guns began firing through the coffee trees, was what role the volcanoes would play in the future legends that he and his comrades were now creating for their country's children.

The first line of proletarian soldiers fell like a row of sliced banana trees, leaving the second line naked to the hidden glint of metal barrels protruding between the coffee branches. The machine guns laughed again, and sliced into the second row. Those who were not hit ran into the hills.

Paco's head burst with pumping blood. He ran, dropping the machete in the field. He fell into a crevice between two steep hills, where he tried and failed to hold his bursting breath. Bullets cracked through the hills; he could hear them between the intermittent explosions of the distant volcanoes. The machine guns had been driven into the countryside. They shot out sporadically, at times close enough for him to see the spit of fire from the barrel and the shadow of the jeep where the weapon sat. Paco did not move. He looked up at the moon, so bright and clear, then dove into a shadow just as a volcano spoke. There he remained. For long periods of time, the machine guns worked, throwing the sharp bullets about the hills and trees like metal seeds. He remained unmoved, though his throat tightened and almost coughed forward a cry. He squeezed down all noisy emotional reac-

481

tions, especially when a boot stepped two feet away from his face, then stopped for a moment. The other boot followed, then they remained there until a cigarette dropped to the ground, and the red glow looked toward Paco as if to tell the smoker something before one boot covered the glow in a habitual manner, and walked away.

Paco remained still long enough for the moon to disappear behind a hill to the west. Breathing had become all important. The rhythm of his breath rose and fell, barely enough to keep him from passing out. When the guns shot, his lungs snatched the air to keep from screaming.

As the moon disappeared from his sight and left the trees to cast a long shadow eastward, the machine guns settled down. They were no longer out here in the hills of coffee. They had retreated to some other place, perhaps back to the Guard House. After a long wait, he pulled away, out of she shadows where he was hiding. He picked himself up and moved between the two tall hills. When he walked around to one side of the eastern hill, he could hear the guns in the distance, but they were muffled by the hills in between. He walked slowly, at times stopping for long pauses, figuring out how he would return to the safety of the town where there would be no shooting.

Three hills stood between him and El Comienzo. The moon settled far to the west, and the light of a new day just began to trickle over the sky, enough for him to see the faded bark of the trees around him. He crossed the first hill. The machine guns sounded clearer, yet still sporadic. On the second hill, something punched through him, a sharp realization, which made him run as he panted.

"No, it can't be..."

On top of the third hill he looked down and saw El Comienzo. The population as a whole ran through the streets, and the machine guns turned left and right, mounted on geared-up jeeps that left a trail of arms and legs jerking and flopping against adobe walls. The people ran, with no direction or destination. Three jeeps drove the roads, circling about, returning again. The guns aimed directly to the side, moving left and right, cutting through doors, into glassless windows.

Paco ran down the hill. On the edge of town lay the carcasses of pigs and horses, of children and goats, a lone dog. As he ran into town,

A Fire in the Earth

he had to slow his pace to keep from stepping upon the remnants of a decreasing population. With no sense of reason, he ran up the mound. No one stopped him.

The sun moved higher with the strength of a sigh and displayed the refuse of an official order. Bullets had worked on the town's walls like an ice pick. Wails echoed behind the walls. Three screaming children wandered outside and walked among the piles of skin and muscle.

From where he stood, Paco could see it all. For a transient moment he seemed protected there, as if the guards would not look for anyone hiding upon the open mound. From the mound he looked up, and in the new daylight he could see that some of the Comenzaños had found a destination: They were running south of town, up the hill, toward the private ranch house, toward the open gates of the fence. There, at the opening, stood his sister. She called out to the crowd of townspeople who were huddling through the small mouth of protection. Through the deluge of cries and of final gunshots he could hear her voice, yelling out orders to people who still ran parallel with the fence, screaming at them all the way until they found the gate. She turned toward some guards outside who shot at the people before they reached the gate. Rosa cursed at the guards in the voice she had inherited from her mother, a voice that would frighten mad dogs away.

Villagers already inside the fence ran toward the hotel. They retreated to the closed establishment as Rosa had ordered them to do. People on the outside fell with a cut-off cry as metal sang through them.

The guards, ignoring the screams of the benevolent *patrona*, moved up the hill toward the gate, where she stood like a thin, shaking sentinel. From the mound Paco could see his mother behind Rosa, pushing the crowd of people toward the hotel. Laughter burst through his tears as if he were witnessing some sort of salvation. He fell down the mound to the street and sprinted toward the ranch.

As he ran he looked up. Don Enrique was straddling the gate with his daughter Regina helping him forward. Rosa ran out and grabbed the old man. Both women helped him through the gate. Regina screamed back, searching for her little girl Consuelo. There, to the

483

right of the gate, several steps away, the child stood crying, frozen. Rosa ran out again. She grabbed the girl and shook her toward the opening. As she turned, Rosa saw Paco. She sprinted like some angel out of the protection of her kingdom to save a soul from an apocalypse. Yet her body was real, and it stopped the flying lead that had been aimed at the girl Consuelo who now ran through the gate. There, half a hill above him, his sister's body came down.

Paco stared as silence rushed through his skull. His sister fell forever toward him. She reached forward as if to touch Paco before her chest met the grass.

Romilia was running behind the gate. An approaching guard was quicker than she, and he rushed to the opening and pushed her back while shutting the massive gate closed. He quickly explained to the well-known mother of the *patrona* with a forced respect that it was for her own good. "Ma'am, the people, they have tried to revolt. This is for your own safety." An outside lock wrapped the gate and fence together and clicked closed. The guard pushed the key into his pocket just as four hands wrapped around Paco's upper arms. Though a knee punched into him and several fists came down upon him like some fleshy stoning, Paco heard his mother's cry, a scream that fell against the tall poles of iron and steel.

There Romilia stood, watching stony men in uniforms and rifles carry away that young, flinching body of her son, while below her lay the lovely, fallen form of her daughter, a lithe, white rose cut by accident. As she wailed, Romilia's arms and hands beat violently against the metal bars of protection.

♒

In the following days the new god of this earth proclaimed his demands to all. "We must purify the land. We must cleanse it finally, once and for all, of this filth that has infested even the soil of our great little country, a stain on our earth that has been among us much too long. So kill every man who holds a machete."

At first, even some of El Brujo's main officials hesitated, knowing that the majority of the population owned a machete. But to balk meant to allow the growth of the ideological disease, one which had broken out like bleeding cancers all over the country wherever a batch of farmers turned angry at their way of life and a communist sat nearby, feeding them with propagandistic flames. "So do as I say," demanded El Brujo.

When morning and evening passed that first day, his uniformed angels went out to the world with rifles of rapid fire. There was much work to do.

On the outskirts of towns they set up the mechanics of their vocation. They rounded up all the men who lived nearby and brought them to a field. There they placed shovels into the farmers' hands and told them to dig a long and deep ditch. The men worked, all in a row of two-hundred individuals. They dug side by side, tossing dirt to a long pile that stretched over the small grade of land. They spoke nothing to one another, for the angels had forbidden them that. There was little to say about their digging, or about the jeeps behind them that had soldiers crawling about like green, spotted grasshoppers, constructing with metal pieces and wood and rubber the weapon that pointed toward them. There was nothing left to tell as the soldiers gave the men string to tie and weave their own thumbs with the thumbs of the men standing to one side, then to the other side, until all was organized, and all had been tied together like a string of paper men, making it so easy to carry out El Brujo's order. The gun on the back of the jeep spat at them while the vehicle drove parallel with the newly dug trench, playing dominos with body after body as they fell back in perfection. A bulldozer behind them cranked up to finish the beauty of the order. Children and wives jumped with screams into the trenches like cats kicking away from a fire. They did not stop the bulldozers.

The new rite proceeded like a well-performed liturgy. Efficiency reigned in this new kingdom, and by the evening of the second day El Brujo handed more orders over to his retinue. The angels announced to the whole country to go to such-and-such a building in the capital in order to receive such-and-such papers that officially stated that you had not nor ever would have had any connection with the Communist Party.

There the people flocked. They thickened the lines with their need, their desire, to get hold of those papers, believing in that final act of law and consideration for the population. So strong was their faith that they stood unmoving as the burst of machine guns geared around the corner and followed the line for as long as it stretched, until it reached the building.

The third, fourth and fifth days followed with the consistency of a giant farmer sowing a field with bodies instead of seeds. It was a major task, so large that some of the families began to complain of the stench that stretched from city to city. Those few who were friends of El Brujo asked if something could please be done, and so it was. The angels tossed gallons of fluid and dropped matches and cigarettes to the piles. The mounds of arms and legs and gutted abdomens burst into balls of flame that rose to a strange heaven, rolling smoke to some hungry being. El Brujo looked from his palace window and saw that it was good.

The act of the new creation continued for several more days. Thousands of machetes had fallen from the hands of those who had been the source of El Brujo's problem. "Those natives, the Indians, those who are suckered so quickly by that ideology, they are the root of the problem. How I hate them." El Brujo had shown his efficiency, had burnt the country's root down to its deepest earth, that indigenous, deep, dark root buried so profoundly into the rich, black land. It had been a stubborn plant. Yet El Brujo raised his arms in a blessing upon the land and said to his companions, the families of the kingdom, "I give this all unto you, a new earth, ready for you to use." His companions raised their glasses to him. They drank from deep goblets of elixir that clogged their heads of the final wisps of stench rising from that burning root outside.

∿∿
∿∿

"Come here and smell my gun."

It was still the first day in El Comienzo. The angel, Geraldo Castillo, sat upon a chair at the bottom of the mound. To his right and

A Fire in the Earth

left stood two soldiers. He leaned an elbow on a knee and cradled a pistol in his hand.

Hermes Alarcía, the husband of Marta the breadmaker, leaned on his knees against the ground. No clear words came from his mouth, only the quiver of broken, throaty noises.

"I said come here, you fucker. If you do not smell my pistol then you are a communist and afraid. He who is without sin knows no fear."

Hermes fell forward. He crawled the distance from the front door of his home toward the sitting captain. Behind him Marta screamed. Suddenly her scream was cut off. Hermes jerked his head back, but could not see her. He did see, on the bread table in his home, one of his daughter Lupe's legs jerking under the weight of a green-clad body. Again the command came from the chair, "Move nearer." Hermes reached the captain, who placed the pistol low, toward his lips.

"Go ahead, suck it."

The cold barrel pushed against Hermes' teeth as if to chip them. He obeyed. Hermes sucked against the taste of iron. He looked up at the captain. "Very good, very good," said Castillo. Then he pulled the trigger.

"Bring the next one over," said he, over the dispersing sound of the report. The second man was Leonardo, the carpenter. A guard dragged Hermes' headless body away.

This scene occurred four times before Castillo looked over his right shoulder toward Paco. Paco had wondered beforehand if Castillo knew of his presence, for the captain had given no sign of acknowledgement. Now it was obvious. Castillo yelled out in perfect English, "Come here, you prickhead hair-egg son of a bitch."

Paco stood and began to walk. A gun stock kicked him between his shoulder blades and brought him to the ground.

"You will come here to me on your knees, like everyone else has."

Paco crawled forward. When he reached the chair, again the gun was lowered.

"Suck it, boy. You owe me."

Paco spat on the gun and on Castillo's hand. Two soldiers grabbed him and held him to the barrel.

Marcos McPeek Villatoro

"You have become braver as you have grown up, Colónez. Not running away, like when we were kids."

The captain shoved the barrel into Paco's mouth as the two guards held him. Castillo pulled the gun back and forth, in and out. Paco could taste the spattered blood of his four dead predecessors. Castillo smiled. "Very good, very good." Again he pulled the trigger.

Nothing happened except the click. "Goodness, no more bullets." He laughed only slightly. "Put him up with the other lines."

They carried the suddenly-heavy Paco to the back of the mound. He passed out, dropping like a filled sack.

The mound had been used for few things in the past years. Depleted of its richness, it had remained fallow during more recent seasons. Every two years they tried to grow beans on it, and sometimes tomatoes or other vegetables. But decades of hunger had forced them to misuse the mound. After those first seasons, they had used it less, opting for the risk of planting between coffee rows, where there was still some good soil. Until now, the mound had been left alone. Then came Captain Castillo, who decided to be creative. "Dig the trench in a circle, around the middle of the mound." The captured men huddled together on the street. The soldiers encircled them and handed out shovels. One of the soldiers dropped the tool onto Paco's chest. "Wake him up. Get him working."

Paco dug. About twenty-five farmers worked with him, for that was all that could fit around the waist of the mound. The others stood, gathered in large crowds, held together by pointed metal. Periodically, Paco looked up, glanced at the little kingdom on top of the hill, surrounded by guards. An order belted over Paco to dig deeper into the center of the mound.

They worked without ceasing for the whole morning. At midday the guards sat down in the shade to eat oranges. Some, those with metallic strips of status dangling from their chests, slept the afternoon away, while those of lesser rank stood guard. Finally the master of them all, Castillo, awoke with a grunt, heavy from the weight of the heat. He grumbled to his men, "Get started. Do thirty at a time."

Someone brought out a thick roll of string. Those who dug the circular grave were the first to be tied. One of the officials demanded

A Fire in the Earth

them to tie one another's thumbs and leave the final, free extensions to be tied by the guards. Paco refused. Again, he was kicked, then tied. He slowly bent back up again. Slight vomit fell from his mouth, and his eyes encircled the remnants of the deluge before him, those piles of burning limbs and abdomens on the edge of town. A soldier approached him and, after tying his thumbs to two men from Piricón who stood beside him, shoved his fist into Paco's groin. The youth bent forward. It suddenly occurred to Paco how many times he had been cut in two like that. He remained doubled over, with a tear running over his dusty nose and his hands shaking not from his own fear, but from the moaning and trembling of the two men at either side of him. The pain that ran through his stomach left no room for his own inner trembling, nor for any reaction to the several rifle barrels that had circled the mound. He did see the mouths of the guns as they aimed upward, straight into his face. The fire burst forth, and the weight of his comrades kicked him into the ditch. He stared at the bluest sky for a momentous eternity until the next circle formed, casting shadows upon his vision. The bullets burst and dropped the shadows upon him.

The guards continued their work until nightfall. It took seven circles to finish. Between the orders of shooting, silence walked dryly among the little town's streets, as no one stood about. No one cried aloud. A few still were actually alive, hiding, hoping that by staying in their quiet, noiseless back rooms it would appear that they were dead, that they no longer existed.

Silence walked, sometimes crawled, all the way up to the top of the hill, beyond the fence. There people stood, those who had saved themselves, a handful in comparison to the bodies strewn all over the hills. They watched, horrified, to what was going on down in their El Comienzo. The corpses had all been heaped together. All but the white body of the dead *patrona* in her well-made dress. It had been carefully handled and taken back inside the fence of the ranch house. The guards almost demanded that the people inside step out. Then the one in charge decided not to push it, not to order that those who hid in the hotel be handed over. Their accidental shooting of Rosa Reyes had already put them in a precarious position. Thus they too had joined

489

the stalking silence, and except for the periodic explosion of packed gunpowder and the cries that followed, the afternoon passed quietly.

Doña Romilia had fallen into one corner of her cheese shed. Her wrinkled, wizened face rested against the adobe wall and wood planks, as if to push through them. The people inside the fence—the survivors—later found her. They stared at her, wondering for the moment if she was among the living or the dead.

♒

"That is all for today," Captain Castillo said. "Throw the matches to this shit."

A guard whispered to him that there was no more fuel left, that more would not come until tomorrow. "Fine. We will burn tomorrow. Let the people live with the smell, so they will not forget." With that, they left town.

The darkness became even deeper for Paco. He knew that night had come. He had shifted his weight as much as possible, pushing the body that lay upon him to one side with his legs. Yet the weight of seven dead men pushed against him. He could feel his wound to his left side, staining his shirt. But he was alive, and more than alive, for an energy pumped through him, something he could not define at the moment.

He worked on bringing his tied left thumb closer to his mouth. Then he chewed at it, grinding with teeth that tore like a dog's. He tasted the blood that dripped from the hand of the dead man to whom he had been tied. The fingers of the Indian flopped against his own chest as he worked with the string. Only one strand remained. It bit between two of his molars and tore into his gum. He brought his tongue under it, lifted the weight of the hand and the string, then tore it with one bite. His left hand was free. His thumb pumped with the ache of the taut cord. He tried to free it, but failed. He turned his attention to his right hand, which still lay under several hundred pounds of wet flesh and bone. He pulled at it until it came out from under all the weight, still tied to the thumb of the dead man to his right. His body shuddered. He worked the dead arm through the mass of limbs and again began cutting with his teeth.

Though still buried under the dead bodies, his freed thumbs ached from the tight cords, and he tore at them like an animal caught in a toothy trap until he cut them off. Blood pumped through his blue extremities. He found it almost impossible to move them. They flopped to one side like dead flesh. At the moment it did not matter. He tore through the mass of arms which had fallen in an almost uniform pile. Only two or three abdomens lay in the way. With grunts and heaves he dug himself out of the grave, pulling and pushing through layer upon layer of death until his arms reached upward and touched nothing except the coolness of the night air. He spat out laughter as he slowly pulled his head through the top layer of skin and muscle.

Below him stood the town at night, his hometown, with no lights, with only a moon showing the way up the hill to that old ranch house. Some lights burned in the hotel windows. Up there life dwelled, silent and in mourning no doubt. He laughed and wept as he pulled up further away from the stench. He could say nothing, not even whisper, as if he had forgotten how to speak. His caged lungs coughed away the stench of blood and shit that had leaked out of the bodies and onto his own. He breathed in the air. It smelled of many things—smoke, stench, new winds that came from the east. He put his hands to his waist to rest, and felt his own blood, warm, beating out of a side wound.

From his cloth belt fell a small packet, the gift from Romilia, which held the lock of hair of some old ancestor and a devout ancestor's rosary. It dropped on the mound and rolled down its side before coming to a stop near the edge of the cellar door. He would pick it up as he walked down the slope. For now he only breathed in the slightest sense of wind, blowing over him like hope. He looked up again at the ranch house. He could see a man standing by the grave of his father. The old, highly respected *patrón*, Patricio Colónez, wore a hat as he walked around, checking out the inventory of food that Rosa had collected. The figure shook his head in affirmation toward the harvest of a good heart. Patricio raised his chin, and Paco could almost see that strong face. In English Paco's father spoke through the wind, *There is a difference between strength and power, son, remember that.* Paco laughed aloud, and he saw that there was hope. He believed as he looked up to the departing moon. Paco turned to his side to look one last time in mourning at those that had fallen with him. It was then that he smelled the wisp of a freshly burning cigarette. It brought his eyes to the top of the mound where a real man was squatting down, with the shadow of one of those perfect, long barrels resting on his lap. The uniformed shadow flicked the match away, toward Paco who had just raised himself from the dead.

"Hello, prickhead hair-eggs son of a bitch," fell the words that failed to blanket the click of a deadbolt.

As that speeding lead bit into Paco's pure heart, the voice of a fallen white rose whispered him a question: *You are following your beliefs. You do have beliefs, true?* The belief in the many, the belief of that power, that strength; believing, never seeing.

The angel, Castillo, tossed the rifle over his shoulder. He walked down the hill toward his jeep, and in his mind wrote a report that would assure him the eradication of his shame.

There was one man who managed to escape. No one knew him. He had found a bottle of the strongest rum from the abandoned, bullet-riddled bar of The Other Place and had carried it with him through the night until it was finished. Not even the morning sun could give him pain, for he awoke with the elixir still deep in his slow veins. He stumbled toward the cellar of the mound. Before entering it he stood to its side and pissed a long stream upon its slope. He barely glanced at the newest fallen body above him, for such a sight had become too common for him to give it any heed.

Next to his left foot lay a black pouch. He picked it up, thinking it was a tiny money bag. Perhaps money would someday be useful again. His gnarled, numbed hands clutched at the packet three times before picking it up, and his buttocks fell to the mound while he worked at opening it. The little strings were knotted together, and he tore with maladroit fingers until it finally opened. He mumbled to himself with

492

a glee. He pulled the rosary out. His face scowled when he looked at the sixty beads and the crucifix. "What is this shit?"

The drunk flung the prayer tool to one side, dug his numbed fingers into the pouch again. He pulled out an old leaf, which unwrapped in his hands. The white hairs took hold of a slight gust of wind to look for a ride of freedom. "Ah, fuck, nothing!"

He crawled toward the opening of the cellar door. His foggy reasoning told him that the guards would be back, and his inebriation pushed him to prayer, that they not look in here. For safety, he worked with the fallen door and leaned it upon the opening, which gave him complete shade. He did not hear the black ones arrive, circling in their usual pattern before ruffling their feathers toward the ground. They landed in a legion. It was simple to see that something or someone had been very good to them.

Epilogue

Romilia picked herself up from the corner of the cheese shed. No one stood inside except her. A long string of black hair finely streaked with white fell over her face. She leaned against a pole and looked out. Daytime had come again. Outside the shed she could hear people milling about, talking. All of them were labriego voices. They spoke of practical matters, what to do, what were the first steps to take, how long should they stay, where would they go? Sobs and wails from men and women rose and fell in a sporadic harmony.

Romilia walked through the door of the shed. A handful of them turned to her and fell silent. Their stares, sad and curious, searched the ground. She walked before them, straddling their multitude. She pulled a shawl over her head.

At one end of the crowd stood Don Enrique, Regina, and Consuelo. Romilia barely nodded to them, as if offering some cryptic approval. She walked to the malinche tree that had grown forever beside the ranch house-turned-hotel, the same one from which her boy had swung to scamper into the nights of his childhood. In its shade lay the body of her daughter. Next to it kneeled her little son, sobbing. Rosa's body had been placed there by the crowd in a respectful manner. Her eyes had been closed, her arms crossed over the wounded chest, and a serape covering her to the neck. Romilia grabbed Jesús and held him.

"Where is your brother?"

"With Olga."

They did not move for a long while. When she did, she gently pushed him away with a kiss on the forehead. "Go get Olga and your brother," she said.

He obeyed. Romilia then bent down to the body and slowly leaned over. She stared, unmoving. At times she cocked her head to one side as if in wonder. Then she brought her head down and kissed her daughter upon the forehead. The cold of death touched her lips. Romilia finally pulled herself up and sucked in cool morning air, like an animal snorting rage. She turned to the waiting people behind her, and her wet, wrinkled eyelids opened wide. She stared hard, as if to cut an opening into the crowd. It worked, for they separated, allowing her to see the fence, the locked gate, and those guards, walking back and forth, so tall and erect, rifles upon their shoulders. She stood and walked to them.

"Get out of here. Get away. This is private property. You will leave it!"

The guards turned. One of them protested in sound, military fashion, explaining the threat, the need for security.

"You...fucking PACK OF DOGS LEAVE! LEAVE NOW!"

The guards turned to one another. After a moment of disciplined discernment, they walked down the hill.

Romilia turned. She faced the crowd. It was a large number. Most were from El Comienzo. Many were Indian. They looked upon her. All their eyes tried to express something—gratitude, sorrow, something undefinable.

Behind Romilia, down the hill, burned the bonfires of gasoline and flesh. The mound gave off the greatest amount of smoke. Romilia began to speak, though the balls of the gasoline igniting below threw shudders into her words.

"This, this land is all...is all open... We have much food, it will last us, and we have room, enough room. We will, work together..."

She rambled, barely pointing with a weak arm to the barn, the house, the hotel, the gardens. Her eyes glanced over to her daughter's body. Romilia drew in a breath and raised her head up to them all.

"This is your home, yes. You are all welcome. Welcome to stay."